A *LESS THAN ZERO* ROCKSTAR ROMANCE

TIMELESS

KAYLENE WINTER

TIMELESS: A Less Than Zero Rock Star Romance
Copyright © 2021 by Kaylene Winter
Cover photography and design: Regina Wamba
Cover Model: Enrico Ravenna
Formatting Cat at TRC Designs

All rights reserved. No part of this book may be reproduced, scanned or distributed in any manner whatsoever without written permission from the author except in the case of brief quotations embodied in articles or reviews.

This is a work of fiction. Names, characters, businesses, places, events, locales, and incidents are either the products of the author's imagination or
used in a fictitious manner. Any resemblance to actual persons, living or dead, or actual events is purely coincidental. Certain real people, businesses, locations, and organizations that are referenced are used in a way that is purely fictional.

shouldn't be surprised by adding one more thing to the list. Like mom spending Christmas with us this year.

And staying at Carter's house.

"Jesus, Zane. Snap out of it." Carter clicks his fingers in front of my face. "I asked you a question ten times, what's going on with you?"

Despite my best efforts, my mind is a jumbled mess. That's what's going on. So many things are changing drastically. At light-fucking-speed. My bandmates, Ty, Jace, and Connor are burned out. After nearly a decade of nonstop recording and touring, they've tired of living in a fishbowl. Ready to begin new chapters. Blah. Blah. Blah.

We had a vote, and it was three against one. I lost. We are officially on hiatus. Which fucking sucks. Because I know what this means.

The end of LTZ.

I feel it in my bones.

LTZ is my fuel. My identity. Playing music keeps me sane. Balanced. So, when my bandmates are moving on to new chapters without me?

It fucking hurts.

Probably because my own happily ever after blew up in my face.

"Nothing. I'm just tired," I lie.

"Bullshit." Carter's voice is kind. He's been through it. He knows.

His phone buzzes as we pull into Alaska Airlines arrivals at Sea-Tac. He picks up and squints over at the sidewalk where hordes of people are waiting to get picked up. "Yeah, we're here. Ah, there you are. Yeah, the black Audi. Okay. I'm pulling over."

I see my mom waving at us. Surreal, I tell you.

We park. I jump out of the passenger seat. She's standing next to three large suitcases. Good god. How long is she staying? She floats into my arms. Mom's graceful that way. My entire face is covered with her kisses. "Zaney," she coos.

"This is a surprise." I hug her tightly.

She steps back. Thumbs the lipstick off my cheeks. "Well, your grandparents are in Minneapolis with your uncle. When Carter invited me to spend Christmas with my son, I thought, why not?"

"Lianne." Carter acknowledges my mom. Kinda like a giddy teenager. His eyes sparkle. "Let me get your bags."

WTF?

A few people begin to recognize my dad and me. I can always tell when they start to whisper and point. Some pretend to be talking on speaker phone even though the devices are pointed toward us. Recording us. Just a day in my life. And Carter's. Mom's too, on a lesser scale. All of us are high-profile in our own professions.

I motion to the Audi. "Let's get going unless you want this little family reunion to be broadcast all over YouTube."

"Jesus, fuck." Carter opens the door for my mom. "Sorry about this, Lianne. I was hoping to just have a low-key airport pickup."

My mom slides into the front seat, laughing. "The low-key ship sailed long ago as far as you two are concerned."

We navigate back onto I-5 in silence.

"Let's check out the new Mission on our way home?" Carter looks over at my mom and grins. "Construction is coming along."

"That sounds great." She settles back and smiles over at him.

I'm trying to read their body language.

Unsuccessfully.

Twilight Zone, I tell you.

I slump back into the back seat. This night is getting weirder and weirder. I bury myself in my phone until we pull into the parking lot of what will soon be Seattle's premiere midsize concert hall. Three stories.

World-class restaurant. Bar.

It's going to be epic. Just what this city needs with so much development going on displacing music and other arts venues. When I notice a black Toyota Highlander parked close to the front entrance, my heart plummets. Shit. The *last* person I want to see tonight is Fiona.

She's my childhood friend. Business partner.

Among other things.

So many other things.

Recently, I made a vow about our situation.

Stop. Making. A. Fool. Outta. Yourself. Son.

I'm just not quite there yet.

Despite my misgivings, we enter through the back entrance using my key. The entire place is dark. We just passed an electricity inspection, so I try the switch and the entire place lights up. It's still a construction zone. Over the next six weeks, the flooring, tile, stage, painting, and trim out will be done. By the end-of-March completion date, the facility will be state-of-the art.

"Wow, you guys!" Mom twirls around like the ballerina she is. "This is breathtaking."

"Who's there?" I hear an angry voice and heavy clomping footsteps approaching. "I've got a fucking gun and I'll fucking blow your head off."

Instinctively, I leap in front of my mom. "Jesus, Fee. It's just me. I've got Carter and Mom with me."

"What the fuck, Zane?" Fiona Reynolds appears from the shadows, her fuchsia hair the perfect contrast to her black-rimmed blue eyes, which squint at me with annoyance. She's wearing red-plaid pants, chunky black boots, and an oversized black sweater. Her voice softens when she sees my folks, yet her arms remain crossed defensively. She tilts her head up. "Hey, Carter. Lianne, it's been a minute."

My mom strides to Fiona and practically squishes her. "It's been way too long. Sweetheart, I'm so glad to see you."

Fiona's arms are like noodles at her sides until she reluctantly reaches around my mom and hugs her back. "Um, yeah. It's good to see you."

"Don't worry. We're just looking around for a few minutes. Mom's spending Christmas with us. Carter and I were over at Ty's house earlier. Ty got engaged to Zoey tonight," I babble. No matter how hard I try, my tendency to spew out more information than anyone ever asks for always kicks in when I'm deep inside my head.

Little known fact: I'm almost always deep inside my head.

I've just gotten good at hiding it. Most of the time.

In other words, word vomit is my tell.

So is joking. Bouncing off the walls. Getting lost in music.

"I'm very impressed." Mom turns to Fiona. "You've all gone through so much to get it to this point."

A wave of agony passes across Fiona's face, likely at the thought of— well everything. She covers it up quickly. "Onward and upward, I guess."

"You must be tired," Carter says to my mom. I notice Carter touch the small of her back and gaze into her eyes. I raise an eyebrow at him, and he moves his hand away.

Mom catches the look that passes between me and Carter and steps aside. "It's getting pretty late."

"We'll head out then. See you later, Fiona." Carter and my mom head toward the back exit.

I don't move. Fiona and I are eye-locked into a showdown stare. "I'll be there in a couple of minutes." I wave them off.

Fiona looks weary. She's so tense, her hands are balled up in fists. She glares at me. Except no, that's not it. She's pleading with me. But for what? "Just go with them Zane. Let's not do this right now"

I step toward her, run my hands along her forearms and unclench her fists with my fingers. Her long, black nails dig into my wrists when she grips them tightly. I lean in, my mouth is right up against her ear. "You. Can't. Make. Me."

Fiona shivers. Her breath hitches. "Stop being such a child."

My cock stiffens. Strains against my jeans.

"I haven't been a child in a very long time, and you know it, Fee." My lips drag along her jawline and then press against hers. I don't kiss her, exactly. I simply take her in. Her sweet, orangey essence permeates my entire being. Her soft skin feels like silk. Her blue orbs bore into mine until she closes her eyes, and her entire body relaxes against me.

Us. Together. Close like this. It's our safe space.

It's always been our safe space.

Abruptly she pulls away. "I can't, Zane. I told you, I can't."

"You can."

"Fine, I *won't* risk it."

"Pushing me away won't work." I close the gap between us, wrapping my arm around her shoulder. "We promised never…"

She runs her fingers through her pink hair and looks up at me. "The stakes are too high. If I have to sacrifice us, I will. I *have* to. You know that. You've always known that."

Ouch. Direct hit.

Yet, something about the contrast between the snarky tone of her comment and the pleading look in her eyes gives me pause.

She's scared.

She needs me.

The most precious thing in the world is at stake.

Finally, I know what I have to do. I've probably always known, but I didn't see it until this moment. It's up to *me* to break the destructive pattern we've fallen back into.

A-fucking-gain.

Oh yeah. I'm fucking done.

Done with the push and pull.

Done with the yo-yo.

Done with her excuses.

Done with mine.

Done. Done. Done.

I may not have control over much in my life, but I do have control over this. And I'm not waiting one more minute. I turn and gently cup her jaw with both hands on either side of her face. I touch my forehead to hers. Our eyes meet. She blinks up at me and places her hands over mine.

This time, she's *going* to listen.

This time she's going to *hear* me.

Because if she doesn't?

I've made up my mind.

I'll end this situation we find ourselves in for good.

For my sanity. And for hers.

CHAPTER 1

AGE 6

"Zane! Where are you?" I blow the hair out of my eyes and peer around the giant mountain-shaped fountain in Broadway Playfield. Hoping to catch a glimpse of my best friend. We've been playing hide and seek but he's too good of a hider. I'm not a good seeker.

Now I can't find him.

I run around to the other side of the dome, hoping he's in the shallow pool area. Nope. He's not there either. It's like he's vanished into thin air. I hate it *so much* when he does this.

Spotting the icky men's restroom, I figure it's exactly the kind of place he'd hide. Knowing Zane and all. Just to see me squirm. I pinch my nose between two fingers, hold my breath and charge inside. So disgusting. The stalls are caved in. It's dirty. Stinky. The toilet is stuffed with paper towels and overflowing with yucky liquid.

So gross.

And no Zane.

Coughing to get the smell out of my throat, I bolt back outside. Shielding my eyes from the sun with my hand, I turn slowly in a circle and look around the big grassy area. A bunch of older kids are playing hacky sack on the soccer field. Zane isn't with them. I run toward the trees separating the field from the sports fields. He isn't near the baseball diamond either.

There aren't many people here today. He's usually easy to spot. Not many boys our age have long hair like Zane's. He wears different clothes than most kids. Cool clothes. Like the black skull sweatshirt and rolled-up blue jeans he has on today.

Where could he have gone?

I have no idea what to do. Zane's dad brought us here, then disappeared into an apartment building across the street from the park. Not before warning Zane and me not to leave the playground area. He promised to be right back. Two minutes, he said. But he was gone for a really long time. We got bored and started playing hide and seek in the park.

Maybe Zane went to look for him?

No, Carter warned us not to follow him. Zane always does what his dad says. Always.

Jeez. Now all I can think about is how mad my mom is going to be when she finds out Carter brought us here. She hates this park even though it's a short walk from our apartment. She says there are weird vibes here. Weird people doing weird things. She's going to freak out.

I'm going to be in so much trouble.

Since I can't find Zane, I decide to go back to the playground where Carter told us to wait. Hopefully he'll find me if I'm back where I'm supposed to be.

Soon.

I'm trying to be brave but I'm really scared. My heart is pounding so hard. My scalp is all prickly. I've never been alone in a public place and I don't like it one bit. I run as fast as I can toward the playground. As I get closer, I see a man is sitting on the bench by the slide.

I slow down to see who it is.

Omigod! It's Carter. He's put on a knit cap and sunglasses. It's his costume. To disguise himself when he's in public. Dad says he gets really embarrassed when people recognize him. I guess he's famous or something.

I'm so happy that I take off running again. Then I remember Zane's missing. I skid to a stop. What am I going to say? I mean, I have to tell Carter. Even if he's not around much, he's still Zane's dad. And an adult. He'll know what to do.

I tiptoe toward the bench. Carter is hunched over. His arms are crossed tightly around his chest. He's not moving. Is he asleep? I don't really want to wake him up if he's tired.

Except I need to find Zane.

"Carter?" I whisper as I get closer. "Are you awake?"

His mouth is open partway. He doesn't answer.

"Carter?" I tug at his soft brown coat. "Wake up. I can't find Zane."

I jump back when he slumps over and his head hits the seat on the bench. He still doesn't wake up. My heart races.

Calm down. He's fine. He's just taking a nap.

I hear a noise behind me and whip my head around to see where the sound came from. I don't see anyone, so I turn back to watch Carter lying on the bench. I hope he's okay.

I wonder what to do.

"Guess who?" I nearly jump out of my skin when a hand covers my eyes and a familiar voice shouts into my ear.

"Zane!" I pull away before turning around and shoving him. "You scared me. Where were you? You're so mean."

"I'm not mean." He holds up a single yellow daffodil. "I saw this and wanted to pick it for you."

My heart melts into a puddle. I love this boy. Zane always does sweet things for me. I immediately forgive him.

I always do.

"Thank you. It's so pretty." I take it and peer into Zane's dark-brown eyes. His curly black hair hits his shoulders. His crooked smile makes me feel squishy inside.

He's my other half.

Our moms say so anyway. And it feels true. Zane was born just a couple of months after me so we're practically the same age. Our parents are best friends, so we have spent nearly every day together since we were babies.

I can't live without him. When we're apart, it feels like something is missing. I throw my arms around him. "I was really scared that you got lost."

Zane squeezes me back super tight. "Fee, don't be scared. I was just over by the flower bed. Don't worry. I'll never, ever leave you."

We press our heads together and rub. Head snuggles. That's what we call it. I smile and then remember Carter is sleeping on the bench.

"Is your dad sick?" I poke at Carter's jacket. "I couldn't wake him up."

Zane doesn't seem worried. He grabs my hand and pulls me toward the jungle gym. "No. This happens all the time when he comes home from tour. Let him sleep for a bit. We can go swing until he wakes up."

Hand-in-hand we skip toward the playground and sit side by side on the swings. My feet don't quite reach the ground, so I move myself back and forth on my tiptoes. "Next time will you promise to at least tell me where you're going?"

"Yeah. Okay. I'm sorry." Zane smiles at me, looking up from under his hair. "I just got moony."

Moony is what Zane's mom, Lianne, calls it when Zane's mind starts spinning. He sometimes gets an idea in his head and can't focus on anything else. My mom says that Zane is a genius. I think so too. He's the smartest person I know. Even if my friends at school think he's weird. I wish I were smart like him.

My dad says that I have a smart mouth.

Whatever that means.

I kick my feet out and start pumping my legs. Zane copies me. It doesn't take long before we are flying through the air on our swings. We go higher and higher until I think I can touch the sky with my toes.

Zane shouts at me as our swings swoosh past each other, "I want to marry you, Fiona."

"What?"

"I said I want to marry you!"

"We're only six."

"I don't care." Zane drags his feet on the ground and launches himself off his swing. He grabs the chain on mine and I come to a stop. "I think we should get married right now. Then you will never worry about me leaving you again."

"You're crazy." I giggle as Zane picks up the daffodil he carefully placed on the grass.

"This can be your bouquet." He hands me the flower.

"What do we do?"

"It's easy. I, Zane Rocks, take you, Fiona Reynolds, to be my wife." Zane puts his hand over his heart and shuts his eyes dramatically. "Now you go."

"Okay. I, Fiona Reynolds, take you, Zane Rocks, to be my husband." I twirl around with my daffodil.

Zane waggles his eyebrows. "Now we get to kiss."

"Ewww! You didn't tell me that, Zane," I squeal.

Zane grabs my hand and yanks me to him. "We have to, or we won't be legally married. Don't you watch TV?"

I shut my eyes tightly. "Fine."

"No, you have to look me in the eyes when we do it!" Zane whines.

My eyes flutter open and Zane presses his lips to mine. Our wide eyes stare at each other. He pulls away quickly.

"Are we married?" I ask, wiping my lips with the back of my hand.

"Yep. Now no one can ever break us apart. And we can tell everyone at school I'm your husband."

We hear a thud and look over to where Carter has fallen to the concrete. His arms are flopped out to the sides and his sunglasses hang off his face. The eye we can see is staring into space.

At nothing.

Is he dead?

"Daaaaad." Zane speeds over to him and pounds on his chest. "Wake up! Dad!"

Carter doesn't move. Not even a little bit.

I burst into tears and run to Zane, who is screaming bloody murder. I wrap my arms around his back and squeeze. "Zane, stay with your dad, I need to get my mom."

"No! Don't leave me, Fee," Zane wails as he continues to thump on his father's chest. "Dad! Wake up! Are you dead?"

I'm bawling uncontrollably. "Zane, I've got to get help."

Zane flings himself on top of Carter like his whole world is falling apart. I've never seen him like this. He never cries. He's always happy.

Someone is yelling from the sidewalk outside the park, "Fiona? Zane? Fiona?"

My mom.

"Mom, we're over here!" I jump up and wave my arms wildly. My mom, Faye Reynolds, is with Lianne Rocks, Zane's mom. My godmother. They hurry toward us. I can tell the minute they spot Zane beating on his dad's lifeless body.

Their calm-mom faces are gone.

They look afraid.

No, terrified.

Which makes me terrified.

Carter hasn't moved. His eye still stares into space. Lianne runs to him and pulls Zane away, shielding his eyes. She's now screaming like her leg has been cut off. Some of the kids at the park start to gather around us to check out what's happening.

"Faye, can you take the kids to your house and call 9-1-1?" Lianne notices the people staring and strategically positions herself so they can't see Carter. "I'll stay with him until help comes."

My mom nods, picks me up and grabs Zane's hand. We turn and walk in the opposite direction, leaving Zane's mom holding Carter's head in her lap. When we get out of the park, Mom puts me down and we all run toward our apartment. She stroke's Zane's head. Wipes his tears with her thumb. "Don't worry, Zane, I'll call for help. Your mom will take care of your dad. It will be okay."

Except it wasn't.

My life was never the same again.

CHAPTER 2

AGE 7

My mom is crying.

Again.

She's trying to be quiet, but I can hear her.

I throw down my Xbox controller and bolt to the stairs. If I'm stealth, I can lie flat on the top step, peek through the rails into the living room and listen to what's going on. It's hard for me to sit still, but sometimes it's worth it. Like now. Mom's sitting on the edge of the ugly green couch in her ballet practice clothes with her face buried in her hands. Her pretty red hair is falling out of her bun.

My grandma, who has the same bright-green eyes as Mom, is next to her. Rubbing her back. "Li-Li, you did the right thing. Carter can't be trusted around Zane."

My dad. They're talking about my dad. I haven't seen him since Mom and I moved to Colorado to live with my grandparents.

The worst day of my life.

I keep quiet so I don't miss out on anything. It's all a confusing blur about why I don't see him anymore. I know he was really sick on the day Fiona and I got married in the park. Then I couldn't wake him up. I thought he was dead. I remember Fiona's mom bringing me to their apartment. We had a slumber party for a couple of sleeps. Mom picked me up and we drove straight to Sea-Tac airport.

Now we live in Denver.

I didn't even get to say goodbye to Fiona.

Or my dad.

I miss him.

I want to go home.

I hate it here so much.

My new school sucks. The teachers are mean. They say I'm too hyper. That I can't stop talking and interrupting class. I'm just trying to make friends because no one likes me. The kids at my new school think I'm weird. I have no one to play with at recess. Every single day they make fun of my hair. My clothes. Pretty much everything about me.

Yeah. I really, really, really hate it here.

I *really* miss Fiona.

My mom's crying so hard I can barely understand what she's saying. "Mama, I don't want to keep Zane from Carter. I sent him the custody papers the lawyer drew up. He's trying to get clean. He wants us to come back home. For us to try again."

"And you'd even consider that?" Grandma claps her hands together. "In my mind you *are* home. You're just getting back on your feet. Please don't uproot your son for a man who doesn't deserve it. Do you really want to risk having that sweet boy finding Carter dead from an overdose? Because that's what's going to happen. He'll be traumatized for life. That's the risk you're taking. It's not about you, sweetheart. It's about Zane."

Overdose? What's an overdose?

My mom stretches out her legs and rubs her thighs. She looks so tired. "I'm so confused. Zane's not happy here. He doesn't have Fiona. Or his dad. I miss my friends too. My life there."

"Stop it. Right now. What kind of life did you have? Carter was always on the road with his band. He was never home. He was never a father to Zane. If Faye hadn't helped you out with him, you wouldn't even have a career!" Grandma paces back and forth across the floor. She's clenching and unclenching her fists. As if to keep herself under control. When she heads in my direction, I curl up to make myself small so she won't see me on the stairs. "You've worked your ass off to regain your status as a principal dancer, Lianne. Are you willing to throw that all away? For a goddamn druggie? He isn't good enough for you. He definitely isn't good for Zane."

I shove my fist in my mouth. I want to yell at Grandma that she's wrong. My dad was the best. The *best.* We had so much fun. I'd sit on his lap and we'd play his guitar. He gave me zerbits on my belly. We picked strawberries and ate them right off the vine. We'd walk in the woods and talk about my Native American relatives.

I miss everything about him.

I just don't understand why he's not here anymore.

Mom wraps her arms around herself. Tears stream down her face. "I will *always* love Carter, Mama. He loves Zane. He's—"

"Love is not always enough, baby," Grandma interrupts then kneels in front of Mom and hugs her. "Don't put this off anymore. Secure custody. Get you and Zane into some counseling. You're an amazing mother. A talented dancer. A kind person. This obsession you have for

Carter is going to destroy you both if you don't come to terms with the fact that he's a drug addict. You need to be an adult now, sweetheart and do what's right for your family."

Wait? What's a drug addict?

"I know. *I know.*" My mom's voice is small. Hushed. "I will never be able to unsee his eyes staring into space that day. Or forgive him for OD'ing in front of our son and then disappearing from the hospital to get another fix. I'm scared. He wasn't using when we met. Now it has a hold on him."

"Which is why you moved here. To get a clean break. If you keep talking to him, Li-Li, you will never move forward."

"He's Zane's father, Mom. I will always talk to Carter. One day—"

My grandma slaps the coffee table with her hand. It makes a horrible noise. "That's bullshit. Zane's better off without him."

I can't help but react. Before I can stop myself, I'm flying down the stairs screaming at the top of my lungs. I slam into my grandma. "I hate you! I hate you! I hate you! You can't keep me from my dad. I want to go back to Seattle. I hate it here!"

Mom looks like she's going to faint.

"Zaney," she whispers. "I thought you were asleep."

"I heard *everything,*" I flail at my mom. My entire body feels like I might explode into smithereens. "You said Dad wanted us to move. You're a fucking liar! I fucking hate you!"

"What's all this commotion?" I hear Grandpa say behind me.

I scream at the top of my lungs, "I fucking *hate* it here and I want to go home."

"That's enough." I feel a palm on each shoulder. My grandpa pulls me back against him. "Do *not* use those foul words in this house. Where did you learn to talk like that? And don't you *ever* speak to your mother or grandmother that way again. You are never to speak to *any* woman in anger, young man. Especially your family."

My mom is sobbing uncontrollably. I feel so bad. I hate it when I can't control myself. I break free from my grandpa and lunge for her. She wraps her arms around me. Kisses my head over and over. "Zaney, I'm so sorry. I love you more than anything in the world. You're my precious boy. Let's go upstairs and calm down."

We walk past my grandparents, up the stairs and into my room. She shuts the door and hugs me tight. Her hands cup my cheeks, and she kisses my forehead, wiping my tears away with her thumbs. "I need you to know that no matter what, Zane, it will always be me and you. *You* are my only priority."

"I want my dad."

"I know, baby." Mom sniffs and wipes her tears away. "There is nothing in this world that I want more than for you to have your dad. But the situation is complicated."

My heart hurts. I don't want Mom to feel bad, so I take her hand and squeeze. "I'm sorry for yelling those things, Mommy. I didn't mean it."

"You haven't called me Mommy in a long time." She smiles. "I need to have a grown-up talk with you about your dad. Is that okay?"

I sit on my blue race-car bedspread. Mom sits beside me. "Yeah. Okay."

"I want you to know that your dad has a disease. It's called addiction. When he drinks or does drugs it causes him to make bad choices." Mom's green eyes search mine. "Do you understand what I'm saying?"

"Dad does drugs?" My stomach feels wonky. We learned in school to run and report to the principal if someone offers us drugs on the playground.

“Yes. That day in the park? He left you and Fiona alone in that park to get drugs. He overdosed and nearly died when he was supposed to be watching you both.” Mom pulls me onto her lap. “Your dad needs to get help.”

I wrap my arms around my mom. She smells like flowers. “I can help him.”

“No, baby. You can’t.” She strokes my back up and down, which calms me. “He needs to go away to a special hospital and see some special doctors. It’s hard for him to find the time because his job is being a musician and he travels all over the world to play shows.”

I think about this for a minute. “Why can’t the doctor go with him?”

“That’s a great idea, Zane. But it has to be your dad’s choice. We can’t make him do anything he isn’t ready to do.”

“What happens if he doesn’t go to a doctor?”

My mom doesn’t answer. She just sighs and squeezes me tightly. I squeeze back.

But somehow I understand what she isn’t telling me. At least not out loud.

If he doesn’t get help, my dad’s gonna die.

CHAPTER 3

AGE 8

"Mommy, is the mail here yet?" I burst into the apartment. "Zane's letter should be here today."

There's no answer.

A stack of mail is piled near the edge of the kitchen counter. Eagerly, I flip through the stack addressed to my parents—Gus and Faye Reynolds— and finally find what I'm looking for. My name and address in Zane's careful all-cap handwriting on an envelope filled with musical note doodles. And a picture of a daffodil.

My heart explodes with butterflies.

There's no better feeling than letter day.

I rip it open.

FEE,

HI FROM DENVER.

MY MOM TOLD ME WE ARE GOING TO DISNEYLAND WITH

YOU AND YOUR MOM THIS SUMMER. IT WILL BE SO FUN.

HAVE YOU SEEN MY DAD? I SAW HIM ON MTV. HE SAID HIS NEW SONG WAS FOR ME. I WISH HE WOULD CALL ME.

I HATE IT HERE. MOM SAID WE CAN'T GO BACK TO SEATTLE. I MISS GOING TO SCHOOL WITH YOU. I DON'T HAVE FRIENDS HERE. THE KIDS MAKE FUN OF ME ALL THE TIME.

MY NANA GOT ME A KITTEN. HIS NAME IS CECIL. HE'S BLACK WITH TAN STRIPES AND BITES MY HAND. AT LEAST HE'S MY FRIEND. AND YOU ARE TOO.

WRITE ME BACK.

LOVE, ZANE

Sighing, I relax into my dad's recliner. After reading and rereading Zane's letter a few times it finally sinks in. He's not ever coming back. I can't believe his mom would just take him away from me. And his dad. She's so mean. And selfish.

I hate her.

Even if she is my godmother.

"Fee, are you home?" My dad Gus's voice booms through the front door. He appears in the archway between the kitchen and living room, where I'm sitting. My dad is like a big teddy bear. He always wears his brown-plaid jacket over a band T-shirt (today it's Mookie Blaylock) and skinny black jeans. His long, dark curly hair is pulled back into a low ponytail which pokes out from under a slouchy, gray beanie with "The Mission" logo embroidered in yellow letters. "Ah, there you are!"

"Daddy, is it true that I'm going to Disneyland?" I run to him and throw my arms around his ample waist. "Zane said so in his letter."

Effortlessly, he picks me up and secures me against his side. I love being in his arms. He smells like Christmas all year long. "Yes, it's true. Your mom and I talked it over with Lianne, and we think it would be fun for you kids to take a summer vacation together every year. What do you think?"

My heart beats wildly. It's the best idea ever in the history of all ideas. "That's so cool! Are you coming too? Is Carter?"

"Ah, sweet girl." He strokes my hair and twirls a piece around his finger. The skin next to his eyes crinkles as he smiles at me. "Carter and I have to work. It will just be you, Zane, and your moms this year. Won't that be fun?"

I drag my nose along his nose and flutter my eyelashes on his forehead. My dad loves butterfly kisses from me. "I'll miss you. Zane misses Carter, he said so in his letter. Carter never calls him."

"Is that so?" Dad's lips press into a thin line. He looks away for a second, as if he's thinking about something then focuses back on me. "I'm sure there is a reason. I'll talk to him."

"Promise?"

"Of course." He presses a kiss to my temple and sets me back down on the floor. "Is your mom here?"

"I don't think so." I sit back down in the chair to reread Zane's letter while my dad heads back to their bedroom.

A few minutes later he comes back. He seems irritated. His big hand tugs on his beard as he looks around the apartment before collapsing onto the sofa and picking up the remote. We watch *Wheel of Fortune* together for a few minutes when my mom breezes in. Her arms are full of groceries.

"Hey, you two. I thought I'd just make us some sandwiches tonight." She sets the bags on the kitchen counter and pulls out some bread and deli meat. "I don't feel like cooking."

My mom *never* feels like cooking, for the record.

Dad gets up and joins her in the kitchen. Their voices are low so

I can't hear what they are saying. It isn't hard to figure out they are fighting. Again. I pretend to focus on the TV.

"I'm heading out, sweetheart. See you in the morning." My dad waves to me, his huge smile directed at me is a lot different than the angry frown he wore when talking to my mom.

I'm not surprised. With shows at The Mission every night of the week, my dad's very rarely home at night. My mom, however, is seething mad. I can tell by how she slams the mayonnaise and mustard on the counter as she puts together our sandwiches. She's muttering things under her breath that I can't quite hear. From her scowl, I'm guessing her thoughts about my dad aren't very nice.

I tiptoe into the kitchen and hug my mom from behind. "Let me help."

"It's okay, Fiona." She turns and shoves a plate with a ham sandwich into my hands. "Here you go."

I carry it to the kitchen table and eat it. Mom stands at the counter with her own. I inhale my sandwich so I can grill my mom about our vacation. "Mommy, I got a letter from Zane today. He says we're going to Disneyland."

"Oh, good. I was waiting for you to get the letter before I told you." She pops the last bite of sandwich in her mouth. "It will be good for you and me to have a change of scenery."

"I can't wait."

"Me either, sweetheart." Mom grabs our empty plates and puts them in the sink.

"Are you mad at Daddy?"

She looks over at me from the kitchen. "Fiona, please promise me something."

"Okay." I'm not sure what I'm supposed to promise, but I don't want to disappoint my mom.

"Don't ever give up your own dreams for a man." She looks out the window above the sink. "You'll only be disappointed."

A sliver of fear invades my heart. I don't know what my mom means, exactly. Except, she doesn't seem happy. Every time she and my dad are in the same room, they fight. It's scary. I don't want her to take me away from him. Look at how sad Zane is without Carter.

I decide then and there I'll try to be better.

I won't sass. Or swear.

I'll learn how to cook, then maybe Daddy will stay home and have dinner with us.

I just want things to be normal again.

Except I can't really remember what normal is anymore.

CHAPTER 4

AGE 9

I hate waiting.

I hate sitting still even more.

Tonight, I'm sitting on the front porch doing both. My dad is coming to pick me up for dinner. He's in town with his band. They're playing a show tomorrow in the middle of their world tour. I'm not allowed at his concerts, so tonight is the only time I'll get to see him until next year. We made really fun plans. Just me and him.

Hamburgers and shakes.

We'll play guitar at his hotel.

We'll order room service and eat ice cream.

I'll show those stupid kids at school that Carter Pope is really my father.

I still have no friends. I still get teased constantly. It sucks. This kid named Greg Smith started a rumor that Carter isn't my real dad. He told everybody in my class that Carter shouted out to his *real* son Zane on MTV. A Zane that isn't me. Now, the whole school says I'm a liar because I don't have any pictures of us together.

I've got to prove he's my dad. Grandma's going to take a picture of us when he gets here. Maybe then they'll finally stop picking on me.

Finally! I hear a car pulling onto our street.

Shoot. The car drives past but doesn't stop.

Grandma peeps out the door. "How you doing, Zane?"

"Fine, Grandma." I smile, even though I'm getting worried.

"Okay. I'm going back in, *West Wing* is almost on," she says before closing the screen door behind her.

I wish my mom were here. Tonight, she has a performance, so she's at the theater. She's never around when my dad comes to visit. She tells me it's so I can spend time with my dad alone without her influence or something. I don't get it.

Adults are really weird.

By the time the sun disappears, I'm feeling really sad. I *know* he isn't coming, but I don't want to go back inside yet. My leg bounces uncontrollably but my eyes remain on the road because I hope I'm wrong. He *promised* not to forget when I talked to him the other night. I even made him say it twice.

Please show up. Please show up.

Like magic, my wish comes true. The headlights of a car appear down the street. I'm so excited I run down the pathway to the front gate. Dad made it! My dad made it! I stand on the lowest rung of the fence and peer over the top to get a better view. A black sedan approaches, slowing down in front of the house. Before I can stop myself, I disobey my grandparents' orders, unlatch the gate and run toward the car.

Just as it speeds away.

I stand on the sidewalk and watch it disappear around the corner.

My eyes fill with tears. I angrily wipe them away. I don't want Grandma and Grandpa to see me cry. They already hate my dad, but they don't understand how busy he is. How famous he is. I hear his music everywhere I go. He's always on TV. I'm *lucky* to be his son. Don't they know? It's not his fault if something came up.

I just need to get over it. Carter doesn't always show up when he's supposed to. All rock stars are busy. I'm a big boy. I'll just... A large hand lands on my shoulder. "Zane, time to come in. I don't think your dad's going to make it tonight."

"Maybe we got the week wrong, Grandpa." I follow him inside. "Or we probably have the wrong day..."

My grandpa doesn't say anything as he walks into the kitchen and pulls out a tub of ice cream from the freezer. I sit at the counter and watch him scoop it into two bowls. He takes some Hershey's syrup out of the fridge and squirts it on top. Then he adds a dollop of Cool Whip and slides the bowl over to me. "Zane, you're getting to be more grown up now. You don't need to make excuses for your father. I want you to listen to me because what I'm going to tell you is very important. Carter was supposed to be here and he didn't show up. I know you feel sad. And hurt. You need to know it's *not* your fault."

I stab at the ice cream with my spoon. "It's okay. He probably has cooler stuff to do than hang out with me."

Grandpa sits beside me at the counter. "Trust me, Zaney. There is nothing cooler than spending time with you. Your father's an addict. He's to blame, not you."

Addict. Guitar legend. The two ways people always describe my dad. Mom takes me to see a nice lady named Dr. June on Monday nights. We talk a lot about addiction. And how it makes him unreliable, which basically means he promises things he doesn't follow through on. Dr. June gave me a few books I'm supposed to read, but it's hard for me to focus. Mainly because a lot of what she says doesn't make sense. I never see my dad, so how am I supposed to know if he's on drugs or not?

"Do you want me to take that?" Grandpa tilts his bowl to get the last of the melted ice cream from the bottom. "Doesn't look like you are too hungry."

"Sure. Okay." I slide the bowl to him.

Grandpa quickly spoons the rest of my dessert into his mouth and then puts our dishes in the dishwasher. "Let's go watch some TV with your grandma."

"Can I just go up to my room?" The last thing I want to do is watch that stupid, boring *West Wing* show that my grandma loves so much.

He ruffles my hair. "Sure. Your mom should be home soon."

Once I'm in my bedroom, I pick up my ukulele and get lost in playing it for a while. Before I know it, I look up to see my mom standing in the doorway with tears in her eyes. I hate it when she cries. "Why are you sad, Mom?"

"Oh, Zaney. I'm not sad. You're so talented. Watching you play. It… It just makes my heart so full." Her red hair is loose around her shoulders instead of her usual tight bun. I like it this way; she looks like a princess. She's so beautiful. She always keeps her promises. I love her so much. "I heard your dad didn't make it tonight."

"Grandpa says it's because he's an addict."

Mom sits next to me on the bed. "Your grandpa's right. We've talked about this before. Your dad has something inside his brain that makes it hard for him to stop craving things that are bad for him. Things like drugs. He didn't grow up in a very good environment, and his own mother and father were addicts too. He's a good man when he's well."

"Why won't he get well?" It's so hard for me to understand all this adult stuff. It seems so easy. Maybe he can take a pill or something.

"I really hope he will get help someday so you can know him." Mom brushes a long lock of hair out of my eyes. "The truth is? I don't know if he will. No matter what, Zaney, I love you more than anything on this planet. I'm trying to protect you as best as I can, but I want you to know how sorry I am that he didn't show up. Again. You're the sweetest, kindest boy in the world. You don't deserve this."

"I know. Dr. June tells me that all the time." I set my ukulele down next to me. "I just wish he wouldn't say he's coming if he's busy. It hurts my feelings."

"I hate that, baby. I really do. There are no excuses."

I lean my head on my mom's shoulder. "I don't think I want to talk to him anymore until he's well. Is that okay?"

"Of course. If you change your mind, that's okay too. He'll always be your dad. I know he loves you. He's just not…" She wraps her arm around me. "If it's any consolation, you're the best thing that has ever happened to me, Zaney. I mean it."

We sit like that for a while, until I get sleepy. Mom tucks me in and kisses me goodnight. I dream of the day when we are all living in Seattle again. Mom, Dad, and me. Fiona, Gus, and Faye.

Except I wake up the next morning. I'm not in Seattle.

I'm still in Denver. Cecil is curled up beside me. I stroke his head. His purring soothes me, just a bit. He gets up, stretches and jumps off the bed which is my signal to get up and feed him. I trudge out to the kitchen and fill his bowl with cat food.

This is where I live now. It's time to just accept it.

I know things will never, ever be the same again.

No matter how hard I wish for it.

CHAPTER 5

AGE 10

"They say it's your birthday
It's my birthday too, yeah.
They say it's your birthday
We're gonna have a good time
I'm glad it's your birthday
Happy Birthday to you!"

Carter and my dad are singing to me in the middle of the dining room at Daniel's Broiler on Leschi. We always come here for birthdays and special occasions. It's not *my* favorite, but it's really fancy and overlooks Lake Washington. I wish someone had asked *me* where I wanted my birthday dinner. I'd have picked Dick's Drive-In and avoided the celebrity bullshit that follows Carter everywhere he goes.

Look, I know I swear a lot for a ten year old. My parents don't give a crap, neither should anyone else.

"Happy birthday!" Carter gleefully leans over to kiss my cheek and give my hair a ruffle. "Gus, I think this is the first time I've been in town for a birthday since Fee was a baby!"

"Wrong. You were at her sixth birthday." Mom glares at Carter through her startling blue eyes rimmed with thick black eyeliner. "You clearly don't remember."

Carter slumps back in his chair and looks down at his half-eaten steak.

Dad growls. "Jesus, Faye. Not *now*."

Mom knows how to kill a mood, that's for sure.

We finish eating in silence. After the plates are cleared, a waiter with a nose ring and long red hair places a giant chocolate cake in front of me. Ten candles are burning on top. He's not paying any attention to me, though. Instead, he keeps glancing at Carter and then looking away.

He's starstruck. They always are.

I tug on the waiter's shirt. "Just ask him for an autograph. Or hand him your demo. Then maybe I can enjoy *my* fucking birthday. *Thank* you."

Six pairs of eyes snap to look at me. I smirk and blow out the candles. I know how to get this lame-ass party back on track. My dad starts laughing. So does Carter. The waiter backs away slowly before turning and nearly running back toward the service station.

"God, Fee." Dad snorts. "You're one in a million."

Mom seethes. "*Jesus*, Gus. Way to encourage her. Fiona, it's not nice to be rude to people."

"Fuck you," Dad mutters under his breath. Mom glares at him.

God, my folks never stop.

Ever.

Carter ignores them. He's still chuckling at my sassiness.

"And you." Mom points at him. "Do *not* forget your son's birthday this year."

His mood immediately shifts. "Faye, I've told you to stay out of my fucking business."

"You should thank me for staying *in* your fucking business," Mom says as she slices the cake and hands me a big piece. "God knows, Lianne has had enough of your disappearing act."

"Stop it, Faye." Dad touches her arm.

She shakes him off and glares at him. "It's true and you know it."

Carter stares at the tablecloth. I feel bad for him. We hardly ever see him anymore, and every time we do my mom is a total fucking bitch. She hates him. For something that happened years ago.

Like I said, she knows how to kill a mood.

"Thanks for a *great* birthday, Mom." I shovel a big bite of cake into my mouth and don't bother chewing before I mumble, "This has been such a *fun* time."

Carter looks up and gives me a small smile. He reaches under the table and pulls out a medium-sized box wrapped in silver paper and a hot-pink ribbon. "I got you a present, Fee."

I carefully unwrap the gift to reveal a brand-new Nokia 7650 cell phone. "Wow!" I squeal and throw my arms around him. "I've wanted my own phone for a long time!"

"Our management company gave them to all of us in the band. It's badass. There's a camera, you can send text messages and there's all sorts of techy hoo-hahs which are over my head." Carter grins. "I bought the same one for Zane's birthday. I sent it to him early and programmed your number in. Maybe instead of writing letters, you can start texting. I know he'd love to wish you a happy birthday tonight."

Mom tilts her head. "It's a sweet gift, Carter. Thoughtful."

"I added it to my account, so don't worry about any of the mobile service fees. It's on me." Carter rests his arm around the back of my chair. "I know Zane misses Fiona. It's all he ever talks about."

"As if you actually talk to your son," Mom mutters under her breath. It doesn't take her long to go from sweet to salty.

"I miss him too." I ignore my mother and kiss Carter on the cheek to make him feel better. "Thank you so much. This is the perfect present."

In the car on the way home, Mom examines the phone. "Just when you are ready to kill him, he goes and does something like this."

"You need to lay off, Faye. You're such a fucking bitch to that man," my dad growls. "He's been sober for three months."

Mom pinches the bridge of her nose. "He deserves it. Every bit of it."

"It was four fucking years ago. He's *trying*. Can you give him a break? *Jesus*." My dad doesn't even bother trying to get along with my mom anymore. It sucks being around the two of them.

Really sucks.

Mom never lets go of that day in the park. I barely even remember it, but she seems to think it's permanently scarred me and Zane. What really scars me is the fact that she brings it up *all the time*. Besides, who cares about Carter. What I *do* remember is how scared I was when I couldn't find Zane. Life without him would be unbearable.

I'm old enough to know that Carter has a problem with drugs and does bad stuff like leave kids unsupervised in the park when he's high. Or disappears for hours before he's supposed to go on stage. Or doesn't take Zane for dinner on his birthday. One time, he showed up at our house wearing nothing but his underwear.

Mom was *really* pissed that night.

I'm also old enough to understand why Lianne moved and took Zane with her. She was afraid. She wanted him to have a more normal life.

Which *sucks*.

I still miss him so much.

So yeah, I'm super psyched about the phone. We can forget the stupid letters and call and text each other every day. Carter is the *best*. The second we get home I race up to my room and slam the door. It doesn't take me long to figure out how to use the text feature.

Fee: Hello?

Fee: Zane?

The phone buzzes in my hand, startling me. I nearly drop it. When I see Zane's name on the screen, I press the green button and hold it up to my ear. "Hello?"

"Happy birthday, Fiona."

I nearly cry with happiness.

"Hi, Zane."

"Did you have a nice dinner?" He sounds a bit sad.

"It was okay. Mom was a bitch to your dad again." I flop on my bed. "The cake was good, though. This weekend some of the girls from school are coming over for a slumber party."

"Dad's not going to make it for my birthday dinner this year. He's going back out on tour, I guess."

"I'm sorry." I hate that Zane doesn't get to see Carter. I also hate that Carter was there for my birthday and won't be there for Zane's. It makes no sense to me that I see Zane's dad more than he does.

He sighs. "I wish I knew what I did to make him stay away."

"It's not your fault." I *hate* being a kid. I can't wait to be eighteen so me and Zane don't have to do what our parents say. They're so stupid sometimes.

"Everyone always says that." Zane sniffs. "I hate it here so much."

When Zane feels bad, I feel bad. There is nothing I can do, and it makes me so *mad.* "Did you do what I told you to do when those kids make fun of you?"

"Yeah."

"And?"

"They smashed my ukulele and gave me a black eye. Mom wants to put me in a different school now."

Zane hasn't changed. He still isn't like the other kids. He's special. He loves people, but he just doesn't quite fit in. He talks too much. It's hard for him to stay focused so he fidgets. I used to protect him when we were in kindergarten. But that was a long time ago. He has no one in Denver.

Adults are so *annoying* sometimes.

"Do you want me to come to Denver and kick their asses?" I offer. Not that I can really back it up or anything.

Zane laughs. "No, I'll be okay. Grandpa signed me up for this Krav Maga self-defense class. I had my first session yesterday. It's really cool. I'm going to kick their asses someday, count on it."

"I know you will, Zaney." And I do. When he sets his mind to something, nothing stops him.

For the next hour we talk about everything in the world. This is so much better than writing letters. Hearing Zane's voice is like medicine. It makes everything so much better. When we finally hang up, I find myself smiling like a lunatic.

The perfect end to an imperfect birthday.

But then, Zane *always* makes things perfect.

Always.

CHAPTER 6

AGE 11

I'm getting too big to spy on my mom and grandparents on the stairs. Cecil always gives me away, anyway. My new vantage point is in the den next to the living room where my PlayStation is set up. Carter sent me the latest model for Christmas together with *Tony Hawk's Pro Skater 3*, *Grand Theft Auto III*, *Halo: Combat Evolved*, and stupid *Mario Kart Super Circuit*.

I don't really like video games, which is one more strike against me fitting in at school. It seems stupid to just sit around all day when you could be doing something productive. Like making music. Or doing Krav Maga at the studio.

I'm still going to kick someone's ass. I just haven't had the chance yet.

Anyway, pretending I'm into games comes in handy. Especially when all the adults are home and have conversations they don't want me to hear. I just have to pretend I'm focused on the screen and not answer when one of them calls my name. They think I'm not paying attention and talk about things they usually wouldn't discuss in front of me.

It's a great strategy.

Before Mom left for her performance, I learned a lot. First, our annual getaway is at a dude ranch in Wyoming. Second, Carter bought my mom and me a house and my grandparents are mad about it.

I can't wait to tell Fiona.

My phone buzzes. She's a mind reader. I just have to think about her, and she calls these days.

"Hey, Fee. I bet you don't know where we're going this summer," I taunt.

"Wyoming," she snorts. "Give me some credit. I'm a way better spy than you are."

She's right. "Crap. How did you find out?"

"Mom told me. How did you find out?"

"My video game spy trick."

"You're so funny. So, guess what I'm doing?"

I hear a lot of rattling and clanging around in the background. It's hard to know what Fiona's up to, she's always doing something crazy. "I don't know, but whatever it is you're loud."

"Cooking!" she squeals. "I've decided I'm going to be a chef when I grow up. I found an old Betty Crocker cookbook at a yard sale today. Mom agreed to buy it for me if I promised to cook three recipes."

Now that I think about it, the last time we were together Fiona was really focused on the food we ate. It's not something that I think about at all. Well, except for strawberries. I *love* them. Other than that, Mom or Grandma feed me, and I eat. End of story. "Cool. What are you making first?"

"Creamy garlic shrimp pasta," Fiona announces triumphantly. "We just got back from the grocery store."

"That sounds pretty good."

"We'll see. It can't be any worse than my mom's cooking."

I laugh. She's so right. I remember the stuff Faye would serve us when I still lived in Seattle. Her scrambled eggs tasted like dog pee. Not that I know what dog pee tastes like. Really. I don't. "Are you going to cook for me someday?"

"Of course. When we get married for real I'll cook dinner every night." There's a loud clang and a thump. "Whoops. I just dropped the cast iron skillet on the floor. It's super heavy."

"Be careful." I hear myself say but my heart is pitter-pattering a million miles a minute. I love it when Fiona talks about the day we really get married. Even if it seems weird to think about. We're only eleven, after all.

There's more shuffling around and another thunk. "Zane, can we talk tomorrow? I'm making a huge mess. I don't want my mom to kill my dream. I better go before she throws a shit fit."

I'm about to reply when Fiona ends the call. Harsh. Even though she knew about the dude ranch, I didn't even get a chance to tell her about the new house.

Oh well, I'll just tell her later. For now, I have a new instrument to learn. I'm super excited. Yesterday, Grandma was telling me about my great-grandparents who were from Sweden. We went up to the attic where she showed me a bunch of old pictures of her as a little girl. I also got to see some of my mom's baby pictures.

Even better? I saw the accordion. Grandma showed me the basics of how to play it and gave it to me to keep. Now, I have the entire night to figure it out.

"Zane," my grandpa bellows from the bottom of the stairs. "Are you ready to go?"

Crap. I put the accordion down and run to find out what my grandpa's yelling about. When I peer down from the top of the staircase, my grandparents are all dressed up with coats on. "What are we doing?"

My grandma tromps up the stairs, grabs my arm and drags me into my room. "We're going to see your mom perform, but we need to hurry. Put on your nice jeans and a sweater."

"I don't..."

"We're going to be late, Zane. Don't talk. Get dressed." She tugs my shirt off and hands me a gray sweater, which I put on. While I change into my black jeans, she practically pulls my hair out of my scalp as she slicks it back into a ponytail.

Twenty minutes later, we walk into the Auditorium Theatre at the Denver Performing Arts Complex to watch my mom as Odette in *Swan Lake*. It's been a long time since I saw her dance. This is a great surprise.

Grandpa leads us through the crowd to the fancy box seats we always sit in. When the curtain goes up, my mom appears. I can't take my eyes off her. There's no one more beautiful in this whole world. Except maybe Fiona, of course.

Anyway, I'm so proud of her. My dad might be more famous, but my mom is a true artist. Every single movement from her face to her fingertips conveys how she feels when she's on stage. I get so lost in watching her float across the stage, I don't pay attention to the story of *Swan Lake*. All I know is she's in a white costume. Then she's in a black costume. She's breathtaking either way.

That's my mom. I'm so lucky.

Afterward, we meet her backstage. All the dancers gather round to hug and kiss me. Her dancing friends love me. They love my long hair. It makes me feel popular for the first time ever. I can't remember all their names but having all this female attention is worth it. One hundred percent.

A pretty woman with dark-cocoa skin runs her hand along my cheek and tells my mom, "Zane is growing up to be absolutely gorgeous. He's going to break a lot of hearts one day."

"Don't I know it." Mom rests her graceful hand on my shoulder and smiles at me. "He only has eyes for one little girl, though. Zane, this is Vanna. She's just joined the company."

Mom has taught me how to be polite to grown-ups, so I hold out my hand. "Hi, Vanna, it's nice to meet you."

"Ooooh, Zane." Vanna flutters her hand in front of her face like a fan. "Don't you get yourself tied to just one woman. Not until you're much older."

"Fiona's a girl, not a woman. Besides, we're already married." I give her my biggest smile.

My mom and grandparents laugh. "Zane pretend-married his friend Fiona when he was six," my mom explains. "They're so cute. They talk every day on the phone."

"He's loyal." Grandpa ruffles my hair. "All Rocks men know how to treat women right."

Grandma chuckles. "Zane never stops talking about Fee this, Fee that. I wouldn't be surprised if they actually *do* get married one day."

Vanna throws back her head and laughs. "Well, I sure wish I were a ten-year-old girl. I'd give this Fee a run for her money. What do you want to be when you grow up, Zane?"

"I'm going to be in a rock band just like my dad. He's the guitar player in Limelight." I cross my arms and jut my chin out. Like I'm proud. Because I am. Then I add, to make sure my mom doesn't worry, "I'm never doing any drugs."

My mom's face falls, but she pastes a smile on. "Of course you won't, Zaney."

I look around. Vanna eyeballs my mom and then excuses herself. My grandparents look a bit freaked out.

What did I say?

"Mom, Dad, let's get Zane into my dressing room." Mom pushes through a door into a hallway that leads to a bunch more doors. Her name is printed in the middle of a gold star on the first one on the left. We go inside. Mom sits at her dressing table. I sit on the couch with my grandma and grandpa.

Grandma's hand covers her eyes like she has a headache. Grandpa puts his arm around her. I look at my mom, who is leaning over resting her elbows on her knees. Her hands are clasped. She's looking right at me. "Zane, I… Um."

I look around at my family, I'm not sure what's going on. We were just having fun in the hallway. "What did I do?"

"Nothing, Zaney. But we need to tell you something before you find out from someone else. Your dad overdosed earlier today," Grandma speaks quietly.

"Did he die?" My voice comes out like a squeak.

"No, baby. He's in the hospital in Los Angeles." Mom sighs. "Your grandparents brought you here tonight because we didn't want you to see it on the news."

I know I should cry, but it's hard to feel really sad for Carter. It isn't the first, second, or third time this has happened. "Is he *going* to die?"

Grandpa coughs. I look over to find him rubbing the bridge of his nose with his fingers. "Lianne, this isn't normal. Can't you see that? You can't continue to—"

"I know it's not fucking normal, Dad," my mom whisper yells, interrupting him. Her cursing shocks me. She's so gentle and patient and kind. I've rarely heard her swear. Everything I know about swearing I've learned from Fiona.

"Don't do this here. We'll get Zane home." My grandma stands. "How long are you going to be, Lianne?"

"Not long. And leave Zane with me." She crosses her arms defiantly. I've never seen her like this. She's like a tea kettle about to boil over. When they leave, she breathes out like she's been holding her breath for a year.

I'm not sure what to do, so I go over to her and give her a hug. She winds her arms around me and squeezes me tightly. "Are you okay, Mom?"

"No. I'm not okay, Zane." She clasps my hands in hers. "I'm so disappointed in your dad."

"Why? He's OD'd before."

All the color drains out of her face. It takes her a minute to find words. "Your grandpa's right. This is not normal. Talking so freely about your father's overdose should not be your life, Zaney."

"You're the one who brought me to Dr. June, Mom. She says it's healthy to talk about your feelings and the things that are going on in your life. Good or bad." Strangely, I feel fine. "I never see Carter anyway."

"I was hoping you'd see more of him. He'd been working so hard on getting sober. After he missed your birthday last year, he went to rehab." She stretches out her long legs and undoes her pointe shoes and flexes and points her feet when they are free. "He hoped if he stayed clean, we could all be a family again. I've always wanted for us to be back together, and it breaks my heart that it wasn't enough of a motivation for Carter to keep himself well."

Tears well up in her eyes. It's always this way when she talks about my dad. "Mom, I don't think you should be sad because of me. I don't want to be around him if he's not well. It hurts too much when he doesn't do what he says he'll do. Maybe you should talk to Dr. June too, so you don't get so upset."

"You're a wise boy beyond your years, Zaney. I *am* sad. I'm sad because he's not a better dad. I'm sad because you've been exposed to things no kid should have to see. Or feel. I'm also sad because I've disappointed your grandparents. They don't want us to move out. Or see Carter, for that matter."

"Is the house we'd move into back in Seattle?" The thought makes me happy. I would be reunited with Fee.

Mom shakes her head. "No. My career is here in Denver now. The house is a couple of blocks from your grandparents."

"Oh." Now, I'm disappointed. "Do you *want* to move?"

She shrugs. "Yes, I think I do. It's time for me to move out of my parents' house. I love the idea of you and me having our own place and making it our own. You'd have your own room to decorate any way you want. We'll still be close to your grandparents, so we'll see them every day."

It actually sounds like a good idea. "Okay, I think we should move too."

"It's decided then." She nods toward the door. "Step outside for a minute and let me get changed. We'll call the hospital and check on Carter on the way home."

I do as she asks and lean against the wall outside my mom's dressing room to wait for her. Vanna walks by and blows me a kiss. It makes me feel bubbly inside. She's so pretty.

"Ready?" Mom emerges, grabs my hand and pulls me toward the back door. "Let's get out of here."

"By the way, you were beautiful tonight. I should come to more shows." I squeeze her hand. "I'm sorry that Carter ruined your special night."

She stops dead in her tracks and looks back at me. "What did you say?"

"Um…"

Mom straightens her spine and narrows her eyes. "You know what? You're right. Tonight was supposed to be a special night for me. Your dad *knew* I was dancing Odette and how much it meant to me. I'm done making excuses for him. Until he's clean for at least a few years, we can't have him in our lives."

I cross my eyes and stick out my tongue. "Duh! We go to enough Nar-Anon meetings. Just remember, we have to figure out our boundaries and set expectations. Remember when Carter didn't show up for my birthday? The night before, he texted me and promised to be there. I told him if he didn't show up, I'd never make birthday plans with him again. And I won't. Not until he proves himself to me."

"I guess I'm not as good a student as you are." Mom looks almost… proud? Yeah. Proud.

"Do you think he'll ever get clean?" We go out the back door and get in her Toyota. "I hope he does."

She starts the engine. "I think Carter's strong. And stubborn."

"Like me?"

"A little."

"He'll do it." I pat her hand.

I'm not sure how I know, but I do.

The real question is, will it stick?

CHAPTER 7

AGE 12

"Holy shit!" Zane launches himself off the golf cart and bolts for the front door. "This is awesome!"

"Language, Zaney." Lianne's hands are on her hips.

He turns and looks up from under his hair. His brown eyes blink up at her. God, he knows how to work it. "Sorry, Mom. I meant to say holy crap."

She shakes her head. "Faye, I don't know what to do about the swearing. Fee, I know you're a nice girl, you don't curse, do you?"

I don't answer, I'm way worse than Zane. Besides, I'm distracted. My mouth hangs open, looking up at the giant tree house we're staying at in Sayulita, Mexico. It's three stories of modern stone and wood with a high, peaked roof, but it's wedged into the trees with floor-to-ceiling glass windows. Tarzan would live here if he were a millionaire.

"Fiona, swears like a sailor." My mom hands me my black-and-white bag and pulls her suitcase off the cart. "I don't get too bothered by it."

Lianne unlocks the door and Zane and I take off to explore the coolest house I've ever seen. Nothing sucks, that's for sure. Everything is super modern. The entire living room is open air with huge pillars that look like tree trunks, which separate the seating area from the kitchen. Every bedroom has its own private bathroom with accordion wood doors that open all the way to the outside too.

"I want to live here." Zane spins around on the upper deck in one of the master bedrooms. He's wearing only swim trunks and flip-flops. His arms are open wide and his long hair whips around as he whirls.

Lianne floats in. "It's beautiful, isn't it?"

"I've never been anywhere this nice." I stand at the rail looking down at the ocean. "Thank you for bringing us, Lianne."

"Anytime, sweetheart." She joins me at the rail. "I always look forward to our trips. This one is going to be really special, I think."

Lianne has always been the most beautiful woman I know. Every year, she's prettier. More sophisticated. Someone I aspire to be. Porcelain skin. Shocking blue eyes. Pink lips. Her red hair is tinged with gold. She's tiny. Everything she wears looks like it was made for her. Her voice is gentle and kind. Today, her beach outfit is a light-turquoise bikini with a white sarong. She's a Disney princess come to life.

Zane bops over, oblivious. "When can we go to the beach?"

My mom strolls in, also pretty but the polar opposite of Lianne. Petite and curvy, with olive skin and dark, wild hair she wears up in a clip most of the time. Mom is bold where Lianne is subtle. She dresses in black or wild, crazy prints. Case in point: her beachwear is a black, studded bikini that leaves very little to the imagination and leopard-print wedge sandals. "Yes, let's take a walk to the Beach Club and check it out."

I look down at my own tiger-striped bikini and wonder if I'll have big boobs like my mom or tiny ones like Lianne. Right now, they're just beginning to swell.

Zane grabs a map from the kitchen counter and the four of us set out on the trail through the tropical countryside to the pool. A few minutes later, when we arrive at the Beach Club, I'm even more blown away. The club is private, we have to show our room key to be admitted. Inside, lush gardens filled with bright flowers line the pathway to the swimming area.

"I'm going in." Zane kicks off his flip-flops and cannonballs into the ginormous infinity-edge swimming pool. "Fee get in here. The water's awesome!"

"Coming!" I pull off my T-shirt and shorts and jump in. I swim over to Zane at the edge of the pool and we look out at the ocean.

"I like your hair long, Fee. It looks really good." Zane reaches over and twirls a lock of wet hair around his finger.

"Almost as long as yours," I tease as I sproing one of his wet curls.

Zane sticks his tongue out at me, then swims to the corner of the pool. He anchors his feet on each wall and his hands on the pool's edge. "Let's play corners. You can go first."

Corners is one of our favorite pool games. I have to swim through his arms and legs and then dive under and swim up so I'm in the corner, all without touching him. Then we switch. We take turns, five rounds each and keep score of how many times we touch each other. Whoever has the least amount wins.

I'm never sure what we win, though. It's just a fun game to play in the pool.

Except this time, Zane seems to be purposely losing. On his last turn, he swims under my legs and the next thing I know I'm on his shoulders and he holds my legs against his chest. "Hey!"

"What? Let's see how far I can swim with you on my shoulders." Zane pushes off to the middle of the pool and we bob along for a while before we topple over, laughing and sputtering.

I glance up at our moms who are deep in conversation, frozen drinks in hand, sun hats pulled down low over their eyes. "Should we go spy on them?"

"Duh." Zane ducks down. "Get low, we'll swim over to the deep end and sneak around the back. They'll never notice."

A few minutes later, we creep up behind our moms and sit behind their beach chairs cross-legged. Zane holds his index finger against his lips and mouths, "*Shhhh.*"

So far, so stealth.

"I'm so sick of Gus spending time at that goddamn club, Lianne." My mom sounds incredibly frustrated. "We still live in a fucking apartment. I feel like I'm stuck. Fiona's getting older, we need a bigger place. At least Carter bought you a house."

"It does feel good. Living with my parents for so many years was tough." Lianne slurps the frozen drink through her straw.

"Yeah, but it sounds so fun to be dating. Any hot dudes on the horizon?"

Zane's face is priceless. He's horrified. He mimes a gagging motion. I cover my mouth with my hand to stop myself from giggling.

"I have so many people that want to date me." Lianne sighs. "How would I ever pick just one?"

Zane just can't help himself. He jumps up. "Mom! You don't *date*. You're too old! That's gross!"

Lianne spins around and wraps her arms around Zane, pinning his arms to his body. "You little spying sneaks. You're not that clever."

For someone so small, she's strong. She maneuvers Zane to the pool and shoves him in before diving in after. He emerges sputtering and laughing. Mom and I jump in after them. The rest of the afternoon we spend splashing around the pool and relaxing in loungers. It's the perfect afternoon.

Later that night, I can't sleep.

Zane and I are in our room, each in separate twin beds. Usually on our vacations, we stay in smaller places or share hotel rooms. Meaning, Zane and I always share a bed. This place is so big, we each have our own bed. I don't like it.

He doesn't seem to mind. I lie on my side, watching him sleep. His dark curls splay out over the pillow. His eyes flutter. Little puffs of air escape his mouth as he breathes. One arm rests across his stomach, the other arm is bent above his head. His fingers wiggle every so often. Like he's dreaming of playing his ukulele.

There's no one on this earth I love more than Zane.

He's always been a cute little boy. An oddball.

But he's *my* oddball.

He's taller this year. With muscles. His hair is still long, but he's grown into it. Zane's still the sweetest person on the planet. Quirky. Full of energy. Like a bouncing ball half the time. But give him an instrument? He can sit still for hours learning it. Mastering it.

I mean, who the hell plays the accordion?

He shifts in his sleep and turns to his side, facing me. His eyes blink open, and he catches me looking at him. "Are you awake?"

"Yeah, I can't sleep."

He stretches his arms out in front of him. "Ummm, you're staring at me?"

I can feel the blush on my cheeks. Luckily, he can't see me. "Yeah. You're growing up, Zane. You don't look like a little boy anymore."

"Wanna snuggle?" He lifts the covers and pats the space next to him on the bed. "I'll cuddle you to sleep"

"Hell yeah." I scramble in next to him and he wraps me up in his arms. I wind mine around his and rest my ear against his chest.

"Better?"

"Yeah. Much better."

He kisses my temple. "These trips are my favorite part of the year. You're my favorite person."

"You're mine too." I give him a peck on the cheek. "I wish we could live here."

"Yeah. Just you and me, though," Zane whispers.

I roll over. He spoons me. We lie quietly for a long time. Just when I think he's sleeping, he whispers, "Fee, are you okay?"

He knows me so well. When we're together it feels like we can read each other's mind. "My mom and dad are fighting all the time. It's really bad."

"Carter?"

"Nah. Well, sometimes. Mostly my mom never stops bitching to my dad about selling The Mission." I bite my lip, then continue, "She says it's a money pit. That it's tearing our family apart. It never stops."

"Wow? Sell The Mission? What would he do?"

"I dunno. That's the thing, he loves it. I don't want him to sell it." I clutch Zane's arms, which are wrapped around me. It feels good to talk about this. It's off-limits at my own house. "My dad is who he is. He's a good guy. My mom makes him feel horrible all the time. I hate it."

Zane squeezes. "Do you think they'll split up?"

"I don't know."

"Maybe it wouldn't be so bad." He interlaces his fingers with mine. "Maybe you and Faye could move to Denver with me and mom. Then we could hang out all the time."

"I wish. Not going to happen, but I'm glad you're my best friend, Zane." My eyes are heavy. Probably because I feel so safe when I'm close to him like this. Like our own protective cocoon.

Zane presses his head against mine in a head snuggle. "Oh yeah? You're my everything, Fee. Sleep tight."

The next thing I know, I feel the bed dip. Someone is sitting by me and Zane. My eyes blink open to see it's morning. Lianne stares down at Zane and me still wrapped up together under the blanket like a giant burrito.

"Good morning, Fee." She brushes my hair out of my face. "Maybe you should get in your own bed before your mom gets up."

I prop myself up on one arm and rub the sleep out of my eyes with the other. Zane snorts in his sleep and flops over to his other side. I'm not sure why me sleeping with Zane is such a big deal. "Did we do something wrong?"

"No, sweetheart. It's just that you're getting older now. So is Zane."

"She's worried that I'll poke you with my morning woody, Fee." Zane's groggy voice is muffled by the pillow.

I'm stumped. "Um, woody?"

"Zane!" Lianne swats him with the back of her hand.

"What?" He half-sits, leaning up on one elbow. His hair's a rat's nest, you can barely see his eyes squint against the light. "*You* said it's a natural bodily function."

Lianne wrinkles her nose. "Of course it is, but you can't say stuff like that to Fiona, it's disrespectful."

My eyes ping-pong between Zane and his mom. I'm clueless about what they're talking about.

"I can say anything to Fee, she doesn't care." Zane yawns and continues. "Fee…when I wake up in the morning, sometimes my penis is stiff. I'm becoming a man now. Sticky stuff called semen comes out of it when I play with it. Mom can explain everything."

I have no idea what to say. That was not what I was expecting.

At all.

Lianne winces and glances over at me.

Could my eyes be any wider? No. No, they couldn't. We had sex education at school, but we didn't have pictures or anything. Hearing Zane talk about his penis this way is a little bit shocking. I guess it never occurred to me that what we learned in class translated to real life. Or hard penises.

Of course, I can't help looking down at Zane's crotch. He grins and covers it with his hand.

"Okay, okay. That's enough. Thanks a lot, kiddo. Now I've got to let Faye know we've had this little chat." She shakes her head at Zane like he's a bad puppy. Then she ruffles his hair. "You're something else, Zaney."

"I know." He nestles into her hand, smiling like a lunatic.

The sound of footsteps down the hall grabs all of our attention. Lianne motions for me to get into my own bed. I scramble up and over just as my mom walks in. "Morning, kids. Oh, hey Lianne." She stops in her tracks when she sees Zane's mom.

"Morning, Faye. Let's go get some coffee. I've got to tell you something." Lianne pops up and sweeps out of the room, motioning for my mom to follow. "Zane? Fiona? Get ready, we'll go down to the beach today."

With our moms gone, Zane and I look at each and start snickering.

Soon, I'm laughing so hard the bed shakes. Tears stream down Zane's face. He clutches his belly and wheezes, which sets me on a whole round of giggles. Every time one of us recovers, all it takes is a simple glance and we launch into another fit of laughter.

Neither of us can stop.

At some point, I hear my mom calling for us to come down for breakfast, which only starts a new cycle. Zane finally manages to shout out a response, "We'll be down in a minute."

By the time the madness ends, I'm exhausted.

Happy.

And curious.

"Is it weird when your penis gets hard?" I whisper to Zane as we shuffle toward the stairs. "It seems like it would feel funny."

Zane blushes. "It actually feels really good. I'm kind of obsessed. Don't tell my mom."

"I won't." I can't look at him, for some reason I'm a little shy. Embarrassed maybe? Like what we're talking about is forbidden. Except it's Zane. We *can* talk about anything. "Was it weird that your mom made me get in my own bed? We've always slept together."

Zane stops at the top of the stairs. "Mom had the sex talk with me. Now that we're getting older, I'm pretty sure they worry about us wanting to do it with each other."

"Do what?"

"Fee-own-uh. Sex. S.E.X." How is he so calm when my heart is beating really fast? I mean, even though I'm comfortable with Zane, this is basically a forbidden subject at my house. Well, there it is. Zane's goofy smile makes me feel comfortable again. "You and me will have sex one day, right?"

I can't help but grin back at him. "Yeah. I guess."

"I mean it won't be for a while. We're only twelve." Zane takes my hand. "Have you had the sex talk with Faye or Gus?"

As if. "No. We did have a lecture on sex education at school. It was mortifying."

He nudges me with his hip. "Nah, don't be embarrassed. Sex is natural. That's what my mom says."

"Somehow, I don't think my mom and your mom feel the same way." I roll my eyes. "She was pissed that they taught it in school without her permission."

Zane drops my hand and starts down the stairs. "Maybe that's why mom acted so weird when she saw us together this morning."

"Zane?" I remain where I am. He turns to face me as I say, "Promise me you won't talk about this in front of my mom. I don't want her to know about me and you talking about it."

"I won't."

I'm not sure why, call it instinct, but I don't want anything to ruin the time my mom and I spend with Lianne and Zane. Something about how Lianne reacted this morning scares me. "I don't ever want us to be apart, Zane. I just…"

He nods. "Yeah. Okay. I get it."

"You do?"

"Fee, please don't stress. Nothing will happen to you and me. Your mom always used to joke about us getting married. She loves me like a son. One day, I'll be her son-in-law, mark my words." He starts back down the stairs motioning for me to follow. "Let's get some breakfast. Just remember, no matter what, nothing and no one will keep us apart. That's a promise."

Just like that, I feel better.

Because I know.

Without a shadow of doubt.

It's me and Zane against the world.

CHAPTER 8

AGE 13

I broke Greg Smith's nose.

On my first day of junior high school.

And I don't feel bad. He had it coming.

The stupid asshole and his shitty friends finally pushed me too far. I can take the taunts. The jeers. The shoves. Even an elbow to the ribs here and there. This time, they tried to take my new guitar at lunch. It happened once in grade school, and it wasn't going to happen again. I have my limits.

It takes me a while to get there.

When I'm pushed too far, it's all over.

Today, for our first day at school, we were supposed to bring something that was special to us. My prized possession is my new 1960 Gibson Les Paul Standard Sunburst. Dad gave it to me last year for my twelfth birthday with the promise he'd teach me how to play.

"Zane, Principal Fitzgerald will see you now." A lady in a yellow dress with white sneakers holds the door open. I walk inside. Sit down. Cross my arms and look at the man in front of me directly in the eye. I don't care what this guy thinks of me. Not even a little bit.

On the morning announcements, I learned our principal likes to call himself "Fitzy." Right now, Fitzy leans way back in an ancient brown leather chair studying me. Actually, probably judging me as a person based on my black skinny jeans, Limelight band T-shirt and long, curly hair. His fingers are steepled in front of his nose and his abnormally beady eyes bore a hole into my face. "Young man, we do not allow fighting in this school."

"Yeah. I know."

"That's all you have to say?" He leans forward on his elbows and gives me what he seems to think is a scary, mind-your-manners look.

I cross my arms and stare back at Fitzy. "I wasn't fighting. No one touches my guitar. Greg Smith tried to take it from me. He's bullied me for years. Taken my lunch. Called me names. Smashed my ukulele. It wasn't going to happen again."

"Zane, you can't possibly justify physically harming someone over a guitar."

I glare at him. "Yes, I can. My dad is the guitar player in Limelight…"

"Wait, you're telling me your dad is Carter *Pope*?" God. Fitzy's starstruck. It's a 50/50 chance whenever I name drop my dad. Or my mom in certain circles. Which isn't often, obvi. For this reason.

"Yeah. He's my dad. So you see, when Greg and his friends were trying to steal the guitar from me, I was outnumbered. It left me no choice but to fight back."

I'm interrupted when the door opens and Grandpa walks in. He takes the seat next to me. "Sorry I'm a few minutes late."

"Mr. Rocks, welcome." Fitzy leans over his desk to shake my grandpa's hand. "We were just chatting about how your grandson seriously injured another child today."

"Oh, I heard what Zane said. I also heard what you just said to him, Mr. Fitzgerald."

"It's Fitzy."

I roll my eyes. I mean, seriously?

Grandpa puts his hand on my shoulder and squeezes. "Just so I'm clear, are you chastising Zane for defending himself?"

Fitzy straightens in his chair. "Of course not."

"Well that's what it sounded like. For your information, Zane's guitar is one of the rarest in the world. It cannot be replaced." Grandpa emphasizes each word by pointing at Fitzy. "It's asinine for anyone to turn this around on Zane when he was minding his own business. He was protecting his property from a thief."

Fitzy is visibly sweating. "Uh. Um. Mr. Rocks… That's not…"

"Stop right there." Grandpa's fierce glare at my principal shuts him up quick. "Start again. You were saying?"

"Stealing and bullying are expellable offenses," Fitzy sputters.

"Good." Grandpa stands, turns and steps toward the door, motioning for me to join him. "Then expel him. This is *not* how the school year is going to go for Zane."

Fitzy's eyes bug out. Wisely, he says nothing more.

We leave and walk silently to Grandpa's red truck, but once we are seated inside, he fist-pumps me. "I knew you'd gain confidence from Krav Maga."

"I've never had to use it in real life until today." I hug my guitar, which rests between my legs. "It was stupid of me to bring the Gibson to school. If Greg had wrecked it, Carter would have freaked out."

Grandpa looks straight ahead at the road. His lips are set in a tight line, which always happens when my dad comes up. I get it. From my grandpa's perspective— anyone's perspective really— my dad is a fuck-up. Luckily, we aren't too far from home and in a couple of minutes pull up to Mom's new house. Her Mercedes is in the driveway, so I thank Grandpa for having my back and head inside.

The new house is cool. We moved in at the beginning of summer. My room is black, gray, and red and is set up like a music studio. I have my own bathroom too. Mom's bedroom is huge, with a deck overlooking the creek, a closet the size of a gymnasium and a bathroom with a cool walk-in shower. Her favorite room is the ballet studio, which has a barre and floor-to-ceiling mirrors.

I find Mom standing at the kitchen counter in a leotard and oversized sweatshirt holding some paperwork. She tucks it under the rest of the mail when she hears me. "Zaney, I heard what happened. Are you okay?"

"Yeah, I was stupid for bringing my guitar to school." I carefully set my guitar case down. "Grandpa was fierce."

"Well, he's something."

I shrug. "As Grandpa said, Krav Maga came in handy."

"I guess. I'm not a big fan of you fighting."

Neither am I, but it sure is nice that I have skills to get myself out of a jam. Plus, fighting is a hell of a lot better than being bullied, that's for sure. "I'm fine. I use it for good, not evil."

"Okay, I just worry about you. Would you mind if I go work out in my studio for an hour or two?" She runs her hand along her red hair, which is pulled back in a bun. Like always. "We can get fast food for dinner tonight. Your pick."

I close the gap between us and hug her tightly. "I'm practically grown up, Mom. You don't need to treat me like a little boy anymore, you know."

"You'll always be my little boy." Mom kisses my forehead and runs her fingers through my long curls and smiles. "God, you are the spitting image of your dad today."

I roll my eyes. She releases me and heads across the hall to her dance studio. When I hear the music playing, I run up to my room. Slam the door and call Fee.

"Hey." She answers on the first ring. "How was your first day?"

"I broke a kid's nose who tried to steal my Gibson." I flop on my bed.

She pauses. I can hear her suck in a breath.

"My grandpa chewed the principal out." I punch my pillow. "How was your day?"

She's quiet. Too quiet.

"Fee?"

"They're getting a divorce. It's official. Oh, and Mom's moving to Bellingham. They're downstairs screaming at each other right now. I'm surprised you can't hear them."

Crap. Fiona's parents have always fought and bickered, so I'm *not* surprised at the news, but that's not what she needs to hear. "Are you okay?"

"I'm pissed." I hear her slam the door. "I swear, if she makes me go with her, I'll just run away. Seattle is my *home*."

"That sucks." I mean, what else is there to say?

"Zane, if I tell you something, will you promise not to get mad?" Fiona whispers.

I hate it when people say that. Fiona is the only one who can get away with such a stupid request. “Oh-kay.”

“Your dad loaned my dad money for the club. My mom found out. She said it was the last straw. That Dad’s friendship with Carter was more important to him than she was.”

Any news about my dad is worth its weight in gold. Fee always has the goods because she sees him in person a lot more than I do. “You know, so far he’s kept his promise to teach me guitar. He’s never missed one of our calls yet.”

“That’s good. My dad said rehab seems to be sticking.”

Fiona means well. She knows more than anyone my history with Carter. Unlike my dad, her dad is cool. Responsible. She spends a lot of time with him. I know she wants that for me too. “He told me that after he got out of rehab, his band decided to take time off so he could recover. Every night at seven he Skypes me and we play guitar for an hour. Mostly we just jam. We don’t really talk or anything.”

“At least you’re spending time with him.”

“Yeah. Playing with Carter makes me feel normal. It’s like something inside me is wired to play music.”

“It comes easy to you.” Fiona’s voice is soft and soothing. “You’ve taught yourself to play the weirdest instruments. Who plays the ukulele? Or the accordion? Or the banjo?”

“Me, but the Gibson is fucking killer. It’s changed everything. I’m obsessed with the guitar.”

“You better be,” she says, laughing. “My dad said it’s worth thirty-thousand dollars.”

Whoa! I didn’t know that. “It’s cool to watch Carter play. Music is effortless for him too. It’s the one thing we have in common. “

Music is really all I think about. Playing calms me. It allows me to focus and get out of my head. It gives me confidence; I don’t give two shits about what the kids at school think anymore. I have an outlet.

Dr. June thinks it's great therapy, whatever that means.

"It's good that your dad is so encouraging, Zane. He's really trying. That's all you can ask."

"Yeah, but I still don't really know him. I'm trying not to get my hopes up. I mean, who knows how long he'll keep up this routine. I've been disappointed by Carter too many times. I'm not about to get comfortable now."

Fiona is the only person on this earth who knows the depths of my frustration with my father. She never pities me, she just supports. She's my best friend. "I get it."

"It pisses me off that he hasn't brought up his overdose. Or addiction issues. Or apologized for not showing up all those times when he said he was coming and didn't. I keep my feelings to myself, though. I'm afraid I'll come across angry. Maybe drive him back to drugs."

"Zane, if he goes back to using, it would never be your fault."

"All I know is when he does slip up, I don't want that to be on me."

Fiona's silent. She has no concept of what it's like to have a parent who doesn't want anything to do with you. I don't want her to know. Because it sucks. I don't say any of this though. She needs me because her world is being shaken up. "Enough about me and Carter. It's old news, and I'm sure it will be fine. It will be fine for you too, Fee. Everything will work out."

"I doubt it." Fiona sighs. "I'm actually a little scared."

"Remember what I said last summer?"

"About your penis?"

I laugh. "No. About us."

"Yeah."

"Do you believe it?"

"I want to."

"Tell me what I said."

"You said no matter what, nothing and no one will keep us apart," she chokes out through her sniffles.

"Believe it. I always keep my promises. Even if I have to go to Bellingham to get you." I shut my eyes. Fiona's the most important thing in my life and always has been. I can't wait until we're adults and can live our own lives. "Do you feel better?"

"You always make everything better."

I hope so, because it's always been me and Fiona against the world.

Nothing will ever take her place.

Ever.

CHAPTER 9

AGE 14

Zane's long, dark hair is whipping around his face in the wind as he leans over the rail of the ferry. He's so tall now. Handsome. Dangerous-looking in his black skull hoodie and skinny black jeans. We're on our way to Roche Harbor in the San Juan Islands for our annual two-week summer vacation with our moms.

Something I look forward to every year.

"So, I was thinking about something that I want to run past you." Zane pulls back his hair into a knot out of his face. His chocolate-brown eyes sparkle. "I'm calling it Operation Seattle."

Ferry wind is no joke. I raise an eyebrow and plait my long, dark hair into a braid so it doesn't get more tangled. "I'm listening."

"Carter's been clean for a couple of years now. We're still Skyping. It's actually been cool. He's taught me all of his guitar tricks." Zane rubs his chin. He wears a few silver rings now. They glint in the sun. "I think I want to move to Seattle to live with him during high school."

"Ha. Like your mom will ever let *that* happen."

He tilts his head. "I have a whole year to convince her."

"Zane, are you crazy? Your mom doesn't trust Carter. She'll never believe he'll stay clean long enough for you to move in with him. Just don't get your hopes up." I cross my arms over my chest. I notice Zane keeps glancing at my boobs, which have developed a lot over the past year. His looks make me feel equal parts self-conscious and equal parts zingy.

"You're wrong. She's always wanted me to have a relationship with him." Zane mirrors me by crossing his arms over his chest. "But I also agree. It won't be easy to convince her to let me go. On the other hand, she only has a couple more years left as a dancer. I know the only reason she's turned down roles in London and Chicago is because of me. It would be nice for her to be free to have a cool experience. Maybe I just need to finesse it a little."

I can't get over how much Zane has grown up. How thoughtful and caring he is, despite all of his disappointments over the years. He's also so incredibly good-looking. Swarthy. His cheekbones are like blades. His lips are supple. Supple? I didn't even know I knew the word supple. Anyway, I find myself staring. "What are you going to do?"

"I'm still figuring it out. But the best part of the plan is you going back to Seattle to live with Gus. Then we can go to high school together." Zane is bouncing up and down on his heels as he speaks. "Our halves will be reunited."

I laugh bitterly. "Now I *know* you're crazy. My mom is *not* like your mom, who actually *wants* things to be better with Carter. She fucking hates my dad. She makes it impossible for me to see him. I haven't been back down to Seattle since we moved. She makes him come to

Bellingham if he wants to see me."

"I know. That sucks." Zane throws an arm over my shoulder and my heart rate speeds up. "Let's give it a think. We'll come up with a plan."

I lay my head on his shoulder and he squeezes me closer. It's August and the weather is warm. The sky is blue and cloudless. The air smells like salt and freshness. We watch the ferry's wake over the side of the boat. In this moment snuggled up to Zane, I can picture it. Us together in high school. The perfect couple. I'll take business prep courses and work my way through *Mastering the Art of French Cooking*. Zane will play music and get even more ripped practicing Krav Maga. We'll walk the halls of Garfield High together.

How cool would that be?

A dream come true.

Too soon, Roche Harbor comes into view. We pry ourselves apart and head to the lower decks to meet our moms at the car. We sit in the back seat with our pinkies locked on the drive to the hotel. Sneaking glances and knowing smiles. Our moms chatter away up front, oblivious. Zane strokes the top of my hand with his thumb. We interlace our fingers.

It's natural for us.

The next two weeks are filled with hikes, picnics, a whale-watching boat ride and a lot of doing nothing. Our moms love to sit by the pool and drink wine while we swim and lie out in the sun. In the evenings, we go for dinner. Eventually all of us end up by the fire pit throwing out songs for Zane to play on his prized Gibson guitar. Singing along. He's absolutely incredible. None of us have been able to stump him. It's like he's a walking songbook.

Being with Zane this year feels different. Last year when we were in Hawaii and had separate hotel rooms, he snuck into mine to help me sleep every night. Just like we did in Mexico the year before. We just slip into our usual patterns. Best friends. Confidants. Partners in crime. Kid stuff.

Except things are shifting between us.

I *know* I'm not crazy.

We are constantly touching. Hugging. Holding hands.

Finding ways to stand or sit beside each other.

Watching each other.

The love we have for each other is different.

More grown up.

Just being around him makes my heart flutter.

The time passes by too quickly. I want to freeze every moment we have together so we never have to goodbye. A year is too long.

And yet, tonight is our last night. The moms have gone to bed. We stay up. Zane strums his guitar while I sit by the fire and make smores with the fancy chocolate I bought in town. And the homemade vanilla marshmallows I whipped up earlier today. I'm trying to absorb every minute we have, but I can't deny that I'm feeling blue. Leaving Zane every year takes a toll on me. I feel so empty when we are apart.

This year is going to be unbearable.

I'm deep into my thoughts, when he gently circles my wrist in his fingers and takes the twig from me. I glance at the marshmallow at the end of it. It's black as coal and smoking.

"Did you want to kill it or eat it?" Zane grins.

"I guess I spaced out for a sec." I get lost in his eyes, which are boring into mine.

He wraps his arm around me. I lean my head on his shoulder. "Whatcha thinking about?"

"You." I look back up at him and smile. Our lips are millimeters apart. A sense of awareness passes over his eyes like a wave. I lick my lips. He sucks in a breath.

Then lowers his mouth to mine.

It's not our first kiss, that ship sailed when we were six.

Oh, but this one is so very different.

At first, it's innocent enough.

But then our lips part and our tongues tentatively touch. Taste. Explore. It's like we've discovered pure magic, that's how profound the moment is. He tastes every part of my mouth, swirling his tongue against mine. He caresses my face with both hands, moving my head. Thumbs caressing my cheeks. My hands run through the tangles of his hair and stroke his nape.

Our bodies press closer and closer together.

We make out for what seems like hours, and I never want to stop.

Ever.

He shifts his position to fully face me but doesn't break our connection. Instead, he deepens it by pulling me onto his lap so I'm straddling him. His arms wrap around my waist. Mine wind around his neck. Our mouths furiously press together. Needy. Desperate. When I lock my legs around his waist to get even closer, I feel him. Through his board shorts and my cut-offs, he's stiff against my center.

So that's what his hard penis feels like.

Good.

I pull away in surprise and look down between us and then up into his eyes.

Even by the firelight, I can see he's blushing. It doesn't stop him from yanking me back against him. We pick up where we left off and our hands are everywhere. Stroking. Caressing. Clutching. We grind against each other frantically, building to something I don't quite understand.

What I do understand is I didn't know what heaven was until now.

We are so utterly lost in each other that we don't realize we have an audience.

"Fiona! Zane! What the fuck is going on here?" my mom screeches. We fly apart. Zane's lips are swollen and his hair is everywhere. I can't imagine what I look like. I frantically try to pull myself together. What we were doing felt like the most right thing I'd ever done in my life. Like destiny.

Because of this, I'm not so much mortified that we got caught as I am by my mom's reaction. I glance at Lianne, who is right behind my mother. Her eyes are soft. She's not angry. Not even a little.

"Faye, we were just kissing." Zane's eyes are like saucers. "Did we do something wrong?"

"No, of course not, sweetheart," Lianne soothes, just as my mom growls, "*Yes*!"

Zane and I look at each other, confused.

I pull my sweatshirt around me. "Mom, stop. Don't make a big deal about this."

"Big deal. *Big deal*?" Steam is shooting out of my mom's ears. "If you think I'm going to stand by and watch you throw your life away on this boy the way his mother did on that worthless, *drug addict* father of his, you've got another thing coming."

Metaphorically, the record screeches.

Zane's face.

God.

Zane's *face*.

He's utterly crushed.

"Mom!" I scream angrily.

Lianne gasps and runs to Zane, looking over at my mom. "Faye, you had no fucking right to say that. I'm going to need you to apologize to my son. Right now."

"Like hell I will." Mom crosses her arms and doubles down. "I'm *glad* I finally said what I've been thinking all of these years. I've tried to bite my tongue. But I won't for one more minute. Zane is turning out *just* like his father. Anyone can see it from a mile away. He's obsessed with that stupid guitar. He's been leering at Fiona for the past two years and was about to fuck my fourteen-year-old daughter on a public beach. *She's fourteen*! Oh hell no. Over my dead body."

Zane stares into the fire like a zombie. A shamed zombie. Faye Reynolds scored a direct hit. Lianne whispers something to him, he just shakes his head. He won't look at me.

My mom storms over, places her hands on my shoulders and attempts to spin me around toward the hotel. I struggle and break free from her grasp. "You're crazy if you think you'll keep Zane and me apart. He's my other half. You've said it yourself."

"Don't test me, Fiona. This vacation is over. O.V.E.R. This friendship is over. We're taking the next ferry home." Mom starts back up the walkway. "I fucking *mean* it. Say goodbye to Zane and Lianne, because this is the very last day of this stupid tradition. There won't be a next time."

When she's out of sight I kneel by Zane. He looks at me with tears in his soulful, brown eyes. My heart breaks. I take his hands in mine. "Don't listen to her, Zane. We have a plan. I don't agree with anything she said just now. *Please*."

He still can't meet my eye.

"Sweetheart, it's best if you do what your mom says." Lianne strokes my temple. "We'll be fine. Let her cool down. Zane will call you tomorrow."

I squeeze his fingers between mine. "Zane, remember—no matter what, nothing and no one will keep us apart. Not even my mom."

He finally looks up. A tear rolls down his face.

His expression says it all.

Like he knows life as we've known it is over.

Like he knows my mom *will* keep us apart.

Like he knows, despite our vows, everything has spun out of our control.

CHAPTER 10

AGE 15

The last year of junior high is ruining me.

Fiona and I haven't spoken since Roche Harbor.

No letters. No calls. Nothing.

Not for a lack of trying on my part. Her mobile number was disconnected. Faye won't answer my mom's calls. I guess she never cooled down. She definitely made good on her promise to split us apart. To say I was stunned by the things she said to me would be a lie. Every time we were on vacation together, Fiona's mom would get her little digs in. Never in front of Mom. Or Fiona.

Oh, I always knew how she felt about me. About Carter.

It never occurred to me she'd follow through and keep me from Fee.

That's going to change.

Operation Seattle is about to be put into motion.

The annoying Skype tune blares through my laptop. It's time for my nightly call with Carter. He's been consistent, I'll give him that. We still don't talk about anything personal or deep. After losing Fiona, playing guitar with him for an hour each night is as much as I can manage.

Even now, I'm wary.

He disappointed me too many times over the years.

He seems to be okay with my boundaries.

"Yo, Zane!" Carter's sitting with his Gibson. Today, I've got the new Rickenbacker he sent for my fifteenth birthday ready to go. He squints into the screen. "Ah, that's sweet. I can't wait to hear it."

We play for a while as usual until it's time for me to disconnect. He looks like he wants to say something. "What's up, Carter?"

"Can I talk to you about something that is long overdue?" He scrubs his chin with his hand. "I think it's time I come clean about some things with you."

"Yeah, okay."

"It's kind of deep." He seems unsure of himself.

I'm not sure what he wants from me. He's the grown-up. "I said it's okay."

He coughs and puts his fists over his eyes to compose himself before he looks at me through the screen. "I'm sorry. Saying it won't change anything, I know that. But I'm determined not to ever slip up again."

It's all I can do not to roll my eyes. I've been in Narateen for a long time. He's working the steps, as he should be.

"Um. Well. Anyway. I'm sure you were able to Google this shit, but I tried to kick heroin for years. I overdosed in the park when you were little. I know you remember trying to wake me up. The truth is, I left you and Fiona alone to score and then I OD'd right in front of the two of you."

My mouth drops open. I never thought he'd admit it. "Yeah. I know.

It was really fucked up."

"I know. I'm not proud. What's even worse is that wasn't my rock bottom." Tears well up in his eyes. He looks off into the distance and says more quietly, almost to himself, "It wasn't even my fucking rock bottom."

Faye's hatred of my dad makes a lot more sense now.

"The last time I overdosed, the guys in my band staged an intervention and kicked me out of Limelight. That's why we took a long break and have cut back our schedule. I know your mother thinks that losing the band scared me straight. But it wasn't. When I was lying in the hospital thinking about all the ways I did you wrong? I realized I turned into my own father. The thought of you having a dad with no redeemable qualities made me sick."

"Yeah, don't make staying sober about me, Carter." I parrot things I'd learned over the years and were ingrained in my body. "You've got to stay sober for you. For the record, I'm glad you're clean. I really hope you stay healthy."

He nods. "I want that too. Of course, I'm taking it one day at a time but in a few months, I'll be three years sober. I haven't slipped. I know I'm not going to. I've never felt better."

"Zane!" I hear Mom downstairs. "I'm home."

"I gotta go, Mom's home." I click off without really saying goodbye to Carter. It's time for a conversation with my mom.

She's going through the mail at the kitchen and looks up when I stand in front of her. "How was your day?"

"Shitty." I cross my arms and glare at her. She's surprised, I've never even raised my voice at her. I'm usually the perfect, loving son. "Are you ever going to let me see my dad?"

Her face drains. "What do you mean?"

"Carter's doing really good. He also just got finished with some twelve-step apology bullshit."

She sits on the kitchen stool. Rests her face on her hand and just looks at me.

"I want to go stay with Carter in Seattle. It's time for me to know him."

"Zane..."

"No!" I turn and bound up the stairs, yelling as I go. "All I have is stupid Skype guitar lessons. He hasn't missed one in years. Carter has really changed. He said he wants to be a better dad. It's time I got to spend real time with him. *Please*."

And so after *serious* discussions about his addiction. And boundaries. And backup plans, I'm at Carter's huge mansion on Lake Washington. We're sitting in his sunken living room in comfy corduroy chairs staring at each other like strangers. It's been a few years since I've actually seen him in person. Skype guitar lessons aside, now that I'm here, I can't believe how uncomfortable this is. And how different his life is from mine in Denver.

He picked me up in a fucking Bentley, for God's sake.

"I'm glad you're here." Carter breaks the silence.

I stare at the custom inlaid wood floor and take in the opulence of this home. "Yeah?"

"Should I say what I need to say?" He drums his fingers on the armchair. "I'm sorry that this is so awkward. That I've been so absent over the years."

I look up at him. Confused. Didn't we have this exact conversation a few weeks ago? I suppose I need to indulge him. It's important to get on his good side so I can keep my promise to Fiona. "I can admit it. I wasn't prepared to be a father. Your mother and I were very young.

These are not excuses, but you were born when I was only a couple years older than you are now."

I look out at the expansive lawn and the lake outside his floor-to-ceiling living room window. "And?"

"And what?"

I walk over to the window to get a better look. I can't help but snark, "You were a young father, blah blah blah. That's not why you were a bad father. How did you become an addict?"

"I'm not sure what your mom told you."

"Nothing." I twirl my hair around my finger. "She's not spoken of you much at all."

He winces. Nods. "Well, the basics are I grew up on the Puyallup Indian Reservation until I left at seventeen. My dad died of a heroin overdose when I was young. My mom died of cancer right after you were born. She was a tribal advocate. Addiction runs on both sides of my family. I always knew I was predisposed. For years, I was able to control it. Then I couldn't. I nearly lost my life. The band. I did lose you and your mother."

"Boo-fucking-hoo." I can't help myself. I also can't help but think coming here was a terrible idea.

Carter gets up and stands next to me. "That's fair enough."

"I don't really remember you at all, Carter." I'm pissed because my eyes fill with tears, so I want to lash out. Hurt him. Even though I remember everything. Every. Single. Thing. My emotions are all over the place being here. "Mom said that we were all happy when I was a baby, but I don't remember any of it."

"Come with me." He's on the move, motioning for me to follow.

We head upstairs to a spare bedroom. It's overwhelming. I don't even know where to look because it's filled with all sorts of Limelight stuff. On the walls. On shelves lining the walls. In the closet. Almost every surface is filled with everything from T-shirts to bobble-head figurines to gold records. I'm in awe.

"Whoa!" I turn around and around, taking it all in. "It's like a museum of Limelight."

He's digging in a drawer and holds up some photos. "Here, look at this."

I decide to fuck with him a bit and point to a picture of Gus with Fiona. "Wait, I remember her. What was her name?"

"Fiona. You were born a couple of months apart. You spent nearly every day with her when I was touring and your mom was dancing at PNB." He hands me another picture. "This one is in the back of a club called RKCNDY. That's you in the stroller. There's your mom."

"Whoa." I trace baby me with my finger. I can't believe he can't remember that Fiona and I have been in each other's lives up until last year when I nearly came in my pants making out with her. I mean, he gave us both phones when we were ten so we could talk to each other. It doesn't make sense.

Except it does. He was probably using and doesn't remember.

I feel like I'm in a warped world talking to him sometimes.

It must be strange losing such big chunks of your life.

"Zane, I wanted to be a good dad. I did. Your mother was the love of my life." He rests his hand on my shoulder. "I don't want to blame it on a disease that I have. I take full responsibility for being a world-class asshole. I'd like to try to make it better, though."

He seems sincere, so I give him a break. "I want that too."

And I do. I really do.

"Wanna play some tunes?" He gestures to the stairs. "Practice room's downstairs."

The rest of the summer is a blur and a bit of a disappointment. My plan to have him help me get to Fiona is a disaster. Fiona's mom has a restraining order against Gus, and he's currently battling for custody. Carter can't risk doing anything that will interfere with Gus's case, so he won't take me to Bellingham.

So now I'm stuck here for the summer without any way to get in touch with her. I hope she knows I'm trying to keep my promise to her. She's never stopped being my everything. I love her. With every ounce of my being. Especially after what happened between us.

Her long, dark hair. Sparkling eyes. Creamy skin. Lush, soft body. She's the only one for me. My every fantasy. My wet dream.

Literally. Every day. My wet dream.

Part of me wants to go back home to Denver and sulk. Except, at least here in Seattle, I'm closer to Fiona. I suppose I need to give this thing with Carter a chance.

So I do.

He and I stick to the same basic routine. Sleep in. Eat. Spend the day into the wee hours of the night playing out our feelings. Except now we no longer play cover songs. Carter's showing me how to create music. How to collaborate.

I never knew how much I needed it.

Needed him.

Our dual guitars.

Speak our respective truths.

Even when we can't say the actual words.

Too soon, the date I'm supposed to fly back to Denver approaches. I miss my mom. I miss my grandparents. I miss Cecil. I don't miss Colorado. Or my school. I decide I'm going to follow through on "Operation Seattle." I'm going to move to Seattle for my first year of high school.

Make more of an effort to know my dad.

Hopefully, Gus will win his court case and then I'll be here waiting for Fiona as soon as it's over.

Yep. Seattle is where I'm supposed to be.

A few days later, we sit eating steaks at a fancy restaurant called Daniel's Broiler when I finally get the courage to bring it up. "Carter? I've got to come clean about something with you."

He's mid-chew and raises an eyebrow.

"Mom and Faye Reynolds have remained friends ever since we left Seattle. Fiona and I have always written and called, she's still my best friend. The four of us have been on vacations together every summer since her parents got divorced. I'm here with you this year because all of that is over now. Last year, we got caught making out at a campfire. Faye lost her mind, said some shitty things about you and about me. Now, she's cut me off from Fiona."

Carter shakes his head back and forth vigorously, as though he's trying to clear a lifetime's worth of cobwebs. "Jesus. Fuck. Gus never said anything."

"Well, probably because Gus has to be careful. I need your help, though. I really need to get a message to her."

Carter sighs. "I really don't see him as much as I'd like because next to you, sobriety is the most important thing in my life, Zane. I've stayed away from The Mission so I'm not tempted to drink. Fuck. It's selfish of me not to check in on him more. I've not been a very good friend."

One thing that has impressed me about my dad is how completely humble he's been about his addiction. Carter is quite possibly one of the most famous musicians on the planet, but with me he's just my dad. My imperfect, mess of a dad. Except, he's not that messy. He's actually really responsible. Careful. Kind. I didn't expect for his heart to be so big.

"Ehrm, about that. I just finished ninth grade. Mom has me enrolled in high school in Denver, but I'm wondering if you'd be open to me transferring to high school in Seattle. Garfield isn't too far from your house, and it has an excellent music program. I'd come in as a sophomore, not a freshman." I decide to just toss it out there and see where it lands.

Carter's eyes widen. He puts his fork and knife down and reaches for my hand, gripping it tightly in his. "Are you serious?"

"Yes. If you want me to be here."

His entire face crumples. Tears spill down his cheeks, but he quickly wipes them away. He gets up and pulls me into the biggest bear hug of all time. "Of *course*, I want you here. That would be awesome!"

He sits back down. He smiles. Takes a bite of steak. Looks up. Smiles.

I swear, he's like a little kid.

"I'll tell Mom," I say through a mouthful of au gratin potatoes. "She'll be more likely to say yes if it comes from me."

"Zane, you don't need to 'manage' me." He makes air-quotes with his fingers. "I'm an addict, not an infant. I'm also your parent. I'll discuss this with your mother."

A few weeks later, I move in with Carter and enroll at Garfield High for my sophomore year. The timing works out perfectly. Mom is able to accept a guest role with the New York Ballet on loan from the CB. She's been surprisingly supportive about giving Carter a chance even though I know she's still skeptical. I promise to visit her for Christmas break, spring break and a couple of months next summer.

In the back of my mind, I know that as long as Carter keeps it together, I'll stay here for high school.

So I'm feeling a bit smug.

My plan has worked perfectly.

Except for the most important part: Fiona.

Now that I'll be in Seattle for good?

Getting back in her life will be my top priority.

CHAPTER 11

AGE 16

My heart is ripped out and bleeding.

Each morning I hope to wake up from this nightmare.

But, I don't.

It's hard to believe how drastically my life has changed in two years. Moving to Bellingham sucked. But after my mom snapped when she caught me making out with Zane, the suckiness is off the charts.

I'm basically in prison.

It's killing me.

Growing up, I always had a lot of freedom. Now, it's like she's on a mission to be in control of everything I do. Everyone I see. It's been such a drastic change. I don't have anything to look forward to anymore.

She won full custody. Seeing my dad is nearly impossible.

She's also successfully cut me off from Zane. I don't have any way to get in touch with him.

If she had her way, I'm sure she'd cut me off from *life*.

She says it's for the best. I'm not sure for who.

Any sane person would know that isolating a teenage girl from the people she loves is quite the opposite of being "best," right?

Tell that to my mom.

No, don't. You don't want the wrath of Faye Reynolds.

Ask my dad.

I used to love school. I had friends. I played soccer. I was even supposed to be a cheerleader. My days were filled with activities, socializing, and fun. It made my mom's constant grievances bearable.

Of course, every summer I had Zane, which was *everything*.

God, she never fucking shuts up about all the things that piss her off. The Mission. Carter. The apartment we lived in. Seattle. There's no limit to the things that bother her.

Still, I never thought in a million years she'd try to ruin Dad's life.

And mine.

But she did. And here I am, staring at the glass doors of Bellingham High School. Trying to work up the courage to go in when there's nothing for me inside those walls. A group of girls push past, jostling me on purpose. A tall blonde with low-cut jeans and a crop top actually shoves me. "Move it, psycho."

I step aside but keep my foot in her path causing her to stumble in her six-inch Jessica Simpson platforms. "Clumsy much?" I smirk and look off toward the parking lot.

A chorus of "bitch" follows from Clumsy and her friends.

I ignore them.

They're the least of my worries because I'm at the end of my rope.

And I have no one to turn to.

Fuck it.

I need a mental health day. A place to escape. I decide to go to the library. Not the school library, the public library. It's only a short walk. Yes, that's what I'll do. I'll bury myself in books and shut off my phone. The repercussions will be worth a day of peace and quiet.

When I arrive, I see a row of computers with free Internet access. Mom doesn't allow it in the house. My options at school are limited. My phone only has basic features. Certainly, no online capabilities. Suddenly, I'm feeling jazzed at the opportunity to surf all my favorite gossip sites for an entire day. I sit at a corner terminal, which is open to Facebook.

An idea formulates.

And then I'm typing like a madwoman.

Within minutes, I've created a Gmail account and a new Facebook profile. I don't have any way to upload a picture of myself, so I Google a random photo of a daffodil and upload it instead. Glancing around, even though no one is looking at me, I zip up my hoodie and pull my black skull cap down low on my forehead. I've got to be stealth, after all.

I type: *Zane Rocks*

His Facebook page fills the screen. Zane's deep-brown eyes peer out from under a green beanie. His long, curly hair is just past his shoulders. Angular cheekbones are smattered with black whiskers. He sits on a stool with his Gibson resting against his leg. He wears black jeans and a tight black T-shirt over defined muscles. A chunky silver chain is draped around his neck. Leather cuffs enclose both wrists.

Holy fucking moly.

He's so manly.

Gorgeous.

No. Drop dead gorgeous.

Mine.

I scroll through his profile to discover he's in Seattle. At Garfield High School, just like he planned. Other than that, there's not much to his online presence. He clearly doesn't spend a lot of time on Facebook. There are only a few posts of him and another long-haired, good-looking guy. Maybe Zane has finally made a friend.

I keep staring at his picture, though. It feels like he's looking right at me.

Waiting for me.

Even though I know it's a stupid thing to think.

Except it's Zane.

My other half.

At least he used to be.

Before I can stop myself, I add him as a friend. I'm not sure what I thought would happen, but of course there's no response. He's at school right now. I can't help but stare at the screen like a zombie. Nothing.

I read Perez Hilton and a few other gossip sites. Still nothing. Finally, I force myself to get up and walk around. Miracle of all miracles, there's a copy of *Twilight* on the shelf. I tuck myself into a cozy chair and get immersed in Bella and Edward's vampire world. A few hours later, I check my watch and then my phone. *Fuck.* I've missed several calls from my mom.

Shit's going to hit the fan.

The clock is ticking, so I have to make the most of my remaining freedom.

I stop by the computer terminals on my way out and log on to my new Facebook account. My heart races. No, it actually thunders out of my chest. There are messages waiting for me.

Zane: Fiona?

Zane: Fee?

Zane: Talk to me, I've tried to get to you, but I don't know where you are.

Zane: Fee answer me.

Zane: Are you okay? Tell me you're okay!

Zane: Where are you?

Zane: Tell me everything!!!!!

Zane: Fee? I miss you so much. I have to go to class. I have so much to tell you please please please call me. My number is 206-555-0000.

I quickly program it into my phone and save it under the name "Lisa." My mom checks it every morning and evening, so I can't really use it to talk or text Zane. I don't want to lose his number. I stare at the screen, wondering what to say. What I *should* say.

I have nothing to lose, I decide.

Fiona: I miss you more than anything. I'm still in Bellingham. I'm sorry I haven't called or written. I've been grounded permanently. My mom forbid me to ever see you. I don't really get to see my dad. Living with her is a nightmare. I'm not okay, Zane. Nothing about what is going on is okay. I need you.

Before I can overthink it, I hit send.

And pray.

When I get home, I swear, my mom's gone off the deep end. My entire room has been torn apart. "Where have you been all day? Don't lie to me."

"I was at the public library reading." I decide on the truth.

She just stares at me. Like I'm an alien.

"I see you were busy tearing apart my room." I step over all of my clothes, which are piled all over the floor. I begin hanging them up. "Did you find something interesting?"

"You are a shitty daughter, Fiona."

"Yeah, yeah. Well, each day with you is a real fucking treat." I continue to straighten up my room without looking at her. "You're a bitter, joyless bitch. It's like you love ruining my life."

She lunges for me. Grabs my arm and yanks me to her. "Shut the fuck up, you ungrateful little girl. I'm the only one who has protected you from the *drug addicts* your father has brought around you. I'm the only one who cares about your future."

"I hope you left a mark; I'll report you to child services so I can go live with my dad." I rip my arm away from her grip. "I'd give anything to get away from you. *Anything*."

Her face crumples. She pushes up the sleeve on my T-shirt to see my arm. Sure enough, you can see the imprints of her fingers. There will be bruises. She sinks to the ground. I know what's next, and I'm right. She begins to sob uncontrollably. "I'm sorry, Fiona. You have to understand, I just want to keep you safe. I'm your mother. I love you."

I continue to straighten up my room while she cries. This isn't the first time we've gone through this insanity. She becomes frantic if I'm not with her. I can't go anywhere but school, and even then she demands to know exactly what time I'll be home. She texts me non stop throughout the day, even during class. If I don't answer her, she calls incessantly.

I'm drowning.

So no, I don't feel bad for taking a day off for myself.

Not even a little bit.

No matter what comes next.

"Just let me go live with my dad." My mom's emotional outburst is over, she's leaning against the wall watching me put the last of my clothes away. "I want to finish high school in Seattle."

"No."

"Yes."

She leaves the room. I hear her bedroom door slam. She won't be back out tonight. When I glance down at the floor, I spot my phone. She didn't take it with her tonight! I pick it up and flop on my bed. Relishing the silence. It all hits me at once. I was in touch with Zane.

I have his phone number!

I dial.

No answer.

Fiona: It's Fee I just tried to call you.

Nothing.

I stare at the screen for two solid hours.

Finally, he responds.

Zane: I'm calling you in five.

My heart races. I run to the bathroom. Throw my pajamas on. Shut my bedroom door and climb into bed. Just in time for the phone to ring.

"Ohmygod I've missed you so much," I blurt out the second I see his call coming in. I don't even wait for it to ring.

Zane's voice is deeper, huskier. "Fee, I've been out of my mind trying to figure out a way to find you."

I immediately start to cry. Hate myself for it. For being anything like my mom. But I can't help it.

"Fiona, you're scaring me." Zane's voice is soft, concerned. "I just got my driver's license, text me your address. I'll come get you."

"You don't understand." My voice sounds like hiccups. "My mom has me under lock and key. She's made all sorts of accusations against my dad to keep me from him. I'm afraid to do anything that will make her even more vindictive. I can't let you come here because he could get in trouble."

"Shit."

"Yeah. Tell me about it." I regain my composure. "What about you? How are you?"

"I'm good. I moved to Seattle with Carter. I even have Mom's blessing. It's going really well." He pauses. "He's clean. It's really different now."

I'm curled up in a ball now under the covers. Hearing his voice is so comforting, but it also makes me unbearably sad. "I'm glad. It's ironic right? You found your dad and I've lost mine."

"It will be okay."

"I don't think so, Zane."

"Trust me, it will work out."

"I told my mom I wanted to live with my dad tonight."

"And?"

"She freaked out and locked herself in her room. Luckily, she forgot to take my phone. She usually only lets me have it when I'm at school." Telling him this is so embarrassing.

"Wow. No wonder I haven't been able to reach you." Zane sighs. "I've been worried that I took things too far that night."

"What? No!" I speak too loudly and immediately my adrenaline is through the roof. If my mom hears me talking, she'll realize she doesn't have my phone with her. "I think about that night all of the time."

"Me too." His voice is low also. A warm feeling pulses through my body because the tone of his voice is so grown up.

I press my palm to my forehead. "Do you have a girlfriend?"

He laughs. "No, nothing like that. I do have a real friend though. Carter's practically adopted him."

"Oh?"

"Yeah. His name is Ty. He's an amazing singer and a great guitar player. We're pretty much outcasts at our school." I know Zane is smiling, I can feel it through the phone. He's genuinely content for the first time, well, ever. It's like our roles have reversed.

"I'm happy for you, Zane." I yawn, despite myself. I don't want to hang up, but the day has taken a toll on me. "I need to tell you that I've saved your name as 'Lisa' under my phone just in case Mom finds it."

"We can talk every day now, Fee."

"No, you need to let me reach out to you. I'm serious." My voice comes out harsher than I want it to. "When it's safe for me to text or call, I'll be in touch."

"Fee…"

"Yeah?"

He clears his throat. "I miss you. I really miss you."

"Me too. So much." I pinch the bridge of my nose. I've needed to hear Zane's voice more than I ever realized. "I want to see you so bad."

"I do too. When we hang up, promise me you'll text me your address. I'll come up with a foolproof plan."

"Okay."

Even though I'm exhausted, I keep talking to him. Who knows when I'll get the chance again? I've got to make the most of this opportunity. We chat for another hour because neither of us can seem to bring ourselves to hang up. Finally, my battery flashes and I have no choice but to say goodnight.

It's the first time I go to bed with a smile in a very long time.

Having Zane back in my life will make me happy again.

I just know it.

CHAPTER 12

AGE 17

Tyson Rainier is my first male best friend. Ever. Aside from Fiona, he's my favorite person. We like the same clothes. We're both obsessed with music. He spends a lot of time at my house now. Writing songs. Practicing. Hanging out. Studying.

Well, let's not get too crazy. Neither of us are really academic.

We do enough to get by.

Even though he's a lot more serious than me, it's like we're the same person.

If I didn't have his friendship, losing Fee would have been unbearable. She never sent me her address. I haven't heard from her in many months. When I think about it—which is often—it hurts. Spending time with Ty and creating music fills the void she left.

"Maybe you should just stay here." We're jamming in the practice room. "Carter could show us how to use the recording gear."

"Fuck, I'd love to spend all weekend here, but I can't. I've got to work. I have two doubles." Ty shakes out his hair, which is just inching past his shoulders.

"C'mon, Ty. We're just getting started!"

"Look, Zane, I've got bills to pay. Your dad says I need vocal lessons. If I lose my job, I won't be able to afford them. I'm not trying to be a dick, but you have no idea what it's like to…"

He never finishes his sentences when he brings up his life. Before he says too much, he catches himself. Ty is *so* careful not to let me—or anyone else— in. His family life is mostly a mystery. He told me he doesn't know who his father is and that his grandparents are dead. He lives with his mom, but I haven't met her. Or been to his house, for that matter. My guess is she doesn't provide for him. I'm not sure if her problem is illness, addiction, or something else, but I don't know any seventeen-year-old kids who work as much as he does.

I don't pressure him for details. Our friendship is too new, and if he's not comfortable talking about it, so be it. I feel bad he doesn't seem to have any family. Even when Carter was at his worst, I've always had my grandparents. And my mom.

Long story short? Me butting into Ty's business won't help.

One day, hopefully he'll feel safe enough to confide in me. Until then, I try to be a good friend in more subtle ways. "Why don't you at least keep your guitar here at the house so you don't have to worry."

"Could I?" He's so earnest. As if he's shocked that anyone would do anything nice for him.

"Yeah, I mean we're writing and rehearsing here anyway."

"Young dudes, it's sounding great." Carter opens the door to the practice room. "Ty, are you staying for dinner?"

"Nah, I've gotta work. Thanks, Carter." Ty throws on his beat-up black leather jacket and skulks out, leaving his guitar on the stand.

When we hear the door close upstairs, Carter looks over at me. "He's a talented kid. I'm glad you have a friend who's interested in the same things you are."

"Yeah." I realize my voice sounds a bit dreamy. Part of me is a bit confused at my feelings for Ty. Especially considering how messed up my head is about losing contact with Fiona. I know it's because of her mom and all the custody drama. My heart wishes she could just make some small effort letting me know she still thinks about me.

About us.

God, what I'd give for just a quick Facebook message. Or text. Or letter.

Anything.

Carter raises an eyebrow but says nothing. He picks up and strums Ty's guitar and makes a few quick tuning adjustments. "He needs lessons, maybe I should talk to his mom."

"I don't think that will help." I pick up a random bass guitar and pluck at it. "He's pretty tight-lipped about his home life. He just left to work a couple of double shifts to 'pay the bills.'"

"Hmmm." Carter gets lost in a melody he's playing. I add a snappy bass line and we jam for a half hour or so.

"Can I ask you something?" I set the bass down and decide to just dive into this conversation. "Fiona got ahold of me on the down low a few months ago. She was frantic to get away from Faye. I haven't heard from her since. I'm worried. I feel helpless."

Carter rests his arm over his guitar and squints. "Yeah, um. Well, as you know, Gus lost custody after Faye made up some story about drugs at The Mission. There's a restraining order, so he's petrified of doing anything that will hurt his chance to see her. He's willing to ride it out because she's almost eighteen."

"That sucks, Carter. When I talked to her, she was a mess. She told me she wanted to move to Seattle to live with Gus."

"It's not our business, Zane." Carter shuts his eyes and sighs. "I wish I could do something, but I'm the root of so many of their troubles. Faye has never forgiven me for what I did at the park. What happened with your mom. Or for lending Gus money. For so many things."

"But *I* never did anything. I miss her. Can I go see her?" I practically beg.

"Well, your mom told me she had a falling out with Faye..." He winces. "Over a little make-out session by the fire? Ring any bells?"

Shit. "You talk to Mom?"

"Of course. In order for you to stay here, she checks in with me every night. Mostly Skype, but sometimes if she's busy, by text."

Huh. Weird. "Well, I love Fiona. She loves me. We didn't do anything wrong, Carter. It's not fair that just because all of you parents have issues that we suffer. I want to see her. I need to know she's okay."

"I don't know, Zane. For now, my best advice is to wait it out. *Please* don't do anything impulsive. I know you have a bit of a streak that you inherited from my side of the family, and if you can try to channel your mother a bit it will do you a lot of good." Carter tentatively cups my shoulder and squeezes. We haven't really had a lot of physical interaction since I've been here. I think he's waiting for me to take the lead, but it's so awkward.

Still, it feels good to make progress.

To have a sober dad I can finally talk to.

Finally, after all these years.

A few weeks later, Ty and I are in the music room tuning our guitars in preparation for our debut performance at the end-of-the-year talent show. I'm in a foul mood. Fiona still hasn't been in touch. It's coming up on a year since we spoke. Two since I've seen her beautiful face.

I've kept my promise to Carter not to reach out to her. I don't want to get her in trouble by calling the number she called me from. Still, it hurts on such a deep level that she hasn't made any effort. It's the first promise she's broken to me. She never even texted me her address.

I hate to say it, but after a year, I've nearly lost any ability to believe in all that "other half" bullshit.

"My dude, are you okay?" Ty places his hand on my shoulder. It's been months since anyone has given me even a simple hug. Carter is still so hesitant, and I've grown up with an affectionate mom and grandparents. I can't help but lean into Ty's hand. He studies my face and wraps his arms around me.

It's a little weird, I'm not going to lie.

But I like it. Need it.

Embarrassingly, I'm overcome with emotion. Before I know it, I'm hugging him back. Tightly. It goes on for a tad longer than an ordinary hug with a friend should.

Confusion sets in.

Do I have feelings for Ty?

We pull apart, pick up our guitars and head out toward the auditorium.

"Have you ever, um?" He speaks quietly as we walk through the courtyard.

"No, you?" I glance over at him.

"No."

"Girlfriend?"

"Nope. You?"

"Nope."

We continue to walk in silence until my uncontrollable urge to fill up silence kicks in. With a dose of impulsiveness, of course. "I think we should get it over with. Maybe tonight after the show."

Ty looks at me like I'm crazy. "Get what over with?"

"Get laid. We're musicians, the ladies will be throwing their panties at our feet when we get done with our song. It comes with the territory. There's a reason Carter shoves condoms at us all the time." I'm babbling. Being moony as Mom used to say. I can't help it. I need to push all thoughts of having my first time with Fiona out of my head. She's clearly not interested in friendship with me, let alone having sex with me. "Unless…"

"Unless what?" Ty looks like he wants to flee.

"Unless you want to fuck *me*." I just can't help myself. I've got to know if that's how Ty rolls. "I'm just sayin'."

Ty's face gives me all of the answers I need. He's not horrified, for which I thank God. I couldn't be friends with a homophobic asshole. He's just completely afraid to hurt my feelings. "Um, dude. It's not like that…"

"I was just checking, I mean how could you resist all this." I swoop my hand up and down my body and give him my biggest toothy grin.

"It's hard." He rolls his eyes and grabs his junk. "Really hard."

And just like that my man crush is squashed. Ty is my friend and brother through and through. Nevertheless, I'm emboldened. "I'm serious, though, about getting the job done. We should just do it."

"No one at this school is interested in me like that, Zane." Ty stops before the door to the auditorium. "Even if they were, I don't really have time for a girlfriend. I'm not into fucking some rando either. Don't you even *listen* to your dad?"

"Of course I do, but it's complicated. I know he's trying to be a father-figure every time he goes on and on about all of the things he rambles about. Part of me can't help but think he wishes he'd used one with my mom." I word vomit and immediately wish I could retract the last statement. TMI and all that.

Ty raises his eyebrow and thankfully says nothing.

I shut the fuck up too.

Minutes later, we're on a real stage for the first time ever. We play an original ballad called *Storm*, and I've never felt so empowered. Together, we are completely on point. Our guitars are in perfect sync. Our vocals blend effortlessly. When the song ends, the crowd of students, teachers, and staff jump to their feet and lose their minds. I'll admit, it's a total fucking rush.

Total fucking rush.

Our first gig.

Our first real audience.

They love us. The feeling is impossible to describe. An energy that permeates every molecule of your body with sunlight and fireworks. The applause doesn't die down, so we play a second and third song until we reluctantly leave the stage.

The high from what just happened in that auditorium is better than anything I've ever felt. When I see Ty's face, I know he feels the same way. We created magic tonight. I can't wait to get up there and do it again. And again. And again.

"Zane, right?" A gorgeous black-haired girl with the most beautiful mocha skin and startling blue eyes leans on me backstage. "You guys were awesome. I'm Kedra. This is my friend, Melissa."

A petite blue-haired girl waves and gazes up at Ty with lust. "You're

Ty?"

"Um, yeah," he sputters and looks over at me.

"We need to put our instruments away, ladies." I take charge. It surprisingly comes naturally. "You're welcome to come with us to, um… Chat."

Ten minutes later, we're making out with our respective fans on opposite sides of the band room. When I look over, Ty's girl pulls out his dick—which is seriously the size of an elephant trunk— and impales herself on it. He pulls her off to put on a condom before resuming.

I guess we're doing this then.

Kedra unzips my pants. Before I know what's happening, I'm sheathed and pumping into her on a bench across the room. I barely realize what I'm doing and then it's over. I'm no longer a virgin.

Shit. I'm no longer a virgin.

And I didn't lose it with Fiona.

Like we talked about.

My heart sinks.

I'm just like Carter, I can't keep my dick in my pants.

And now I can't take it back.

By the time I get home, the energy I felt earlier is completely depleted. Mortification has set in. I'm feeling the opposite of the high from the show. Devastated about what I've done.

What I've lost.

Carter's already in bed, not that I'd talk to him about what just happened. He'd turn it into another lecture about condoms and the "realities" of the rock-star lifestyle versus the perception. I don't need him to tell me that I fucked up royally.

I feel it all the way down to my toes.

How could I?

I know better, I've lived with Carter's impulsive behavior my entire life.

Am I just like him?

I need to see my mom. New York is only a week away, and I'll have two months with her in a city I've always wanted to visit. My phone pings. Thinking it's Ty, I almost ignore it. I'm not ready to face him either. Except it's me. Curiosity wins out, so I take a look.

Fiona: Are you there?

Fiona! Why tonight? After all these months?

God, she knows.

Are we really that connected? I'm so embarrassed. It's almost too much for me to talk to her right now. Except if I don't, then who knows when I'll be able to get in touch with her again. I need to suck it up.

Zane: Fee!

Fiona: Can you talk?

Zane: Always.

The phone lights up. "Hey."

She's crying. "Hey."

"What's going on?"

"I'm sorry I haven't been able to contact you. After last time, Mom has me on an even shorter leash. Luckily she left my phone on the kitchen counter when she went to bed, so I grabbed it to call you. I'll be in trouble tomorrow, but it will be worth it." She's calmer now, her voice isn't as shaky.

"I'm glad you did. I've missed you. I've been so worried about you."

"I miss you so much, Zane. I never stop thinking about you. About us."

"Me either." The words stick in my throat because I wasn't thinking about her when I was fucking Kedra. Well, I was because I'm never not thinking about Fiona. I just fucked her anyway.

"Zane. I've been trying to figure out how to see you," she loud whispers. "I was thinking. Maybe you could ask Carter to let you borrow his car to visit me."

Fuck. Why couldn't she have called me last night?

Why?

"Shit, Fee. I already asked. He told me that if he gets involved it's going to make it a lot worse for your dad. Gus doesn't have any custodial rights over you, which could be made permanent if he does anything to violate that restraining order."

"Why is this happening?" Her voice is frantic. Desperate. "Could you just lie and tell him you're going somewhere else and come see me? Please?"

"Fee, I'm leaving for New York in two days to spend a few weeks with my mom. When I get back, I'll do anything to see you. I promise." I'm not sure how to soothe her.

To help her.

"Oh." She's utterly defeated. I hear it in her voice. I feel it in my bones.

"I played my first show tonight. Ty and I won the school talent show." I change the subject, forgetting that it's taking me down a dangerous path. I don't *really* want to tell Fiona that I've had sex. Maybe I don't have to. On the other hand, we don't keep secrets. Ever. She'll find out eventually, right?

But God, how can I hurt her any more than she's hurting now?

Fuck. This is a disaster. I have no idea what to do.

Her voice is soft. "Oh, Zane. I'm sorry I'm so selfish. I didn't even ask about you. How did it feel to be up on stage?"

"Like nothing I've ever experienced before. Like I was born for it."

"You *were* born to be up there, silly. Look at who your parents are." She sniffle-giggles. "You're going to be rich and famous and leave me behind, aren't you?"

"Never!" I protest. "Why has it taken so long for you to get in touch? I've been so sad without you. I thought you left me behind."

"Oh, I skipped school. Got caught smoking outside. During detention, I made out with one of the football players which, apparently, is frowned upon."

Wait, what?

"You made out with a *football* player?"

She's silent for a minute. "Um. Would that be wrong?"

I think back to a couple of hours ago when I was balls-deep inside of Kedra. "I guess not."

"We're not dating, Zane." Fiona blows out a long breath. "Right?"

I don't answer. The truth is, I don't really know what we are to each other. Which doesn't explain why my chest feels so tight. Why my heart is so sore.

I'm so fucking confused right now.

"Zane?"

"You're right. I guess." It's only then I feel anger bubbling up in my chest. The only time I ever feel—felt—this way is when Carter flaked on showing up for a visit. I've been desperate for Fiona for nearly two years. Faithful to something that hasn't ever been defined. She's dating other people? Suddenly, what I did in the band room doesn't feel wrong anymore. "I mean, how could we be dating when we haven't seen each other in so long? I mean, I lost my virginity tonight."

"Wait, *what*?" Fiona's voice is a wheeze. Shocked. "Did you just say what I *think* you said?"

"Yeah. After the show a girl followed me back to the band room and I just decided to go for it." I don't exactly want to hurt Fiona, but the image of her making out with another guy kills me. Dead. At this point, I can't help what comes out of my mouth.

Of course, I don't tell her that right before she called I puked my guts out because of the guilt.

"Wow. Okay."

"Are you mad?"

Her voice is so quiet I can barely hear her. "I guess our ship has sailed, then. Huh, Zane?"

"You sailed it first, it sounds like."

"Sure. Yeah. That's exactly what I did."

"You're still my best friend," I lie. She's so much more, but I'm overwhelmed by the entire evening. I really have no idea what to say. How to unsail the ship.

"I'm gonna go, Zane." Fiona's voice is like ice. "Have a good time in New York."

"Have fun with the football player."

She hangs up the phone.

Leaving me in a room of silence.

Devastated.

It's probably the last time I'll ever hear her voice.

And the last words I'll ever say to her were mean.

All I really wanted was to tell her that I love her.

Because I do.

Godfucking dammit. I do.

CHAPTER 13

AGE 18

I didn't blame Zane for giving in to temptation last year. Not that it didn't hurt, because it did. His confession about fucking some girl in the band room sent me into a spiral. I couldn't eat. I couldn't sleep. It made the hellhole I was living in worse.

I wallowed.

I acted out.

All because I lost Zane.

Nothing's ever hurt so badly.

Life kept going on around me. Nothing changed. I was miserable. Cooking didn't even cheer me up. Then one day I realized nothing *would* change unless I did. Once I had that particular revelation, I adjusted my attitude. I truly couldn't rely on anyone in my life, including Zane. It was time for me to grow up and move on.

I made a vow to never, ever allow myself to get that attached to any one person ever again. My mom was right. Don't let anyone get in the way of your dreams.

It wasn't worth it.

Self-sufficiency. That's my motto. I have a Faye-approved job waiting tables at a downtown diner. It keeps me busy. I've saved a lot of money. Seattle is a dream of the past. I have a new plan.

In a few short weeks, I'll execute.

"Mom, I'm home." I throw my backpack on the counter and grab a bottle of Evolution orange juice from the fridge and pour it into a big glass. Armed with delicious, delicious OJ, I open my graduation packet and shuffle through all of the things I need to get filled out. There are caps and gowns to order. Invites.

Mom appears at the back door and kicks off her muddy boots before joining me in the kitchen. Her gardening hobby has done wonders for her well-being and our dinners. I have fresh vegetables and herbs to play with in the kitchen. The new boyfriend Jonas, helps too. She's much happier now. "How was school?"

"Meh." My days at Bellingham High are practically over. Senior prom. The graduation ceremony. Parties. None of them are on my radar. I just want my diploma at this point so I can get the hell out of Washington. Despite both my parents pressuring me to go to a traditional college, it isn't for me. In a few short weeks, I'm heading to New York to attend culinary school.

Not exactly what my folks want for me, but it isn't their decision. I'm paying for it myself. Besides, they both lost their right to tell me what to do years ago. I try not to allow bitterness to creep into my psyche. People are flawed. That's okay. Doesn't mean I'm going to allow it to rule me.

I'm not turning into my mother.

"I'm proud of you, Fiona." Mom washes the dirt off her hands in the kitchen sink. "It's been a rough transition over these past few years, but I think we've all come out of it okay in the end."

I don't argue. I'm pretty sure me not harping on and on about Zane Rocks is the reason she believes this. She thinks she broke us apart, and she did. Goody for her. "Sure. I guess so."

"We got this today." Mom hands me a crisp, white invitation with purple-and-gold accents. "Zane's graduation invitation."

I keep my expression neutral. Even though my heart twinges at hearing his name spoken out loud. He broke my heart in a million pieces. No reason to sugar coat it. The last time we spoke, I tried to lighten our chat by joking about detention. Making out with a football player. As if any of that could happen on my short leash. Not only did my joke fall flat, it cratered.

He actually believed I'd do that to him.

I probably should have. He'd moved on from me and our promises. Threw his virginity away on some groupie in the band room instead of waiting for me. I hate admitting my mom was probably right. He's just like Carter. No doubt he's fucked a bunch of other girls by now.

Except I know better. That's not who he is.

"Fiona?" My mom shakes the invitation at me.

"How special. Should we send him one of mine?"

"Yes. I think we should."

"*Really*, Mom? Doesn't anyone get my sarcasm? You seriously— after all of these years of keeping us apart— want to invite Zane like nothing ever happened?"

"Don't start, Fee." Mom crosses her arms. "We've been over this again and again. You didn't see the entire situation the way I did. You were unnaturally fixated on that boy. I did what I had to do to protect you from ending up like Lianne. You're an adult now, my job is done."

Infuriating. Simply infuriating. "God, Mom. Thanks for all of your goddamn faith in me."

My mom sniffs. "I do have faith in you, Fiona. I didn't have faith in Zane after I caught him mauling… and once he was living with Carter—"

I cut her off. No matter how hurt I am, I can't hear her accuse Zane of something he didn't do. Ever fucking again. Despite everything, if I had to choose between my mom and Zane... "Stop it. Let's *please* not fight. It's in the past now."

I finish my juice, rinse out the glass and head toward my room. She follows me down the hall. "I spoke to Lianne, you know. Apologized. Made amends of sorts. She'll be in Seattle for Zane's ceremony with her folks. It's the week before yours. I think we should go."

"Uh-huh. *No*." It's so annoying that everything—including rekindling what I thought was our most treasured friendships—is on mom's timeline. *She's* the reason why I was cut off from my best friend. My family. It's all I can do not to scream. I'm just trying to hold it together until I can get the fuck out of her house. All I know for sure is that if I had a daughter, there is no *way* I'd treat her the way my mom has treated me for the past few years.

"Your dad will be there too, of course."

WTF?

Now, I can't help myself. "Jesus, Mom. You practically ruined my relationship with my own father. What's going on with your redemption tour? You've tried to extricate our past like cancer, are you sure you won't combust on site if you let them back in?"

She ignores me. Things are always on her terms, not mine. "Lianne asked about you."

"Well, I'd hope so, she's my fucking godmother." I roll my eyes.

Mom rests her fists on her trim hips and studies me. "She asked about college and I had to tell her you weren't going."

"Culinary school *is* college."

"I bet your dad wouldn't approve. Believe me, I know firsthand how hard it's been to keep that stupid nightclub of his going. Let alone a restaurant. Cooks make shit money."

I dig my nails into my palms in exasperation. If there's one thing I've learned, it's to *not* take any advice from my mother.

"You're eighteen. You can do whatever you want now. Even if I think you should stay here with me and go to Western."

"Mom. Please. Not a fucking chance." God, she's pushing every single one of my buttons today. Well, every day.

"Fine, but I'm going to invite Lianne and Zane to yours." Mom waves her hand at me and flounces past on her way to her bedroom.

He won't come, I know it. Neither will Lianne.

What we had is over. Killed dead thanks to my mom. It's been four years since I've even seen him. A year since we last spoke. I never gave my mom the satisfaction of knowing what happened between us, and I never will. It's none of her fucking business.

She gave up that right a long time ago.

On the big day, it's unseasonably hot. The sun is beating down on me and the rest of my graduating class as we sit in the unprotected football field in the middle of the stadium. Thank God, I wore shorts and a tank top under my black gown. I'm already roasting, I'm not sure how the kids wearing suits and dresses are surviving.

I don't particularly want to be here, but I figure since my dad and mom are going to make nice for a day, I might as well give them a photo opportunity. Call it a last gift from me before I blow Washington State forever.

As I thought she would, Lianne declined the invitation. She has a performance. A good excuse. Mom never heard from Zane. I'm relieved, the last thing I want today is drama.

I guess I'm just mentally prepared to let my past go and embrace my future.

After the ceremony, I make my way to where all the parents are waiting. I nod at a couple of classmates. Only to be polite. I don't have any real friends here. Never really bothered since I was on house arrest.

"Fiona! Fiona!" I hear my mom's voice through the crowd. I can't see her even when I stand on my tiptoes. I try to follow her voice and run smack dab into a wall of solid muscle. It's almost comical. I bounce off and nearly fall on my ass.

Except strong hands grip both my shoulders to stop my trajectory.

Familiar hands.

I'm afraid to look up. Petrified. I can't help it though, it's magnetic. When I do, Zane's brown eyes gaze tenderly down at me. His voice is deep, soft.

Home.

"Hey, Fee."

Before I can think about all the reasons I shouldn't, I fling myself at him and he wraps his arms around me. He's so tall. And muscular. His chin rests on my head, his long, black curls cascade around my face. I bury my nose into his chest and breathe him in. He smells like heaven. If heaven smelled spicy. Earthy. Citrusy. Everything around me fades as if I'm in a dream.

A dream where Zane and I are the only two people on the planet.

When I become more coherent, his hand runs up and down my back to keep me taut against him. I cling to his trim waist like a lifeline.

How completely stupid I've been.

Zane will never be out of my system.

Never.

He's part of my bloodstream.

"Holy fuck. You're so fucking beautiful, Fee." Zane releases his grip on me and kisses my forehead. He runs his fingers through my hair. He looks at me like I'm the frosting on a cupcake and he wants to have a lick. Then he hands me a bouquet of daffodils. "I couldn't wait to finally see you again. Happy graduation."

I have so much to say, but my dad appears beside me. His long hair is tied back in a leather string. He wears a smart blue suit and a black tie, which shocks me. "There you are, Fiona. Ah, I should have known you'd be with Zane."

I untangle myself from Zane to re-tangle myself in my dad. I haven't seen him much as a teenager, but at least my mom removed the moratorium once or twice. When the court made her. "Dad, you look great!"

"I clean up okay." He drapes an arm around me and holds up his smartphone. "Should we take one of those selfie things?"

"Here, let me, Gus." Zane rescues me from certain disaster. I pose with my dad and my mom slips in beside us like we're one big happy family.

So. Fucking. Weird.

I'm blown away for the second time in the span of ten minutes when Carter walks up behind Zane. He's wearing nice jeans, a black T-shirt, and a gray-checked sport coat. His dark, curly hair flows long and loose exactly like Zane's, except with a few stray gray strands. It's uncanny.

They're nearly identical now that Zane has grown up. "Fiona, look at you. You're gorgeous."

I nestle myself into Carter's side. He smells like a muskier version of his son. "Carter, I'm so happy to see you."

"Zane, Carter, you'll come out to dinner with us?" My mom rests her hand on my shoulder. I'm not sure who replaced my mom with this bot-woman. Not an ounce of snark. Not a modicum of bitchiness. I seriously can't remember her *ever* being nice to Carter.

Zane and I look at each other. Our telepathy is fully intact.

WTF?

He and I burst out laughing. His eyebrows quiver with happiness.

God, I've missed him. It's like no time has passed.

Almost.

An hour later, at a little bistro in Fairhaven, Zane and I sit next to each other at dinner. My bouquet of daffodils is in a vase in the center of the table. I look around at our parents dining together after being at odds for so many years. I can sense Zane peering at me from under his hair. His signature move has been perfected. I furtively glance his way without moving my head. I can't help but smile while I study my menu.

Fuck. I love this man.

When our meals arrive, Zane and I quietly eat while the adults talk and laugh like nothing has ever separated them. There's no way I can make sense of this night. Plus, I'm all woozy from the thrill of sitting so close to Zane. I've never had alcohol, but I'm pretty sure I'm drunk on the events of this bizarre day alone.

Especially when Zane's hand finds mine under the table.

I sigh and grip his fingers tightly. I feign interest in the conversation but I'm not really listening. All my attention is on the warmth of his hand. The slight scrape of his blunt nail against my palm. My nipples are tight. My pussy is clenching and unclenching of its own volition. My breath is erratic.

Despite my reaction, I just can't look at Zane right now. It would be like staring into the sun. I can't afford to blind myself to the reality of the situation.

As much as I want him back in my life—and there's no question that I do—too much has happened between us.

I need—must—carve out my own path.

It's all or nothing for me with Zane.

At this point in our lives, it's going to be nothing.

Zane leans over and whispers, "Let's get outta here. We really need some time alone."

Still avoiding eye contact, I silently nod and stare at my half-full plate.

Well, the "nothing" can wait until tomorrow.

"Parents, I'm going to take Fee on a drive." Zane stands, moves behind me and pulls out my chair. He fixes my mom with a look. "It's been too many years. Fiona and I have a lot to catch up on."

My mom narrows her eyes, "Fiona..."

"I'm going." I glare at her and stand. My legs are wobbly. I steady myself by gripping the table until I find my footing. Before we leave, I kiss my dad's forehead and give Carter a hug. "This is *my* day, and I'm spending the rest of it with Zane."

Zane holds out his hand to Carter. "Keys?"

Carter looks over at my dad. Then Mom. Like he's asking permission. Dad nods. Mom burns a hole through Zane's forehead with her laser-stare. Just like that, Faye is back with a vengeance. The crunchy dynamic returns. I don't care. Their old business isn't mine anymore. Or Zane's.

With Carter's keys in hand, Zane and I practically skip out to his Bentley.

"Well, this is fancy." I run my hand along the leather in the passenger seat.

Zane adjusts the driver's seat. "Nothing but the best for Carter."

He's clearly uncomfortable now that we're alone. Still, he looks at me, willing me to look back at him. And I do. His soft, black sweater is pushed up to his elbows. His black jeans are dotted with grommets. Designer no doubt, they sure didn't come from Target.

"Nothing but the best for you." I waggle my finger at his outfit.

His smile lights up the small space in the car. Suddenly, I feel really, really shy. My insecurities about our relationship whoosh over me. Fucking band-room girl. I look out the window in case I start to cry.

I guess it isn't a good idea, me being alone with Zane.

Zane reaches over and takes my hand and places it on his thigh. Then he covers it with his and interlaces our fingers. "Where did you go?"

"I dunno, Zane." I gaze back over at him. He's the most handsome man I've ever seen. Will ever know. He's the perfect mix of Carter and Lianne. Something's so different about him. There's nothing left of the insecure kid I grew up with. He's like a panther. Oozing sex appeal. Confidence. Kindness.

He's too much for me.

Except, his eyes shine with tears. "I miss you, Fee. You have no idea how much."

I shut my eyes and feel my own tears roll down my cheeks. "Zane, I don't..."

"Shhh." He cuts me off with a squeeze of my fingers. "Let's just be in the moment. *Please*. Because this is the best moment I've had in forever."

CHAPTER 14

AGE 18

Nothing prepared me for how stunning and womanly Fiona has grown up to be. Her long, sleek, dark hair flows like a waterfall down her back. She's tiny but voluptuous in her sexy denim shorts and black ribbed tank top that leaves nothing to the imagination. Smooth, creamy skin. Curves of a pin-up model. Sad, aqua-blue eyes fringed with long, black lashes.

She's breathtaking.

She's still my every wet dream.

My dick is attempting to drill its way out of my jeans.

Which is so inappropriate given the circumstances.

Then again, it also seems like destiny.

I don't know my way around this little town but see a sign for *Marine Park* a short distance from the restaurant. The sun is still fairly high in the sky, and I need to get out of this car before I do something stupid. Like kiss her senseless. I pull into the parking lot thinking we can take a walk or something.

Anything to cool myself down.

Anything to quell the energy zapping between us.

Which is overwhelming.

Apparently, Fiona feels the same way because she practically leaps out when the car comes to a stop and takes off down a path without me. Luckily I'm a lot taller, so it's easy to catch up. I follow her over dusty train tracks to a clearing. God, the Bellingham waterfront is gorgeous. Endless deep-blue sea. Sandy beaches lined with driftwood. Tall, thick fir trees for miles. A few boats gently rock on the horizon.

Even better, we're alone. She sits on a bench overlooking the beach. I nervously join her and can't help myself from holding her soft hand. My thumb strokes her fingers. Her long, shiny nails are painted black. After a moment, she leans her head on my shoulder and sighs. "That was the weirdest dinner I've ever been to."

"Right?" I chuckle. "Did you feel like you were in the *Twilight Zone*?"

"Um, yeah. Who took my mom and replaced her with a robot?"

"Oh, the Faye we all know and love made a raging comeback right before we left." I lean my head against hers. Head snuggle. That's what we called it when we were little.

We sit in silence for a while. I'm not sure how I lived so long without her.

God, I missed her.

God, I missed this.

I need to talk to her, but I don't know how.

Like always, Fiona picks up on my energy. We're just wired that way and nothing will ever change it, I guess. She lets my hand go and rests her elbows on her knees. A few seconds later, her forehead touches her forearms. I know she's hurting. Hell, I am too. I'm not sure where to go from here. I just want *us* back.

"Fee?"

"Don't say anything. It's okay, Zane," she whispers.

My knee starts bouncing. Energy courses through my body. I guess we're going there. Fuck. "Fee, you've got to know. I wanted it to be you. I always *thought* it would be you. And then I got caught in the moment with Ty…"

She looks up, shocked. "What?"

"No, no. Not *me* and Ty." I squeeze my eyes shut, knowing I just have to be honest with her. "For a hot second I thought I might be attracted to him, but no. It's just that he's the only other person I've ever been as close to as you, Fiona. He's like my brother and I was a bit confused. What happened was we played the talent show and afterward these girls followed us back to the band room…"

Fiona pops up and storms off toward the water lapping at the shore. I leap up to follow her. As I approach, she holds her hand out to keep me at bay. "I'm not trying to shame you, Zane. I have no right to tell you what to do with your body or your life. But… But…after Mexico. And the San Juan Islands. It's stupid, but I guess I just always thought that it would be you and me… I wanted…"

She bursts into tears.

I fold her into my chest and wrap my arms around her. "I'm sorry. I'm so, so sorry," I whisper over and over. "I hadn't heard from you in so long. I thought you'd forgotten about me. That stuff with your parents… I was just trying… Fuck. I don't know…"

I burst into tears too.

We hold each other, crying like babies. Our lost friendship. Our lost first time. The forces that kept us apart. All the minutes we could have had together. Fucking wasted. We were torn apart by the very same parents who told us it was our destiny to be together. It sucked. It wasn't fair. We've never done anything but love each other.

"For the record, it was over in two seconds. I've never… Well, it was only that one time, and I've felt sick about it ever since." I hug her so tightly to make sure she can feel my energy through our clothes. "Fee, you know you're it for me, right? I love you. I wanted it to be you. It's *always* only you."

She tries to push me away, but I don't let her. "Please don't say that."

"It's true. You *know* it's true. And I know you love me too. I *feel* it."

She looks up at me. Her blue eyes sparkle through her tears. She clutches my sweater in her fists and yanks me down toward her, capturing my lips in an angry kiss. I can't help but groan and grab her ass with both hands and hold her against my body as our tongues war. It isn't a pretty, romantic kiss.

It's feral. Desperate. Needy. Our teeth gnash together. I taste blood on my lips but I can't stop. Neither can she. I cup her ass and lift her. She locks her legs around me and grinds against my cock which has never, ever been so hard. Knowing we are in the middle of the park and could get caught any moment, I manage to open my eyes for a second to suss out the situation. Through some shrubs, I spy a hidden picnic bench. A perfect secluded nook.

Without losing any momentum, I maneuver us over to it. My hands rest on Fiona's hips and I boost her up to sit on the table. She lies back so her legs are dangling off the edge, drapes her arms above her head and looks at me. Her breath is labored causing her fantastic tits to jiggle underneath her tank top. The next thing I know, I'm standing between her legs, cupping her breasts and running my thumbs over her nipples, watching them bead into hard points.

Fiona squirms under my touch. Her head lolls from side to side. I lean over and feather kisses on her forehead down her cheeks and to the soft space between her neck and ears. Then I suck and lick her neck and her earlobes, pinching her nipples to my rhythm. Her hands wind through my hair. As lost in the moment as I am, things are moving fast, and we really haven't talked. "Fee…"

"Keep going, Zane. I want to have my first with you. Right here. Right now." She looks at me. Pleading. "No more waiting."

I shake my head. "But I thought…"

"There was no football player, you idiot." She reaches for me. "You're it for me too."

I'm blown away. All of this time I thought… "Wait, what?"

"Zane. I want you to fuck me. Right here. Right now."

"Um, okay. But anyone could find us here, Fee." I try to be the voice of reason. My self-control is for shit, but I'm giving it some effort. "We're in public."

She locks her feet around my legs and pulls me toward her. "I don't care. We deserve to have a redo. Our first time together was stolen from us and this is our opportunity."

It's hard to argue with her point of view, and I don't really want to. So I kiss down her neck and lift her tank top over her head. Her full tits strain against a black bra. I pull down the straps with my thumbs and nuzzle them. Perfect brown nipples stand at attention. My lips fasten around one and then the other and Fiona moans and squirms.

I'm going to come in my pants. There's no getting around it.

I have to take a breath.

When I move away, she seems to understand that it's not because

I don't want her. It's because I'm overwhelmed by what's happening. I cup my cock and squeeze. Shut my eyes and breathe. If we're doing this, I need to make it good for her. First, I need to gain a bit of control.

Fiona is undeterred. She unbuttons her shorts, lifts her hips and shimmies out of them, taking her black bikini underwear along for the ride. Her index finger rubs the top part of her pussy in a circle, causing her to moan and buck. I'm fascinated. Despite what she probably thinks of me, my day-to-day life is consumed with music. Not sex.

Now it's all I can think about.

"What are you doing?" I wheeze, not able to look away from her long black nails against her most private parts.

"Rubbing my clit." Her other hand now is pinching her nipple. "I've been cooped up like a prisoner, in my free time I learned how to get myself off."

"Wha… What?" My dick swells and balls tighten.

Fiona licks her finger and resumes. "I read romance novels from the library. The sex scenes are incredible. Once I learned to make myself come, it's become part of my evening routine every night. Sometimes more than once. It's awesome."

My pea-brain explodes.

"Ohhh. Ohhhh. God." I erupt in my pants. I can't help it. There's no way to help it. I cup my junk. "Shit."

Her eyes are hazy. I realize she must not know what just happened when she dips her finger into her folds and holds it up to me. "Do you want to taste me?"

I don't need to be asked twice. Without a second thought, I bend down and suck her finger. Her mysterious, sweet essence tastes like honey on my tongue. I look up at her and smile. "Delicious. You're delicious."

Then all rational thought leaves my brain and primal instinct takes over. I lean over on my elbows, which rest against her hips. Using my thumbs, I spread her pussy lips apart. She's glistening. Her scent fills my senses. I look up to find her watching me. Her hips writhe in anticipation.

Ah, hell.

I go for it. Fasten my lips on the spot she'd been rubbing and discover a hard little nub. I lick and swirl my tongue around it. Watch to see if she likes what I'm doing. She stuffs one fist into her mouth, the other claws my hair for grim death. I keep lapping at her until she bucks against my mouth. Her entire body shudders and she moans. Low. Keening. I don't stop.

Suckling. Tasting her.

I'd do anything to keep those tremors going for as long as I can.

Despite the mess I made in my pants, I'm still as hard as a steel pole. Aching to be inside her. To do it right this time.

After a while, Fiona pulls me away from her by my hair. "It's too intense. I can't take any more, Zane."

I stretch my body over her and kiss her lips. She's surprised but gets into it. I suckle her tongue and ask, "You taste good, right?"

"Yeah." Her cheeks pinken.

"Have you tasted yourself before?"

Now her cheeks are redder.

She's blowing my mind.

"Fee, you do realize that when you were playing with yourself, I literally came in my pants?" I cradle her head between my elbows and stroke her hair with my thumbs. "I'm pretty sure I don't really know what I'm doing."

"Well, if that's not knowing what you're doing, I'm not sure what to say." Her eyes search mine. Questioning. "Can we, um?"

"On this picnic table?"

She nods. I look around. No one is here.

"Are you sure?"

She looks into my eyes and asks, "You're clean?"

I nod vigorously. "Yes."

She sucks in a breath. I press my lips to hers. They part and we give each other little kisses. When she relaxes a bit, I seek out her tongue and suck on it. Languish. Slowly bring us back into the rhythm that's all ours.

Where no one else is in our bubble.

With Fiona, I don't need experience.

Our bodies know *exactly* what to do.

My fingers find their way to her slit and I explore her pussy as we make out. She's sopping wet and slick. I push one finger inside her, causing her to gasp. Slowly I stroke in and out. In and out. In a moment of inspiration I search for her little nub with my thumb and rub it the way she did. We resume kissing and I push two fingers inside her and repeat what I just did.

Soon, she's squirming and clenching around me.

I stand, pull off my sweater and T-shirt. Unbuckle my belt and undo my jeans. My cock bursts out of the top of my damp boxers. I give it a couple of pumps before pulling my pants and briefs down to my knees. Now that I'm exposed completely, Fiona's eyes are wide. She sucks in a breath and bites her lip and says with a cheeky grin, "Oh, Zane. I'm finally seeing your stiff penis."

I take her hand and bring it to my shaft. "You can feel it too."

She strokes me tentatively. "Are we doing this? For real?"

"Only if you want to. There's no pressure from me, Fee. Never." She circles my crown with her index finger and thumb, nearly causing my head to pop off my neck. "I want you like I've never wanted anything in my life. It's your choice, though. Always."

"I want you so badly." She guides my cock to her opening. She strokes me back and forth against her wetness. Her thumb flicks over my crown. "Has anyone ever touched you like this?"

"No," I groan.

"Have any girls sucked on it?"

Her brazenness is killing me. My cock jumps in her hand. "Jesus. Fee. No."

"Then I'll be your first." She sits up and takes me into her mouth. Sucks. Licks. Looks up at me with her blue eyes and smiles. Her tits jiggle. Holy fucking shit. Never in my wildest imagination—and believe me I've beat off to this vision hundreds of times— did I comprehend how incredible Fiona's real-life lips would feel wrapped around my cock. Her tongue swirls around my tip. She releases me and kisses up and down my shaft. Then she sits up and begins the cycle again.

God, I've got to read romance books. Holy hell.

My hands cup her face as she plays and explores. When she gingerly cups my balls, I nearly shoot off in her mouth. Instead, I jump back and my dick bobs against my stomach in the fresh evening air.

"Did I do it wrong?" Fiona's lips are plump and swollen. From my cock.

Jesus. Hold the fuck on, Zane.

I quickly take her in my arms and kiss her. Tasting us together. Fucking amazing. "No, you did everything right. Whatever you were doing was the best thing I've ever felt. I was about to come in your mouth. I couldn't let that happen twice in one night."

She rests her hands on my hips and looks down at my cock. "That would be okay. You tasted so good."

I can't think. Nothing I've ever been told about sex registers. All I know is that I've got to be inside Fiona. Right here. Right now. Claim her. Make her mine. I hold myself at her entrance. Flick my tip around her opening the way she did earlier. She's still soaking wet for me. "I think this is going to hurt a bit."

"I don't care. I want to feel you inside me." She leans back and shuts her eyes. Her hands rest on my biceps. She anchors her feet against the edge of the table and her knees fall open to make room for me. "I've dreamed about this moment since I was fourteen."

So have I.

I push inside just past my tip. It's glorious. Warm. Wet. Tight. So, so tight. The sensation nearly kills me. "Look at me, Fee. *Please*. I want to see your face when I'm inside you."

Her blue eyes blink up at me. I lean over her and cradle her head with my arm and kiss her. Slowly. Lingering. Using shallow thrusts, I work my way inside her. Realization hits me all at once. Even though I technically lost my virginity in the band room that night, right now is the *real* deal. *This* is what sex is meant to be. I push all the way in. She winces and then relaxes.

I press my forehead to hers. Head snuggle. We stare deep into each other's eyes. Into each other's souls. My hips rock into her as slowly as I can muster. Her nails trace up and down my back. She pulls my hair. Grips my ass. There's no way I'm going to last. Fiona's going to be my addiction.

I know it.

"Is this okay? Does it feel good?" I whisper.

She squeezes her thighs against my hips and moves against me. "God, yes. It's incredible. I'm so full of you. I can't believe this is really happening."

That's when I lose all control. So does she. I buck into her. She thrusts up to meet me. She reaches between us and rubs her little button furiously in circles. Almost like magic, she cries out. Her channel tightens around me. My lips swallow her moans. I can't hold back one second longer. My come floods out in endless spurts. This orgasm is harder, longer and more intense than I ever thought possible. It's impossible to stop pumping into her. She feels too good.

Too right.

When my body comes to a rest, her hands grip my ass, keeping me there. Still joined. Like we've always been in our hearts. And now, finally, with our bodies.

Our kisses are sweet. Reverential. Satiated.

When I finally pull out, our combined fluids spill down her thighs.

Both of our eyes go wide as realization dawns.

My heart beats out of my chest. The evidence of what we just did is undeniable. "Oh, Fee. God. I'm so sorry."

"It's okay." She watches as I grab my T-shirt and use it to wipe her up a bit and then myself.

"Are you on the pill? I didn't even ask you. I'm so stupid." I pull up my pants and buckle them. "Carter's going to kill me."

"What?" Tears spring to Fiona's eyes. She puts on her bra and tank top. I pick up her shorts from the bench seat and hand them to her. "Why would Carter even know about this?"

Without answering, I look around at our surroundings in disbelief. I've just fucked my best friend. My heart and soul. The girl I haven't laid eyes on in four years. We should be basking in the glow of our first sexual experience in a real bed. With rose petals. Champagne.

Instead we're scrambling to cover ourselves in a public park.

I grip her hands and bring them to my lips. "I love you, Fee. I mean it. I don't regret what we did. It's just…I should have pulled out… I didn't think."

"I'm not on the pill." She clutches my fingers. "But Zane, would it be so bad if I got pregnant?"

No, it would make me the happiest guy in the world.

My thought surprises me, but reality sets in as we watch the sky turn from blue to pink, purple and orange. "Fuck. We're practically the same age as our parents when they had us."

She glances up at me. Sighs. "It makes our childhood a little more understandable, huh?"

"Yeah." I nod. "Carter and my mom weren't ready to have me."

"Neither were my parents."

My arm drapes over her shoulder and I pull her against me. "We'd be different."

She doesn't answer. For the next half hour we sit watching the sunset until the sky darkens.

"Give me your phone." I hold my hand out. She pulls it out of her pocket. I type in my number. Carter's address. My email. All of the ways to get in touch with me that I have. Then I call myself and program her number into my phone. "We are never losing touch again. Promise me. Especially if…"

She kisses me. "The odds are slim, Zane. It's not the right time in my cycle."

"Either way, whether it's now or later. One day we'll have our own family, Fiona Reynolds." I kiss her nose. "If that day is nine months from now? I'm fine with it. You are my other half."

"Do you really still believe that?"

"Yes. With all of my heart." I place her hand on the left half of my chest. "We're still married, after all."

She laughs and shoves me playfully. "We were six."

"It was forever, don't you forget it." I flash her my cheesiest smile.

Our lips gravitate toward each other again. We kiss until the moon is high in the sky and our lips are bruised. Her face is raw from my whiskers. I have a hickey on my neck. We're branding each other. There's no hiding what we've been up to from our parents. How we've reconnected. And I don't give a flying fuck.

As far as I'm concerned, after tonight, it's none of their business.

Ever again.

"I should get back." She hops up and holds her hand out to me. "My flight is early."

"Graduation trip?"

"Um… I'm moving to New York for culinary school tomorrow."

The record scratches.

Why didn't Gus say anything on the drive down? Did he know? I can't believe she's leaving after I just found her again. Unbearable sadness blankets my heart.

"It's a long drive. Are you and Carter going back tonight?" Fiona's voice sounds like it's far away.

"Yeah. Carter has a charity show with Limelight tomorrow night," I hear myself answer.

When we return to Faye's house, a big graduation cake sits untouched on the counter. All the parents are waiting. Watching us both intently. Faye scowls at me but plays nice—well as nice as she can be. Gus is oblivious. Carter's gaze says it all. He knows something went down.

Faye serves us dessert close to midnight. It tastes like cardboard.

Then we all say goodnight.

I kiss Fiona goodbye on the lips in front of everyone.

Just *because*. It's time our parents got used to it.

Especially if…

By the time Carter, Gus, and I head back to Seattle, my mind is whirling. From the back seat, I stare out the window reliving the magic of me and Fiona. God, she might be pregnant. I was careless. We both have plans. If we have a baby, our lives will be on an entirely different trajectory. Fuck. Did I just repeat the sins of my father?

No. I push the negative thoughts out of my head.

What's done is done. There's no use in wondering about what-ifs. If she's pregnant, I'll do whatever needs to be done to support her and our child. Even move if she wants to stay in New York. I know Ty and I have plans, but Fiona's the most important person in my life.

God, I hope she's not pregnant.

Not because I don't want to be the father of her children. It's because I want Fiona to follow her own dream. To taste freedom after being under Faye's thumb for so long. She deserves a chance to get back to the feisty, sassy tell-it-like-it is person she is deep down inside. I don't want her to feel trapped. Stifled. Tied down.

No. She needs to be free.

We belong together, there's no doubt in my mind.

Especially after what we just shared.

The purest form of love.

It's just something inside me… Call it instinct. Call it psychic power. Call it whatever the fuck you want. It doesn't really matter. I know.

Know.

If I push Fiona for something she's not ready for?

It will be all over for us, before we even begin again.

CHAPTER 15

AGE 19

Graduation day was magical. Like a dream. An ethereal notion that, after four years of dealing with my mother's neurosis, I couldn't count on as real. My mom and dad actually played nice, not even one bicker. She allowed Carter to celebrate with me.

And of course, Zane.

Always Zane.

Seeing him again, well. It immediately put us right back to where we belonged. Like nothing had ever separated us. Losing my virginity to him was…gah. Like fulfilling my destiny. Where only the two of us mattered. Sex with Zane? Soooo much better than what I fantasized about for so many years. Feeling him moving inside me. His lips on my nipples. My pussy. Taking his fat cock in my mouth. Our kisses. The emotions flowing between us.

After years of unwilling separation, Zane and I were briefly "us" again.

Only better.

He's always lived inside of me.

Now, he's actually been inside of me.

Where he belongs.

Such an intimate connection with my other half means I know, on a cellular level, that he loves every part of me. The good and the bad. My confidence. My insecurities. Who I want to become. How I need to get there. Experiences we need to have. Together. Apart.

We're finally growing up. Learning how to adult.

So yeah, us together. It was *everything*. I couldn't have asked for anything more.

Well, except for the forgetting birth control part. I still cringe when I think about our conversation afterward. How I actually said it wouldn't be so bad if I got pregnant.

Why I said it.

It was only on the plane ride from Seattle to New York that I was able to process what went down that day. Well, not just that day. I'd lost faith in him. But he never wanted to break his promise to come for me. After we talked, I understood the truth. He didn't know what was going on with me and Mom. How could he have from a couple of phone calls where I whined about my mom like every other snotty teenage brat?

Osmosis?

ESP?

Sadly, I came to horrific realizations about myself. Realizations I'm having a hard time coming to terms with.

I'm like the gift that keeps on giving. Acting like an asshole because I'm scared to be truthful with him. From the day I arrived in Hyde Park, New York, nearly two weeks ago, I've barely answered Zane's texts.

Dodged his calls.

My excuse? Settling into student housing. Finalizing my financial aid. Finding a job. Now that I've completed these tasks, I'm out of distractions. It isn't fair to continue avoiding Zane. Not when I have news.

Before our life-changing sex in the park, my mind was in a different place. In the moment when it became clear where things were going, I had a singular moment of desperation that I acted on but I'm not proud of. You see, I didn't want to lose him ever again—couldn't lose him again. I needed insurance.

So I let him fuck me without a condom knowing there was a chance I'd get pregnant.

I'm coming to terms with the fact that —for a moment— I was just another man-trapping, lying liar-pants cliché.

And that I did this to the one person in the world who has always had my back.

Confessing my sins to Zane should be my top priority. But, like I said, I'm an asshole. I haven't been able to face him. Except, today's the day. We're talking soon. Hopefully, we can move forward somehow, even though I wouldn't blame him for telling me to go fuck myself.

Either way, I want to start this new phase of my life with a clean slate.

I'm looking out the window of my dorm room in Hudson Hall at the Culinary Institute of America, waiting for Zane to call. I can't believe I'm here. My excitement level is at its peak. Culinary school is what got me through high school. It's what I daydreamed about when I wasn't pining for Zane. I taught myself how to cook. To bake. I'm good at it.

And I *love* it.

While there's nothing I want more than to have Zane back in my life. I also want *this*. I don't know what he expects. Or even wants for himself.

We haven't talked about that stuff yet.

I just know I have to do what's right for me.

My phone buzzes and I nearly jump out of my skin.

"Hey, Fee, I'm sorry practice went long." Zane sounds out of breath. "We have our first show at the Vera Project in a couple of weeks. We're trying to get ready so we don't embarrass ourselves."

When I hear his voice, I can't remember why I was dreading this call. It's Zane. I can tell him anything. "No worries, I'm just relaxing before school starts on Monday. My roommate hasn't shown up yet; I hope she's not a nightmare."

"Ah, you get along with everyone. By the way, I'm so proud of you for following your dream. You're going to kill it." God. He's incredible. He doesn't even mention me avoiding him. He's just there for me. Like he always has been.

The lump in my throat is huge. I can barely choke out, "Thanks, Zaney."

"Are you okay, Fee?" His voice is soft. "You'll be great! You're the most confident person I know."

"Confidence hasn't been my strong suit for a while." Tears stream down my cheeks. "I'm so ashamed of myself. I… I…"

"Shhhh. It's just me. We're just us. Talk to me."

"I… I…got my period this morning."

"So, uh." He pauses. "You're not…"

"Nope." I pop the "p."

"Are you okay?"

"Well…" My voice breaks. "I have to tell you something. I'm not proud of what I've done and you're probably going to hate me."

"Fee, can we Skype? Please?" Zane's calm voice turns frantic. "You're scaring me. Let me see you."

My voice sounds small. Pathetic. "Okay. I need to set up an account. Give me five minutes and I'll text you my deets."

"Don't ditch me, or I'll be on the next plane out there. I'm serious," I hear him say before I hang up to fuck around with my computer.

It takes a few minutes to download the Skype app to my Mac, set up an account and text him my handle. Going through these motions pisses me off. Reminds me of how my mom cut me off from everything for so long and I don't even have basic technology setup. No one will ever stifle me ever again.

That's a promise.

Seconds later, the Skype tune fills my dorm room. Swallowing hard, I click to accept the call. There he is. In all his budding rock star glory. Dark-brown eyes peer out from under a green beanie. Curls sproing free around his forehead and neck. Biceps bulge under his tight, black T-shirt because his hands are clasped together, like he's stressed. "Fee. God. You're upset. What is going on?"

Crap, I can see myself in the little video thumbnail. No wonder he's worried, I'm a mess. I smooth my hair down and wipe the mascara from under my eyes with my thumbs. Eke out a smile. "I'm such a disaster, Zane."

Zane leans into the screen so all I can see are his pupils. He makes a peace sign and points it at my eyes and then back at his. "Look into my eyes. You can tell me anything. *Anything.*"

I figure it's time to rip the bandage off. "Fine. That, um…night? I *wanted* to get pregnant." My breath hitches. "Being with you in that perfect moment when you and I… The thing is, I knew I wasn't on the pill. I wanted you to come inside me. So I could have the chance at something *permanent* that bound me to you. To get back what we had. Something that would make sure we never get separated again."

He doesn't react, only cocks his head and zeros in on one word, "*Had*?"

"Yes, *had*. You know as well as I do that what we had was severed. By the distance between us. By the lack of communication. By things that happened." I bury my face in my hands. "The truth is? I didn't believe in us anymore. I lost all faith. I, uh, figured our relationship was kids' stuff, I guess."

Zane takes a deep breath. Pinches the bridge of his nose with his fingers. Exactly like Carter. He looks off into the distance before focusing back on me. "It wasn't only you. In high school, when you Facebook messaged me and we talked and I never heard from you again. I didn't understand what I did wrong. You never got in touch. I was so hurt. So *sad*. Then I made the mistake in the band room… and you picked *that* night to call me? After all those months? The guilt has eaten me alive, Fee. It should have been you. Us."

Whoa.

"Oh, God. Zane."

"So don't beat yourself up. I was selfish that day too. I—uh—finished inside you because part of me wanted the same thing. Something to keep us together. Because I missed—miss—you, Fee." Zane nods. Wipes the corner of his eyes with his thumb. "Being without you isn't an option for me. Don't you get it?"

"I do. I really do." I don't want him to hurt or blame himself anymore for things that were out of our control.

Zane's eyes are wide. Horrified. "Jesus. Fuck. I hate what happened to us. I wish I knew…"

I shake my head. I can't tell him why. It will hurt him too much.

He bites his lip. "Was it me?"

"Us." My eyes squinch shut. Fresh tears pool and spill. "My mom was *obsessed* with keeping us apart. All in some insane need to *protect* me."

"Why the *fuck* are our parents so obsessed with us not repeating their mistakes?" Zane fumes, pounding his fist into his palm. I swear, I can see steam coming out of his ears. "Carter's the same with all his talk about condoms and not getting tied down. Every time he says something like that, it makes *me* feel like a mistake."

My breath hitches.

How could Carter be so insensitive?

"You're not a mistake, Zane. You're the best person in the world."

For a few moments we just look at each other through our respective computer screens. Something passes between us that makes me settle into the type of calm I haven't felt in years.

I press my finger to the screen and Zane touches me back virtually with his. "I used to think adults—my mom, grandparents, I won't put Carter in that category yet—knew everything. I'm so fucking mad at what's happened, Fee. What a Goddamn mess. Don't let them define us. It's time for you and me to make our own way in the world."

"I'm so ashamed of myself. I thought the worst of you. My imagination ran wild. Visions of you fucking other girls consumed me. In the end, I gave up on us. I should have *known* to trust in you. In us."

"I begged Carter to let me come up and see you, but I just couldn't risk…with your dad… Fee, I will never abandon you. Not for any reason. Not as long as I live." Zane scrubs his face and squinches his eyes. Like he's been waiting for years to tell me this. Because he *has* waited for years.

"I know that now."

Zane's smile fills the screen. "When your mom sent me and Carter an invitation to your graduation? I've never been so happy. There was no fucking question."

"And instead of having this talk, I tried to trap you." My chin drops to my chest in mortification.

"We tried to trap each other." His chest heaves. He shuts his eyes. When he opens them, tears spill down his cheeks. He looks away from the camera as if he's trying to compose himself. "We don't need traps. We are us. Now that we're adults? We make the rules. Nothing and no one will keep us apart ever again."

"I'm so sorry," we say in unison.

Which at least makes us laugh.

Good God, the angst. The tension. It's unbearable. It's never been who we are.

"Well, you're not pregnant then?" Zane looks around, as if to see if someone's listening.

"No. Horrible cramps. Blood flowing."

He wrinkles his nose and raises his eyebrows. "Um…"

"Sorry."

"You're one of a kind. I love you, Fee." He shakes his head at me, grinning.

My heart beats a mile a minute. "I love *you*, Zane."

"Seeing you again was the best thing that's ever happened to me. I miss you. I just want…"

"For us to be friends again?" I ask hopefully.

He's silent for a long time, which is unusual for Zane. Ordinarily, he needs to fill the empty spaces with words. To get moony. He's watching me. Studying me. Finally he speaks, "Aren't we *more* than friends now?"

"I'm not sure how to answer that." My fingers bridge my chin and forehead as I stare intently through the screen at him. "We're thousands of miles away. I need to focus on school. You're starting a band."

"Yeah, but we've been separated since we were six years old and we've always been in touch. Practically every day, the past few years aside."

"And we've always been friends." I shut my eyes. I want more, but it's not realistic. Not right now.

He leans back on his bed and holds the laptop against his knees. "Of course we're friends. *Best friends*. But I can't stop thinking about having sex with you, Fee. I want to fly out to see you. Stay naked for days. *You're* who I want. Who I've always wanted. Fuck our parents. Let's be *together* together."

"We can't," I say, but the words stick in my throat. He's saying everything I've wanted to hear for the past four years. He's been honorable. He didn't give in to my hysterics. Instead, by waiting for my mom's invitation, he did the right thing by me. My family. So we could be *us* again.

Without hiding.

Still, the timing isn't right.

His face says it all, he's crushed. "Don't say that."

"I'm not saying it has to be that way forever, but we do have to consider that our parents—as ridiculous as they've been acting— split up because they got together before they experienced the world."

"We're *different*."

"Zane, we need to be smart. I want what you want. Here's what I think we should do."

He listens intently as I explain.

We discuss.

Negotiate.

Within the next hour, we've figured out a brilliant love hack. It's unconventional. Foolproof. With a dose of batshit crazy.

Just like us.

"Are we good?" I blow him a kiss through the phone.

"Yeah." He smiles. "You're the smartest person I know."

For the first time in years, I actually sleep through the night.

Because I've got Zane back.

And he's got me.

On our own terms.

No one will *ever* come between us again.

CHAPTER 16

AGE 20

I'm behind the stage at The Vera Project, an all-ages nonprofit space on the Seattle Center grounds waiting for Ty. The community of young musicians and artists has been a lifeline, especially for Ty, for the past couple of years.

Ty jogs up and taps me on the shoulder. "My dude, I'm sorry. I couldn't get off work early."

"No worries, we're not on for another half hour." I look up from my Gibson. "Go do your vocal warm-ups, you have time."

His look of relief is palpable. "Thank God. I'll be back in a few."

Right before we go on stage, the hair on the back of my neck prickles. Although we've played in front of our peers many times, the energy in the room feels different tonight. Like something great is going to happen. We start the show and instantly, Ty and I lock in. Connect, almost psychically.

Unlike anything I've ever experienced.

In perfect sync.

His vocals are blowing my mind. It's the first time he's allowed himself to really let loose. In public, anyway.

It's fucking *awesome*.

From the day and hour he first sang in front of us, both Carter and I have been in awe. Effortlessly, his deep-baritone voice grabs you by the throat and pulls you in. But it's the other subtle elements that dance around his multi-octave range.

Sensuality.

Sorrow.

Cheekiness.

Angst.

Raw vulnerability.

Then, suddenly, he'll howl, like a wolf when the moon is full. That's what gets you in the glands. Makes you pay attention. You can't help yourself.

All of that aside, tonight is my first glimpse of the performer he's destined to be. He's working the stage. Lost in our songs. Not one ounce of self-awareness. Or shtick. Simple, immersive indoctrination.

I'm blown the fuck away.

So is the audience. Everyone's eyes are riveted on us.

Us.

He spurs me on. I shut my eyes and just let go. *Feel*. My fingers, wrists, arms…they do what they were born to do. Eke every last emotion out of my Gibson. We're in perfect harmony. He growls. My guitar soothes. He croons. I pluck cheekily. He holds a note for an ungodly amount of time. I unleash and shred over the top of him. It's like all of the hard work we've put in over the past years has permeated our entire being.

The music builds.

There's a push and pull.

A Yin and Yang.

We are a perfect immersion.

The crowd loses its mind. Like nothing we've ever experienced, including the talent shows and every other shitty gig in between. We were posers then. Now, for the first time I understand. *Really* understand my dad. Why he toured all those years and had a hard time coming off the road. Because there is not one thing to compare this feeling to.

This rush.

I just know it's addictive.

We play twelve songs and by the time we leave the stage, we're exhausted from the exertion of it all. Backstage, we hug each other tightly.

"Why do I feel our lives are about to change?" I pat him on the back. "Our hard work is really paying off. Dude, you were amazing. How did it feel?"

Ty cracks a slight smile. "I missed a few notes, but fuck. It was awesome."

"I want to play more shows. We need a band, dude. *Stat*." I put my Gibson in its case.

Ty twists his hair up into a knot. "I'm frustrated. Who else do you know to jam with? We can't be a duo forever if we're going to take it to the next level."

"Yeah, well, I guess we should go out there." I nudge him with my shoulder.

We head out into the crowd and chat with a few friends. Fans. Ty's not really great at this stuff, but I make him stick by my side while I network for the both of us. It's important for him to come out of his shell a bit more if he's going to be the front man. I've come a long way from that bullied little shy boy. Talking to people is actually fun for me.

Especially after a show like this one.

When everyone wants a little piece of us.

A willowy beauty with black hair touches my bicep and licks her lips. "You were incredible. Where'd you learn to play like that?"

Jesus. It's incredibly easy to pick up the ladies when you're in a band. I shake my hair and peer at her from under a stray lock. "Lots of practice."

"I'd love to feel your fingers on my strings." She bites her finger suggestively and winks.

Inwardly, I roll my eyes. But I need to play the game. "Ah, well. You're so sweet but…"

"Don't tell me you have a girlfriend." She wrinkles her nose. "You're too young to get tied down."

She's definitely gorgeous. Big tits I can't help but notice because they're literally shoved in my face. My dick stirs a bit, but she's not really worth it. All these band chick girls are the same. They don't know me. Or really want me. "No. No girlfriend. Another night, I'd be tempted to say yes, but I've got somewhere to be, sweetheart."

"Ah, bummer." She hands me her number, which she must have already had ready to go. "Call me when you have a night off. I'll make it worth your while."

I take the paper and flash her a toothy smile. "Sure. Thank you."

Variations of this exchange happen every time we play. So far, even though Fiona and I have an understanding, I haven't been tempted. Nor do I call any of these gals.

FaceTime sex with Fiona is so fucking good, I have no interest.

Just sayin'.

Across the room, Ty is buried in his phone, so I head over. He hangs in there. He really tries. When I see him fading, the night is over. We're about to leave when a super-tall buff guy with curly, reddish hair and a dude with long blond hair stop us. Blond dude says, "Hey, would you guys have time to grab a coffee?"

"Um…I've gotta work in the morning." Ty, predictably, tries to back out.

"Aye. So do I, we just want to have a word. We've been lookin' for a singer and guitar player, so we have. Thought it might be worth a quick chat." The big guy has a faint accent I can't make out.

Ty and I look at each other. He nods. I'm fucking psyched. I can feel my energy level zing out of control, and I don't give two shits about trying to control it. Something inside me knows these guys are the ones. We end up at the iconic 5-Point Cafe a few blocks away drinking shitty coffee in torn-up vinyl booths, which feels appropriate somehow.

"My dudes, what's your story?" I try to get down to business knowing Ty won't last long.

The blond guy, Jace, pulls out his phone and fires up a video. "We've been playing in a cover band while I was in college. Here, you can have a look."

Ty and I hover together and watch a few songs. Solid. Tight. Jace has mad skills, but isn't overly showy. He's just a cool, cool cat behind his kit. For such a tall guy, Connor really rocks. He's not in your face, just a solid performer. He's decent on backing vocals, harmonizing easily with his bandmates.

I'm impressed.

Really impressed.

"You guys sounded great tonight." Jace is such a laid-back guy. All business. He leans back in the booth with his cup of coffee and blows on it. "What do you say about jamming together? See if we gel."

Fuck yeah!

I can't stop myself, I'm excited. These two are the missing pieces. I talk Jace's ears off about music. Influences. Favorite songs. Riffs. Things I hate. Things I love. Not really even thinking if my energy is off-putting. Besides, who the fuck cares? Moony or not. I am who I am. Right now, I need to determine if these guys are worth *our* time.

Sure, I know that sounds arrogant. But whoever we decide to play with will have access to my dad, and I'm not about to bring dudes who are looking for social currency into my life.

Neither of them seems like scenesters.

Or crazy Limelight fans.

Still, you can never be too careful.

It's nice to have lively conversation with someone, though. Ty's not a talker. By any stretch. I could see Jace and me becoming good friends. Getting into mischief. Working the room. Having fun.

Connor is a bit older. Very intimidating. There's a quiet intensity to him. Some would call him broody. He's tight-lipped. Kinda like Ty, in some ways. All he's divulged is that he works construction in a family business and wants to pursue music full time.

With the right people.

Ty, of course, stays mostly silent. I can tell he's impressed, though. Probably because we haven't met musicians of this caliber yet. After two hours of drinking shitty coffee, I'm sold.

Channeling Carter, I turn on my charm. "Look, instead of jamming, why don't we just join forces? What's the worst that could happen? Could you guys meet us at Vera next…"

"Friday." Ty nods at me.

"Friday." I raise my cup to Jace, who clicks it.

"Slainte." Connor raises his cup and clicks ours.

Ty follows.

As far as I'm concerned, it's official. I'm in a band.

I guess we'll need a name.

Afterward, Ty and I walk back to my car. He sums up my feelings succinctly. "Thank fuck."

After I drop Ty off at his apartment, I return home to find Carter puttering around the huge black-and-white chef's kitchen he just had installed. Perfect timing. "Guess what? We finally found a drummer and bass player."

"Yeah?" He offers me a cup of tea, which I take.

I pull up the YouTube video to show him.

He watches. Nods his head to the beat. "Solid. Yeah. Solid."

"The drummer, Jace? He's a marketing major. He built up his college band's following on YouTube to over five thousand subscribers. He wants to do the same for us." This part of our conversation tonight really excited me. How great would it be to have a guy in the band who could handle that stuff?

Carter snarls, "That social media stuff is bullshit. He's got to be a good drummer first and foremost."

"He *is* a good drummer. Better than good." I roll my eyes at my old-school father stuck in the 90's. "Social media is how people my age connect with fans, Carter. If we can build up a solid following, it can get us noticed a lot faster."

"Well, you know I'll do what I can to help you guys. Are you going to practice here?"

"Probably. We're meeting them at Vera next Friday first. I didn't tell them you're my dad yet."

Carter's face falls for a second but he catches himself and pastes a smile on. "Yeah, no need."

I clasp my hand on his shoulder. "There is a need, but I'm not bringing strangers into our house if I think they're using me to get to you."

His eyes soften. He sighs and clasps his free hand on my other shoulder. I pull him to me and give him a hug. Carter's still getting used to affection. I'm worming my way in. He wraps his arms around my neck and squeezes.

We've come a long way in just a few years.

Dare I say my life is perfect?

Mom's cool.

Dad's cool.

Fiona's cool.

Maybe, just maybe, I finally have the band I've been dreaming of.

CHAPTER 17

AGE 21

Nearly two years ago, Zane and I made a plan after I was brutally honest about my need to spread my wings. It was important for me to be free to experience life for a while. Make my own choices. Mistakes. Be independent. With no limits. No judgment.

Zane has been so supportive, on every level.

He's been incredible.

Understanding.

We really figured it all out. A way to have it all but have each other too. Zane's going to be a legendary rock star, just like his dad. He'll have Grammys. Platinum records. As for me, I'll be a famous chef. If all goes as planned, the first woman to earn two Michelin stars in the US. Then, maybe a cooking show, or a line of pots and pans. Dishtowels. Cutlery.

I want it all.

At this point in our lives, we need time and opportunity to achieve our goals. We're in different states. Following different paths. We love each other and are best friends, but our support for each other's dreams is more important right now.

If he's going to be my best other half, I don't want to hold him back.

Contain him.

Put restrictions on his life.

That didn't work out too well for Carter and Lianne. Or my folks, for that matter.

Our rules, which we affectionately refer to as our "love hack," allow us to explore our freedom during these years we won't be together. Quite honestly? Even if someone dared to disagree? They can fuck off. We know what works for us, so we don't expect to be judged for our own choices. Besides, we're brilliant.

1. When we're in the same city, we hook up. As much as possible.

2. When we're not, we're free to fuck other people.

3. Condoms are mandatory. No exceptions.

4. No kissing. No oral. No dates. No sleepovers (yes, that's four rules in one, sue me).

5. We shall never discuss any of said hookups with each other.

Ever.

Done and done.

The last one is probably the most important. Why put something out there that would cause unnecessary jealousy? There's no need for it. No one will ever come between us again. We belong together. We just can't *be* together right now.

As for me, I've really not felt the urge to be with anyone else. Naked FaceTiming Zane is enough for me. More than. He can get me off better than any random I'd pick up in a bar. So why bother?

I'm the happiest I've ever been.

It must be that sweet, sweet feeling of being in control of your own destiny.

Six months into my stint at Le Bernadin, I'm officially the Commis Chef in the meat section. Chef Ripert has never promoted someone so quickly to this position, which is a huge accomplishment. Today is the first of a rare two-day-off stint after fourteen days on.

And it's spring break.

Time off isn't really good for me, though. It's on days like these I climb the walls a bit. I pine for Zane if I'm not busy.

I try to stay really, really busy.

But I miss his touch.

His smell.

His hands on my body.

Fucking him. Without condoms. Nothing in-between us.

Yes, I'm on the pill. I'm not that stupid little girl anymore.

Late last year when I was home for Christmas, Zane fucked me raw in the band practice room. On multiple occasions. He ate me out in Carter's kitchen. I blew him in my dad's office at The Mission. I doubt Zane will ever get the smell of sex out of his car. His back seat got quite a workout. In multiple locations. We wanted to relive the sneaky high-school-kid sex that we were deprived of.

Can you believe our parents still have no idea we're anything more than platonic friends?

We like it that way.

Less messy.

More private.

Zane made it to New York once for a long weekend. My gem of a roommate, Petra, graciously stayed with friends so we could be alone. Three solid days of marathon fucking later, I couldn't walk right for a week.

But it's now seven months since I've seen him in person. I can't leave New York because of school and my new prestigious job. Zane's schedule isn't much better. His band, Less Than Zero, is gaining a ton of momentum. Their drummer is a marketing whiz and Zane is his social media guinea pig. Following Zane's antics on YouTube and Instagram has become my obsession.

I'm not alone, LTZ's fan base is multiplying every day.

Which is so cool. I want him to revel in the band's success. Soak it up. Enjoy all the perks.

Really, I do.

Which is why I've decided to finally take advantage of our love hack. I just need a well-hung fuck-buddy to get some sweet, sweet relief. I'm in the process of activating a Plenty of Fish dating account when my phone lights up.

"Zane, what's going on?" I accept his FaceTime request and his gorgeous, goofy face fills the screen. He's had a haircut. It's a bit shorter, his curls bounce around his shoulders as he walks through his house. Holy hell. He's shirtless. A fresh, colorful tattoo stretches above his left nipple across his chest and over his shoulder.

He holds the camera back. "Do you like my new tattoo?"

"Is it fucking real?" I shriek.

"I have to keep up with you." He strokes the gorgeous street-art-inspired pink rose emerging from out of bright orange flames, surrounded by vivid-green, winding leaves. "It's badass, right?"

"Yeah. Wait, I see letters. What did you write on yourself?" I squint into the screen.

Zane lowers the screen to his left pec and I'm able to make it out.

Choose your battles.

"What does it mean?"

Zane pans the phone back up to his face. "It's something my grandpa always told me when I used to get bullied. It's why he wanted me to learn Krav Maga."

"Wow, that's really cool." I rub the Egyptian eye on my left inner wrist. I have a hummingbird on my outer right arm and many small symbols of my personal milestones in various locations across my body. Miniature eggs and bacon on my ankle. A fuzzy wise owl on my bicep. Stuff like that. "Be careful, Zaney. It's very addicting."

Zane winks. "I'm already planning my sleeve."

"Sexy." I waggle my eyebrows.

"How's the new cook job?" His grin is wide. He likes to tease me about my mom's condescending description of my career choice.

I don't even bother explaining the difference between a cook and a chef to her anymore.

Not that she and I talk much.

Our relationship hasn't really healed yet.

Maybe it never will.

"All's good. It feels good to have a couple of days off," I say after sticking my tongue out at him. "Oh, I meant to tell you. The new video of you jumping out of the amp case to scare Connor was the funniest thing I've seen in a while."

"Yeah, his complete inability to see the humor in it made it even funnier. It's blowing up our social media. Jace is a fucking genius. Our YouTube channel just hit ten thousand followers."

My inner snark can't help but come out. "Ooooh. You're so famouuuus."

Zane smirks before propping his phone up on his dresser so he can put a shirt on. Lord, the man is a specimen of male perfection. In my current sexually needy state, I want him naked.

God, I have a one-track mind.

He's babbling on about band stuff as I try to push the visions of myself tracing the indents of his six-pack with my tongue out of my mind. It's no use, my replacement memory is of him coming all over my tits and painting it on my lips with his finger.

My pussy clenches.

"Take your shirt back off," I growl and flop back against the pillows resting against my headboard.

Zane glances into the screen. "Oh yeah?"

"Yeah." My voice is nearly breathless with desire. I shove my hand down the front of my black leggings and begin to fuck myself with two fingers.

"Fuuuuck." Zane's eyes are hooded. "Pull those pants down so I can see what you're doing."

I remove my hand and suck on my fingers one by one. Then yank my pants and panties off and lose my sweatshirt and bra too. "Like that?"

"Oh, yeah. Jeez, Fee. Your nipples are so hard." Zane shuts and locks his bedroom door. "God, I want to taste you. Tell me…"

"I'm tangy. A little sweet." I trace my tongue along my index finger. "Mmmmm."

His eyes are nearly black now. "You're trying to get me to come in my pants again, aren't you, Fee?"

I giggle and cup and pinch my nipples. He's not wrong. Ever since graduation day, I'm dying for a repeat of that monumental moment. Hasn't happened yet. He's learned tremendous self-control.

Zane steps out of his jeans. God, he's commando. His cock is thick, long, and hard against his belly. He pumps a couple of times then uses his thumb to rub the glistening moisture all over his bulbous tip. With his other hand he positions the camera so I can see his cock up close.

By now I've taken out the suction cup vibrator that Zane sent me and coat it with lube. It's an exact replica of his penis, down to the veins. Such a great visual when we do video sex. When he looks back into the camera, I'm deep-throating his cock-clone. I do it up. Swirl and lick and taste. Hollow my cheeks and let his model shaft slide against my inner cheeks and then back down my throat.

As if it were really him.

He groans, listening to me suck him.

His hand beats his shaft faster and faster. His face is a beautiful grimace as he tries to hold back.

"Let go, I want your come all over my tits, Zane."

My dirty words do the trick. He erupts all over his stomach. Spurts and spurts of come coat him. Like he's been building up for months, which surely can't be the case.

Not that I'd ask.

It's against the rules, after all.

"Now it's your turn. Fuck yourself with my cock, Fee." Zane's eyes are still half-mast. One of his fingers traces through the sticky mess and spreads it around his flat belly. "Ride me hard."

"I will." I affix the suction cup of Zane-the-vibrating cock to my small nightstand, turn it on low and straddle it. Fully intent on impaling myself and coaxing a deep internal orgasm out of this little sesh.

"Slowly." Zane's pumping himself again. "Lower yourself slowly, I want to watch it disappear inside you."

I do as he asks. He's a visual man. Nothing turns me on more than him telling me exactly what he wants to see me do. And me doing it. He always knows what I need. I position the cock at my entrance and sink down millimeter by millimeter. Feel every ridge as it enters my body.

I imagine that it's really Zane.

By the time it's fully inside me, I'm gushing like a geyser.

"Lean back a little, so I can see it in you." Zane's eyes are like saucers. His cock is fully engorged again, he's gripping it in his fist. "Rub your clit. Pinch your nipples with your other hand."

I give him the show of his life and get lost in the moment while doing it. My eyes flutter shut as I imagine it's Zane circling my clit with his rough finger. Stroking my body with his hands. Cupping my breasts and thumbing my nipples into diamond-hard peaks. Without realizing it, I'm undulating like a mad woman on the clone-cock.

Canting my hips.

Searching for—oh…oh… Found it. Jesus.

"That's it, Fee. God, you're so fucking beautiful." I hear Zane's breathless encouragement. "Keep fucking yourself with my cock."

I lean way back, bracing myself with my hands on the back of the nightstand. My tits are thrust forward and jiggle with each movement. I'm so wet now, the cock is effortlessly sliding in and out of me. Each stroke hitting my G-spot at the perfect angle. There's no way to control myself now, I'm on the brink of insanity.

Or pure bliss.

It's hard to tell.

My orgasm rips through my body like a wildfire. I scream like I'm being burned alive.

Because I am. With a passion so intense, I'm sure it will never flame out.

Vaguely, I hear Zane moan, "What are you doing to me? I'm coming again. So fucking hard." I manage to open my eyes just in time to see his face contort with his own rapture. He ejaculates almost as much as before, coating his hand completely.

"I needed that. So much." I disengage myself from Zane's fake shaft and flop on my bed. I prop the phone up so I can see him. He's in a similar position.

We smile at each other.

"FaceTime sex is so hot." Zane's eyes are a bit sleepy. "You wiped me out."

My eyes are heavy too. "I wish you were here."

"Yeah, me too. We've got to find some time to spend together before you graduate."

We chitchat for a bit. Make various air-plans to get together that will never happen. Talk about how badly we miss each other. Then hang up.

The loneliness is suffocating.

My mind races for hours after our sexy call. I pace around my tiny studio apartment where I can practically brush my teeth from my futon. I came to New York to prove something to my parents. To prove being a chef is a great profession. To take back control of my life after living in prison with my mom.

But I've also been trying to prove something to myself.

That I can make it on my own.

And I have been. No doubt.

It's just that I can't deny my stubborn heart wants to be with my long-haired guitar prodigy back in Seattle.

But it doesn't really matter what I really want. I know Zane better than he knows himself. He deserves to go out into the world and explore. To live a rock star life. Not have to worry about being faithful to me.

Unless he wants to, of course.

God I hope he wants to.

I'll just finish up school.

And wait it out.

Until we can be together for real.

Isn't our love hack genius?

Yeah.

Right.

CHAPTER 18

AGE 22

"Dude, are you ready?" I put my arm around Ty. Usually, before we go onstage he's shaking like a leaf. In a state of panic. Ty's a fucking rock god, maybe he finally is beginning to believe it himself.

This isn't our first show by a long shot, but it's the first one at The Mission. We finally draw enough people that Gus is giving us a shot. The show sold out weeks ago. Hundreds of people are here to see us. I'm so fucking excited, I can hardly stand it.

First, I need to make sure my band brother is okay.

"I'm so ready." Ty shakes out his hair. His voice is strong. Confident. "This is so fucking awesome, have you seen the crowd?"

I've caught a glimpse. It was important to me that none of us interacted with the audience before the show. We've stayed smooshed in a tiny room next to the stage where we can hear but not see the crowd.

I love my bandmates. So much. We have different personalities, yet we all complement one another. Connor is fixing a broken string while Jace films him. Ty's bouncing on his toes. The three of us are about to embark upon a journey that's going to change our lives.

I know it.

Deep in my bones.

"Fuck yeah!" I can't control my energy anymore. I jump up and down, unable to contain my excitement. We need a tradition. A going-on-stage band tradition. I thrust my fist out and yell, "Fist pump!"

The guys look at me like I'm nuts. I keep my fist suspended. Waiting. Eventually they all hold out their fists and we knock knuckles. Connor bolts out the door and takes the steps to the stage two at a time. Jace follows. I salute Ty and run up onstage with my trusty Gibson.

Once I'm plugged in and ready, the three of us lock eyes. Jace nods to Connor. Connor nods to me.

Here we fucking *go*.

Mirroring Carter's stance from back in the day, I spread my legs wide and strike the first chord to our new song *Catatonic*. Then I really let loose. The intro to this song is one of my best creations, and I fucking shred.

I'm consumed.

In utter heaven.

When I get to Ty's cue, I glance off stage and see him at the bottom of the stairs wringing his hands together. Nodding to the beat. He catches my eye and nods. There's something phenomenal about watching him in the seconds before he performs. Like Clark Kent changing into Superman. Shy, sweet Ty disappears, and he transforms into a rock god super-fucking-hero.

And when he takes the stage. *Fuck*. He stands with his arms spread wide, looking toward the rafters. Commanding. Sexy. Powerful. The entire energy of the room immediately shifts. All eyes are on Ty.

Mesmerized.

Waiting with bated breath.

Then he lets out a keening wail and we proceed to blow the roof off the place. Carter loves to describe Ty's voice as the combination of Chris Cornell, Geoff Tate, and Johnny Cash. He's so fucking right. I glance out into the audience to see the entire crowd singing along. Jumping up and down. Throwing shit on stage. Losing their minds for Less Than Zero. My band.

Our band.

Fuck yeah. This is what I'm born to do.

Nothing feels like this.

Nothing.

My need to be on stage is clearly in my DNA. Carter's renowned as one of the most entertaining guitarists of all time. Don't get me started on my mom. She's the poster-ballerina for every magazine, blog, and article on ballet. I can't fight my destiny.

I don't want to.

It's my privilege and honor to make *every single person* here feel like I've personally invited them.

A few songs in and Ty's energy shifts. Not in a bad way. More like a taking-it-up-a-notch way. As if that were possible. He's staring at a couple of blonde girls in the front row. He has never, in the six years he's been my honorary brother, reacted to anyone this way. It's fascinating to watch him try to get their attention by upping his game.

It makes me happy; I'd love for Ty to get his rocks off.

God knows, the rest of us do.

After the show, I'm on a high like no other. A zillion women crowd the stage where I sign all sorts of items. I'm chattering away but not really paying attention because I'm watching Ty actually head out to the ladies he was looking at. A curvy redhead asks to sit next to me and take a selfie, which I gladly accommodate. Big mistake. Suddenly, everyone wants their own picture with me.

The rest of the guys are no help. Ty's in the crowd awkwardly hitting on the shorter blonde girl. Connor's texting someone. Probably his girlfriend. Jace is breaking down his kit. A heavily made-up redhead shadows him. A few minutes later, Ty skulks back with a dazed look on his face. When he jumps up to help load out it gives me the opportunity to extricate myself from the fans.

"Who's the girl?" I nudge Ty.

He actually blushes. "Her name is Zoey. She's the most beautiful girl I've ever seen."

I look out into the crowd and the object of his affection is looking at us. "She's pretty. You gonna actually hook up with her?"

"I hope so." He dangles the keys to our van on his finger and disappears out the back to pull it to the loading dock.

I spot Fiona heading in our direction and I dash over to intercept her. I'm taken aback by how stunning she is. Her hair is sleek and shiny. She's wearing a leather corset that causes her ample tits to spill out over the top. Black skinny jeans that are shredded practically everywhere. Her startling blue eyes are emphasized by dark shadow and black cat-eye liner. Red lips.

She's still the woman of all of my dreams—both wet and dry. I want to drag her into the office and fuck her from behind.

Oh, and I will. I push that thought to the back of my head for a moment and ask simply, "What did you think?"

"Incredible. Seriously." She touches my arm. "I'm really proud of you."

Her words mean more to me than anyone's opinion in this room. Before I can stop myself, my arms are wrapped around her. She hugs me back tightly. We break apart, but I keep my arm around her when I steer her to the stage where the rest of the guys are.

"Ty, you remember Fiona." I snap my fingers in front of his eyes. "Fiona Reynolds, this is Tyson Rainier."

"Hey," He's clearly distracted. He's craning his neck looking for someone at the front of the room. Probably the blonde chickadee. He doesn't really acknowledge Fee at all, even though he knows she's my best friend.

He just doesn't know she's also my great love.

No one does.

I'm hoping to change that this summer.

Even though my attention has to be nearly a thousand-percent focused on LTZ right now? I'm sick of the love hack. I've never used it. I'm not sure if Fiona has either. Either way, it's time to put it to rest.

Time for us to be a real couple.

Fiona wiggles to set herself free, but I keep my arm tightly wound around her waist. She rolls her eyes at me. In her snarkiest of snarky voices, she addresses our lead singer, "Nice to see you again, Tyson. Will I settle up with you?"

As if.

"You're breaking my heart, Fee." I grab her hand and pull her back to the office. "You'll settle up with me!"

She unlocks the door and we go inside. I slam it behind us and lock it. "Tell me what you really thought."

"I told you. You were incredible." She pulls a fat envelope from the front of her jeans and slaps it on the table. "At least you'll have gas money for the big tour."

For some reason, I've become the business manager of the band. For someone who was shit at math in school, it still cracks me up that the guys want me to take care of the money. When I was tasked with the role, I decided to study up. Carter gave me a book called *All You Need to Know About the Music Business* by Donald Passman, and I studied that fucker until I nearly had it memorized.

If I'm going to do something, I'm going to do it all the fucking way.

I lean back against the desk next to Fee and pull off my T-shirt by gripping the neck from the back. Then I shake out my hair. Fiona's gaze scans the muscles in my chest and my tattoo, which she hasn't seen in real life yet. I smile. "See something you like?"

"Is that how you take a shirt off like a rock star?" She narrows her eyes.

"Are you calling me a rock star?"

She doesn't answer. Instead, she rips open the envelope and begins counting out the door money. I watch her intently, willing her to look at me. She's struggling not to, I can tell. When she finishes her calculation, she hands me a wad of cash. "Three thousand."

"Fuck, That's awesome. I take the loot from her and put it in a fresh envelope she hands me. "We might even get to go through the McDonald's drive thru on tour."

She laughs. Her eyes crinkle at the sides. Her perfect cupid lips part to show white, gleaming teeth. Her features just, well, soften. Fiona's the most perfect, beautiful woman on the planet.

I reach out to tuck errant hair behind her ear. Impulsively, I bend and press my lips to hers. At first, her lips part and our tongues briefly touch. My hands cup her face when our kiss deepens. We're about to get lost in a sea of kisses when abruptly, she pulls away.

"No, Zane. We're not going down that path. Not with your band here. And my dad. And Carter." Fiona crosses her arms in front of her chest.

"What path?" I slip back into rock star mode and drawl, "There's no path."

She pinches the bridge of her nose between her thumb and forefinger. Her long nails are painted blood red. "C'mon, Zane."

"Oh, this is happening." I waggle my eyebrows. "You are a little minx who didn't even tell me you were moving back to Seattle. Talk about surprise tonight. I might need to spank you."

She peers at me. Glares more like it.

God, how I love her.

"It happened fast. I got the job offer and…"

This is news to me. "Wait, what job offer? I thought you were back for Gus."

"I am, but hinting around about coming back to help him went nowhere. He's not having it. He insisted that I stay in New York because I was promoted to sous chef..."

"Yeah, you were killing it."

"Well, when I was offered the head chef position at Tom Douglas' new fine dining restaurant, I couldn't say no. It feeds two birds with one seed." She brushes something invisible off the front of her pants. "It's opening at the end of the year. I start in a couple of weeks on menu prep and recipe building. Hiring my kitchen staff. Refining the design in the kitchen."

"Wow, that's incredible news."

She's literally beaming. "Now I can keep an eye on my dad, but let him save face."

"I'm so proud of *you*, Fee. Look at us living our dreams."

"Yeah." Her voice is soft. Her eyes lock on mine.

My heart beats through my chest. Video sex aside, we haven't been this close in so long. I take a chance and press my lips to hers once more. A friendly, chaste kiss. I pull back to gauge how she's feeling. Her eyes are at half-mast. Lips swollen. She licks her lips and blinks up at me.

We press our heads together for a snuggle. I rub her back. One hand strokes up and cups the back of her scalp. My lips touch hers again. Just. Barely. She relaxes into me and a little mewl escapes before we're ravaging each other.

In a frenzy, I grip her hips and lift her so she's sitting on the desk. Nudge her knees with my thighs. When she opens them, I step in between and yank her against my hard length. Then I get to work loosening the strings that tie the leather corset so her tits bounce free.

Her gorgeous, succulent breasts. I take her taut, brown nipple in my mouth and suck and nip. Fiona moans. Her long nails thread through my damp hair holding me where she wants me. I devour her tits. Both of them. While I feast, I unbutton and unzip her jeans. Slip my hand into her panties.

She's soaking when I insert my fingers and use my thumb to circle her clit. Our mouths smash together as I stroke her deeper. Rub her faster. "Zane," she moans. "Oh, what are you doing to me?"

Encouraged, I pull her jeans and panties down to her knees. She leans back on her elbows when I kneel between her legs. Lord, Fiona's a sight to behold. She's pinching her nipples with her fingers. Oh my Lord, she's so fucking sexy. Curvy in all the right places. Soft.

Made for me.

I dive in. Lick along her seam. Drink her in. Lap and suckle and reacquaint myself with heaven. My fingers fuck her, curling, seeking.

I flick my tongue on her clit and suck hard. Flick. Suck. Fuck. I know exactly what to do for her. Fiona's body is an instrument.

My most precious instrument.

Her legs smoosh against my head when she comes. She chokes back her cries of pleasure with her fist shoved into her mouth. Her thighs quiver against my ears as she shudders through many aftershocks.

I love every minute.

The longer she comes, the longer I get to lick her until her tremors subside.

Eventually her body stills.

Fiona flops back on the desk. Her eyes are closed. Her chest heaves. I pull up her jeans. Button and zip. Then I carefully reassemble her top, lacing her back into it. When I finish, I see her watching me.

"What about you?" Fiona whispers.

I lean over her and kiss her. Giving her a taste of herself. It's a beautiful kiss. Sweet. Hopeful. Promising.

"Later." I stroke her cheek with my thumb. "Your place or mine?"

"Come to my apartment." She wraps her arms around my neck and I pull her up to sitting. "Whenever we're together, why does it always feel like time stands still? Like we're where we're supposed to be."

"We. Are. *Timeless.* Fee."

"What do you mean?" I can barely hear her she speaks so softly.

I grip her face between my hands. "No matter where we are in our lives. No matter how long we are separated. No matter who has tried to keep us apart, both of us know that what we have transcends time. Transcends space."

She smiles, but behind her eyes Fiona closes down.

Lately, this is her reaction when I go too far with my woo-woo talk about us.

Shit.

"I've got to get out there before Dad comes looking for me." Fiona hops up. A little shaky. I steady her.

We step back out into the club and she hurries away from me toward the bar. I watch her go and wait. And wait. There it is. She glances back at me and smiles.

God, I'm glad she's home.

She's the best thing in my life, hands down.

Despite all the bullshit we've endured during our childhood. The baggage from our parents. Our crazy upbringing.

The long distance.

We've survived.

Some might say, thrived.

And that's saying something.

CHAPTER 19

AGE 22

I couldn't stay away from him a minute longer.

Under the guise of my dad's minor health scare, I hightailed it back to Seattle. In reality, I wanted to be back with Zane. So I left my job at Le Bernadin. Not that working for Tom Douglas is a step down or anything. It's just that Seattle doesn't have any Michelin star restaurants. I might have just shot myself in the foot on achieving that dream.

All because of my stupid heart.

God, I'm so impulsive.

Moving to Seattle now, when Zane's only going to leave.

Four months from now on September 23. When LTZ goes on tour.

Reality is setting in. When he's away, I'll be here in Seattle. Alone. Well, there's my dad. Other than him, I'm essentially starting over.

Again.

All because I wanted four months of quality time with Zane. It's working out spectacularly. We fuck and kiss and hang out and hold hands. Watch movies and head snuggle and create memories. I cook for him. He plays guitar for me. We're taking this time to just love each other for a bit.

Is impulsive behavior so wrong when the outcome is so incredible?

I mean, I even rented my own apartment for us to hole up in. We are free to be naked and fully explore each other's bodies without fear of getting caught. Jesus, I get wet and squirmy just thinking of all the creative ways we've had sex so far. And all the things we want to try.

We're like kids in the candy store. Super loud, screaming, satisfied kids.

Don't get me wrong, we spend a fair bit of time together with both of our dads. We purposely avoid any resemblance of sexual affection when we're with them for now. After years of navigating my mother, as far as we're concerned there's no reason for our parents to know what we're up to.

Like the fact I just got Zane off by jacking him while licking and suckling his perineum and inserting my thumb in his asshole. He came so hard he smacked his head on the wall. He returned the favor by locating my G-spot and sucking my clit all at once. My first combined internal and external orgasm caused me to squirt to our mutual delight.

It's like unlocking little sexual treasures, all of this experimentation.

God, we're insatiable.

Everyone around us is clueless.

Which is just the way we like it.

"We should get downstairs. Ty is bringing Zoey to the barbecue. Carter will be back soon. So will the guys." Shirtless Zane zips up his designer moto pants. I still can't help but openly admire every single muscle on his body. And his growing collection of tattoos. Like the intricate black, white, and red sleeve on his right arm with a giant clock and the word "Timeless" written in script across his bicep. He got that one for me. "Stop looking at me like that. You're making me hard again."

"You're always hard." I cup my breasts and thumb my nipples. Lick my lips for good measure.

He hisses.

Rather than get him worked up any more, I roll out of his bed and put on my bra and tank top. I can't find my panties. "Looking for something?" Zane dangles them from his finger.

I lunge at him, but he shoves them down his pants.

"Give them back, it sucks for a girl to go commando in jeans."

"Deal with it. You can get them yourself later at your place." He toes into his kicks and runs his fingers through his hair to untangle his sex-head. Dabs a little of his sexy-smelling spicy patchouli citrus oil on his neck. Grins at me in the mirror when he sees me watching him.

Reluctantly, I finish dressing and join him at the dresser. I use his brush to tame my own wild locks and thumb the smudges from my eyes. A quick coat of powder and fresh coat of red lipstick is as good as it's going to get tonight.

"You're so beautiful, Fee." Zane's watching me, his eyes hooded.

I pinch more than an inch on my waist. "Don't fuck with me. I'm getting fat from all of the recipe testing."

"I love every part of you, Fee. You're fucking gorgeous. For the record, you're also delicious. I want to eat *you* all day long." He wraps his arms around me and nuzzles my ear. "Let's get downstairs before we start up again."

"You do a *fine* job of eating me." I follow him out the door. He takes my hand and leads me down the back stairwell where we should be able to slip outside no worse for the wear. Instead, he nearly smacks into Ty and a girl with wide, hazel eyes and wild blonde hair as we descend into the kitchen.

"Hey, Zane. Fee." Ty drapes his arm around her. "This is Zoey."

She's young. A little scared rabbit who smiles nervously. "Hey."

"Ahhh, so you're the girl that's stolen our guy's heart," Zane blurts out and throws his arm around her other shoulder so she's sandwiched between them.

I scoff. "Didn't you just play a show at her house?"

"Um, yeah. But I left early." He gives me a pointed look. "I didn't actually *meet her* meet her. Right, Zoey?"

Ty rolls his eyes at Zane and takes control of our introduction. "Zoey, Fiona Reynolds is the daughter of Gus Reynolds, who owns The Mission."

"Oh, that's cool!" Zoey's reaction is genuine. "Nice to meet you."

She seems sweet. Immature, maybe. But nice. "You too."

"Well, you guys are late, the food is probably ready. Let's go eat!" Zane's energy kicks in. He leads us all to the big sliding door leading out to Carter's huge backyard.

My dad and Carter are busy cooking the salmon on the grill. Shit. We didn't hear them come back. Zane joins them like nothing's amiss. The three of them place mountains of food on the picnic table.

After Zoey and I help Connor and his girlfriend, Jen, drag extra chairs around the firepit, we pile our plates high and sit around the fire. Dinner is simple. Delicious. Even with as much training as I've had in the culinary arts, it's a luxury to eat other people's food.

As per usual when LTZ, Carter, and my dad get together, the entire discussion revolves around band business. I zone out for a bit and daydream about ideas for a lamb dish for the new restaurant until it's almost time for me and Dad to leave for the club. I get up and collect everyone's plates. To my surprise, Zoey helps me.

"So, you're Ty's girlfriend?" I'm not all that interested but attempt to make small talk when we go into Carter's house to throw away the garbage.

"Yes, we've been together for a couple of months." Her face lights up. She's got it bad for Ty. Silly girl. "Are you Zane's girlfriend?"

"Uh, no." I make a show of rolling my eyes to throw her off the scent. "He's not capable of keeping his dick in his pants, so I'm not about to get my heart broken."

Of course, I don't let on that when his dick is out of his pants it's usually inside my pussy. Or my mouth. Or my ass.

Or that I'm *actually* about to get my heart broken when he goes on tour.

"Oh." She's clearly shocked by my crassness. I take mercy on the poor girl, she's got a good one who is quite possibly as sweet as she is. "Don't worry, I'm pretty sure Ty's a saint. So is Connor. Zane and Jace? Meh."

We're back at the firepit, so of course everyone hears what I just said. Zane smiles to himself as Jace snarks, "Musicians aren't meant to keep it in their pants. We're too young to be tied down."

"I got into a lot of trouble not keeping it in my pants." Carter stands by the fire rubbing his hands.

Everyone laughs. But me. And Zane, who glares at Carter.

It's not funny to us.

I glance over at Zane, who winces then covers his reaction up with a wide smile. Fucking Carter. What a shitty thing to say in front of his son. I love him, but he's a train wreck sometimes. Hence, why we don't let on about our relationship to him.

"Zoey, Ty tells us you're going off to college in a couple months." Carter sits back down in his chair.

Zoey squirms in Ty's lap. If he didn't have a gigantic boner before, he probably does now. "Yes, I'm going to Western this September."

"Ah, that's great. It's important to get a college degree," my dad offers unhelpfully. "I'm hoping Fiona will finally agree with me."

I'm pissed, but I won't show it in front of this crowd. I grit my teeth. My job at Tom Douglas is still under an NDA until they issue a press release. Zane is the only one who knows about my new job. "I like helping you run the club, *Dad*."

"Speaking of which, we need to go." He stands and motions to me. Zane tries to catch my eye, but I take off for the front door without glancing back. It's time to get the hell out of Dodge. Once we're in his truck, Dad pulls out of Carter's neighborhood. "It's so nice to see that after all these years, you and Zane are still close."

"Yeah..." I look out the window. I'm angry at him. And hurt.

"Sweetheart, is something wrong?"

"Dad, why do you always put my career down? I've worked hard to get where I'm at. With no financial support. Well, any *real* support from either you or Mom. You belittled and embarrassed me in front of Zane and his friends. I have a four-year culinary degree with restaurant management from one of the most prestigious schools in the world. And, if you must know, I'm back in town because I'm the executive chef at a new restaurant. My career is actually way ahead of every single person who was at that barbecue tonight. Well, except for you and Carter."

He stares straight ahead at the road.

"Dad? Did you hear me?"

He doesn't answer me for a long time. Finally, he looks over at me.

Reaches over and pats my knee. "Fee, I'm sorry. So sorry for so many things. I just want what is best for you. I guess I don't want you to follow in my footsteps."

"I'm a chef. How is that following in your footsteps?"

"This service industry is tough. Long hours. Transient. You're married to the job." He pulls into the back parking lot of The Mission. "It's impossible to have a normal relationship. It tore our family apart. It tears a lot of families apart."

"Then why do you still do it?" I unclick my seatbelt but don't move. This is actually one of the first real discussions I've had with my father as an adult.

He turns sideways to face me. "It's all I know. I don't have a college degree."

"You don't need to have a college degree to be successful, you know. Don't forget that I've worked in some of the top restaurants in the world. I've been a fucking brunch cook in Brooklyn. I'm a certified sommelier. I can wait tables with the best of them. Oh, and I know all about the financial side of the business too."

"I wouldn't have been able to make the changes you've implemented at The Mission without you. I *am* proud of you, Fee. You're the best thing I've ever done. Truly. If this is what you really want to do, I won't ever say another word. The last thing I want is to make you feel bad. You're my little girl."

My heart melts. After all, that's all you ever want to hear from your dad. We go inside and I check on the bar. Watch the first band. Hang out with Dad. It's true, this club is his home. Everything about The Mission is Gus Reynolds. Everyone loves Gus Reynolds. The problem is, there aren't enough people here on a Friday night. It's dead. My phone buzzes in my pocket.

Zane: whatcha doin?

Fiona: bbq still going?

Zane: Y jam sesh in a few

Fiona: u coming 2 my place tonight?

Zane: coming heh heh

Fiona: you're stupid

Zane: no you're stupid

Fiona: ok beavis I'm heading home nobody's here

Zane: nooooooo come back over here

Fiona: no car yet, it's on my list

Zane: Find Pokey & tell him to drive you over or there's this thing called Uber…

Fiona: ha ha

Zane: I miss you

Fiona: we can hang out tomorrow

Zane: don't make me beg it's unbecoming

For fuck's sake, I *can't* resist Zane.

Which is why twenty minutes later, I'm back at Carter's house with Pokey and a couple other of LTZ's roadies. As stupid as it sounds, I feel a little less conspicuous walking in with them rather than returning to the scene of the crime alone.

Like a stupid groupie.

Speaking of which, Zoey is there with yet another blonde girl. A few other hangers-on are scattered about. LTZ sounds amazing, but I'm not really into all of this cock-star shit. When they finish jamming, I figure everyone will go home, but no. Only Zoey and her friend leave. The rest of the gathering moves to the firepit.

It's quite the cast of characters. Ty stares off into space with a goofy lovesick look on his face. Groupies fight over Jace. Drama ensues.

Connor and Jen snuggle together like the perfect, normal couple they are. Pokey, the roadies whose names I can't remember, and Zane are deep in a discussion about their tour.

Not my favorite subject.

I really just want Zane and me to be alone. Unfortunately, it's nearly 2 a.m. when everyone finally leaves.

Rather than go back to my place, we tiptoe quietly up to his room even though Carter's room is on the other side of the house and he couldn't hear us anyway. Once inside, Zane closes and locks the door. He undresses quickly. I do too.

We don't need words.

We need each other.

I imagine our naked bodies are like silhouettes in the moonlight peeping through the blinds. He cups my breasts and pinches my nipples. As we back up toward his bed, I stroke up and down the entire length of Zane's shaft. When the backs of my knees hit his mattress, he spins me around and clasps my wrists at the small of my back with one hand.

Zane bends me over his bed and kicks my legs apart, I can't help but moan in anticipation. His free hand sneaks between my legs and he drags his fingers along my slit. I'm more than soaking for him.

"Taste." He touches his fingers to my lips. I suck his fingers in my mouth and lick hungrily. Zane's cock nudges my opening and with one cant of his hips, I'm full of him. So full. My cheek is pressed into the mattress. My arms are captive. Right now, the only thing I can or want to comprehend is how amazing it feels to have Zane fucking me from behind.

Zane releases my wrists and grips my hips. Pulls nearly all the way out and rams back in. Over and over. Hard and fast. Our bodies slap together.

We're porn-star fucking.

It's exactly what I want.

Need.

It doesn't take long before I'm close. He reaches around to rub my clit, exactly how I showed him the first time we made love. I come with a shriek I try to muffle in his mattress. He bites down on my shoulder when he empties his load inside me a few seconds later.

I'm wrecked, but damn if he doesn't crouch behind me and eat me out so thoroughly, I shatter again all over his face.

This. This is why I'm here.

Liar. It's so much more. Just tell him.

Exhausted, we climb into bed. I lay on his chest, listening to his heartbeat. Our legs are tangled together. He pets my hair. Stares up at the ceiling.

"Are you okay?" I kiss his chest. "You seem a little off."

He sighs heavily.

I wait. He'll tell me what's bothering him. On his own time.

"Do you ever wonder if you belong anywhere?" His voice is shaky.

"All the time."

"Yeah?"

I stroke his new tattoo with my nail. "Tell me what's going on."

"It was a weird night. After you left, for some reason I word vomited about the time Ty and I lost our virginity in the band room. I couldn't stop myself. It makes me so mad when I get moony. I still can't seem to stop myself. I hurt Ty's feelings. And Zoey's."

"I'm sure they'll survive a Zane tornado." I twirl one of his curls around my finger and don't ask what I really want to know. "Ty's pretty gone over her. Is that weird for you?"

He nods. "I don't get it. He doesn't really know her. She's so young. The timing is bad, we're leaving for six months. It's not like a relationship can sustain that, right? We should know. That's why we invented the love hack."

My heart squeezes when he confirms my worst fear out loud. "Yeah. For sure."

"Fee, tonight I overheard Carter talking to Ty about me. And Mom."

"Well, fuck. What did he say?"

Zane doesn't answer right away. When he finally does, it makes me want to thunk Carter on the head. "A lot of the usual bullshit advice about not getting too serious. Using condoms. Blah blah blah. What really stung is he used himself as an example of what *shouldn't* happen. Like *I* shouldn't have happened. Like I was a *mistake*. As you know, this isn't the first time, either."

"He didn't mean it that way, Zaney." I wrap my arms around him. "I know he didn't."

He rests his head against mine. "I guess. He didn't know I was there. And he did correct himself. That's why I'm upset. It wasn't fun hearing what Carter said."

"He loves you, Zane. But there's a reason we're smarter than they are. It's why we came up with the love hack." The words singe my tongue, but I persevere. "None of our folks have been stellar examples of how to navigate relationships. Even your mom sucks at it. On the way to The Mission, I had to yell at my dad about his stupid condescending comments about college tonight."

"Yeah! What was that all about?"

"Some *bull*shit." I wag my finger.

"Do you realize that we're already three years older than when our folks had us? I can't even imagine having a three year old right now." Zane goes still for a second. No doubt remembering our own carelessness the first time we had sex. That it actually *could* have happened to us.

"I know, we dodged a bullet," I say, though I don't really believe it. The wind is out of my sails, though.

"Fee, what I'm trying to say is the scariest thing about tonight is my realization that Carter was right. I'm actually more like Carter than my mom. I'm impulsive. I get lost in my own world. I can be completely inconsiderate."

I can't argue with him there, but he means well. "Zaney, don't get down on yourself. No one holds that against you. I think it's cute. It's part of why you're so awesome."

"You think I'm *awesome*?" Zane raises one eyebrow. Smirks.

I silence him with a kiss. He's trying to play it off, but I know this man. He needs comfort. Reassurance. From me. I nudge him over on his side so I can spoon him. My hand rests on his ripped stomach and I press my upper body flush against his back.

"Wanna know the one thing I'm the most scared of, Fee?"

"What?"

He takes my hand and moves it up so it's pressing against his heart. "It's my addictive personality. I'm also just like Carter in that way."

"You're not addicted, Zane. That's crazy talk."

"You're wrong."

I squeeze him from behind. "What in the world are you addicted to?"

Zane turns his head so he can look me in the eye.

"Don't you know it's you? Fiona, I'm hopelessly addicted to you. It scares the fuck out of me sometimes."

And that comment cements it. In that moment, I decide to put him first. Like he did for me when I went to school. It doesn't matter if I never needed our love hack.

He does.

It's time for him to be a rock star. And all that comes with that life.

Even if I'd love to get rid of our arrangement and have him brand me as his, he's not ready for that level of commitment.

I need to stand behind what I asked of him four years ago.

And now allow him his freedom.

Without repercussions from me.

Even if it's going to kill me if he fucks anyone else.

At least I won't know about it.

Fuck.

Turns out, I'm not all that smart after all.

CHAPTER 20

AGE 23

Every single day of being a rock star is awesome.

Some days are just easier than others.

Today is not one of those days.

I just completed six solid hours of press with no one to help. I'm fine with it. I guess. I'm certainly not going to complain about my band's success. It just wasn't supposed to be this way. LTZ started as a dream that me and Ty had together. From practically the day we met in high school, he and I knew we'd be here one day.

We plotted. Planned. Rehearsed. Created.

Never in my wildest dreams did it occur to me that he'd be so disconnected from the actual experience of it all. It fucking sucks.

It sucks that most days I wonder if he's going to make it to the next show.

It sucks that he just can't get over what happened with Zoey.

It sucks to be alienated from my best friend.

In some respects I'm lucky, I guess. Fiona and I have been religious about keeping our shit locked down tight. As far as I know, no one but us has any clue about how much we mean to each other. That's how we like it. Somehow, years ago, we unlocked the key to a successful long-distance relationship. We have it all figured out. Because we know what true love really is.

Unconditional.

Judgment free.

Supportive.

Trusting.

We live, sleep, and breathe all four elements because of our brilliant love hack. I'm so glad I never told Fiona I wanted to put an end to it. Now that we're on the road and having success? It's the smartest thing she ever did. If my parents had done what we're doing, who knows if they'd have stayed together.

When I'm in town, we're exclusively together.

When I'm away touring, we're both free.

Fiona's right. As much as I don't like to think about her with someone else, fucking doesn't actually mean anything. It's just sex. A physical release. How lucky am I to have a woman like Fee in my life? Someone who is on board with a modern, practical relationship.

Once things settle down with the band and with her career? That's the time for monogamy. We'll get there someday; in that I have no doubt. Married. With our own house. A bunch of kids.

Just not for a decade or so. Not if the band continues on this trajectory.

Fee is crazy busy too. Between helping Gus at The Mission and her executive chef position at Seattle's hottest new restaurant, Market

Seafood, Fee's working all the time. She's pulling twelve-hour shifts at least five days a week. If her texts are anything to go by, she really doesn't have any days off.

She doesn't want anyone "fucking up her menu," as she so eloquently puts it.

As for me, LTZ is exploding. Beyond anything Ty and I ever hoped or dreamed back in the Vera Project days. We have record sales. Our songs are played everywhere. We have millions of followers all over the world. Our tour's been extended multiple times because we keep selling out.

I hope this goes on forever.

Because I love it. Every. Single. Second.

This is what I was born to do.

Same with Jace. Connor too.

I'm beginning to question if this lifestyle suits Ty. And he's the one we need the most.

"My dude, can I come in?" I rap on his dressing room door. He finally convinced management to give him private space at gigs. He claims he doesn't want to disturb us with his extensive vocal warm-up routine.

I know the truth.

He needs somewhere to escape.

For his own mental health.

Ty opens the door, looking every inch the rock star. Shredded jeans. Black Dr. Martin boots. White tank. Wild, long, dark hair. "What's up?"

"I'm just wondering how the writing's going. I heard you playing a really cool melody earlier. I miss working through songs. Just me and you." I plop down on the sofa after grabbing a plateful of fruit.

"Yeah. I'm sorry about that, Zane." Ty sits next to me. "I'm really trying, you know."

"Is it helping?" I say through a mouthful of strawberry.

Ty cocks his head. "What?"

"Writing about her."

"Yeah. I guess." He checks his phone and changes the subject. "You ready?"

It's always been like pulling teeth to get him to talk. It's even worse these days. Good thing he's the most professional of the four of us. He takes his job very, very seriously. Always upping his game. Tonight's no exception. Barcelona is probably the most phenomenal show we've played to date. Ty leaves everything on stage and more.

After the show, we all shower and head over to the VIP area for the meet-and-greet portion of the night. Aside from playing the actual gig, this is my favorite part. I love to interact with our fans. Love. It. I don't care that Ty will disappear after ten minutes. Or that Connor is broody and awkward AF. Or that Jace manages me to death. It's all part of our band rhythm.

The four of us make a perfect team.

The VIP parties serve another purpose for me. It's where I find my hook-ups. You see, I'm literally always horny because I miss Fee. So, so much. Except, unlike when she was at school, nowadays it's virtually impossible to have video sex with her. Our schedules are too busy and the time difference is brutal.

I need something to take the edge off.

To release my sexual tension.

I've fully embraced the love hack.

Plus, I've implemented four additional rules for myself that Fee doesn't know about.

First, I *never* choose anyone who looks remotely like Fee. There is no substitute for the real thing, after all.

Second, an NDA is mandatory.

Third, my bodyguard takes their devices as soon as they sign. There's no way I'll risk some rando taking a bed selfie with me while I'm sleeping. No, fucking way. I'm not risking anyone posting some bullshit on social media that Fee could see.

Finally, used condoms come with me when I'm done. I dispose of them myself. Our fans are awesome, but I'm not naïve. No way will any tiny Zanes show up unexpectedly. Fiona's the only woman who will bear my kids. And I'm the only man who will father hers.

Truth.

Anyway, tonight should be easy pickings. The VIP area is lit. Everyone in Spain is gorgeous. Well-dressed. On point. I don't waste time identifying my target for the evening. Across the room I spot a pink-haired girl with funky buckled boots. Jace has his eye on her too, which is perfect. I'm gonna mess with him a bit. I make him take pictures with some Spanish royalty guy to keep him from hitting on her. *Mr.* Deveraux is super annoyed that I'm interfering with his game.

Which. Is. Hilarious.

As for me, I'm leveling up. Royalty dude brings me to a private house party at an enormous mansion. I throw back a gin and tonic. Do a bit of requisite hob-nobbing with the Spanish elites. Then I'm ready to hook up and get the fuck out of here. It doesn't take long for me to find a willing redhead heiress, who I drill in a marble bathroom as big as Carter's living room.

I'm satiated and back at my hotel by six a.m.

I empty the condom down the sink, toss it and check my phone.

Perfect timing. Fiona's just off work.

Zane: call me when you get done I have a day off

Fiona: I'm home tonite

Zane: tonite's tomorrow… calling

"Hey! Isn't it super early there? Are you just getting home?" Fiona answers before the phone even rings.

I chuckle. "Hello to you too."

"How's Barcelona?" Fiona has my itinerary at all times. She's my emergency contact. She has my passwords to everything too. "Are you going to do some sightseeing?"

It's the last thing I want to do, believe it or not. "Nope, I'm sleeping all fucking day."

"You never experience the amazing cities in Europe. I literally hate you. I'm not going to keep sending you restaurants to try if you don't appreciate it. You're pissing me off, Zane Rocks," Fiona scolds good-naturedly.

I don't answer, instead I press the FaceTime button. She accepts and her beautiful face fills the screen. She doesn't have any makeup on. Her hair is piled high on her head. I squint, not sure what I'm seeing. "Did you dye your hair?"

"Surprise!" She reaches up and pulls out the clip. Her once-dark locks are now fuchsia pink. She fluffs her hair out around her shoulders. "What do you think?"

She's fucking stunning. "I love it, Fee."

"Yay!" Her smile lights up the screen.

God, I love her. I love seeing her face. Hearing her voice. "Stop being mad at me. I'm waiting to go to all of those fancy restaurants with you. *We* should do that stuff, not me and a bunch of guys who won't appreciate it."

"Awww." She beams. "You're a silver-tongued devil."

I guess that was the right answer.

My heart squeezes. God, if only she could be here with me. Truth be told, I've avoided video calls because they are bittersweet. Despite our arrangement, I can't help but feel a bit guilty. It's hard for me to reconcile being balls-deep inside another woman an hour ago and talking to the woman I love now like nothing happened.

Oh, I know I'm not cheating on Fiona. But…in these moments it sure feels like it. I always feel just a teeny bit sick inside.

I really only want to be with her.

It's just not possible right now.

"What's wrong, Zane?" Her face falls. "Did something happen?"

I smile to reassure her. "No, just another long night. The show was fucking amazing. I went to an after party for a bit."

She's silent. Tries to hide the wince when she figures it out. I see it, though, and it's a knife in my gut. I know Fee won't say anything. Sometimes, I wish she would, except she's the one who came up with the love hack. And she's stubborn. Instead, she changes the subject. "Are you guys ever coming home?"

"Fuck! I forgot to tell you. Yes. Management said this is our final extension. I'll be home in a couple of months. We have three weeks off, then we're going to LA to work on the new album."

"I bet you're excited to sleep in your own bed."

"I'm more excited to sleep in yours." I waggle my brows.

"Crap, I didn't tell you. I moved back in with my dad." She props the phone on her knees and winds her hair back up in the clip. "He had a stint put in; I need to look after him. Make sure he eats right and everything."

Shit. This is a great example of how disconnected I get being on the road. "No, you told me. I just forgot. I remember you said that. Is he at least trying to take it easy?"

Her face falls. “He’s so bull-headed. I’m doing what I can at The Mission. I go early in the morning to do his books. I stop by after every shift to check on him. He’s killing himself.”

“Why doesn’t he just sell the club?” Carter already filled me in on some of the details and how he’s been trying to convince him. “It makes no sense.”

“He’s determined to preserve The Mission’s legacy. So many famous bands have gotten their start there. My dad believes it’s his purpose in life.”

I shake my head. “I don’t get it.”

“I do.” Fiona leans back, giving me an amazing view of her tits. “You haven’t been home in a while. It’s getting a little scary here. With all of the tech expansion, clubs are shutting down left and right. He doesn’t want a developer to buy it only to tear it down.”

“He owns the building, he could just let someone else run it.”

“Zane, the property taxes have quadrupled. He’s really struggling. The only way it’s still going is *because* he owns the building. A new owner would raise the rent to cover the property taxes and he’d never be able to pay that much every month.” She’s getting agitated. “I may be an executive chef, but I don’t make enough money to help financially.”

My bank account is fat. Our first royalty checks are in and I know just what to do with the money. “Fee, I can pay the taxes. Let me help, I have good money rolling in now.”

“Don’t you think Carter already offered?”

My heart sinks. Of course he did. He’d never let Gus down. “Well, great! Problem solved.”

“Not so much. My dad won’t take Carter’s money. He certainly won’t take yours.” Fiona buries her face in her hands. ”Nothing I say or do will convince him. He’s cutting off his nose to spite his face.”

"Fucking Gus."

"Yeah, you could say that again."

"Fucking Gus." I give her my cheesiest smile. Only to cheer her up.

It works. I'm rewarded with her adorable grin.

We catch up for a few more minutes, but soon Fiona's eyes are drooping. She yawns. Then blinks and opens her eyes wide, as though she's trying to stay awake.

"You're falling asleep, Fee. I'll let you go." I don't want to hang up, but I'm exhausted too.

"'Kay." She makes a kissy face at me. "I miss you."

"Oh, Fee." I bury my face in my hands.

"Zane, what's wrong?"

"I really miss you. When I have to hang up, it hurts," I say through my fingers.

"I know."

"Can we go somewhere when I get back? Alone?" I look back at her through the screen. "Would you be able to get the time off work?"

"Yeah." She reaches out and touches the screen. "Let's make it happen."

"Promise?"

"Promise."

We hang up. I sit on the edge of my bed for at least another hour. Thinking. Brooding, more like it. I remember to put the *Do Not Disturb* sign on before I finally crawl into bed. As bone-tired as I feel, I can't sleep.

Yeah, my "arrangement" with Fiona feels stupid.

No, it *is* stupid. Colossally so.

We've spent so much of our lives trying to avoid the mistakes of our parents. The mistakes of our friends. The mistakes of everyone who has ever been in love before.

Why?

To protect our hearts? Nope. Hasn't worked. To avoid getting hurt? Nope. Hasn't worked. To stop feeling left behind? Nope. Hasn't worked. To take control of our lives? Yeah. But, no.

It. Hasn't. Fucking. Worked.

I lie staring at the ceiling in my hotel. Brooding, and I'm not a brooder. I'm a fixer. There's nothing more important than fixing this mess I've made.

Bottom line: I don't have any control over my love for Fiona. I don't want her to be with anyone but me. It's time I told her so.

I know what I need to do.

First, I'm never fucking anyone else again but her. I never want to see that look on her face again. She's *it* for me, so I'm putting an end to this madness. No more love hack going forward. As far as I'm concerned, Fiona and I already have what everyone is searching for. We've always had it. Always will have it.

I'm done hiding.

She's my future.

I'm ready. God, I've really always been ready.

It's time she knows it.

And *believes* it.

CHAPTER 21

AGE 24

Zane's sitting on a giant piece of beechwood, staring out at Sunset Beach. We're spending a few days in a private cabin on Lummi Island. How he managed to book us at Willows Inn, I do not know. Chef Wetzel is one of the most coveted chefs in the country. Reservations are impossible.

Somehow he's made it happen.

A late birthday celebration for me. He was still on tour on the actual date.

"We should go, dinner's a pretty big event." I run my fingers through his long curls. Breathe in his intoxicating spicy, earthy citrus scent. "I'm so excited, I can't believe you pulled off such a huge surprise."

He looks up. Smiles his goofy Zane smile that I've loved since I was born. "Let's get over there."

The atmosphere is spectacular. Thick wood beams. Eclectic

furniture. Huge stone fireplaces. Herbs, fresh bread, and lavender candles deliciously permeate the dining room. We're seated slightly away from the other diners in the prime table overlooking Lummi Bay, where the sun is on its way to setting.

It reminds me of the Bellingham sunset when we made love for the first time all those years ago.

One might think that I'd indulged in dinners like this before, being a trained chef and all. But, no. Tonight is a rare treat. Even when I worked in New York, it was tough to find time to venture out of the kitchen to experience a tasting menu by a renowned chef.

Oh, but tonight is worth it.

Dinner is presented in courses of multiple little bites. All exquisitely prepared and plated like art. Each course is paired with its own wine that complements the food. As a sommelier and chef, I'm in literal heaven to just sit back and enjoy. Enjoy, I do. I can't decide whether my favorite dish is the seared spot prawn with black gooseberry, the deer tartare with spicy radish, turnip, apple, and juniper, or the kohlrabi cooked in sea water then grilled in seaweed oil. I'm pretty sure I moan with every bite.

"I love watching you eat." Zane's staring at me. "I have the biggest hard-on right now."

"Mmmm." I take a bite out of my buckwheat doughnut dusted in rose sugar and dunk it in caramel sauce. I make sure to run my tongue over my lips slowly to catch all of the sugar. "Delicious."

"You're killing me, Fee." Zane sips the 2013 Foris Moscato. It's funny watching Zane drink such a fancy wine. It's also hilarious that the two of us are all grown up on an overnight trip having dinner in one of the most celebrated restaurants in the world.

Once dinner is finished, we take a few selfies with guests who recognize Zane. A big guy from his high school is particularly pushy, but Zane handles it well. He's firm, direct, and kind. Being the child of two famous people really has honed his celebrity skills. He's adjusting to fame well.

It's a half-mile walk back to our cabin. Lummi Island is sparsely populated. Most of the people here are staying at the Inn, so our stroll is quiet and peaceful. The fall air is still warm. The scent of pine and salt water dances on the breeze. We meander. Holding hands. Sneaking kisses. The night is so beautiful, we decide to sit on our back porch overlooking the beach.

The waves gently lap at the shore.

It's the calmest I've felt since he left.

I curl up into Zane's side. His arm rests around my shoulder. Our heads snuggle. He twirls my hair around his index finger. I sigh contentedly, "It's so quiet here. I bet this is culture shock for you."

"Actually, it's nice." He kisses my temple.

"Are you going to tell me what's bothering you?" I stroke the anchor tattoo on his right arm. "You've been deep in thought since you got back from tour. What's up?"

"Don't be silly. I'm good. Tell you what. Last one to get naked is a rotten egg." Completely ignoring my question, Zane pops up, runs inside, throws his shirt on the floor and dives onto the bed. I'm on his heels. I hop around and manage to unzip my skirt, which falls to the ground. Zane whistles. I lean over, pull my blouse off and do a little shimmy before tossing it on top of the skirt.

"Likey?" I pose with my hands on my hips.

"Get over here." He's sitting on the edge of the bed in lotus position. I sit across from him cross-legged because, damn it, I'm not as flexible. I still wear my gray-and-black herringbone bralette, black boy shorts and knee-high socks. Nothing wrong with some naughty schoolgirl visuals, I figure.

Things get heated quickly. We stare into each other's eyes. Our chests are heaving. He holds his hands up. I press my palms against his. We breathe. Take in each other's energy. It's intense. Too intense. I reach over and grab a decorative pillow off the bed and smack him in the head.

"What the fuck?" Zane howls. Then grabs his own pillow and peeks around it with a mischievous grin. He smacks me back. Soon, we're in a full-blown pillow fight. Laughing so hard it feels like I've done a kajillion sit-ups.

This is us. Me and Zane. We're not emo. We're not angsty. We have fun. We can do anything. Anytime. Anywhere. Like smash pillows in each other's faces one minute. And fuck each other senseless the next.

As if reading my mind, Zane's expression changes. He's not laughing anymore. He's the big bad wolf. In a quick, fluid motion, he grabs my pillow, throws it behind us and tosses me down on the bed. Holds my wrists above my head. Grinds his cock against my core.

"You. Are. So. Fucking. Sexy." He punctuates each word with a thrust.

I lock my legs around his ass to hold him against me. "Some sick moves there, son." Our mouths crash together. He keeps my arms captive and presses his body against mine. Just enough so I can feel his weight but not crush me. He swivels his hips and I can't help but moan, feeling his hard length press against my pussy.

"Let me up." I stare into his brown eyes. He releases me without question. "I'm taking care of *you* tonight."

"Oh yeah?" He cages my head with his arms and hovers his lips over mine.

"Yeah."

We roll over so I'm straddling him. I splay my fingers and stroke his face with my palms, careful not to scratch him. I had my nails done for this trip as a treat, my chef duties aren't normally conducive to manicures. My palms travel down Zane's chest, over his nipples, across his washboard abs. Using my thumbs, I hook the waistband of his boxer briefs and pull them down, revealing his impossibly hard cock bobbing against his defined abs. He takes himself in hand and pumps as he kicks his underwear off and to the floor.

"Well, well. I guess you did miss me," I say right before my lips seal around his shaft and fingers. He releases his cock and holds my hair up so he can watch me take him deep. His dick slides along my tongue to the back of my throat. I swallow his tip, just the way he loves it.

There's a method to my madness. I alternate deep-throating with sucking and licking him all over. Zane's hands grip the sheets. His hips buck to the rhythm of my mouth. I hold them still to keep him focused on the gold-star head he's getting.

"Good God, Fee." His eyes are closed. "Stop for a sec. It feels *too* good and I want to be inside you when I come."

I pull down my boy shorts and toss them on the ground but leave my socks and bralette on. Gripping his cock in my fist, I guide him into me. Bareback. I trust he's followed the rules. I know he won't put me in a position of catching something from one of his groupies.

He has nothing to worry about with me. Anyway, we don't talk about it—per our rules— but I'm pretty sure he can't say the same thing. I mean, VIP party is his code word.

I think.

Maybe I should just ask…

No, it would fucking hurt to hear about…

Shut up, Fiona.

It doesn't matter. Now we're back where we belong. And nothing… *Nothing* feels as good as fucking Zane raw. I won't give it another thought.

My hands splay across his abs. He reaches up and pulls the cups of my bralette to the side so my tits spill out. He pinches my nipples. Hard. Then he strokes them with his thumbs to soothe. Pinch. Stroke. Pinch. Stroke. Each time sends a zing straight to my clit.

Needing a bit more, I lean over so my breasts dangle over his lips. Now he sucks my nipples one after the other. Then nips them. Suck. Nip. Suck. Nip.

Exquisite.

My hips grind against him in a circular motion to find the exact angle I want. Ah. Got it. With each stroke, his crown rubs against my G-spot with just the right pressure. My mouth lolls open. Every muscle in my pussy and abdomen clench in a spectacular release. I ride waves of pleasure that roll through my body. My clit spasms against the base of his cock. Zane wraps his arms around my waist to hold me in position so I can extend my orgasm.

Oh, and it keeps going.

It's intense how hard I come with him. Like I'm electrocuted in a good way.

When I can take no more, my body liquifies and I collapse on top of Zane. He rolls us over and pumps himself into me so hard the bed moves. Bangs into the wall. Dents it, there's no doubt.

He holds himself up on taut, muscular arms and floods me with his release.

There's nothing better than being filled by him.

We stay connected until our breathing returns to normal. He rolls off and I resume my position tucked under Zane's arm. He surprises me by wrapping both arms around me and squeezing. I hug him back tightly. We're locked together in a way that feels reverential.

Did he miss me?

Does he want to be exclusive with me?

Can we stop this love hack?

Please?

I can't even let myself go there. He's only back in town for a few weeks, then he's leaving again. He'll always be leaving again. Every time he goes, it's harder to recover. Yet I can't *not* be with him.

He's *my* Zane.

At least when he's in town.

I'll take whatever part of him I can get.

After several minutes of being tightly entwined, Zane releases me. He watches me pull off my socks and bralette and lie back down facing him. His finger traces my jawline. We are so close our noses are touching. He whispers, "Can we just kiss for a while?"

Aw, fuck. See? This is why I can't ever stay away. Zane has my heart so wrapped up with his sweetness. His earnestness. We make out lazily. Exploring. Savoring. We play tongue swords. Kissy face. Love bites. It becomes a game to see how many ways we can kiss each other. Believe me, there are a lot. And we are creative.

When our lips are puffy, raw, and quite possibly chapped, we settle back down. I flip over so Zane's the big spoon. He cups my belly. He claims to love its soft roundness. I'm not gonna stop eating—it being my job and all—so that's a good thing, I guess. I'm so comfortable just being with him, I don't ever worry about how much I weigh or how I look. He has always loved me just the way I am.

And I love him back. Unconditionally.

Let him in. Take a chance. Tell him how you really feel.

"Carter nearly broke up the band, Fee." Zane speaks so softly into my hair that I can barely hear him.

My eyes fly open, but I don't move. "What did he do?"

Zane tells me about Carter's interference with Ty's relationship. I'd already heard a bit from my dad and Carter mentioned something about fucking up once or twice. I didn't realize how much it had affected the band dynamic. How stressed Zane has been for over the past two years. He kept a lot of that stuff to himself.

Fucking Carter.

I turn to smooth his hair from his face and kiss his forehead. "I'm sorry you went through that."

"Why does he do this shit, Fee?" Zane flops over on his back.

I prop my head up on my elbow and study him. "Who knows. We're like a broken record on this subject. Our parents' obsession with making sure we don't repeat their mistakes. Sounds like Carter extended that to Ty. Thank God you and I kept things locked down from their interfering asses. If Gus or Carter knew about us, I'm sure you would have gotten the same lecture."

"I'll tell you what's pissing me off." Zane's mouth is set in a line. "We would be married by now if my dad and your mom hadn't interfered with us."

Um, what?

I have no idea what to say.

Say yes.

"I'm being serious." Zane slaps the bed. "Don't you think?"

"You think we'd be married?"

"Well, yeah. I mean, we *are* married if you count our wedding in the playground." Zane waggles his eyebrows. "Seriously. I've given this a lot of thought, Fee. In fact, since I found out about Carter it's all I can think about. I've watched this entire thing go down with Ty. He's a shell. A broken man. I'm not sure if he'll ever recover. I didn't understand how he could love a girl he only knew for a couple of months. But I realize now that love comes in all forms, and you should fucking treasure it when you've got it. He really loves that girl. Even after everything. He's going to talk to her dad on our break and hopefully reconnect with her."

I sit up. This conversation is taking a turn I hadn't expected. "Well, that's good. Maybe they can work it out."

"Sure. Yeah." He shakes his head. "That's…um, not really my point. What I meant was you and I shouldn't be in the shadows anymore. We're in love. We always have been. I don't want to be without you. I don't want us to hide. Why the *fuck* are we scared of what our parents think? I was talking to my mom…"

"You talked to Lianne about us?" I try to keep my voice neutral, but I'm not okay with this. We had an agreement. No parents.

"Yeah. When I was on the road, I talked to her." He looks at me like I'm an idiot. Like I should have known this.

"So she knows about us hooking up?"

"What?" He looks at me confused.

"Your mom knows that you and I are fuck-buddies."

Zane launches himself off the bed, agitated. Really, really agitated. More like irate. "Can you *please* stop calling what we do 'hooking up?' *Fuck buddies*? Hooking up is what you did with whoever you did it with. *Hooking up* is what I did with hundreds of groupies. I know we're not supposed to talk about that because of your *stupid* love hack rule, but *you and I* are not hooking up. Hooking up doesn't *mean* anything. Don't call what we do together 'hooking up.' We *make love*. We are *forever*."

I bury my face in my hands. He's saying everything I've wanted to hear for two years.

Kinda?

Because did he just say *hundreds* of groupies?

WTF?

"Fiona?" Zane's in front of me. He removes my hands from my face. "What's going on?"

"You tell me." I shake him free but look at him in the eye. "I think you've had some conversations in your head with me that never happened."

He looks at me, dumbfounded.

"And what do you mean we would be married?" I'm also entirely confused. "You're just getting started with LTZ, Zane. You're about to go record another album. Then you're leaving on tour again. Maybe we could have this discussion in a few years. When we're ready. You've just amped up the pressure. We've never been about pressure."

"Fee? Don't you love me like that?" His brown eyes are sad, his voice is shredded.

I take his hands in mine. Kiss his knuckles. And say the hardest thing I've ever had to say in my life, because it's not how I truly feel. The thing is, even though I love him. *Really* love him. Now is not our time. "I love you more than *anyone* on this planet. Which is why I'll never tie you down, Zane. I'm not going to be that person. I don't ever want you to feel guilty about what you do when you're on the road."

"That's not fair. *You're* the one who wanted—freedom." Zane's flabbergasted expression infuriates me for some reason.

"For the record, I haven't been with anyone else. *Ever*. I certainly don't want you to miss out on fucking the *hundreds* of groupies you have at your disposal." I wag my finger when he tries to interrupt me.

"I'm not slut shaming you. Not in a million years. I know I'm the one who gave you free license to do what you want. I guess you chose to—um, be just like your *dad*. If fucking *hundreds* of groupies is where your head and dick are at, then you're not ready for me. For us. And that's okay. I'm not mad at you. Just don't get ahead of yourself. Or me. We can't be together, let alone fucking *married*, until that part of your life is out of your system, Zane."

His face crumples in agony. Tears spill down his cheeks. In all of the years we've been each other's person, I've never hurt him like this.

I've said something he'll never be able to unhear.

It's irreparable.

Irreversible.

He sputters, "It wasn't where my head was at. Ever. It never… *you're* the one who said… Fuck. I thought… I, um."

"Zaney," I whisper. I realize how badly I've fucked up. Somehow, I've gaslighted my other half. He didn't do anything wrong. He didn't do anything I hadn't encouraged—given full fucking permission—him to do.

I want to hug him. Touch him. Soothe him. I don't do any of these things, because I know my touch will disgust him right now.

I know one other thing, too.

He's going to leave me. For real this time. I pushed him into it.

"No, Fee. It's okay." He sucks in a breath. "The truth is, I've never wanted to be with anyone but you. And I never will. You've always known how I feel. My heart is crushed. I thought—*assumed*—now that I'm back, we were finally in the same place."

I've always only wanted you, too.

"Nothing has changed, though. We can still…" I try to explain. "You're my person."

He thumbs the tears from under his eyes and stands. "No, I'm not. All of these years I've thought… God. Here I was thinking how lucky we were. How smart. How woke. I'm a fucking idiot. We are two very stupid, immature people who have fucked up the only thing that has ever mattered in this world."

What have I done?

Yet I dig myself in deeper. It's like I can't control the shit that comes out of my mouth. "You're about to record another album. Go on the road. LTZ is destined for greatness, Zane. I'll be there for you every step of the way in spirit just like I always have been. I'm just not going to be the girl that holds you back, don't make me be her. *Please.*"

All I ever wanted was him.

Forever.

I'm punishing him.

Protecting myself.

He's right. We're two very stupid people.

"Look, Fee. I can't pretend I'm not completely goddamn devastated." He closes himself off from me completely right before my eyes. "I can't be with you in here tonight. I'll sleep on the pull-out in the living room. Let's just go home tomorrow. As far as I'm concerned, this weekend is over."

"No! Please. This doesn't have to change what we have going, Zane. You're in town for a few weeks before you leave to record. We have so many fun plans," I plead. I'd give anything to rewind the past hour.

Anything.

"No. This changes everything, Fee. At least for me." He grabs a pillow from the bed and heads into the living room without a backward glance.

I don't sleep a wink.

The next day Zane drives us home.

We exchange only the barest of pleasantries.

He drops me off at my apartment.

No kiss goodbye.

Nothing.

When I open the door to my dad's apartment, it hits me.

I've spent a decade protecting my heart.

From the only person in the world who deserves it.

And now he's gone.

CHAPTER 22

AGE 24

It never occurred to me that Fiona and I wouldn't make it. When she came up with the stupid, fucking love hack, I knew she wanted freedom after being cooped up for so long. I gave it to her.

Even though the thought of her with someone else killed me.

Then, when I did the same thing on the road, I realized how easy it was for me to fuck without intimacy. Without feelings. Purely physical. I came to terms with it.

Figured we were even in some truly fucked-up way.

I always knew. *Knew*. We'd end up together.

Maybe I've known since I was born. That's probably a lie. The day it *really* clicked was her high school graduation. The day we made love for the first time. From that point forward, it was clear. We were imprinted on each other. Ruined for anyone else.

My entire faith in our destiny was restored.

I never questioned it. Not even once.

It *sucks* being so wrong about your entire life.

Well, at least I got one thing right. I'm sitting in my living room. The guys are here. So is Carter. We're listening to the final masters of our new album, *Z*. Even I can't believe we created what I'm hearing. I have prickles all over my body.

Carter has produced an album that will make us legendary.

The lyrics are all Ty. From *Shine* to *Down* to *Butterfly*, I couldn't be prouder of my brother. My best friend. He's channeled his despair about Zoey into pure lyrical magic. Connor and Jace have come so far since the first album. Their musicianship is top notch. Years of touring does that. It's made us tight.

This recording truly feels like a collaboration. Not just a couple of guys playing the songs Ty and I wrote. We created this album together.

As for me, I know I left everything I had on the table. I can hear it in every single note.

I had no choice.

It was the only way for me to cope with Fee and me blowing up to smithereens. No one on earth knows the depths of my devastation. Not even my mom. After all of the shit we've all given Ty for the past three years, I'm not going to put my band through it again.

No fucking way.

Every day, I pull on my happy, positive pants. Without fucking fail. Fake it until you make it. Manifest your destiny. Gratitude. And all that bullshit.

I've read all the self-help books on my e-reader. There are hundreds of hours to kill on a tour bus, after all, I can't play guitar and write songs all the fucking time.

"This is the most raw, explosive album I've ever heard." Carter is standing at the big picture window staring out into the black night. "You've had a taste of fame. I hope you're ready for what comes next."

Connor, man of few words, mutters, "Fuck."

"Fuck, *yeah,* you mean." Jace is sitting on the floor leaning against the sofa. "I can't believe that's us."

Ty doesn't say anything. He's wrecked. Slouched on the couch, his arm flung over his eyes. We're all a bit wrecked, truth be told. This album is a culmination of months of recording, tweaking, reworking. My dad's first producing gig. He's as much a part of this as we all are.

I'm so ready for the next phase. In a couple of days, we're back out on the road. Australia first. Then Asia before heading back here to the States and supporting this latest release. It will be our first headlining tour. It's already sold out in most of the venues.

"Guys, we have an early start. I'm out." Carter salutes us and heads upstairs to bed.

A few minutes later Jace and Connor get up and I walk them out, leaving just me and Ty. I join him on the couch. It's funny, we haven't been alone all that much over the past couple of years. I'm glad it's just us.

Without Ty—or me—there would be no LTZ.

"It's more than I ever hoped, you know." I knock his knee with my knuckles. "Your lyrics are incredible. I know I keep saying it, but do you feel cleansed? Even a little?"

Ty looks up. Shakes his head. "I'm not even sure how I feel. One thing's for sure, it's time for me to start living again. She's gone. It's over. Even if I don't want to, it's time to accept it."

"Yeah."

"Fiona hasn't been around in a while. Did something happen with you guys?" Ty's sincerity overwhelms me. "I didn't want to say anything. I just noticed, that's all."

It's funny. I've never confided in Ty about Fiona. No reason, I guess he just wasn't in the place to hear about us, with Zoey and all.

Now, however, I could use a shoulder. "We had a major misunderstanding. I fucked up. She was mad and said some hurtful stuff. I haven't talked to her in a long time." I word vomit my history with Fiona. I can't help myself, I've needed someone to talk to for months.

"It fucking sucks when you try to do all the right things but still don't have control of your own destiny." Ty shakes his head sympathetically.

I punch my fist into my palm. "Yeah, it's such bullshit."

Ty studies me. "You're a good person, Zane. You took me under your wing when I had no one. So did Carter. You both have big hearts that you wear on your sleeve."

"I'd give anything for a do-over."

"I'd give anything to talk to Zoey. Have a real conversation. Get closure or whatever." Ty sighs heavily. "At least you're on speaking terms."

"We're not really. It's all too raw. I did send her a text telling her I needed a bit of time. And space."

Which I do.

So does she.

It's been four months and my head's still a mess.

It doesn't mean she's not always on my mind. I live for the bits and pieces I overhear eavesdropping on Carter and Gus. Market Seafood was featured in a national magazine. *Eater Seattle* has the restaurant on its hot list. Top Chef is wooing her to compete in the *Bravo* series. She's, apparently, not interested in that kind of notoriety.

She's unapologetically Fee.

God, I love her. I'll never stop. Even if I fucked things up so badly she'll never be able to look at me the same way again.

I jump when the doorbell rings. It's nearly midnight. I'm not scared, Carter's security takes care of the door. He has all sorts of crazy fans that try to meet him. Now, I do too. Anyway, we take precautions.

"Zane?" Lester calls out. "There's a young lady here to see you. Fiona Reynolds? Gus's daughter?"

Ty and I look at each other wide eyed. Freaky.

Or not. It's me. And Fee. Not really all that unexpected.

"Jesus. Did you conjure her up out of the blue?" He stands and moves toward the door. "I'll head out so you guys can talk. Maybe you can have a better outcome than me."

Lester leads Fiona into the living room. She's breathtaking. Always breathtaking. I can't look at her face just yet, but I take her in. Flowy, hot-pink hair floats around her neck in waves. Denim cutoffs over black tights. Low-cut black v-neck. Combat boots.

"Fee." Ty acknowledges her as they cross paths. "Shit. Are you okay?"

My head snaps up to look into her eyes. Mascara runs down her cheeks. Her beautiful eyes are bloodshot. I rush to her side. "What's wrong?"

She looks at Ty, then me and sobs.

I rush over and take her in my arms, eyeballing our singer. "Ty, maybe you…"

He takes the hint. "Yeah. I'm outta here."

I walk her to the sofa. I sit and pull her into my lap. She wraps her arms around me, buries her face in my neck and cries. My head touches hers in a snuggle. We don't speak. She needs to let it out. I cup her head with one hand and rub her back with the other. Eventually she settles. With a big sigh, she slumps against me. "I fucked up so bad, Zane. I've ruined everything."

"It's not that bad." I cradle her. "We just needed some time to get our heads straight. Nothing will ever ruin us, baby. Never. I'm sorry. So, so sorry." She shudders. Setting off an entirely new wave of tears. I kiss the top of her head. "You're scaring me," I whisper.

Fiona scrambles off my lap. "I don't know why I came here."

"Stop." I gesture for her to sit, and she does. "It's okay…"

"No, it really isn't." She uses her sleeve to wipe her face. I jump up and dash into the powder room, returning with tissues. She grabs a big wad and dabs under her eyes.

"Shhh. Just tell me." I take her hand and stroke the top of it with my thumb.

She hiccups. Holds her nose and looks up. "I'm so fucking sorry, Zane. I should have done everything differently. I *hate* the love hack. I've always wanted to be with you. Only you. I've been lying to myself. To you. For so many years. I don't want you to leave on tour without—"

"Fiona!" My heart soars. "That's the best news I've ever heard. I…"

She holds her palm up to stop me. "There's more. You need to hear me out."

"I will. In a minute. First, can I play you the album? The only people who have heard it are me, Carter, and the guys. I really want your opinion." I have a diversionary tactic of my own. From the terrified look in Fiona's eyes, I'm pretty sure I don't want to hear the "more." Not yet. Without waiting for an answer, I get up and press start, cuing *Z* to start at the beginning.

I settle back in the sofa and pull her against me. Breathe her in. No matter where she goes or what she does, her orange blossom fragrance smells like home. I've missed her so badly. The opening bass chords of *Down* begin. We are quiet while we listen to the entirety of the album. By the time it's over, she's calmer. Her eyes are closed, but she's not sleeping.

"Fucking brilliant," she murmurs. "You really are a prodigy."

"So you like it?"

"Zane, it's a masterpiece. I'm so proud of you. I really, really am." She sits up and throws her arms around me. "It's so… I don't know. It's like you've poured every ounce of yourself into it. Your beautiful soul shines through."

All I can do is smile. Her opinion, in many ways, is the one I wanted before it's released to the world. Despite everything, she's what matters. Always.

"Before you tell me whatever it is that's bothering you, I want you to know, I love you Fee…"

"Zane."

I squeeze my eyes shut.

"I love you too." She takes a deep breath. A tear trickles down her cheek. "I love you more than anyone in this world. I wish I'd listened to you up at Willows Inn. I wish I could take everything I said back and say yes. Marry you. Be together. All of it. But I've done something that can't be undone."

I can't believe my ears. I'm so fucking happy. "Whatever it is, we can get through it. We belong together, Fee."

"We do. Except, now we'll never be together. It's my fault. We won't get through what I'm about to tell you." She shakes her head in resignation. "We've always been honest with each other so..."

"Please, just tell me." I'm desperate. There is literally nothing I can think of that would make me give up on her.

On us.

She takes a deep breath. "After our, um…fight. I was at probably the lowest point in my entire life. You were away recording. After you told me you needed space, I didn't want to bother you. We left things…"

"Badly."

"Yes." She bites her lip. "Well. Um. A few weeks ago, I was at the club closing up, and a guy came in and asked about you. He seemed so nice. He looked familiar, but I couldn't place him."

My blood begins to boil. If this is going where I think it's going… Well. Murder. No. Torture then murder. My hands clench into fists as I try to remain calm and let Fiona get out what she needs to say.

"Anyway. It turns out it was that guy from the Willows Inn." She starts shaking.

"Who?" I blurt out.

"Corey Johnson?" She blinks up at me, devastation permeates her blue orbs.

"Fuck! Yeah, I remember." I can't hide the disdain from my face. "I never got to tell you the truth. That guy fucking hated me. He jumped Ty one day after school and coldcocked him. Said horrific stuff. I took him out before he could get out another vile word. It was nothing but a black eye, but because Carter's, well, Carter, Corey and his dad threatened to sue. His dad's a big land developer in Seattle. Rich as fuck. Carter paid him off. I think it was a lot of money."

Fiona's eyes are wide as saucers. "Well, I had no way of knowing that. Fuck. Well, that makes this so much worse."

"What did he do?"

"Okay, Well, we got talking. I…I…Zane, I needed someone. I had no one after our, um, disagreement. You and I weren't speaking. I couldn't talk to my dad. Or my mom, for obvious reasons. I'm the boss at work, I just haven't made a lot of friends between my job and trying to help..."

I take her hands in mine. "It's okay, Fee. You don't need to justify."

"But I do. I was just so sad. I missed you so much. Like I said, I needed someone..."

Then it all hits me like an ice-cold bucket of water over my head. I brace myself.

"The next thing I know, he's kissing me and I'm kissing him back. I was confused but also so sad in that moment. And mad too. Mad at myself. Mad at you." She sucks in a breath and shakes her hands out. Then sits up straight. "No. No. That's fucked up. I'm not going to be some sort of victim. I made the decision. I let him fuck me, Zane. I let it happen. He didn't force me. I just..."

"Don't tell me anything else, Fee. I can't... We weren't together. You didn't do anything wrong. I just can't hear about you with..." It's too agonizing. That's the truth.

"The only thing going through my mind during...was you telling me how you'd slept with hundreds of groupies. The thought of you with anyone else—let alone hundreds of them— hurt me so much, Zane. I know it's what I told you we should do, but I guess I just... I didn't think you'd go there. Because I never did."

I squeeze my eyes shut. Her words slice me deep. I'm in so much pain. More than anything I've ever felt in my life. I can't believe we ever thought our relationship could withstand the love hack.

It can't.

It won't.

"I'm pregnant."

She keeps talking but I can't hear what she's saying. Two little words end my life as I know it. It's quiet in my head. Like a blanket of snow. Her lips are moving, but everything is white noise.

She's right.

We can't come back from this. *I'm* supposed to be the father of her kids. *Me. Only me.* Not Corey *fucking* Johnson.

She's ripped my heart out and shredded it to pieces.

"Zane?" Fiona waves her hand in front of my face. "Say something."

It snaps me out of my trance and I'm so devastated I can barely see straight. "Wait a minute. You didn't use a fucking *condom*? You broke our sacred rule?"

"No! We did use one. It just broke. More like ripped in half." She squeezes her eyes shut. Tears seep out and roll down her cheeks. "I was on the pill…"

"We'll say it's mine," I mutter. Then I say it louder. "We'll say the baby's mine."

She cocks her head. "No. Zane. I can't lie. I won't. I may be an asshole. I may not deserve you. I may be the stupidest person who ever lived by fucking things up with you, but I'm not a liar. After all of the custody shit my dad went through, I can't…"

"Have you told him?" I'm completely gutted. Somehow I'm still going through the motions of asking her questions I know I'll want answers to.

Even if every word is like an ice pick to my heart.

She nods. "He wants a paternity test."

"That's predictable. His family owns half of Seattle, Fee. They're ruthless." I feel like I'm going to throw up when I voice my worst fear. "Are you with him now?"

"No. No! Of course not. I don't want anything to do with him. But he will have rights. To the baby."

"So you're keeping it?" Good God. My entire world is falling apart.

Fiona rubs the soft swell of her belly. "It's funny. I keep thinking about our moms being pregnant with us. Especially with this little being growing inside me. He or she is part of me, Zaney. Yes. *Yes*. I'm keeping my baby. Because it's *my* baby. I'm going to try to be the best mom I can be. Regardless of how I got here, I'm here. I can't—won't—run from it."

My heart seizes. I hold out my hands and I'm shaking like an old man. "Why? Why would you even bother to tell me if you won't be with me?"

"Because you've been my everything for my entire life, Zane. I couldn't let you go on tour thinking I didn't feel the same way about you. That we weren't everything to each other." Fiona cries softly. "It's my fault that we never had a chance. And it's my fault that this little person isn't ours. Not yours."

"Fee…" My voice cracks with anguish.

"I'm not your other half, Zane. Your other half would have been more careful with your heart. I've always only wanted you. And I still do. And I always will. I just don't *deserve* you." She kisses my cheek. "You're the best man I know, Zane. I'm here to *really* set you free. So you can find the woman who does deserve you. The best person in the world."

She gets up and walks out of the room.

I hear the heavy front door click.

And she's gone.

I didn't think things could get worse after Lummi.

But now I *really* know what rock bottom feels like.

CHAPTER 23

AGE 25

With Zane, I thought I knew what love was.

Oh, I was a fool. Nothing compares to what I feel for this little girl.

Not. A. Thing.

Fuck, I know it sounds trite.

My little Mia is a true miracle.

Earlier this year, I assumed my nausea, vomiting, and headaches were tied to my heartbreak over Zane. Or what happened with Corey. It didn't even register that I missed my period. I finally went to the doctor to get tested for STDs. Luckily I was clean, but I found out the mystery flu I couldn't shake was an unexpected pregnancy.

The day I found out, I was in shock. It's the only explanation why I showed up on Zane's doorstep to drop the mother (pardon the pun) of all bombs on him. My hormones were all over the map. I didn't think it through. I just reacted.

I needed the one person I could count on. It was so selfish of me. It wasn't until I unloaded my news that I realized what I'd done. How badly I hurt—no, destroyed—him. I couldn't believe he wanted to claim Mia as his.

That's when I *knew* I didn't deserve him. I hadn't deserved him for years.

Because I would have killed and dismembered him if the situation were reversed.

We'll never come back from this. It's the first time we've ever been separated where it feels like a void, not a pause. After I left, there have been no texts. No calls.

Nothing.

It's one hundred percent my fault.

I put the final nail in our coffin.

Oh, the karma gods have punished me, though. My pregnancy was unbelievably rough. On literally every level. I was a vomitron for nearly six months. Some days I could barely get out of bed. I lost weight and was malnourished. My energy was nonexistent.

Not to mention the depression.

Luckily, my boss and the company support me. My previous work ethic has been rewarded. Instead of being fired, I was promoted to a more administrative role. A lot of it is remote, I don't even need to be in the kitchen. It pays more too.

That's the good part.

The bad part is ongoing and, frankly, scares the living shit out of me.

Dealing with Corey is an absolute nightmare. From the day I broke the news of my pregnancy, he's been litigious. I receive threatening letters from his big law firm nearly every week. Everything from accusing me of extortion to demanding in-vitro paternity tests to slut-shaming to threatening my dad's business.

Today, I received the most recent communication—a draft of a lawsuit demanding full custody if I don't waive all parental support and sign a waiver and release that he's not her father.

Yeah, even I couldn't figure that one out.

I learned quickly that Zane was right about Corey. He's a self-entitled, hypocritical, douchebag asswipe. With too much money at his disposal.

A poor excuse of a man who, unfortunately, *is* the father of my child.

Which leaves me torn. Mia *should* know her dad. Her *real* dad. Right?

I can't help but believe that Corey will change his mind someday when the shock wears off. On the other hand, waiving support and getting him out of our lives was a way out for me. And my dad. My savings dwindled down to nothing due to the legal fees I accumulated.

It was his strategy. To bankrupt me.

Look, I'd gladly spend every penny I have to protect my daughter. But, I also need to feed her.

The stress of dealing with him has taken its toll on my health—and possibly Mia's. I'll probably never fully recover from the complications of my pregnancy. I developed preeclampsia and was on bedrest for nearly three months. Even though I followed everything my doctor asked me to do, ultimately I developed HELLP syndrome. Mia was born via cesarean at thirty-three weeks.

Almost two months early.

I nearly stroked out on the delivery table.

When I stabilized, it was two weeks before I could see her. She was on a ventilator until her lungs could more fully develop. I won't ever shake the trauma of seeing my tiny, fragile daughter connected to machines with tubes everywhere.

Little by little, day by day, things got better. My mom and dad put their ongoing differences aside and rallied around me. Every one of Mia's little victories was a celebration for all of us. Taking her breathing tube out. Holding her. The day she was oxygen free. The day her feeding tube was removed. Finally being free of the incubator. Changing her first diaper.

Because she was premature, Mia is monitored regularly to make sure she's developing properly. It's really scary, though. There are so many potential complications to wrap my head around. I'm just concentrating on keeping her happy and healthy.

That is my *only* focus.

Today, after fifty-one days, we are finally home.

Well, back to my dad's apartment. Again. When I was pregnant, I rented my own place but now that I'm facing my own health issues, I need extra help. The preeclampsia has likely quadrupled my risk of developing high blood pressure and doubled my risk for heart disease, stroke, and diabetes. I need to rest and get stronger.

I'm not even thirty, and I now have a permanent preexisting medical condition.

And the sweetest, loving newborn whose father doesn't want her.

"Is she sleeping?" Dad whispers. I'm sitting in the big recliner. Mia's swaddled in a *Shake Rattle & Roll* blanket dozing on my chest.

I nod and stroke her tiny back. "She's out."

"You need to get some rest, Fee." He sits on the couch next to me. "Do you want me to take her for a bit?"

It sounds like heaven, but I find it very difficult to let anyone hold her. I never want her to feel like I'm not right there with her. We've already been through so much together. "Um. Sure..."

"You know that I took care of you all day when you were first born when your mom was at work." He reaches for Mia. "Those hours were the best of my life. Just you and me."

"I didn't know that." I hand her to my dad, a bit reluctantly.

She squirms a bit but settles on his chest. It's sweet to see her nestled against my dad's burly body. He's a big man. His hair is still long, but now it's gray. He's wearing his ever-present lumberjack plaid shirt over a band T-shirt. Today, it's vintage Pearl Jam. His hands are big and strong and cradle my daughter—his granddaughter— tenderly.

"She's so beautiful. She looks exactly like you." He smiles down at her. "There's nothing like it, is there?"

His comment brings a tear to my eye. "Nope. She's perfect. In every way."

He looks up at me, grinning from ear to ear.

"Dad, I'm sorry about all of the trouble..."

He holds up a finger and shakes his head. "Nope. Not a word. She's not any trouble. You are my baby. So is she. I will always be here for the both of you. Until the day I die."

"Oh, Daddy." Tears stream down my face. The first I've let fall since the night I confessed everything to Zane right after I found out I was pregnant. There's been no time for me to feel sad. Or scared. Or anything. I've been busy being strong.

Trying to stay positive.

Dealing with Corey.

Fighting for my health.

Keeping Mia safe.

For now, I just need to let it out. So I cry. Not loud. Nothing dramatic. Just a steady flow for a good fifteen minutes. Mia rests peacefully in Dad's arms. He watches me thoughtfully until I regain my composure.

"Tears cleanse the soul," he whispers. "Each one is a blessing."

He's so right. I actually feel better. Stronger.

"Fee? I know it's not my business. But I guess I always thought that you and Zane..."

"I know. Me too," I admit. "It's not his fault, though. I'm the one who wrecked us. I was too scared of ending up like..."

"Your parents?"

Ding. Ding. Ding.

"Yes, if I'm honest, Dad." The only way forward for me is being brutally honest from now on. "Zane and I suffered a lot because of what was happening with all of you. It got into my head. Both of our heads, really. I pushed him into an arrangement that neither of us really wanted. Neither of us were honest with each other until it was too late."

He settles back into the sofa. "Becoming a parent changes you. I can't pretend to know what goes on in Faye's head. I will say this. When she and Lianne found Carter in the park when you kids were little, it changed her profoundly. She was never again the goofy, carefree go-with-the-flow gal I fell in love with."

"I don't ever remember Mom being carefree. Or goofy."

"She was. All four of us were. We had so much fun together. We were invincible. Thought we had it all figured out." He stares off into space as if he's picturing those times. "Back then, the idea that I would be able to turn a shitty rat-infested club into the go-to venue in Seattle and Limelight would become the biggest band in the universe was laughable."

I tuck my feet underneath me. I've never talked with my dad about his past. He's ordinarily very closed off. "But you did."

"Yeah. We did."

"Okay. What went wrong with you and Mom? I never really knew. I remember you guys fighting a lot about Carter and the next thing I know, we're in fucking Bellingham."

"It's simple. I covered for Carter. She viewed it as the ultimate betrayal. I viewed it as my brotherly duty. Both of us were wrong." He shifts Mia a bit and settles back against the cushions so he can face me more directly. "He went to rehab for the first time right after Lianne and Zane moved to Denver. He wanted to reconcile. So did Lianne. There was talk of them moving back here to try again, but Lianne's mom wanted her to give it a year. When she told Carter, I guess it sent him over the edge. Maybe it would have happened anyway. Who knows. Bottom line is, sobriety didn't stick until almost a decade later. I knew he was using, but I kept it from your mom and let him come around you after what happened in the park. When he went into rehab the second time, well… The jig was up."

"Zane and I always knew that Carter was in and out of rehab."

He's visibly shocked. "How?"

I look around the apartment and pointed. "Um. Paper-thin walls. Loud yelling voices. Zane would eavesdrop on his mom and grandma. We talked about it all the time. Exchanged information. If we hadn't, Zane wouldn't have known a thing about Carter."

"Fuck."

"It doesn't explain why Mom went off the deep end. She literally ruined high school for me."

He scrubs his goatee with his free hand. "She was scared to death for your welfare. Now that you're a mom, maybe now you have some perspective, huh? I'm guessing you'd protect this little angel with every molecule in your body. Cut your mom a bit of slack. You probably don't remember how bad Carter was when he was using, sweetheart. It wasn't pretty. He treated Lianne… Well, poorly. He wasn't ready to be a dad. Not the way I was. Poor Zane didn't stand a chance with Faye."

"How are you ever ready?" I hug myself. "I'm scared to fucking death."

He laughs softly and kisses Mia's sweet head. "Yeah, and you never lose that feeling. That's something no one ever tells you. Consider yourself warned."

"Great. Good to know." I mock shudder. "It all turned out to be such a mess, didn't it?"

"Yeah. Yeah it did. And it happened in a blink of an eye." He closes his eyes and breathes deeply.

I can't help but feel closer to him. As a child, you think the adults have all the answers. Yet here I am. An adult now. With my own newborn whom I love more than life itself. And no fucking clue what I'm going to do. Or how my life went off the rails. Or why I let the love of my life slip through my fingers.

It all happened in a blink of an eye. Just like my dad said.

"I've been so careless with Zane's heart. I thought we had all of the time in the world. That we were invincible. I've ruined everything." I feel the tears stream down my face again. "Do you regret what happened with you and Mom?"

"Your mother and I had very different ideas about life, Fiona. Her folks didn't approve of me. They were in her ear from the day and hour we got married. Growing up on the reservation, Carter and I shared similar traumatic family histories of addiction and abuse. We also experienced beauty. And hope. A deep connection to the earth. Prayer. Above all, acceptance." Dad's voice turns from soothing to passionate. Mia squirms awake. "We live in a nation that has enacted policies to marginalize and disempower us. Yet, we have endured. You see, it isn't your mother's fault she grew up with stereotypes that my people are ignorant and culturally uncivilized. It's ingrained in her upbringing."

I'm mesmerized by my father. He's always been so peaceful. Calm. Under all circumstances. For so many years I resented what I perceived as weakness. That he didn't fight to see me. Now I realize it was something different. "Dad, I think what you're telling me is that you accepted where things were in our family, but you never gave up hope of what could be."

"Yes. That's exactly it. You are wise, Fee." Dad stands up and hands me my sleeping daughter. "Remember. A mother will do almost anything to protect her child. It's instinctive. I may not have liked or wanted what happened, but I respected your mother's process. And I always loved you. What good would have come out of a long custody battle? Now, your mother and I are peaceful. Parenthood is a long game, Fiona. You, my beautiful, talented little girl, are going to be the best mother. You will make the best decisions for your precious daughter. In these things, I have no doubt.

"I love you, Dad. Thank you." I grab his hand and squeeze.

"You are my sun and moon." He kisses my head and goes to bed. "Try to get some sleep."

Mia and I sit in silence for a while. She nudges my breast with her little nose. Her mouth opens and closes, even though her eyes are squeezed shut. I pull my shirt up and she latches on. I stroke the swatch of dark hair on her head and make a decision. An easy decision, it turns out.

I'm going to follow my gut.

I don't want shit from Corey.

Tomorrow, I'm going to do what's best for my daughter. I'm signing the papers and he'll be out of our lives forever. I never want my child to feel unwanted. Altruism aside, there's no logical reason for me to fight for her legal right to know a father who doesn't want her.

I've made a lot of mistakes in my life when I ignore my instincts.

Losing Zane is the biggest.

Now that I'm responsible for this tiny human?

I have no more room for error.

CHAPTER 24

AGE 25

The past year is a total fucking blur.

Rather than wallow in my heartbreak, after I learned about Fiona's impending motherhood, I immediately turned my shit around. Why wouldn't I? It was time for me to live in the moment. Enjoy LTZ's success. Connor might be hung up on some actress, but Ty, Jace, and I are on a tear. Three single—and I must say, good-looking, rock stars— on tour across Asia, the US, and now Europe. Fuck yeah, we're playing, partying, and fucking our way around the world.

It's been glorious.

Truly.

For the first time in my life, I have no one to answer to. I don't worry about what people think. Or about consequences. With success comes access to some of the coolest experiences I could ever imagine. Unlike the last time we were on the road, I make sure to build in time to take in local culture whenever possible.

For instance, Connor and I took private ninja training lessons in Kyoto, including learning the art of throwing stars and shooting a blowpipe. The four of us stayed in a glass igloo in Finland to see the Northern Lights. Ty and I climbed the Sydney Harbor Bridge. I've visited the Vatican, the Great Pyramids, the Taj Mahal, and many other places most people only dream of.

I must admit, though, my favorite experiences are all related to music. I took acid in Joshua Tree with five of the world's most revered guitar players. I won't mention names, but trust me. It was phenomenal.

In Cambodia, Jace and I joined a drum circle after eating a feast of crickets, scorpions, and tarantulas. The drumming was cool, the bug eating? Not so much.

Carter and I jammed with a jazz band in New Orleans after he surprised me at our show there. We blew the roof off, they had to sneak us out in disguises once the word got out. In Vienna, Ty and I took in Beethoven's 5th Symphony at Musikverein. Transcendent.

In my downtime, I've learned how to play some unusual instruments. The bodhran, didgeridoo, flute, violin, and electric piano.

Ultimately, I need to stay really busy. I'm still me, after all. Filling every single second of time means I don't have any space in my day that allows me to think. To reflect. To contemplate my life. To wallow in what could have—and should have—been.

I'm looking forward, not backward.

I need to be present at all fucking times.

As for Fiona? The subject's completely off-limits. Dad told me she had a daughter about a year ago. That's all I know.

I don't ask for details.

I don't want to know.

I just can't…

I've made it very clear to both my parents.

I mean, why bother? She moved on without me. In retrospect, the writing was always on the wall for us. I just chose not to see it. Her bullshit about not holding me back and us seeing other people. Nope. Not going there. Too much of a dagger to my heart.

I don't need what-if bullshit to pollute my mind.

The band has too big of a problem to deal with.

In addition to fucking literally any woman within a ten-foot radius, Ty's substance use is out of control. I blame myself. And our fucking publicists. He's on a path to destruction, and, despite my long history of Nar-Anon, I'm the asshole who's led him to where he is now.

We all did.

In Australia, we convinced him to let loose. To let go of his inhibitions.

We pushed him time and time again to "just get over" a woman he's never going to get out of his system.

Believe me, I should know.

And now here we are.

History is repeating itself. Except it's not me. Ty is the one who's on track to be the Carter of our band.

Sure, he pulls it together for our shows. I *know* the pattern, though. If he doesn't get the blow under control, the hard stuff is next. If that happens, LTZ will be no more. We are nothing without Ty. Even if I lost the band—which would be devastating—I could never forgive myself if something tragic happened to my best friend.

In an effort to keep Ty from temptation, I've taken over as the LTZ media spokesperson. Only to keep Sienna and Andrew, our asshole publicists, from putting Ty in compromising situations. Which they love to do. They think they're so clever. Trotting him around with models, actresses, private island parties, drinking, drugs.

All the trappings.

Oh, I see through it all. Growing up with two famous parents makes it easy to spot fakers who attach themselves to celebrities for their own social currency. Jace gets it too. He does his best to shield Ty from the madness, but he's more cerebral than me.

I'm reactionary.

I lose my mind when Ty acts like a puppet and does whatever they ask. Protecting Ty is classic codependent behavior. I know it. But, as far as I'm concerned, it's necessary in this moment. To keep the band on track.

Even though it's *infuriating.*

Triggering.

Every single day, I'm petrified he's going to die.

Just like Carter almost did that day in the park.

Until we, as a band, come up with a more permanent solution, I'm off drinking. And drugs, although, for obvious reasons, I've only ever tried weed. Well, and the acid that one time. Luckily, my addiction isn't substances, but I'm not taking any chances.

For now, I'm trying to forget Fiona by fucking her out of my system.

I'm in a sexually experimental phase. Zero regrets. Zero guilt. I won't lie, it took me a while. For a few weeks after I learned about Fiona's pregnancy, I couldn't get it up to save my life.

My sexual appetite was nonexistent.

I finally got my mojo back by watching other people fuck. LTZ's success definitely has a lot of perks. One of which is access to exclusive, discreet, private sex clubs. Pretty much anywhere in the world. It's become my vice.

At first, all I did was whack off to staged sex scenes. Once I felt more comfortable, I decided to open myself up to new experiences. Find out what really turned me on. Sex toys rule, I'm a big fan. I tried bondage. Not for me. I hired a dominatrix. It was funny and not sexy at all. Participated in an orgy in Berlin. Definitely not my thing. Too complicated and not enough genuine connection.

I still fuck hot women I pick up at our VIP parties.

This time without Fiona's stupid bullshit love hack rules.

Just mine. NDAs. No devices. I dispose of the condom.

Every. Single. Time.

My phone finally buzzes with the call I've been waiting for. I connect to see my mom's delicate face fill the screen. Her strawberry-blonde hair is loose around her shoulders. "Hey, Mom. Wow. I don't see you with your hair down that often. Hot date?"

Her cheeks pinken, but she doesn't answer me. "Zaney. You look so good. How was Belfast? I'm hoping to get over to see you in Paris, but I don't know my schedule yet."

"It was cool." I settle back on my bed in the hotel suite. "We're here for a couple of days before our next show in Edinburgh, I'm due to meet Jace and Connor for a *Game of Thrones* tour in an hour."

"I'm so happy you're experiencing more of the culture this tour."

God, if she only knew. "Yeah. I don't have too much free time. I like it that way."

"Always busy. What did you want to talk to me about?" Mom's concerned, I can see the furrow in her brow.

I take a deep breath. "Ty's going down, um…a path. I don't know what to do."

"Crap. I thought it was something like that. I was worried it was you, though, so that's a relief." She visibly relaxes. "How bad is it?"

"It's bad. And it's my fault." I tell her about Australia. "I *know* better. I let him down. Now he's snorting coke like it's going out of fashion. I don't think he even remembers half of the girls he fucks." I pinch the bridge of my nose, then pull my hand away. "I'm just so worried…"

"That he'll end up like Carter. Yeah, well. It sounds about right." Mom shakes her head as she finishes my sentence. "God, I'm so sorry this is happening. Zane, you need to remember that Ty is responsible for his own life choices. You are both grown men. You can't save someone who won't save himself."

She's right, and I hate it. "I know."

Mom gives me the kind of encouraging smile that only your mother can do. "Maybe you should talk to your dad. You've never discussed his addiction. He can take it. I promise you. He might have some words of advice from his perspective."

We catch up for a bit longer before I head out to meet my bandmates. Only to find that I've been ditched by everyone. With nothing to do, I go on the *Game of Thrones* tour. Me and a couple of the crew. Mainly, so I don't have to be alone today.

Too many thoughts.

Too much pain.

A few weeks later, I watch Ty as he stares out the window. The French countryside, blanketed with fields of lavender, whiz by. The relaxing scent permeates the air. Carter and I sit across from him in the custom van that is speeding down the motorway toward a secret location we'll be staying in for the next week.

An entire team is waiting for us. Lisa Kinkaid, a therapist from LA who specializes in celebrity counseling. An addiction expert. Private chef. Personal trainer. It's a week of wellness. Hopefully, healing.

Connor and Jace are the only people who know where we're going. Well, so does our manager, Katherine. I made sure our publicists don't have a clue. They think we're in an entirely different town for an entirely different reason. I'm not leaving anything about this semi-intervention to chance.

To be fair, Carter arranged most of it. Dropped a hundred grand so we could stay at *Alpilles* near *Saint Remy de Provence* in France. We arrive at the expansive, noble eighteenth-century estate nestled in the middle of five hundred acres of olive groves, vineyards, gardens, park, and woodlands.

The clean, gray stone facade looms. It's fucking epic. The entire property is secluded and private. The residence itself is a combination of modern amenities and traditional French decor. I've really never seen luxury like this.

And I've gotten used to some of the finer things in life.

The wellness team have been here for a couple of days to get everything ready. The property concierge escorts Ty, Carter, and me to our suites, which are more like full apartments. My room overlooks the most stunning gardens I've ever seen. So peaceful. Tranquil.

I can't wait to wander the grounds with my acoustic Gibson.

After we're settled in, Carter introduces Ty to the team. Everyone explains who they are and what their role is. Carter and I ask him to accept the help. There's not any contentiousness at all. Ty is not only cooperative but touched by the effort.

He's agreed to a complete immersion. Intensive one-on-one counseling. Nutrition. Exercise. Meditation.

While Ty does the work, Carter and I spend our time together.

Mostly in the gardens visiting, playing music, and relaxing. On the last day of our stay, I know it's time to exorcise a few of my own demons. About what's happened with Fiona. My history with Carter.

I really want to heal.

I couldn't be in a better location.

"I guess I shouldn't be too surprised at Ty's strength. He's always been willing to take responsibility for himself," I say to Carter. He and I are sitting in the middle of an olive grove with our guitars. "He's very remorseful about his behavior over the past few years. He promised me he's going to do what it takes to break his patterns and battle his demons."

Carter strums his Breedlove and looks up at me after a while. "I don't know if Ty's an addict, to be honest. He's gone through a lot in his life. I think he'll be okay. He's definitely not like me. Although, who the fuck knows."

"Can I ask you about it?" I glance at him tentatively before plucking a few more notes.

"About my addiction?"

"Yeah."

He starts playing a Limelight song, *Long Way Down.* I join him. We finish the song before he speaks again. "I've been wondering if you'd ever want to talk to me about it."

I set my guitar down next to me. "I think with all of this therapy shit surrounding us, I need a bit of my own."

"Okay, well I'm an open book, Zane." He leans back against an olive tree. "Where do you want to start?"

We spend hours in the olive grove talking about my childhood and how his absence affected me. We're both raw. Brutally honest. Angry. Self-reflective. Humble. He answers every question I throw at him. By the end of our conversation, we're both crying. It's probably the most cathartic experience of my life.

"I love you, Zane. I hope you know that you're the best thing that ever happened to me." Carter embraces me in a full bear hug. "You've initiated hugs with me, but I didn't know how you'd receive it if I did. I was so ashamed of the kind of dad I was. Well…wasn't."

I cling to my father. "I love you too, Dad. I have all of these memories from when I was little of you kissing and cuddling me. Eating strawberries. Part of me wondered why—"

"Stop." He grips both of my cheeks in his rough hands and kisses my forehead. "I'm not great with emotions. They scare me. I grew up believing that I wasn't good enough. It doesn't matter how many records I sell. How many accolades I get. There's a little voice inside me that's always telling me I don't deserve what I have."

It's a profound moment when you realize that your parents are flawed human beings just like you. They are a product of their own childhood. Their own experiences. Their own trauma. Happiness. Memories. Mistakes. Triumphs.

Just trying to do the best they can.

"I can honestly say, you've turned into the best dad I could have ever hoped for." I throw my arms around him and squeeze Carter tightly. "What you've done for me? For Ty? You *are* selfless. I forgive you for everything. I don't want you to live with that burden anymore."

By the time we get back to the chateau, we're drained. We have dinner with Ty and we all recap our day. Ty seems committed to a new way of life, but only time will tell if he can turn things around.

The next day we leave to meet up with the guys in Madrid, and I'm actually happy. On a deep level for the first time in two years. The next chapter of my life is beckoning, and I'm not looking back.

I feel hopeful.
The past is where it belongs.
Behind me.

CHAPTER 25

AGE 26

I'm walking through mud.

No, I'm getting sucked under by quicksand.

Mia sits on the marble-tiled mortuary floor in a spit-up-stained sweater. Wailing her pretty little face off while I try to wrap my head around that I'm here. In a creepy room filled with caskets.

Waiting to pick out one for my dad.

Surreal doesn't begin to cover it.

"Let me see if she needs a new diaper." My mom swoops her up, tickles her belly and sniffs her bottom. "Whew! I think that's the problem."

Barry, the funeral director, sits across from me and flashes his faux-empathetic half smile. "I know this is a difficult time. Don't feel rushed. Look around. I'll be right here to answer any questions. What is your budget?"

"Could you give me a minute with my mom, Barry?" I smile sweetly when I really want to rip his eyes out. One at a time. He skulks out and I bury my face in my arms, which are folded on the marble table.

My mom steps up behind me. Mia's on her hip, clutching her lamb that used to be white but now is a grayish green. "Gus wouldn't want you to spend a fortune on a stupid casket, Fee. Get something reasonable so we can move on. These places are a racket."

"Yeah, I know." I scan the room. *No* to the pink pearlescent. No to the cherry wood veneer. *God no* to the praying hands light-blue number. Or the black lacquer with gold trim. The economy galvanized metal casket it is. Very rock and roll.

Just like my dad.

I realize there's something fundamentally wrong with me. I should be crying right now. I should feel devastated. At the very least, sad that I've lost him. Desolate that Mia will never remember her grandfather.

I mean, what the fuck?

I'm going through the motions.

Taking care of business.

I'm numb. All I want is to get this over with.

Which cements the fact that I'm a terrible human being. My dad has been my whole world since I found out I was pregnant. He's basically been Mia's second parent. My rock. Why can't I cry for him?

"Have you received the coroner's report yet?" Mom rocks Mia back and forth. My daughter's bright-blue eyes are blinking shut. She's trying to stay awake but failing. Thank God for small favors. "It's so hard to believe Gus is gone."

"Massive heart attack."

My mom rambles on about his bad diet and poor lifestyle choices. I tune her out and study the table. Then Barry is back. I point to the casket I've chosen. "Ah, yes. That is a nice choice." His eyes flick to an expensive-looking engraved silver casket on the opposite wall. "I wonder. It is your father, after all. You might consider…"

"Look. I've made my choice. I'm not in the right headspace for a sales pitch. My dad wouldn't give two fucks about what casket he was buried in. I just need to pay you and make arrangements to bury him at the plot he paid for at Greenwood Memorial Park. It will be a very small gathering."

"You don't want a viewing? Or a church ceremony?" Barry's eyes are wide with disapproval, though, to his credit, he tries to disguise it.

I shake my head. "I'm having a life ceremony at The Mission, the club he owns. It's what he would have wanted, trust me."

Although I say this with confidence, who the hell knows.

Does anyone really plan to die at age forty-seven?

I just need to get through the next couple days.

That's what I tell myself.

Two days later, Mom, Mia, and I stand huddled under a huge, black golf umbrella. Leave it to Gus to arrange for a stereotypical cinematic rainy day to be put in the ground. The driving rain is so heavy, it's practically sideways. I don't mind, though. Somehow it gives me some comfort to know that my dad is angry up there.

He didn't want to leave us. I know that for sure.

I see a black Range Rover pull up. The only other person I invited was Carter, so it must be him. I watch as he parks and gets out of the car. Opens his own large umbrella and huddles under it but doesn't move. I'm about to call out to him when I see another figure emerge from the passenger side and run over and join him.

Don't pass out.

God, don't let me pass out.

"Is that Zane there with Carter?" My mom adjusts the hood on her black wool coat to get a better look.

My head whips back around to stare at my dad's casket. I focus intently on the huge spray of white and red flowers. I clutch Mia tight and bury my face in her neck. The tendrils of her black hair blend with mine seamlessly.

Once I got pregnant, I never bothered dying it fuchsia again. I simply cut off all the pink ends. I'm back to black. It's grown out to shoulder length now.

Yes, I'll focus on any random thing but the fact that Zane is here.

Zane is here.

I can feel his energy zing around me as he and Carter near. The closer he gets, the stronger the force. Now, the pressure in my chest is almost overwhelming. My diaphragm begins to shudder. Blood rushes to my ears. I can't hear. I can't focus. I'm like a volcano waiting to erupt.

My back tingles when he stands behind me.

The comfort in his spicy, earthy, citrusy scent fills my senses.

But the eruption happens when he wraps his arms around me. And Mia, who clings to me tightly.

Tears burst free in wracking sobs.

Like liquid lava that has been under pressure for centuries.

I don't remember one specific thing about the ceremony. All I know is that Zane's got me. For the first time in years. Even if I can't see his face, I know. *Know*. I'm secure in his arms. Free to let everything out, and I do.

I cry so hard, Mom takes Mia from me.

Probably so I don't scar her for life. That's how out of control my emotions are.

Hysterical sums it up.

Zane never lets me go. Just squeezes me tighter as I fall apart thoroughly and completely.

After the ceremony, he holds me as I watch my dad's coffin being lowered into the ground. My mom whispers something about getting Mia out of the elements and I'm vaguely aware of Carter walking with them to the car, leaving us alone by my father's grave site.

Zane and I don't move. He presses his head to mine.

Head snuggles.

Maybe it's ten minutes. Maybe it's two hours. I have no concept of time. All I know is that I'm crying. And crying. And crying. Unable to stop. Unable to stand up on my own. Zane supports me. Keeps me upright.

Doesn't say a word.

Doesn't move a muscle.

I'm enveloped in his strong arms and he's with me.

Except, he's not. Not really.

God, I've missed him. Missed this. But it's an illusion. It won't last.

We aren't anything to each other now.

That thought snaps me out of it. Adrenaline surges through my body and I break free from Zane's embrace. My voice is raw. "I've gotta go. People are waiting at The Mission."

"Let's go, then. I've got you." Zane's deep voice is quiet. Steady. I finally turn to get a full-on look at him. Partially to confirm that he's not an illusion. His brown eyes are despondent but strong. Dark curls are tucked under a black skull cap. He wears black Prada sunglasses, even though it's dark and gray outside. Rain runs in rivulets off his black Gor-

Tex raincoat that looks almost exactly like mine.

I allow him to lead me back to the car. He opens the passenger door. I get in and instinctively turn to check on Mia, who is sound asleep in her infant seat. Zane peers over at my mom, who nods. He says nothing. Just carefully shuts the door, but not before making sure my purse strap is tucked inside.

Always so considerate.

"Carter didn't tell you Zane was coming?" My mom rests her hand on my leg as she starts the car.

I shake my head.

I can't speak.

How can I, when I can't even *think*?

Too soon we're pulling into my dad's designated parking spot behind the club. I have no idea how I'll get through the night. What do I say? Am I supposed to provide comfort to the hundreds of people who will be here to pay their respects to my dad?

They'll be here in a couple of hours.

Somehow, I manage to get Mia out of her car seat and into the club. Mom and I take her up to the office where my dad has a full setup for a baby, including a playpen. He'd often bring her with him to work on the days I needed to go into my company's corporate office.

It's a funny juxtaposition. My baby's fluffy pink-and-white girly stuff smack dab in the middle of Seattle's most notorious music venue.

The Mission is still, by all accounts, a dive bar. Thirty years of abuse has taken its toll. It smells like stale beer and Pine-Sol. The concrete floor has ruts and cracks from thousands of people who have watched some of the most famous bands in the world play the elevated corner stage. Old, faded graffiti decorates the walls, shrouded in wear and tear and abuse. Sharpie doodles. Band stickers. The occasional wad of gum.

The old wood bar my father hand built stands tall and ornate. It divides the entry from the venue. Bottles of booze are behind locked, removable shutters. Decades of names and phone numbers are carved in the chairs and the armrests. The serving station is battered. Two drawers have been missing for at least a decade.

Dad always planned on replacing them, but now he never will.

It will be up to me.

My mom knocks on the door and comes in with Jeff, her husband. "Carter and Zane are downstairs. They're setting up the buffet tables for the caterers. I'm sure you'd like to check that everything is the way you want. Would you like us to watch Mia for a bit?"

There's no way I can go downstairs yet. Not if Zane's there. "Can you handle it? If you send Leif up, he can help me get the slideshow loaded and ready. He's the tatted guy with the long platinum dreads."

"Okay, no problem." My mom bends over and kisses Mia's head. "Take all the time you need. I've got you covered."

The Mission's longtime soundman, Leif, knocks a couple minutes later. Unfortunately, the slideshow only takes a few minutes to upload and test. I put him in charge of choosing music to sync to the photos. The playlist is perfect. He pulls down the projector screens and we're ready.

Except, I'm still nowhere near ready to go downstairs.

Back in the office, I take my time feeding Mia and dressing her in bunny jammies. I sit in my dad's oversized executive chair with her in my lap and read her a couple of stories until she falls slack in my arms. I study my precious daughter as I do every night. Her peaches-and-cream skin. I'm obsessed with her little bowed lip that puffs in and out when she sleeps.

She's so beautiful. And sweet.

My child.

I love her so much.

Voices get louder downstairs. I glance at the clock and realize people are starting to arrive. I can't believe it's already time. Still, I can't bring myself to move. It's too quiet and peaceful up here with Mia. There's no way, I realize, that I'll be able to face anyone tonight. The thought of it makes my heart race.

I'm paralyzed with anxiety.

So I shut my eyes.

It's barely audible, but I hear a faint knock on the office door. My eyes open, but I don't get up and I don't reply. The door cracks open and the one person I want to avoid but am desperate to connect with quietly slips inside.

"Hey, Fee." Zane tentatively steps toward me, his brown eyes burrowing into mine. His curly hair flows around his shoulders. He's wearing an expensive, designer black suit and black tie. Black wingtip shoes with white accents. Snazzy. Understated. Perfect.

I can't find my voice. I just stare at him. Stunned.

Scared.

He kneels in front of me. His eyes flick down to my sleeping baby and visibly soften. A faint hint of a smile passes over his full lips before he looks back up at me. "Mia's gorgeous. She looks exactly like you."

My heart pounds. I can barely breathe.

I certainly can't talk.

Zane rocks back on his heels and stands. He sits across from me on the file cabinet and leans forward, resting his elbows on his thighs. I watch his strong hands flex and relax. He's nervous too, his head hangs down and he sighs. "If you don't want me to be here, I'd understand. I can leave. I just wanted to pay my respects."

If only I could say something. My mouth opens and closes like a fish trying to breathe.

But no words will come out.

He watches me for a few minutes. Nods. His eyes are sad. He stands and walks back over to the door without looking back. When he reaches for the knob, I hear myself squeak, "Wait."

Zane stops but doesn't turn around.

"I'm sorry. I'm so so sorry," I choke out. "I know you're here for my dad. You *should* be here. Please don't leave on my account."

He looks back at me, his eyes welling with tears. "No, Fee. I'm here for *you*."

Carefully cradling Mia's head, I lean over to place her in the playpen. She's had a long day without her usual nap, so she doesn't wake up. Most likely, she's out for the night. I kiss her head and turn to Zane. "I gave up that dream a long time ago."

He squeezes his eyes shut. Sighs heavily. His mouth is set in a straight line, like he's on the edge. His fists clench and then open. Finally, he regains his composure and reestablishes eye contact with me. "You may have given up on me, but I've never given up on you. Not really. I've tried, but I can't. When I heard the news, nothing mattered to me except getting here to make sure you were okay."

"Well, I'm not." I shake my head. "I'm not okay. If you hadn't been at the grave site, I wouldn't have made it."

Zane moves toward me. Grips my shoulders and rubs up and down my upper arms. "Don't forget, Fee, despite everything that's gone down, you and me are timeless. Every day when I see my tattoo, I'm reminded of this. I don't care if I'm not the guy for you. I don't care if you don't love me the way I love you. You're a part of me. My other half. Whether you want me to be or not. If you're not okay, *I'm* not okay. No matter what, I *will* be here for you. For as long as you need me."

My body sags into his. He catches me.

When I let him, he *always* catches me.

"I've missed you. So much," I mumble into his suit lapel. "I can't go down there."

"That's okay. It's fine. We'll stay right here." He leads me to the beat-up olive-green patterned sofa. We sit side by side, but he immediately pulls me back against his chest and wraps his arms around my middle. His cheek rests against the top of my head. "Your hair still smells like oranges."

"Yeah, well. It's always been my favorite shampoo."

Zane takes a deep whiff at my nape. And like countless times in the past, I relax back against him. Except today, it feels both natural and incredibly awkward all at the same time.

Confusing.

"How are you coping?" He takes my hands in his and rubs little circles on my palms with his thumbs. "Really?"

"I'm a mess. There's a ton of shit I have to deal with. His estate. This club. I'm not sure how I'm going to keep my position at the restaurant. Between trying to raise my daughter…"

"Mia."

Hearing Zane say Mia's name again does something crazy to me. Every part of me is zinging with awareness, it's nearly overwhelming. "How do you know her name?"

All he says is, "Fee." But he draws my nickname out. To let me know that he probably knows more about what I've been up to than I gave him credit for.

"She's incredible. Worth every sacrifice. It's the deepest, purest love I've ever had. She's almost fourteen months old and she just started walking on her own, which is awesome and scary at the same time."

"Her father?" His voice is quiet. Shaky.

"Gone. I have sole custody. Corey signed away his rights in exchange for not providing any financial support. I did insist on mandatory medical support if she ever has a medical emergency. Blood donation. Stuff like that."

Zane's arms tighten around my middle when I say Corey's name. Suddenly, I feel self-conscious. I never lost all of the baby weight, and I wasn't a small girl to begin with. He's a mega-star now, dating models and actresses and fucking ten girls at a time. The gossip sites are full of stories about him and all the other band members.

I can feel him breathing against my hair, but the comfort I felt has turned into something else. Suddenly, I feel trapped. Claustrophobic.

"I'm sorry, I shouldn't have brought his name up." I try to wiggle out of his embrace, but he tightens his grip. "I…"

Zane's voice is ragged but hopeful. "He's completely out of the picture?"

"Yes. He's never even seen her."

He now strokes my arm with the back of his hand. Almost as if he can't believe we're together like this and he needs to see if I'm real. "I didn't know that. It hurt too much for me to ask Carter or my mom anything. I didn't want to know anything about you and Corey raising your kid together. Creating a family."

I scoff and arch my neck to look at him. "No fucking way are we a *family*. The night she was conceived was my most colossal fuck up on record. But, Mia is not a mistake. Just so we're clear. She's my everything."

Our eyes are locked. He nods almost imperceptibly. My breathing goes shallow. His lips are right there. A centimeter from mine. My entire body is tingling. He swallows hard.

Then moves his head back a bit.

The moment passes.

As it probably should.

I turn back around and settle against his chest. This is enough. It has to be. I shut my eyes and allow myself this one small comfort. Even if it's only for a few more moments tonight. My ear is against his chest. The warmth of his body and the steady thump of his heart lull me into a state of relaxation that I haven't felt since I discovered my dad's lifeless body last week in the apartment.

I'm transported somewhere.

I hear Zane and Mia's laughter.

Flamenco guitar music.

Warmth and happiness all around me.

My subconscious knows it isn't real.

But every other part of my body wishes it were true.

CHAPTER 26

AGE 26

A few months after Gus's funeral, I'm with the guys in Los Angeles. We blocked off some time in a studio to write and jam. Work through lyrics. Instrumentation. Stuff like that. Get back to basics and figure out the direction of our next release.

We're in the middle of a creative bonanza. Ideas have flowed so effortlessly from all four of us, it seemed stupid not to record them. We didn't have a producer lined up, so Ty and I are co-producing for now.

Unlike when we recorded *Z* with Carter, this album is a true collective effort. Each one of us has shit we're dealing with. The studio has been an outlet. Surprisingly, the music is infinitely more upbeat.

Experimentation. It's actually fun.

Something to look forward to.

Distraction rather than catharsis.

With no pressure.

I mean, how do you recreate a seminal album? Thanks to Carter's good advice when we started, we've never had to share our profits with a record label. Our publisher only charges a nominal administration fee to license our catalog. Even after management takes a cut, LTZ is unbelievably profitable. Each of us have financial security beyond our wildest dreams.

My net worth most likely has surpassed my dad at this point.

Consequently, we have freedom. We don't need to prove ourselves anymore.

Which is a relief.

Except today, I received terrible news.

"What do you mean, Fiona doesn't own The Mission?" I shout into the phone. Jace is laying down drum tracks. It's so loud I can barely hear Carter so I duck out of the studio into the back alley for peace and quiet.

And privacy.

"Gus's estate is finally settled. Apparently, he sold the building to Corey Johnson's dad, Charles, after Mia was born. He never told Fiona about it. You didn't hear this from me, but it's pretty clear that Gus paid Corey and his family off so she would have full custody."

"Wow." I sink to the ground, my back against the building. "What does this mean?"

"Well, unfortunately, Charles just tripled the rent. As part of the sale, Gus negotiated a rent moratorium. Unfortunately, it expired when he died. He obviously didn't expect he'd go so young."

"For fuck's sake, Gus is barely in the ground. How could that bastard do that to her? She quit her job with Tom Douglas to run The Mission full time." My heart races. I cannot stand the thought of Fiona shouldering any more heartbreak. "Could we buy him out?"

Carter emits a long, forceful sigh. "Don't you think I tried? Two years ago he bought the building for ten million dollars."

"Wait, so where is that money?"

"I'm not sure what's left after the estate settled, but probably in a trust for Fiona and Mia."

"Fuck. So if he sold the building for ten mil, how much is it worth now?" My mind begins to spin. The songwriting royalty check I just received was a million bucks. I haven't touched nearly any of my LTZ earnings. I could easily buy this Johnson dickwad out with one wire transfer and *still* have enough money to live on for life. Even if LTZ imploded today.

"Well, the price is now fifty million dollars. Market rate. My realtor thinks there will be a bidding war because of its prime location."

WTF?

I'm not deterred. I could swing that if Carter went in on it. And some of the guys.

Jace peers out of the door and spots me. "Just wondering if everything's okay."

"Carter, let me talk to the guys. Maybe we can all go in on it. I'll call you back." I hang up the phone and follow Jace back in the studio where Ty and Connor are behind the glass listening to the latest take.

I knock on the door to get their attention. "My dudes. I wanted to run something past all of you."

"Shoot." Jace points a finger gun at me.

"Dude! Not very PC," I scold. "Fiona's in a real bind. The owner of The Mission's building is threatening to sell it."

"Wait, I thought her dad owned it." Ty furrows his brow in confusion.

"I did too, but no." I need to explain but don't want to give away

Fiona's personal business. "When Gus passed away, she inherited a real mess. My dad has tried to help, but there's a snafu. Anyway, The Mission is part of Seattle's music history. I don't want to lose it as a venue. Would any of you want to go in on it and buy the building?"

"I'd do it, but I just put an offer on a house here in LA." Ty frowns. "Sorry."

"What the fuck?" Connor fixes him with one of his patented glares. "Why would you move down here? Oh, right. Ronni."

"Connor, stop being so pissy." I jab him in the rib with my elbow. "The focus right now is on The Mission."

"I'll chip in," Jace offers. "My condo's paid off and so is the house I bought my parents."

"Fuck it," Connor growls. "I'll chip in something."

"Great!" I fist-bump my rhythm section and flip off Ty with a smirk. "Carter's in too. He's figuring out what needs to be done, I'll let you know."

"I'm outta here." Connor stalks out, shooting Ty an evil glare.

"I'll see ya in a few hours." I follow close behind him. I've got to get to the bottom of his beef with Ty. It's stupid. "Connor, wait up!"

The big guy turns slowly. "Yeah?"

I size him up. He's clearly bothered by something. "What's up with you and Ty?"

"Ach…don't worry about it." He brushes me off, turning away to head toward his rental car.

"I *do* worry about it." I keep up his pace. "Ty's been clean for a few months, I don't want a beef with you to disrupt his progress."

Connor stops. I watch his body heave in a heavy sigh before he turns. "Dude, don't take this the wrong way, but Jaysus. the coddling of that man is outrageous, so it is."

"What do you mean?"

"He's feckin' grown. He can and should handle his own shite. Ty knows why we have a problem, and I'm not sharin' our business with you or Jace. We'll work it out like men." He points a finger at me. "Leave it be, tend your own garden."

I watch him pull out and speed away, a bit shocked. Luckily, my phone buzzes, saving me from wasting time thinking about Connor's bullshit.

"Zane, you've got to stop." Fiona's exasperated voice fills my ear.

For fuck's sake, does no one appreciate me?

"Hey, Fee." I clench my phone in a vise grip. "What did I do now?"

"I got an acceptance letter from La Petite Academy for Mia today. I know it was you."

"Oh, that." I shake my head, even though she can't see me. "You said you were having trouble getting Mia in. All I did was make a call."

She's quiet for a minute. "Thank you. I appreciate it. It's just that we went over this. I don't want you to buy our friendship back. If we're going to learn how to trust each other again, you need to talk to me first about things that affect *my* daughter."

Ouch, direct hit.

Spending time with Fee after Gus's funeral is going a long way to repair what was broken between us. For a few weeks, I was free of band commitments. Which meant I was able to be present through the huge transition her father's death foisted upon her.

It was where I needed to be.

If Carter had died, I have no doubt she'd have done the same.

Deep down, that's who we are.

Romance doesn't seem to be in the cards for us anymore, though. I'm not sure we'll ever get back to that place. The two of us both royally fucked up in that department. As much as I want her, I'm scared to death to say anything. The vibes she gives me are purely platonic. I guess for now, just having her back in my life is enough.

At this point, I'll take whatever part of Fiona Reynolds I can get.

Well, and Mia Reynolds too. I'm all in. I love that little girl in a way I never knew was possible. The feisty little baby calls me "Unka Zane."

"I'm sorry." Sometimes a simple apology is the best policy. "You're probably not going to be happy with what else I have cooking if you're pissed at me for that."

The bubbling tone of FaceTime ignites and I press "accept." Fiona's blue eyes are hooded with trepidation. "What did you do?"

"Carter told me about The Mission. Me and the guys are going to chip in and buy back the building from Corey's dad."

Her gorgeous face crumples. She bites her lower lip and gazes back up into the phone. I hate that her beautiful eyes now have an undeniable shadow of sadness behind them. Even when she smiles, it's no longer the cheeky, unbridled glee of our youth. What I'd give to erase all her pain. "What's wrong, Fee?"

"They won't sell it to you."

"If I pay market rate they will."

She shakes her head. "No, they won't."

"Why the fuck not?"

"If I tell you this, you have to promise that it stays between us," she begs. When it comes to protecting her, all bets are off. But I'll humor her to find out whatever it is I need to know. "Promise me, Zane."

I keep two fingers crossed behind my back. Like when we are kids. When I catch myself doing it, I laugh to myself. Still, I keep them crossed. "Sure. I promise."

"I mean it. This is life and death for me. I've never told a soul about what I'm going to tell you."

"Okay, I get it." My body involuntarily shivers. Her tone scares the fuck out of me.

"I'm pretty sure Corey targeted me that night…"

Oh hell no. Instantly I'm enveloped in anger. "What the fuck do you mean? Tell me what happened. Right now."

I try to stay calm but...

White. Hot. Rage.

She shakes her head. "Calm down, Zane. If you're going to react like that it's going to stress me out too much. Seriously. You know about my blood pressure."

Shit. She mentioned something about complications from Mia's birth. I make a mental note to get more familiar with her medical condition. I use my Krav Maga mind skills to calm myself. "I'm really sorry, Fee. It's hard for me not to want to protect you. Will you give me some more information?

"Well, um… We, uh... We agreed not…" Fee sputters, but I know exactly what she's referring to.

"*Fuck* the love hack rules, Fee." I point at her through the phone but keep my voice calm. "That part of our lives is dead and gone. From now on, total honesty. It's the only way we can trust each other again."

She shrinks back. I don't care, she needed to hear it. Our stupid rules nearly ended us. And the "us" I'm referring to is still hanging on by a single, miniscule thread.

Unless we can move past it.

Which is why I need to know everything that happened that night. Even if it kills *me*.

Or kills us. For good.

"Okay, Zane. Okay," Fiona whispers and visibly steels herself.

My heart throbs. I love this woman so much; she needs to feel safe with me. "Fee, look. I'm sorry. There's nothing you can say to me that will affect how I feel about you. Okay? I promise."

She wipes a tear away. Gulps. Nods. Her voice is so soft, I can barely hear her. She looks off in the distance as she speaks. "Gus wasn't feeling well that night. I came in to close after work. It was last call. I was behind the bar closing out the till when Corey sat down and ordered a drink. He looked familiar and I told him so. We played a flirty game about how I knew him. It felt good. Light. Fun. Eventually, when I couldn't figure it out, he said he was your friend from high school. Reminded me that we met briefly at Willows Inn."

I punch my fist into my palm. "That fucker, he was *never* my friend."

"Well, I didn't know that. You never said a word about him until the night I told you I was pregnant." Fiona narrows her eyes.

I shake my head. Try to calm myself again. None of this is Fee's fault. "Fee, I'm sorry. I don't mean to be so aggro. It's just…"

"It's okay, Zane." Fee purses her lips. "This isn't easy for either of us."

I nod. "Let's just get it over with."

"Fine. He said I looked sad and somehow he got it out of me that we broke up. I didn't realize… Anyway, he basically offered me a shoulder to cry on."

"What did you tell him?" I know Fiona isn't stupid. She wouldn't tell a stranger personal details, would she? My heart thunders out of control.

Her shoulders hunch over. She hangs her head. "I said we had an arrangement. I didn't say what, but… Well, it wouldn't have been hard to read between the lines. I'm sorry, Zane. I was devastated by what happened in Lummi. I wasn't in my right mind."

What a goddamn fucking disaster. That being said, I don't want her to feel worse than she clearly does. I tamp my feelings down. "It's okay, Fee. Go on."

"He acted super nice. Gave me a big hug. Encouraged me about our relationship. Told me it would work out. Then he…um. Kissed me. I pushed him away at first, but I couldn't help but think of you with all of those girls. I started to cry. I wanted to hurt you. Maybe get back at you. Even though it was me that pushed you into it, I wasn't thinking clearly in that moment."

"I was a grown man, Fee." There's a lump in my throat the size of a grapefruit. "I made my own choices. I didn't have to…shouldn't have…"

"No, you did nothing wrong. And you thought that I… Looking back, Jesus. Zane, why did we think that was okay? I was—am—so stupid." Tears stream down her cheeks. "That stupid love hack destroyed us. You are really the only thing that has ever mattered to me. Until Mia, of course."

"Stop. What's done is done. We can't change it, we need to look forward. To the future. Finish the story so we can move on."

"Maybe. Okay. God, Zane. How do I tell you this?"

"It's okay. I can handle it, Fee." I nod.

I can't fucking handle it. Not even a little

Fee closes her eyes and continues, "Fine. I locked up the club. Then I asked him if he could make me feel better. I'll spare you those details. At first, it was— fine. But once he…um. Well…when it was happening, it took a turn. He got really rough. I didn't know what to do. I didn't feel like I could stop him since I initiated the whole thing. God, by that point, I was sick to my stomach about what we were doing. I…I just wanted to get it over with. After, um, he was done, it was obvious that the condom tore. He freaked out. Told me I tried to trap him. I promised I was on birth control, which I was."

She breathes in and out a few times. Puffs out a burst of air. "The whole situation scared the shit out of me. My bouncers had gone home. I realized how vulnerable I was. How stupid. All I could think about was getting him gone. With every ounce of bravado I had, I told him it was time to leave. That's when he grabbed my jaw and forced me to look at him. His eyes were hard. Cold. His voice was like poison. He said, 'Make sure you tell your boyfriend that Corey Johnson fucked you raw, you nasty, cheating whore.' Then he left. I cried all night. What I'd done was so reckless. Stupid. Then, I freaked out about STDs. Worried about what I'd done to you. To us. I gave him ammunition."

She's crying. Hard. Wracking sobs.

"I'll fucking murder him." My voice is ice cold. I mean every word. Even if there's no hope for me and Fiona as a couple, no one can treat her that way.

Fiona sobs, "Zane. No. Stop. Don't talk like that. It's bad enough—"

"He used you to get to me." I'm wrecked. Utterly wrecked. "I don't know what the fuck I ever did to him, but it doesn't matter. I'll do whatever I need to do to take him down."

Her face hardens. She takes a deep breath and holds her palm up to the screen. "Stop it. Trust me, I've explored every single legal option. When I found out I was pregnant, the first person I told was you. The next day, I tracked down Corey and told him. He raged at me. Told me he knew I was after his money. Threatened to sue me. Then threatened to call the police. I had my phone in my hand and dialed 9-1-1. When the police came, I filed a report for whatever charge would stick, but they declined to prosecute him after interviewing both of us.

"I mean, there really wasn't any prosecutable crime. Of course that's when the custody shit started in full force. You have no idea how much he harassed me with lawyers. I spent all of my savings trying to keep up with the legal bills. All to secure custody of Mia. When I ran out of money, my dad said he took care of it." She looks exhausted. Which doesn't surprise me. What a complete nightmare.

Of course now I'm even more livid. I literally want to smash up a room. Crash a car. Use a baseball bat to knock Corey Johnson's brains out.

Hearing Fee's story guts me.

But also galvanizes me.

"We're going to get the building back," I assure her. "I'll find a way."

Fiona's eyes are tired. Flat. She's clearly spent. "I don't *want* it back."

"What? Why?" I'm shocked. "It's your legacy. Mia's."

She sighs. "Because he will fight it with every ounce of his being, Zane. I don't want to spend Mia's childhood distracted by legal bullshit. I don't want to be stressed. Or angry. Leave it be. *Please*. Right now I have what is important. My daughter. My dad left us enough money. I don't need The Mission. I want to create a new legacy for my daughter."

"You can't let him get away with it, though." The wind is out of my sails. I'm devastated by what's happened to her. To us. To everything we ever knew.

"I can. Because of Mia. She's the most important thing. Not my fucking ego. Not yours. *Everything* I do is with her in mind, and if you want to be in our lives then you need to be on the same page."

"Fee…"

"No, seriously. How do you think it feels for me to go into the place where…"

Shit. Of course.

"Okay. I'll try to let it go." I give her a small smile though my heart is in my shoes. "I just hope you know I can't let *you* go. Ever again."

"I do. I feel the same, Zane. You're stuck with me." She smiles weakly. "Thank you for listening to me. For being there. I know it wasn't easy to hear that."

"What do you want to do now, Fee? Now that you've had some time to think about it?"

She taps her finger on her chin. Her eyes brighten a bit when she says, "Throw a goddamn blow out party as soon as possible. Start fresh. Maybe open a new Mission. A multi-use performance hall. With a diner. And a five-star exclusive restaurant where I can get my Michelin star."

"Let me help you."

Fiona cocks her head. "Really?"

"Yeah."

"No pressure?" She squints. "We can't go back to…"

I look up at the sky and back at her. "I know."

"Okay." This time her smile is genuinely sweet with a hint of sauciness. Like the woman she was before all of this crap.

After we hang up, I feel strangely peaceful after such an emotionally draining day.

Maybe it was the smile.

Maybe it was that she finally trusted me enough to tell the truth.

Somehow, as painful as this afternoon has been, I feel like we've made a breakthrough.

And that's enough for now.

CHAPTER 27

AGE 27

Cleaning up puke. Gotta love it.

I'm in sweatpants and a bra because my T-shirt was destroyed by my nearly three-year-old projectile vomitron. Good God, It's everywhere. In my hair. On the couch. The wall. The floor. I'm going at it one-handed because Mia won't let me put her down.

Unfortunately, that means my clean-up job isn't the best.

"Momma, belly icky." Mia buries her face in my hair and clings to my neck.

Not wanting a repeat, I hustle to the bathroom and gently position her over the toilet and rub her back. "If you have to throw up Meems, try to do it in the toilet."

"Eeeew," she cries. "Not where pee-pee."

"Yes, baby. All the gross stuff goes in the toilet." I'm sure that statement will bite me in the ass at some point, but for now I'm just trying to cope on a minute-to-minute basis. Ah, the joys of single motherhood.

Of course the doorbell rings at exactly that moment. Thank God, my mom's early. I just need a couple of hours to finish up the projected financials for my restaurant. "Mia, stay right here. I'm going to let Nana in."

Quickly, I pull my puke-stained T-shirt and bra off and throw on a clean white tank top, all while scurrying to the front door. When I fling it open, I get the surprise of my life. "Zane? What are you doing here?"

He looks at my raggedy-ass and chuckles. "Not expecting company?"

"Just my mom." I step aside and hold the door open for him.

He fixates on my chest and waggles his eyebrows. "Seems like you're happier to see that it's me."

I glance down to see that I'm nipping out. Yep, there's nothing left to the imagination through the thin fabric. Quickly, I cross my arms over my chest to cover myself. Not before I feel my cheeks flush with heat. Zane breaks into a full-on laugh at my reaction. "Rough day?"

"You could say that." I roll my eyes at him and head back to check on Mia.

He follows me into the bathroom. Mia's dutifully perched over the toilet with her mouth open. Zane crouches next to her and brushes a lock of hair out of her face. "Meems, are you sick?"

"Uh huh. I throwed up." Her huge blue eyes blink up at him.

"Sweetheart, do you need to throw up again?" I kneel next to Zane and smooth my palms over her cheeks.

She shakes her head. "Nuh uh."

"Why don't I go clean up the mess in the living room while you two wash off?" Zane backs out of the bathroom. "You get an A-plus for projectile range, Mia."

She giggles.

"Zane, you don't need to do that." I scoop up Mia and follow him out the door.

He pinches his nose between his thumb and forefinger. "Well, uh. Yeah, I do. You both stink, so the faster we can get everything done, the sooner Mia gets a new installment of *The Flea and the Fly*."

"Fee! Fy!" Mia claps her hands. "Unka Zane tell story!"

There's no use fighting it. Mia adores Zane. He's all she talks about. "Fine, but first we need a bath, missy."

Half hour later, Mia and I are bathed and in clean clothes. She's in bed waiting for her story. I've texted my mom not to come, because there's no reason to put her and Zane in the same room. No love lost there. Even now.

I pop into the living room to check on Zane's progress and I find that he's done an amazing job of eliminating all traces of vomit. He's at the sink, in full rock star regalia, washing his hands.

"Thanks, you." I stroll over and elbow him in the ribs, feeling shlumpy in my jogger pants and sweatshirt, which are in stark contrast to his muscular, fit body in a tight black T-shirt and skinny black jeans. "I hope you didn't get puke on your five-thousand-dollar jeans."

He hooks his thumbs in his belt loops and rocks back on his custom Italian boots. Grins. His hair flops over his eyes. He peeks out from under it, his trademark flirty move. "What? These old things?"

Our eyes connect. The corner of his mouth lifts up.

Electricity. It's always between us.

We just don't act on it. Not anymore.

Building back our friendship is one thing. Romance is another. Letting him into Mia's life? I've got to be careful.

So careful.

It's not just my life I'd screw up this time.

"Mia's waiting for her Fee Fy story." I point to the stairs and back up to let him pass.

He trots up to my daughter, allowing me a few moments of quiet time. A luxury these days. I smile at the thought of Zane and Mia's story hour.

It started a few months ago. Mia lost her shit over a huge, black housefly that landed on the apple slice she was eating. Crying. Screaming. Hysterics. It was something else. With the patience of a saint, Zane turned it all around. He made up a cute little tale of a flea and a fly and their friendship. Now, every time he sees Mia, he tells her the story and adds a little bit more to it each time.

It's adorable. She can't get enough.

She loves flies now.

And fleas, I suppose.

Over the past eighteen months, Zane's been around us a lot. His schedule isn't nearly as intense as it once was, but he's still on the road for a few months out of the year. In between tour legs, he's in Seattle more often, giving him the opportunity to spend time with me and Mia.

Zane is such a natural with her. The perfect honorary uncle. In addition to his Flea/Fly story, he plays games. Spoils her with gifts. Takes her to the beach. Throws tea parties for Mia and all her stuffed animals. He even watches all of her animated movies. Over and over. Sings the songs in *Frozen* at the top of his lungs. Recently, he bought her a tiny pink ukulele and is trying to teach her how to play.

Well, kinda. She just turned three, after all.

Once she's asleep, we are just us. Hanging out. Nothing too heavy. We chat. Joke. Listen to music. Catch up on parts of our lives we've missed over the years. Gossip. He tells me crazy band stories.

We're inching our way forward to trusting each other again.

Hell, who am I kidding? I trust Zane. He's learning how to trust *me.*

When I hear Zane coming down the stairs, I pour us each a glass of my homemade kombucha. Zane's health kick and obsession with fermented food inspires me. I've experimented with a ton of different flavors, mostly using tea infusions.

"Ahh, white tea passionfruit kombucha." Zane reaches for his glass and takes a sip. "Fuck, this is awesome, Fee!"

I raise my glass in a toast. "Thanks."

We take our drinks into the living room of my semi-new townhouse on Alki Beach in West Seattle. My unexpected inheritance allowed me a sense of stability. It's not enough to live on forever. Or to buy a commercial property for my restaurant in Seattle's crazy real estate market.

After taxes, retirement investments and funding Mia's college account, I was able to buy our home in a new neighborhood. So we could have a new life. The money also allows me to take a year or two off to grieve my dad, be present with my daughter and thoughtfully plan the restaurant I hope to open someday.

I still have dreams of Michelin stars.

"How's Ty?" I flop down on my extraordinarily comfortable gray suede couch. The part that's not wet from where Zane cleaned up Mia's mess. "I can't go anywhere without seeing him and that actress."

Zane sits in my rocking chair and steeples his fingers. "Um…it's the most fucked-up stupidity I've ever heard of. Never, in a million years, did I think Ty would agree to a fake girlfriend. After all he's overcome, I can't even…"

He rambles on about it, clearly agitated. After ten minutes of the same repetitive shit, I fake a yawn. Roll my eyes with a smirk. Circle my finger in the air for him to wrap it up. "It was just a polite question, Zane. Jeez."

"Fine, I'll shut up, but *you* brought it up." Zane sips his drink and fake glares at me before a wide smile spreads across his lips. "Wanna know why I'm here a day early?"

"Sure."

"I've done a thing."

"Oh God." I make a display of slamming my palm to my forehead.

"Don't get mad." Zane does his eyes-looking-under-the-hair trick. Again. I swear, it's worked so well for him since we were little, I doubt he's aware how often he utilizes it.

I raise one eyebrow and stare at him.

"Tomorrow, the band's having a surprise benefit concert to raise some money for a worthy cause here in Seattle." He stands and paces, unable to sit still. "For a new Mission. Like the one you've been dreaming about."

My jaw drops cartoon-style. "What?"

"We're posting on social at…" He checks his phone. "Well, shit. How did it get to be past eight? Oh well, it's posted. Here, take a look."

I take the phone from him and read LTZ's Insta. There's a smoldering photo of all four of the guys staring into the camera. Each wearing a Mission T-shirt. The caption reads:

> *LTZ gives back. We got our start in the Seattle club scene, but the one most near and dear to our hearts was The Mission, which sadly closed its doors due to the increasingly greedy developers who are making it impossible to make ends meet. Join us tomorrow at Key Arena. All proceeds will be used to build a new venue in Seattle. Link to tickets in our bio.*

I'm stunned.

The entire band is in on it.

They don't really *know* me.

I'm not sure how to even react at this news.

"Fee?" Zane's knees are bouncing. He looks at me expectantly.

I hand his phone back. Tuck my legs under myself and just stare at him.

I've tried so hard to be at peace in our new normal. Zane seems to have settled in nicely. Not me. Every minute I'm with him I wish I could rewind time. He permeates my very essence. During every waking hour, part of me is thinking about Zane and how much I love him.

How much it's hurt to lose him.

How much I wish we were a couple again.

"Fee?" Zane stands in front of me. Then sits down next to me. His thigh touches mine. Just barely. I keep my eyes fixed on our legs. I'm doing everything in my power not to let him affect me. When the truth is I want things from him I won't ever have again.

Won't let myself have again.

Because I know what it's like to really lose him.

Now that we're in each other's lives again, it's got to be enough.

I can't risk…

Zane cups my cheek with his hand and uses his finger to tilt my head up. Our eyes meet. Just like that, I'm a goner. I'm caught in the eye of a fifty-foot wave. Or a barrel plummeting over a waterfall. Either way, the sheer rush of emotion threatens to pull me under.

Yet, somehow in this moment, I'm also at peace. Everything I've suppressed for years bubbles up to the surface.

It's clear. *So* clear.

I may not deserve him, but Zane is *mine*.

Body and soul.

He's always been mine.

I've always been his.

No. We've always been each other's.

From the day and hour he was born.

Zane studies me. Like he's done millions of times before. The serene look on his face tells me that he knows. *Knows*. That, in this instant, my barriers are down.

There's a crack in my armor.

That I have no choice but to let go. To give myself back to him.

Fully.

I lean toward him and press my lips to his. A chaste kiss, but it's the first time our lips have touched in four long years. His hands cradle my head lightly. He strokes my cheeks with his thumbs as our mouths reacquaint. Over and over again.

Tentatively, I part my lips. He follows my lead. Our eyes never lose contact.

Wordlessly, we seek and give permission for every baby step we take.

I rest my hands on his waist. He pulls one of my legs over his thigh, so I'm half-sitting on his lap. Now, our kisses are more urgent, but not aggressive.

Our hands rove. Explore. Refamiliarize.

Everywhere he touches me is fire.

I burn for this man. No one else.

Ever.

We pull apart. Nose to nose. Breathing heavy.

"Fee?" Zane's voice is a prayer. His arousal presses against my thigh.

I throw my arms around his neck and straddle him fully. My core presses against his stiff cock. Before I change my mind, I find courage to speak my truth. From the bottom of my heart. "I fucking love you, Zane. There's *no one* but you. There will *never* be anyone but you."

"Oh, Fee." Zane is breathless. He cups my ass with both hands and yanks me against him. Moves me back and forth against his erection. Our mouths mash together. This time it's a passion-filled frenzy. Teeth gnash. Groans. Tongues swirl and explore. Moans. Caresses. Gropes. Shirts fly off. Suckles. Squeezes. Cries of unbridled ecstasy.

A fervor unleashed after being pent up for what feels like our whole lives.

My hands tangle through Zane's hair. I grip his head and pull him down to my bare breasts. Hungrily, he suctions my nipple with such force, my body thrusts against his cock seeking relief. My head spins. He plays my body like the guitar prodigy he is.

Drives me so wild, I feel uncaged.

Zane changes tactics. His tongue flickers along my jawline. My neck. Back to my nipple, where he nips and then soothes. Then repeats on the other side. Over and over. Lulling me into throbbing, yearning arousal unlike anything I've ever felt with him before.

It starts at the back of my neck, works down my spine through my abdomen to somewhere deep inside me. Almost involuntarily, my back arches when I come. Every muscle in my entire body shudders from the sheer gratification of what this man does to me.

"God, baby." Zane sighs audibly. "You're so beautiful when you let yourself go." He reverts to achingly slow kisses. Savoring me. Sipping from my lips. Fluidly, he shifts us so I'm lying on the couch with him hovering above me.

He scans my body and hums appreciatively.

I feel *beautiful* with Zane.

He cups my breasts and drags his hands downward, over my stomach (which is rounder) and my hips (which are wider) than when we were last together like this. Zane hooks his thumbs in the waistband of my joggers. I tilt my butt up so he can shimmy them off, which he does and tosses them to the floor.

He presses my thighs apart gently. I let him spread my legs about as wide as they can go.

Opening myself to him.

Completely.

I watch as he hovers above my pussy. His hot breath makes me squirm in anticipation, but he's not in any rush. That much is clear. He licks his lips. Leans down and traces my entire slit with just the tip of his tongue. So lightly I want to scream, but I let out a long, keening moan instead.

Zane smiles up at me and settles between my legs. He spreads my lower lips with his thumbs, exposing my clit. He licks and flickers and suckles the entirety of my pussy, humming and groaning as he eats me out like a fucking boss. When I'm lulled into a sense of erotic complacency, he drags his fingers through my arousal. Taps on my nub, then circles. Taps, then circles. Over and over until my hips gyrate to his relentless rhythm. His lips seal over me and I detonate again with a yelp, thrusting my hips into his face.

"Oh, Zane," I whimper. My body can't stop shuddering. "Oh, God."

He says nothing, just smiles. Stands to kick off his shoes. Pulls off his pants and boxer briefs. Electricity courses through my entire body. I'm overwhelmed with joy and awe that Zane and I are here in this moment. I reach for him and he settles on top of me. I embrace him and burrow my face into his neck. Stroke his warm, muscular body as we writhe against each other.

I'm so lost in him.

In this moment.

"Fee?" Zane nuzzles my cheek. I look up at him, his eyes are pleading. "I want to be inside you."

"Yes. I haven't… I'm safe, I get a shot. As long as you're—"

He holds his finger to my lips and shakes his head. "There is no one else in this room with us. We are pure. We are clean."

Our eyes lock. Everything is clear. Our psychic communication zings, I can literally *feel* what he's telling me through just one look.

He hasn't been with anyone since my dad died.

Because he's been waiting for me.

His lips touch mine and we kiss languidly. My legs loop around him, drawing him to me. He pushes inside my wet heat and groans. Our bodies press together as he cants and rolls his hips. It's been so long, I'm tight. He waits until I adjust and pushes in all the way. He's so deep.

Where he belongs.

We're synchronized in our movements.

Synchronized in our feelings.

Synchronized in every single way possible.

Mind. Body. Soul.

Zane's thrusts become more urgent. Faster. Harder. More intense. Our arms lock around each other. He winces and grimaces. His face contorts with every movement. Rapture. Stamina. Bliss.

When he can't hold off any longer, he braces himself up on one strong arm and reaches between us with the other. He lightly flicks my sensitive clit with just the right touch. My pussy throbs and clenches. My head spins. Soon, I'm matching him thrust for thrust, lifting myself to meet him. Our bodies slap together.

We grunt. We pant. We moan.

My inner walls clamp around him just as he erupts and fills me. My breathing is ragged. Every nerve sparks. Every muscle twitches. We cling to each other. Spent.

A few minutes later, Zane rolls halfway off me, cuddling me close. Our sweaty, naked bodies tangle. He strokes the curve of my lower back down my ass and back up again. Our heads snuggle against each other. "I *love* you, Fiona Reynolds," he whispers.

"Still?" I hear myself ask.

"Always." He lifts his head to look at me, his eyes soften when he sees I'm dead serious. "I've never stopped."

I gaze up at him. Reach up and push the hair out of his eyes. "Zaney."

"My life without you is incomplete. No matter where I am in the world, I can *feel* you. Believe that." Zane kisses my forehead. "My heart and cock don't want anyone but you. I wish you'd fucking remember you're my other half."

"I can't believe you organized a fundraiser for me." I comb my fingers through his soft hair when he rests his head back down against my chest.

Zane relaxes even further against me. "You deserve to have your dream come true just like mine has. We're going to buy a building. Or a lot. Either way, it's all happening. Once you open your restaurant, you'll never have to worry about it being stolen out from under you again."

"I'm sorry." I twirl a lock of his hair on my finger. "I'm so, so sorry for—"

He leans up and kisses me. "All is as it should be, Fee. No more running."

I nod.

"Say it."

I press my lips to his. "No more running, I promise."

His arms scoop under my back and he rolls me so I'm straddling him. "We're together. There's no one else but us now. And Mia."

I nod.

"Say it."

"We're together." I bend to kiss his eyelids. Pepper kisses on his cheeks. His ears. Work my way down his jaw to his lips.

He reaches up and strokes my hair. Traces his finger down my chest and circles my nipple, which tightens under his touch. His cock hardens against my thigh. He grins. "I'm ready for round two."

Me too, Zane.

"Me too."

CHAPTER 28

AGE 27

The show sold out in one hour. I didn't find out until the next morning. I was a little distracted. Fiona and I stayed up all night fucking. Making love. Cuddling. Fucking again. Showering. It's my fault we're both dragging today. I kept us up. We had a lot to make up for.

Plus, I was afraid that if I went to sleep, I'd wake up and me and Fiona would all be a dream.

"Unka Zane." Mia tugs on my jeans. "Fee Fy!"

I crouch down to get eye level with Fee's precocious little girl. Her eyes are the same startling blue as Fiona's. Her long, dark hair is braided. I helped her pick out her outfit today. She wears black-and-white polka-dotted overalls over a tiny white T-shirt. "Sure, Meems. Come sit in the rocking chair with me."

For the next half hour, I make up a new adventure for the *Flea and the Fly*, careful to use different voices for each character. If I mess up, Mia lets me know it. She's curled sideways. One little leg rests over the armrest. The other dangles off my knee. Her cheek is pressed against my heart. She looks up at me. Her thumb is in her mouth.

I wish she were mine.

Over the past year and a half, when I'm in town, I find ways to spend time with Mia. When Fiona got pregnant, I thought her child would be a constant, painful reminder of our stupid love hack. How wrong I was. From the first time I saw her, clinging to Fiona's neck at Gus's gravesite, I was a goner. The entire time Fee sobbed in my arms, Mia just looked at me with eyes wise beyond her years. They never left mine.

She didn't fuss.

She didn't act out.

She just watched me until Faye took her to the car.

In that moment I knew everything in my life happened for a reason. If any one thing had played out differently, this tiny little beauty wouldn't be on this earth right now. Once I came to terms with this truth, every ounce of anger and animosity I had toward our situation disappeared.

The overwhelming love I've always felt for Fee has displaced my anger. And enhanced it by a million times—all because of this precious little girl. I can't imagine my life without the two of them.

If I hadn't shown up for Fee at Gus's funeral, my life would be so different.

I wouldn't have Fee back.

I wouldn't be able to watch Mia grow up.

And now that Fee and I are together…

Stop, Zane.

I'm getting ahead of myself.

We only just reconnected. There's been no specific talk about the future yet. I need to be a bit more patient.

Which isn't my strong suit.

"Zane, I'm heading to the salon—" Fee stops in her tracks when she sees us in the rocking chair. She rapidly fans her fingers in front of her face, clearly a bit verklempt. "Oh, look at you two."

"We're pretty cute, that's for sure." I boop Mia on the nose and look at Fee. "Go. We'll be fine."

She nods. "Okay. Mom will be here soon to take her to daycare. Then I'll see you tonight?"

"Yeah, I'll have someone drop by passes in a few hours. I have a ton of errands, then soundcheck. Try to be there around four. Tell security to bring you to my dressing room. I'll let them know to watch out for you."

Mia dozes off after Fee leaves. I'm on the brink of falling asleep myself when the doorbell rings. Reluctantly, I set Mia down and open the door to see Faye, an older version of Fee and Mia, standing there. "Long time, Faye."

"Zane." She strolls inside like she owns the place.

"Nana!" Mia throws herself at her grandma.

Faye picks her up. "You look especially cute today, Mia."

"Unka Zane pick out." Mia points at me.

Faye shoots me a look. "Is that so."

"Mia, here. Watch *Om Nom* for a few minutes." I grab the iPad and fire up some little animated shorts from the popular game *Cut the Rope*. Mia lays on the sofa and within two seconds, is engrossed in the little green character's adventures.

"Great, distract her with media." Faye rolls her eyes and strolls into the kitchen. "Nice work."

I've had enough of her and her bullshit attitude with me. "Faye, we need to put the past behind us. Fiona and I are together. Just like we've always meant to be. You used to treat me as if I were your own child. I'm not sure what I did to make you hate me so much. It's been very hurtful and confusing to me for many years."

"Oh, cry me a river, Zane." Faye shakes her head. "I was protecting my daughter the best way I knew how."

"From who? The kid who used to love you like you were my second mom?" I cross my arms and lean against the counter. Wait.

"Look. I didn't want Fiona to go through what your mom went through. That's the truth. I could see you going the same direction as your dad from a mile away." Faye shrugs. "If things had kept going the way they were, Fiona would have been pregnant by the time she was fifteen. Then where would she be?"

"Wow. Okay. You're still hung up on something that happened a decade ago. We were fucking kids. I loved Fiona then. I love Fiona now. With all my heart. I'd never do anything to hurt her. *Never*. There's no one on this earth that loves her more than me, that I can promise you."

She scoffs and looks away.

I move to her side and touch her arm. "Faye. Stop. Let us be happy."

"I'm not stopping you. How can I? Fiona has never listened to a thing I say. The second you went through puberty, you only had one thing on your mind. All of us were there when you brought her home on the night of her graduation, Zane. It was so fucking obvious what you two had been up to."

"Yes. It's true. Because we *love* each other. She's it for me. And I'm it for her. She's forgiven you for all that shit you pulled in high school; can't you leave the past in the past?" I stare her dead in the eye. "I'm begging you. Be happy for us. We're all family."

Faye gets in my face. "You have no fucking right to judge me, Zane Rocks. Your mother would be furious."

"No, that's not true. She'd actually cheer me on." I take a step back from Faye. I don't want Mia to think I'm being aggressive toward her grandmother. But I won't back down on this conversation. "Losing your friendship was tough on my mom. She never appreciated the way you talk about me. Or my dad. You hold one hell of a grudge, Faye. How does it feel to be such an angry, bitter woman?"

My words are like a slap in the face. "What did you say?"

"Do you have any idea the damage you caused?"

"Fuck you, Zane."

"Right back at you, Faye. You made us feel dirty. Like what we felt for each other was wrong. For the life of me, I don't understand you." I shake my head. "Did it ever occur to you that if you and my mom had just talked to us about what happened at the campfire the heartbreak of the past decade could have been avoided? We've lived our lives trying to please you. And then to keep our relationship from you. We never had your support."

She slumps against the pantry door. "I did what I thought was best for my daughter. I didn't want her around nightclubs and drug addicts."

"You took her from all she knew and then locked her up and threw away the key."

"Whether you believe it or not, Zane, I didn't want things to turn out the way they did. You weren't around your father when he was at his worst. Gus and I were. A mother puts her child first. Always. Remember that."

"Fiona and I are together. *We* will do whatever it takes to put Mia first. Believe it. If you're going to continue to spread lies about me, then…"

She seems to take that in. I let it sit with her for a minute, but I don't lose eye contact. I'm not threatening her, I'm stating a fact. Fiona's mother is not going to cause harm to my family anymore, regardless of if she thinks she's doing the right thing.

"What will Fiona do when you're out on tour?"

"We will figure it out. The two of us. If we need your help or my folks' help, we'll ask." I glance over at Mia, who is still engrossed in her videos. "Mia's the most important part of this equation right now."

Faye's face softens visibly when she looks at her granddaughter. "She's the most precious little girl."

"I'm sorry for saying some things to you out of anger. It's been building for such a long time. I don't want Fee to feel any more stress. She's had enough to last a lifetime. I'm not going to allow anything to aggravate her heart condition. Besides, there's no one harder on Fiona than Fiona, we both know that. I just want peace, Faye. I want you to be my second mother again." I grip her elbow gently.

She shuts her eyes and her whole body relaxes with a long, drawn-out sigh. "Okay. Zane. I'll try."

"Come with Fee to the benefit tonight. Carter will be there. You can meet the guys. My bandmates are actually pretty grounded, despite what you might have read. You know we're huge rock stars now." I flash her one of my boyish grins.

She smirks. Points at me.

Which gives me hope.

A few hours later, Faye and Fiona are deep in conversation with Ronni Miller, who is here with Ty for some sort of *People Magazine* article. Ronni is cooing over Mia, who looks like a little rock princess in her black taffeta dress. Connor and Jace's parents and respective brood of siblings seem to be everywhere I look. Even Connor's ex, Jen, and her new girlfriend Becca have made an appearance.

For the first time in ages, I'm not putting on a brave, positive front. My heart *actually* doesn't have a hole in it.

The energy in the room is pure positivity.

Well, except for a small scuffle between Connor and Ty.

Which I ignore. Better to keep my nose out of it.

I leave my girls to get ready for the show. Then, it hits me. This is the first time Fiona will have seen LTZ since we've become famous. Before we were well-known, she only saw the Mission show. Then we were off on our first tour and all hell broke loose between us when I got back.

Holy shit, the person I love the most hasn't ever been part of my LTZ world.

And I want her to be part of all of my worlds.

I send my private security detail to escort Fee into my private dressing room. She looks a bit bewildered when the door opens.

"Holy shit, rock star." She surveys the catering table full of fruit, meat, and cheese. A giant bowl of strawberries. Hint Water, a few energy drinks, protein bars. Oh, and a huge bouquet of red roses for Fiona. It's Valentine's Day, after all. There's also a small pink teddy bear for Mia.

"Bawbarey." Mia misses the bear completely, runs over to the food and shoves a giant berry into her mouth.

Fiona and I smile at each other.

"Strawberries are Zane's favorite fruit, Mia." Fiona walks over to the spread. "It isn't polite to take food that doesn't belong to you. Can you ask Zane if it's okay to eat his berries?"

Mia trudges over and stands right in front of me. She holds up a strawberry with a big bite out of it. "Unka Zane? Can I have bawbarey?"

I glance up at Fee and crouch down. "Yes, you may have anything you want."

Mia giggles and throws her arms around my neck. I pick her up and whirl her around.

"Mia! Remember what I told you. Zane is performing tonight, don't get him all dirty." Fiona rushes over to take Mia from me.

"Fee, please don't worry about it. Mia is welcome to give me a hug any time." I blow a zerbit on her cheek. "Zane loves Mia."

"I wuv Zane." Mia kisses me on the mouth. "I marry Zane."

Fiona loses it. She starts laughing so hard she has to sit down. "Wow," she sputters. "Getting aced by my own daughter."

"Never." I kiss Mia's cheek and put her down. She promptly heads back to the strawberries. "So, uh. Had a little chat with your mom…"

"I heard."

"As long as she doesn't try to fuck with us again, I'm good." I saunter over to my girlfriend and cup her face. Press my lips to hers and ravish her mouth.

"Wow." She blinks up at me. "I can't believe I snagged myself a rock star. Thanks for the roses, Zaney."

I wrap my arms around her shoulders and pull her into my body. "Believe it, baby. Happy Valentine's Day."

When I get the signal that it's time for the show, I grab the pink noise-canceling headphones I bought for Mia and place them over her ears. Fiona leans into me and I throw an arm around her shoulders. We are escorted to stage left, where I've set up two chairs for Fee and Mia to sit on.

Pokey nods to me and hands me my Gibson. I gently pull one of the earpieces away from Mia's ear. "Sweetheart, keep your headphones on, the band is going to be really loud. I don't want you to hurt your ears."

She nods. "Okay, Unka Zane."

Fee grips my wrist and I deftly shift so our fingers intertwine. I kiss her lips. "I love you."

"I love you. I can't believe how excited I am to see you play." Her smile is so wide, it nearly falls off her face. "Thank you for all of this. For Mia, I wouldn't have known…"

"Gotta take care of my girls." I kiss her once more, strap my guitar on just in time for Jace's cue. I wave to them as I run out on stage and strike the opening chord to *Rise.* We put on an amazing show despite the fact we haven't been on stage in a couple of months.

Usually, after a hometown show, I'd be the first to mingle with everyone and the last one to leave. Tonight is different. I leave with Fiona and Mia after a brief appearance at the after party. As exhausted as she and I both are from lack of sleep, we make slow, sweet love to celebrate our first official Valentine's Day together.

The benefit is a huge success. After expenses, we clear three hundred thousand dollars for the new Mission. We'll need a lot more than that to build the type of space Fiona envisions. But it's a good start. Carter and I can make up the difference.

It's going to happen. By hook or by crook.

The next few weeks fly by. We hire an architect. Scope out spaces. Hire a team to put together a business plan. Before I know it, I'm due back in LA to finish mastering our next album.

We're also headlining Coachella.

Once the album is out, we're going back on tour. The other guys are grumbling about the pace. They want to ease up a bit. I'm finally beginning to understand why.

Anyway, tomorrow I leave for LA. I'm sitting on Fiona's bed waiting for her to finish washing her face. I look around her bedroom and feel a bit sad. I'll miss sleeping with her every night. For the first time since LTZ started, I'm actually dreading doing my job.

"You're quiet." Fee traces her finger on the design of my rose tattoo as she walks by.

"Yeah." I sigh and pull her down on my lap. Bury my head in her orange-blossom-scented fuchsia hair.

"We're going to be fine, Zane." Fee presses her thumb against my lips. I open and suck. She smiles.

I pull up her tank top and cup her breast. "I know."

Fiona angles her head back to kiss me. I savor her lips. One hand snakes around and burrows down the front of her sleep shorts to find her needy little clit. My other fingers pinch her nipple. She squirms against me.

"I'm going to miss you, so much," I say in between kisses along her neck. "Mia too."

"You'll be back." She angles her head back, so my lips capture hers.

Whoa. Did she really say that?

I kiss her senseless before saying a word. "Yes, I will. I'll always come back for you."

"I *know*, Zaney." She leans back against me. Grinds her ass against my cock. "You can't get enough of me. Or Mia."

That's for sure.

I'm glad she finally knows it.

Feels it in her bones.

We've weathered too many storms to give up our happily ever after now.

CHAPTER 29

AGE 28

The plane touches down and my heart beats out of my chest. I already miss Mia, but she's in good hands with my mom. It's the first time I've ever been away from her. This will be worth it, though.

It feels good to be a bit carefree for a couple of days. Zane and I are doing so well. We are blissfully happy. All of our parents are happy for us. Even my mom. *Finally*. Shocking, but true. I'd worried that Zane's little discussion with her would backfire. But it worked. She's backed way off. Surprisingly, she was the one who suggested I surprise him.

Zane's been in LA for a couple of months finalizing LTZ's new album. Even though he pops up to Seattle when he can, he's on a deadline to deliver the finished master recording. Consequently, we haven't seen each other in person in nearly three weeks, and I miss him.

I need him.

After all he's done to bring us back together again, it's high time I make the effort for my man.

Carter guides me down the stairs of his private jet. We're shadowed by Lester and two of his security detail. It's mind blowing to me how low-key he is for someone so famous. Yet, here we are, arriving at Coachella in utter luxury. With bodyguards. "Zane and the guys are helicoptering in before their set. We have time to catch a couple of bands if you like."

"Yeah. That would be cool." I smile up at him.

A black SUV is waiting for us at Desert Jet, the private airport where we land. It's about a five-minute drive into the back parking lot at the Empire Polo Club, where the festival is held. Lester radios ahead, someone is waiting at the gate. We're guided to a small parking lot next to a giant parking lot where about a hundred tour buses are parked.

I can't help but gape.

"God, Fee. Is this your first time at a festival?" Carter throws his arm around me and we walk toward a balding, portly guy with a long braid for a beard who seems to be waiting for us.

"Yep. Looks like I'm doing it in style." I hip check him. "I'm guessing this isn't how the masses get in."

"Mr. Pope." The man holds out his hand. Carter shakes it. "I'm Billy. Here are your wristbands. Here is my card, call me if you need anything. I'll make sure we accommodate you."

The man helps strap on about half a dozen different colored cloth bands around each of our wrists. Carter's security team gets the same bracelets as us, plus one more. As we step through the gate, I shoot Carter a puzzled look. "What happened to a good old VIP All-Access lanyard?"

"Ah, well there's not really such a thing anymore at most festivals."

He pinches a plastic square that is attached to a bracelet. "This is a RFID chip, each bracelet designates where you're allowed to go. They'll scan it at various places throughout the festival. It allows the organizers to keep track of everyone because your ID is associated with the chip. That's why I had my management office get all your details yesterday. Basically, because we have all of these bracelets, we can get anywhere. Mostly, for security purposes, we'll be behind the scenes."

Which means, in layperson speak, Carter can't really mingle with the masses. He'd be mobbed. I finger through each of the bracelets. Carter explains what each means. One of them is bright pink with "artist" printed in black lettering, it allows us to go to the backstage general lounge areas and to watch most shows from special areas to the side of the stage. Another is pale blue for "guest," which gets us into more private backstage areas. One is yellow, apparently we can hitch a ride on a golf cart with that one. We also have a brighter orange "VIP," a purple "Production," and a black-and-silver one marked "VVIP," which apparently is the most coveted bracelet at the festival.

By this point, we're in a golf cart zipping toward a smaller stage where a band Carter's excited to see is playing. I've already forgotten their name, and they're not really my taste, but it doesn't matter. One of the wristbands allows us to stand at the side of the stage and watch the crowd, so I'm people watching. Slutty bohemian-chic outfits. Crazy hairstyles. Cosplay. Basic fans. Posers. Drunk people. Families with kids. It's a fascinating mix.

Luckily, I studied up ahead of time on festival fashion. I kinda sorta fit in. My bright-pink hair braided into pigtails seems to check a box. I'm a basic festival bitch, but passable. A couple of layered tank tops in black and pink. Cut-off shorts. Ankle boots. Oh, and a black Limelight bandana Carter handed me when the golf cart kicked up a plume of dust, causing me to cough.

"Carter Pope. Good to see you." A striking dude with jet-black hair and ice-blue eyes stands next to us. He nods at me.

Carter pulls down his baseball cap. "New album sounds good."

"Thanks, man."

"Ash, this is Fiona Reynolds, Zane's girlfriend." Carter puts his hand on my shoulder. "Fee, this is Ashley Player, his band goes on right before LTZ."

I extend my hand. "Nice to meet you."

Crazy. I'm living in a whole new world I didn't know existed.

For the next couple of hours, Carter and I explore the most exclusive areas of the festival. We eat a delicious meal prepared by Curtis Stone. Carter introduces us. Turns out, we know a lot of the same people in the culinary world. He chats with us for a long time. Invites me to his restaurant, Maude in LA. Chatting about food really lights a fire under my ass. He encourages me when I tell him about my restaurant plans. Offers advice. Introductions to investors.

Gah!

I realize it's been hours since I checked my phone. I see that I've missed a bunch of messages from Zane.

11:43 am Zane: Hey Fee I miss you

12:11 pm: Zane: Missed FaceTime call

12:20 pm: Zane: Missed FaceTime call

12:21 pm: Zane: Fee, call me

1:01 pm: Zane: Missed FaceTime call

1:49 pm: Zane: Dude! Call me I miss you I have to leave soon for the show!!!!!

2:05 pm: Zane: Sweetheart. Babe. Love of my life. Other half. STOP IGNORING ME. YOU KNOW THIS DRIVES ME CRAZY. Give Mia a kiss.

2:34 pm: Zane: Heading to the show. Love you. Call me when you can.

3:45 pm: Zane: I'm at the venue. Text me when you're free. By the way, I'm getting worried, I know you had a thing today but I was hoping to talk to you before the gig.

"The band's here." Carter's buried in his own phone. He gestures to Lester to get our golf cart. "Should we head back?"

My heart races. I clap my hands together excitedly. "Yes, let's go!"

"Tuck those pink braids under that bandana. Otherwise he'll see you from a mile away." Carter helps me hide them. I smile up at him. He's the sweetest man. Like father, like son.

I hold my phone up and flip the screen to look at myself after he's done. "That should do the trick."

"Fee, you're going to surprise the fuck out of Zane." Carter grins at me as he tucks his own ponytail up into his hat and puts on his shades.

We zip back in record time and slide out of the golf cart. Carter holds his arm out to prevent me from running into a bunch of roadies who are scurrying around doing a set change. I peer up to the stage. You can't see the crowd because a big curtain or some sort of barrier hides what's happening behind the scenes. "Wow, it's so cool seeing what you guys do every day."

"I'm stunned that you've never been to a big show." Carter side-hugs me. "How is that possible?"

I give him a pointed look. God, sometimes he's so clueless. Before I can reply, I spot Ty and Connor making their way to the stage. A few seconds later, Zane jogs to catch up with him. He's so sexy in his aviator shades, tight black T and black shredded jeans. He keeps looking at his phone and frowning.

Carter whispers in my ear, "If we keep out of the way back here, we'll blend in. The boys won't even notice us, trust me. They'll be focused on getting soundcheck done. Ordinarily their techs would handle it, but it gives the crowd a bit of a thrill when they realize the real band is behind the curtain. Just watch."

It takes every ounce of self-control I have not to run up and maul Zane. Of course, I know that every girl out in the crowd feels the same way. I need to exhibit some sort of decorum so I don't embarrass myself in front of my man. It's funny to watch him incognito from our vantage point. He keeps checking his phone and looking around. Which prompts me to shoot him a quick text. I don't want him to worry about me.

Fiona: Have a great show. Love you. Call me after, I'll be waiting.

I see him check his message. My phone pings right after.

Zane: Love you. I'll ping you after. We're all a bit stressed. Jace is missing. Some band drama. Nothing to worry about but can't talk.

"Where's Jace?" I whisper to Carter.

He looks around. "Huh. Dunno. He's usually the responsible one."

Connor, Ty, and Zane take their places on stage. Connor plucks out a couple of notes. Zane follows. The next thing I know, a blur of muscles, tattoos, and long blond hair whooshes past Carter and me. Jace sprints up the stairs to the stage, taking his place behind his kit. He grins at the guys.

"Nice of you to show up, J." Ty speaks into the mic.

"Must have been a pretty good night," Connor's low voice teases.

The crowd goes wild. A chant of "L.T.Z" starts up. It's so loud. I can't even believe this is Zane's life. An entire part of him I've been aware of, but really haven't known because of my own intense work schedule. Well, and Mia, of course. I'm so proud of all that he's achieved. He's bringing joy to so many people. What a rush to have so many loyal fans.

Jace thunks his bass drum with his foot and taps a beat on his snare. The guys join in and run through a couple of covers but finish quickly. Clearly, they are a well-oiled machine. Zane hands his guitar to his tech. Connor does the same. The four of them skip down the stairs and head right past us, but don't even glance our way. Carter nudges me and shakes his head with a grin. I can hear what they're saying as they walk by.

"Jace, where have you been? You haven't blown a gasket, so I guess you haven't heard the news." Zane is on Jace's heels. Clearly agitated, especially because LTZ's drummer isn't paying attention to him. Instead his thumbs are flying as he messages someone. Zane peers over his shoulder to see what he's typing. "Ahh. Poppy. That explains it."

Jace doesn't look up from his phone. He *does* reach out and slug Zane in the arm.

"Ow!" Zane rubs his bicep. "If you expect me to be a genius in the studio, you shouldn't damage the goods."

Jace rolls his eyes.

I can barely suppress a giggle, but manage to keep quiet.

"Carter?" Ty spies us and heads in our direction. This catches Zane's attention. The other guys too. It's awesome to witness the moment that Zane realizes it's me standing next to Carter.

Of course, I can't keep the massive cheesy smile off my face.

We rush toward each other. Just like the movies.

Carter and the rest of LTZ leave us alone and continue on to the dressing room.

"Fee!" Zane smashes his mouth against mine. "God, what are you doing here?"

"Surprise!" I clutch his T-shirt in my fists and yank him back toward me. Our mouths tangle and it's a while before we come up for air. "I flew in with Carter. That's why I didn't answer your texts."

"You. Are. Sneaky." Zane snakes his arm around my waist. Smooches me. We walk toward a gated area. "Is Mia with you?"

"Mom's watching her until tomorrow." I can't help but pepper him with kisses. "I hope you don't have any plans tonight."

He pulls me tighter into his side. "Even if I did, I'd cancel them. I'm blown away, Fee. God, I love you so much. I'm so fucking psyched you're here. I can't believe it."

He's so fucking happy. Coming here was the right move. Seeing the huge smile on Zane's face? It's everything. I want to make him feel that way every single day. "I love you. I couldn't wait one more minute to see you."

At this point, we enter LTZ's designated dressing room. Carter and Ty are deep in conversation. Jace is sitting on the couch with his arm flung over his eyes. Connor intercepts us before we get too far.

"Shite's hit the fan. Ty and Ronni broke up without clearing it through Andrew and Sienna. Jace is furious, so he is. He raked Ty over the coals right before you guys got here. Oh, hi Fee." Connor sighs heavily. "Anyway…"

"Fuck." Zane glances over at Ty, who looks incredibly agitated. "Is he okay?"

Connor nods. "Aye. Surprisingly so. He's more pissed about the press bringing up all of his old shite. Jace is trying to calm down Andrew and Sienna. I gotta give Ty credit, though. He took one for the team to protect Ronni."

Zane and I give each other a look. I can tell he's relieved. "Well, at least it's over. Finally."

"Aye." Connor makes himself a sandwich and plops back down on the couch. The only sound in the room is him munching. The mood is still pretty tense. I'm the outsider, so I don't say anything. No matter what band drama is going on, there's no way I'm getting in the middle of band business.

Besides, I'm still over the moon to be here with Zane.

"Wanna get outta here for a bit?" Zane nuzzles my ear. "We're not on for a few hours. We could grab a golf cart and have a spin around."

"Could we?" It sounds like heaven.

A few minutes later, Zane and I are whisked around the festival grounds by venue security and Zane's new bodyguard, Zeke. Zeke's a handsome but hulking man with dark-brown skin, startling gray eyes and the requisite stern attitude for a man of his profession.

Zane's hair is tucked up underneath a jersey skull cap, despite the heat. He explains it's easier if people don't automatically recognize him. With a bandana over his face and sunglasses, he looks like every other festival-goer. Mostly, we stay out of the main general admission areas, but even the back-end routes give me a glimpse of the sheer enormity of the crowd.

"What do you think?" Zane has me tucked tightly against him.

"Amazing. You guys have really come so far. I can't believe I've missed so much of this."

"You had a pretty intense career, babe." Zane's voice doesn't have any trace of resentment. "Do you think...maybe you and Mia might want to come on the road for a bit before she starts school? Lots of musicians bring their families. It could be a whole new adventure for us."

"I never really thought that was an option. You'd really want a four year old on tour with you?" I blink up at him. Touched on such a deep level.

He pulls down his bandana and kisses me senseless. When we come up for air, I catch Zeke hiding a grin. “Fee, I want you and Mia with me at all times. Wherever I am.”

“I want that too.” I take his hand in mine. Stroke the top of it with my thumb.

When we get back to the backstage area of the Main Stage, things are a lot more lively. Dozens of people are scurrying back and forth. Zane seems completely unbothered. Of course, he’s seen all of this before. Many times. It’s his normal life.

Part of me wonders where all the groupies are. How I pictured it was dozens of scantily clad girls hanging around the backstage area like two-bit hookers. Waiting to snare their rock star. In reality, everyone is really, really busy. There is so much activity. Not a lot of groupies at all.

Zeke holds his earpiece and nods. “Zane, you’re late, the *Rolling Stone* reporter is waiting for you.”

“Shit. Okay.” Zane jumps off the golf cart and holds his hand out to me. “Wanna make it official?”

“What?” I take his hand and follow him to wherever it is he’s leading me.

“It would mean a lot to me if we went in there together. As a couple.”

I’m not sure what he’s getting at, but I’ll do anything to make him happy. “Well, we are a couple. It’s already official.”

“They’ll probably mention you—the existence of you— in the article. Are you okay with that?”

Nothing would make me prouder.

Hand in hand, we enter the press area.

Not realizing that the split-second decision we make to go public will destroy our life as we know it.

CHAPTER 30

AGE 28

Over the past six years, we've played Hong Kong twice, but I know this will be my favorite show here. Maybe ever.

Fee and Mia are joining me, any second actually—their Cathay Pacific flight just landed—to go on tour with me in Asia, Australia, and New Zealand. It's a fairly loose schedule over four months, Manila, Taipei, Osaka, Tokyo, Indonesia, Israel, Malaysia, and Singapore before Australia, where we have two nights in Sydney, then Brisbane, Adelaide, Melbourne and Perth. We wrap up in Auckland, New Zealand, before heading back home to Seattle for more time off.

It's part of the new normal we all agreed to. The guys want more time off to pursue other projects. Hang out with their significant others and families. A year ago, I'd have been pissed. Demanded to keep up our pace.

Now? I get it.

I *totally* get it.

Especially now that Fee and I are about to close on the Columbia City Theater and the building next door to it. In a couple of years, after we get an architect, permits, and all of the other crap that goes into renovating and restoring a venue, we'll be the proud owners of a new arts facility. The *new* Mission.

And Fee will finally have her own restaurant right next door.

We have a lot to celebrate.

For now, we'll finish the Asian leg of our tour, which kicks off with two shows at AsiaWorld-Expo, one of LTZ's favorite venues. When we're touring, I love having back-to-back gigs. It gives us an entire day free from the grind of traveling.

Usually I sleep.

This time, I plan on taking my ladies sightseeing.

Zeke pokes his nose into the door of my dressing room. "They just arrived, should I bring them back?"

"Yeah. That would be great. Thanks, man."

A few minutes later, the door opens again and Mia darts over to me and throws herself in my arms. "Unka Zane. We go to China!"

"Don't you look pretty!" I hold her out so her feet are dangling. "That's a cool looking T-shirt you have on. What band is that?"

"L.T.Z." She points at me. "It Unka Zane's band."

By this point Fiona, looking beautiful in a simple black dress, combat boots, and her pink hair piled high on her head, is at my side, beaming. I lean over and give my gorgeous girl a thorough, sweet kiss. Only then do I greet her, "Hey, Fee."

"Hi." She takes Mia, blushing. "I can honestly say, I've never flown in such luxury before. It was like having our own apartment in the sky. Thank you, moneybags."

"I wanted you to be fresh as a daffodil when you got in." My arm snakes around her waist. "I missed you. I love you so much."

And so our little adventure begins.

Hong Kong fulfills all of my expectations. Our shows are great. The fans love our new material. On the day off in-between shows and the day after, we explore the city.

The energy in Hong Kong is hard to describe. It's eclectic. Vibrant. Strange. Street vendors try to sell you custom suits. The luxury shopping centers are insane. The hustle and bustle is like New York on steroids. Around every corner is something unique, whether it's an ancient temple, guys washing windows on bamboo scaffolding, markets with dozens of dead chickens and ducks hanging by their feet, or a man taking his cat for a walk.

Seeing the world through Mia's eyes blows my mind. She's so smart. Almost exactly like Fiona was at her age. Precocious. Confident. A tiny little spitfire. With a sweet, kind soul. Not once has she put up a fuss. Or thrown a tantrum. Or had a meltdown. She's taking our unconventional schedule all in stride.

Fee is in absolute foodie heaven. She has a list of markets, restaurants, and ingredients that she wants to source in every city. Her knowledge about all things culinary blows my mind. She's passed it on to Mia, who eats *everything*. No chicken nuggets for her. She devours Sushi. Eel. Chicken feet. Rooster cones. The most expensive Wagyu beef.

God, I'm eating stuff I never thought was actual food. But I figure, if a four year old can do it, who am I to say no?

The next few weeks follow more of the same pattern. We have our gig. A few days off in whatever city we're in. The three of us relax. Explore. Eat. I've splurged for the highest-end residential multiple bedroom accommodations in each city. With staff to tend to our every need. This way, Mia has her own room. Zeke has his own space.

And, of course, Fee and I have privacy for plenty of naked time.

I'm so addicted to her, it's insane.

Fiona gazes out at the Aegean Sea from the balcony of our master suite, which abuts a tropical garden. Her black sundress flutters in the breeze. Even I'm blown away at the opulence of this particular five-bedroom penthouse apartment. It's stunning. With floor-to-ceiling windows and balconies that extend across the entire seafront. It's ultra-contemporary, decorated in rich caramels and creams. We have our own private elevator. A swimming pool with a waterfall. Jacuzzi. Sauna.

The perfect place for a ten-day hiatus before we head to Australia. Touring Asia is always a bit of a logistics nightmare, because of the distance and time differences between locations. This Tel Aviv show was a last-minute addition, and since it's a fourteen-hour flight to Perth, management built in a long break so we could recharge.

"I think this was my favorite show so far." Fee keeps her gaze on the spectacular sunset when I open the sliding door to join her on the balcony after putting Mia to bed.

I stand behind her and massage her shoulders. Use my thumbs to work out the kinks in her neck. I kiss her nape. Lick the little daffodil tattoo behind her ear. "Mine too. Mia running out on stage made my entire night."

"She's a ham."

"Maybe a future rock star."

"Hmmm." She cranes her neck to the side. The corners of her perfect little pouty lips curve up. Like she knows a secret.

"Every night is the best night when you're here with me." I bend and press kisses along her neck and chin before claiming her lips.

"Silver-tongued devil." She turns and winds her arms around my neck. Clutches my hair. My hand moves along her ass to under her thigh, I hoist it up and grind my cock against her heat. She grips both sides of my face and gazes into my eyes. "Seriously, though. I feel like every moment of our lives has led to this. I'm so fucking happy, Zane."

This is it. This is the moment. I know it. "Hold that thought. I'll be right back."

Like lightning, I zip through the sliding glass door to my Gibson guitar case. When I find what I'm looking for, I'm back on the balcony in about a minute flat.

"I pour my heart out and you run out like you're going to crap your pants. Way to give a girl a complex, Zaney." Fee's pink hair flutters in the salty air. Her eyes sparkle with amusement.

I skid to a stop in front of her and sink to one knee. I open the black velvet box to reveal a five-and-a-half carat natural pink pear-shaped diamond ring surrounded by twenty half-carat round diamonds in a platinum setting. Then I word vomit, true to my nature

"Fiona Reynolds. I married you for the first time when we were six. I'm hoping this ring is a huge upgrade, but there's no one on this planet for me other than you. Every single day we are together makes me happy. Which makes me want to spend the rest of my life making you and Mia happy. I've been waiting for twenty-two years to do this for real. Will you marry me, Fee?"

"Ohmygod. Zane. Are you for real right now?" Fiona sinks to her knees. I take her hand and put the ring on her finger. "Yes! Yes! Yes! I was hoping this is where we were heading. I didn't want to jinx anything, though. Holy crap. We're really doing this for real?"

"Manifestation, baby." I throw my arms around her and kiss her like a boss.

"I'm manifesting you fucking me like your life depends on it." Fee is already unbuckling my belt. She unbuttons and unzips my jeans and finds me hard as a missile. Before I know it, her lips are wrapped around my cock, which she holds at the base with her left hand. Watching my dick disappear into Fee's mouth with her engagement ring sparkling in the twilight is the most erotic fucking thing I've ever seen.

I grip her wrist and cant my hips to thrust harder. She gags a bit but doubles down and swallows. Oh, fuck fuck fuck *fuck*. She deep-throats me and presses my perineum with her thumb. Wiggles it. The combined pleasure is so unbearably fucking intense, that I can't speak. "Arrrghhh ahhhh."

"Come on my face. Mark me," Fee instructs, kneeling back with her eyes closed serenely. She expertly pumps my cock with just the right pressure. Just the right rhythm. I explode all over her lips, cheeks, neck. Dragging my fingers through my come, I feed it to her. Over and over, she sucks and licks until it's all gone.

I grip her shoulders and lay her down on the cool, stone tiles. Careful to cup her head so she doesn't crack her skull open. I'm considerate like that. When she's safely on her back, I gather her dress and pull it up to her waist. Pull her panties down and go to work.

It's the perfect night to experiment with our special sex trick, which makes her come so hard that we only bring it out on special occasions. Most nights usually qualify as a special occasion but tonight's, obviously, a no-brainer.

Anyway, there's a hard-to-find bundle of nerves just past her G-spot. If I stroke it persistently using just the right pressure, she will feel like she's about to pee her pants. She won't, but it's the critical moment for her. She's got to let me keep going. That's the secret. Now's the time I suckle and lap at her pussy. Give her clit a little lick. Stroking. Stroking.

Oh yeah. It's starting. Fiona's entire body shudders. Convulses. Her thighs clamp around my ears.

She's moaning. Keening. Writhing aaaand yep.

There it is.

She squirts her delicious come all over my face.

I lap it up greedily.

Then I get to suckle and kiss her pussy for a long, long while. Half hour. Forty-five minutes. Who knows? Not to give her another orgasm, the one she just had was way too fucking intense.

I'm helping her recover.

Come down a bit before I fuck her brains out.

Eventually, we make our way into the bedroom suite and we go at it like it's our job. Lost in each other's bodies. Intent on giving each other pleasure that matches the extraordinary happiness we feel. Celebrating that we've actually made it past all of the obstacles. She's going to be my wife. I'm going to be her *husband.*

Holy fuck. Fiona's going to be my wife.

Finally!

The next morning, we're wrecked. But we cover it well and break the news to Mia. She's still a little young to fully understand what getting married means. She seems to love the idea of us all living together.

Next, we call my mom, who is predictably over the moon. So is Carter. We save Faye for last, and she gives us the biggest surprise reaction by bursting into tears and apologizing for ever doubting us. It's an emotional start to our day. Things lighten up considerably during our calls to each of the guys. They're all happy for us.

A few days later, on the private jet ride to Perth, we have a band meeting. Collectively, we decide to take a year off to spend time with our loved ones. Recharge and all that. Technically, the vote was three to one against me. I protested, because our new album is kicking ass. I love touring and playing more than anything.

Other than Fiona and Mia, of course. When I grumbled to Fee about it, she reminded me that Meems would be starting pre-K. They wouldn't be able to travel with us if we wanted her to have stability. It occurred to me that I don't want Mia to have an absentee father-figure like Carter was when I was little.

Father figure.

Wow.

Something I haven't discussed with Fiona yet is adopting Mia. As far as I'm concerned, she's mine. Corey fucking Johnson is a distant, shitty memory. He gave up the most precious person on the planet, and I'm grateful to Gus for everything he did to secure her future. Away from that fuckwad and his scumbag family.

Tonight we're in Perth, my girls aren't at the concert. Mia has a bit of a cold, so we decided to keep her away from the germy stadium. It's weird without them here, but I persevere. Connor and I catch the opening set from a cool local band called the Flying Monkeys.

I'm back in my dressing room waiting for my cue to go on stage when the door slams open. Jace comes barreling toward me. "Um, dude? Something you want to tell me?"

I cock my head because, no. No I don't. "What the fuck are you talking about?"

"Just read." Jace shakes his head and hands me his iPad. "Sorry to be the bearer of bad news."

Over the years a lot of shit has been written about me. Mostly, it rolls off my back. Growing up with famous parents had its advantages. My skin is thick. Unfortunately, none of this helps to prepare me for the rage— the utter, venomous rage— I feel when I read what Jace has shown me. I'm about to throw the device across the room and smash it when Jace grabs it from me.

"My dude, take a breath." He grips my arm. "Fiona and Mia are going to need you to keep a nice, cool head. I'm fucking serious."

Oh God. Fee.

She's going to be shattered.

Utterly and totally shattered.

"I need to call Fiona before she finds out."

Jace sighs. "Yeah. I don't know what advice to give you there. I'm of two minds, but ultimately it's your decision."

He leaves and I sit with my face in my hands. My mind races. I need to call my lawyer. I need to get some advice from Carter.

What the *fuck* am I going to do?

My phone lights up. Of course, it's Fee.

FaceTiming me.

We're telepathic that way.

I might as well answer. There's no way for me to disguise something's wrong from her, but I give it a try. "Hey. How are my girls?"

"What's going on?" Fee squints at me.

"Nothing, I just miss you." I paste on a smile. I know it won't work. I do it anyway.

"Zane." A simple, terse statement. She just *looks* at me. The way she looks at Mia when she's trying to steal a cookie. Fiona's got the mom-voice down pat. It's just never been directed my way.

Until now.

"Well… Um. So… Jace was just in my dressing room. I've been served with a temporary restraining order." I shake my head.

There's a loud thunk in the background. Fee holds up a finger and disappears from the screen for a second before returning. "Sorry, the cookbook I was reading fell off the counter. What did you say?"

"A restraining order. It's bullshit. I'll handle it. Fuck. I better just send it to you. Give me a sec." I forward the document to Fee. "When you read it, please stay calm. I'm begging you. We will figure everything out."

She scrunches her nose. "Well, now you're scaring the fuck out of me. Do you want me to call you back?"

"No, I want to be here with you when you read it. We still have about fifteen minutes before we're due on stage."

I wait patiently as she pulls up the article. I try to regulate my breathing when I watch her expression turn from indifference to anger to horror to devastation in the span of the eight minutes it takes her to read it.

She looks up. Tears spill from her eyes. "I've got to get Mia home."

I nod. "I'll cancel the show."

"No!" she bellows. "No. Don't do that."

"Fee, we need to be united on this. We're getting married. We're a family. I'm going to adopt Mia. We're each other's halves. We can get through it. It will be okay." I babble a shit-ton of platitudes in my absolute panic of Fiona abandoning me.

She's pacing now. Back and forth. Saying nothing. I can see the wheels in her head spinning. Someone bangs on my dressing room door. I scream at them to give me five minutes. "Say something, Fee."

"Pull yourself together, Zane. Go play your show. I need to think. Don't make this worse." Fiona shoos me with her hand. "Just call me when you're done."

Then she hangs up.

Let's just say, it isn't my finest night on stage.

I skip out on all of my after-show obligations and Zeke rushes me back to the hotel.

When the door clicks open, part of me is prepared for Fiona to be gone. She's not. She's lying on the sofa with Mia draped over her, asleep. Fee is stroking her dark hair. Watching me intently as I move across the room to her side. I sit on the coffee table in front of her.

"I chartered a plane. We can all leave whenever you're ready. It's fueled up." I reach over to tuck her hair behind her ear. "Don't worry. I'll get the best legal team money can buy."

She shakes her head sadly but resoundingly. "You and I can never seem to catch a break, can we?"

"Don't say that." I hold my hand out to her. "Come to bed."

She nods.

The three of us cuddle in the king bed. Fee and I cling to each other, but don't really speak. There's nothing to say right now. We had no way to plan for this. It wasn't ever part of any equation. She traces my eyebrow with her fingertip. My hand rubs up and down her back.

Almost like we're memorizing each other.

In the morning, Zeke and I take the girls to the private airport, where the jet I chartered is waiting. Turns out, I can't go with them after all. LTZ has three more shows, and I have no choice but to fulfill my contractual obligations. The penalties are too high.

I need to be with Fee.

But I can't cost my bandmates millions of dollars.

I'm in an impossible situation.

All I can do is help Fiona and Mia get settled on the jet. Mia is easily occupied with her iPad watching YouTube cartoons. I wrap my arms around Fee and whisper words of love. Encouragement. Hope. I twirl her engagement ring on her finger and tell her how much I love her. How I can't wait to marry her. How the three of us are a family.

A few minutes later, I'm watching the plane taxi down the runway.

Gaining speed.

Faster.

Faster.

The wheels lift and the plane gains altitude.

Soars high into the sky and gets smaller and smaller until it disappears into the horizon.

Tears stream down my face as I watch it carry the two people I love the most in this world away.

CHAPTER 31

AGE 29

Four years ago, my dad arranged for me to sign paperwork which I thought was ironclad. Bulletproof. Irrevocable. Twelve lawyers reviewed it. Carter's lawyer reviewed it. We filed all the correct paperwork with the court. The judge signed off on it. Everyone said that Mia was mine. That Corey had voluntarily terminated all of his parental rights.

I relied on this advice.

Maybe it was good advice.

Maybe it was shit.

It's hard for me to know. What I do know is that instead of celebrating my engagement to Zane and starting the process of him adopting Mia, I've spent the past four months and fifty thousand dollars of my restaurant fund fighting Corey tooth and nail over every single clause of the termination agreement.

It's a fucking nightmare. An utter shit show of the most mammoth proportions. All because that stupid *Rolling Stone* article triggered some goddamn vendetta Corey has against Zane.

The restraining order was easily dismissed, after all Corey has no say in who gets to spend time with Mia. He's never even fucking met her, for fuck's sake. In fact, he still hasn't even asked to see her.

I'd hoped by the time Zane got back from tour everything would be resolved. But no. It's gotten worse since he returned and moved in with me.

Legal wrangling for sport. Corey and his father's MO.

Just like when Mia was born, keeping me off-balance is their specialty. If I fight, they fight back harder. Dirtier. If I try to play nice, they double down on their demands. If I do nothing, they petition the court. Claim I'm being difficult. Never in my life have I been so terrified. Off-kilter. Unsure. My entire world hangs in the balance.

Because my child's welfare is at stake.

I'm keeping the worst of this from Zane, which isn't what I want to do. I just know he'd worry too much and it's my mess to clean up. I have an expensive shark of an attorney, and I feel like I'm in good hands. Confident we'll get things under control.

"As I mentioned, we have a new wrinkle. For them, it's a hail Mary for sure, but Mr. Johnson has asked that Mia is appointed a Guardian ad Litem to represent her in the custody case." Skylar Morgan, said shark attorney, is going over the latest legal bullshit with me. I'll be honest. I'm distracted by her. She has more style in her little finger than I've ever had in any part of my body. Her sunshine-yellow shift dress looks perfect against her milk-chocolate skin, a multi-colored scarf is wound around her neck in some sort of intricate knot. Louboutin black pumps. White nails. Cropped black hair with perfect contoured makeup.

I'm envious. Some days, the stress of everything makes it hard for me to want to get dressed, let alone put on makeup.

"Why?" I just want this over with. My only focus—and I mean my only focus—is to end this madness before Zane gets home. Any way I can. Every day this drags on is a victory for Corey. He's a vile human. So is his father. They're only motivated by one thing: Winning.

Skylar taps a pen to her lip. "Fiona, it's really one of the only options they have. Ultimately, they want Mia to be represented by someone neutral. Meaning, he or she won't take your side or Corey's side unless there is a compelling reason. Neutral isn't good for us, because you already have full parental rights. Opposing it, however, makes you look unreasonable to a judge. As you can see, if possible, I'd like to avoid this going any further."

"Um, he terminated his parental rights, isn't that fucking compelling enough?" I practically growl. I can't help it. I'm in a legal whirlpool and I want out. "What is the risk exactly?"

"Unless he acts like a total monster, a neutral representative could recommend that Corey—as Mia's biological father—be involved in her life if he wants to be. If that happens, the judge might be persuaded to toe the door open a bit on reinstating his parental rights. It's still a huge long shot for him, but if he's successful you're back to sharing custody and we'll have to work out a custody agreement." Skylar squeezes my hand empathetically "There's a fair bit of paperwork, and if possible, I'd like to avoid him starting that process. We both know he doesn't really want Mia. He wants something from you. Or Zane, more likely."

"And I told *you*, I'm not going to allow me or Zane to be blackmailed."

Skyler shakes her head, clearly frustrated. "Fiona, Zane has money. He wants to adopt Mia. That's why you made this appointment with me originally. We could put an airtight agreement into place that will take things out of family court. One that leaves no room for error—"

"Stop!" I pound my fist on the table, startling both of us. "You said it is virtually impossible to overturn a permanent termination of parental rights. He either has to prove he was *coerced* into doing it or that I provided him false information. We both know he can't prove either. I don't understand why we can't just let him file the petition so we can get the judge to side with us. He just wants me to rack up legal fees while you try to negotiate something he'll never agree to. You'll see. I've been through this before."

Skylar leans back and crosses her arms over her ample breasts. Studies me. As a senior partner in Finney Cooper, the best law firm in Seattle, and a woman who's been voted best family law attorney for five years running, I know I'm in good hands. The *best* hands if we go in front of a judge. But she doesn't know Corey Johnson. Something is going on, and we need to be smarter.

"I get it. Fiona, if you want me to end him in court, I will. I must remind you that the hearings for this type of action are scheduled out at least six months. He'll keep up the shady tactics. The stress you'll be under won't be good for your health."

"The stress will be nothing compared to me looking over my shoulder for Mia's entire life." I slump down on the conference room table. Fiddle with the projector cord. "Skylar, listen to me. Please. Mia's going to start school in the fall. Zane and I are knee deep in building a new business. A club. A new restaurant. I don't want this hanging over our heads forever."

"How does Zane feel about all of this?" She eyes my giant, gorgeous engagement ring.

"As you can see, we're engaged. We want to get married when

he gets back from tour. He wants to adopt Mia. We just want to be a family." Even thousands of miles away, it's all he can talk about when we FaceTime every night.

Skylar regards me like a witness she's about to cross-examine. "Can we have a frank discussion?"

"Is there any other kind?" I brace myself.

Nothing good ever comes from frank discussions.

"Corey's counsel's most recent correspondence indicates Zane beat Corey up in high school and Carter paid the elder Johnson off to avoid prosecution."

"Yes, that's true." I squinch my eyes together in disbelief. "How is this relevant? That was before I even knew Corey Johnson existed. Over a decade ago."

"Be prepared for him to use it against you. He'll claim that Zane is violent and Mia is in danger. As far as reinstating his parental rights, if I'm reading the tea leaves correctly, he's going to claim that you and Zane were together when Mia was conceived. Your father gave him false information to coerce him to sign Mia over to you." Skylar squeezes my hand. "Look. He wants to drag you and Zane through the mud. Is there anything in either of your pasts that will make you look bad?"

I gulp. "Probably."

"Anything that would look bad for Mia's welfare?"

My chest tightens. I mean, how do I answer that question? Doesn't everyone have something in their past that looks kinda sketchy? "What are you trying to get at, Skylar? Please just tell me."

"Zane. He's a rock star. Is there anything from Zane's past that will look bad if he's in Mia's life?" She looks at me dead in the eye.

"Zane and I have loved each other since we were little kids. We've had years where we've been out of touch, but there's no one I trust more in this world. He went through—well rock star phases, but that's all behind him. He's the absolute best person I know." My heart is clenching. How in the world could anyone think that Zane, the sweetest, kindest most talented man on the planet would be harmful to Mia?

Skylar gets up and stands at the window, which overlooks downtown Seattle and Puget Sound. She turns. "It takes one Google search to find out that Zane's father has a notorious history of drug abuse. He nearly died at least twice. LTZ's social media is full of the band—including Zane— drinking, partying. Zane seems to have been in lots of sexual situations. Sex clubs…"

I just stare at her.

"As I said, a simple Google search."

"Stop. This is insanity." I'm so fuming mad I can barely breathe. I hate hearing about all of this shit. Mainly because I'm the one who pushed him into it when he really only wanted to be with me. So it hurts. On so many levels. "Those days are in the past. Zane was single. He and I are together now. *Committed. Faithful*. He hasn't taken a drink or done drugs in *years*. And even then, it was only a little pot."

She shrugs. "I'm not the one judging you. My point is, Corey will use the past to raise concerns about the present. The correspondence from his lawyers is consistent. Every single letter, email, or phone follows the same MO. He's worried about the welfare of his biological daughter, who he was coerced into giving up. She's in danger because her mother is letting known degenerates around her. He wants his rights reinstated. Blah. Blah. Blah."

"It's all bullshit!" My eyes practically bug out of my head. "He's twisting it all around!"

"Fiona, if you're getting this worked up now in a safe

environment,tell me, how will you react at trial?" Skylar crosses her arms. "I'm trying to get through to you. Is having Zane's past dragged into court really the right thing for Mia? For you? We need to settle this. It's too risky otherwise."

Fuck. Fuck. Fuck.

"What do they want?" I feel completely deflated.

She takes my elbow and rubs my arm soothingly. "We won't know until we ask. I can't go down that path unless you authorize me to do it."

"I need to think about it."

"Of course."

Skyler walks me out. We say our goodbyes at the reception counter when a short blonde girl walks past us. She looks very familiar. Like we've met before. I find myself staring.

"Zoey, meet Fiona Reynolds, one of my clients." Skylar gestures to me.

Her eyes widen with recognition, but she covers it with a smooth mask of professionalism. "We've met before at Carter's house. It's been a long time."

"Ohhhh! That's where I recognize you from." She looks beautiful. I give her immediate props for not dropping Ty's name. After all, he wrote an entire album about her. Then again, she's a lot more poised and mature than I remember. "Are you a lawyer now?"

"Yes, I'll be a third-year associate. I set up companies and nonprofit organizations." She smiles politely, but it's clear she's uncomfortable.

"Well, it's nice to see you again, I'm running late so I've got to jet." I wave and head for the elevators. For a minute, I forget my personal hell because I'm dying to tell Zane that I've had a Zoey sighting.

I don't get a chance until a few hours later, after Mia's sound asleep in bed. Zane comes home and kisses me on the head before settling on the couch next to me. “I’m sorry I’m so late. Ty and I had meetings all day about potentially providing all the music on the soundtrack for an upcoming film directed by Don Kircher. Then Carter stopped by.”

“It’s fine, Zaney.” I try to smile, but know I just look stressed and weird.

He takes my hand and brings it to his lips. “Fee, are you okay?”

“I’m scared, in all honesty.” I fill him in on a few of the details of my meeting with Skylar. “It’s hard to decide what to do. I don’t want to get extorted, and that’s what this feels like.”

Zane twirls a lock of my fuchsia hair around his finger. Lost in thought. “I wonder why he’s doing this now.”

“Skylar wants me to consider offering him a settlement.” I can’t bring myself to tell Zane about anything that will hurt his feelings. Not unless I have to.

Zane cuddles me to him. “I’ve been telling you that for months. We could have had this all behind us.”

“I don’t think it’s the right thing for me to do.” I sit up so I can look at him when we’re talking. This isn’t really cuddle talk.

He sighs. Blows a lock of hair out of his eyes. “Fee, don’t you mean ‘*we*’?”

“Zane, you’ve been touring on and off for months. You’re back for the holidays, then out again for three weeks. Honestly? After today, I’m not sure if you being involved is helping or hurting.” I wince after I say it, as truthful as the statement might be, it’s not the real reason.

If I play my cards right, he won’t ever know.

Ever.

“Wow. Okay. Nice one.” Zane furrows his eyebrows.

Fuck. Mission not accomplished. “Don’t take it like that. I can’t risk—”

"*Your* daughter." His eyes reflect a level of pain that makes me catch my breath.

"Zane…"

"No. I'm sorry. You're right." Zane buries his gorgeous face in his hands and then looks up. "Fee, I live with the fact that she's not my biological child every day. I love her like she's mine. We were supposed to be filing paperwork so I can be her dad, instead I'm in danger of losing both of you."

"You're not losing us. We've fought too hard to get here."

He steeples his fingers over his nose. "Then, let me help. I will literally pay any amount of money to make sure Mia is safe. Please? Let's put this behind us. Get our life back on track."

"I'm skeptical. He's already proved he'll just keep coming back to fight just to fuck with me. I think pushing it to a judge is the only way to put an end to all of this."

Zane gets up and paces. He's incredibly agitated. "God, court is the worst thing. He just wants to use it to drag you, me, and the band through the mud. Get a load of publicity. He's a goddamn *parasite*."

"You're absolutely right." I get up and wrap my arms around him. "That's why I've agreed to let Skylar try to work on a settlement. I can't promise—"

"That's perfect, Fee." Zane cups my face with his palms. Pulls my lip with his thumb. Kisses me. Our tongues meet and explore.

I sink into the kiss and he pulls me in tighter. Being in his arms calms me down so much. I reach down and cup his package, his cock awakens at my touch. "Why don't we get some sleep and table this tonight?"

"That doesn't feel like sleeping." He nibbles my earlobe. "Which is perfect, I'm actually in the mood for fucking some sense into you."

The next thing I know, I'm hoisted over his shoulder, firefighter style, as he carries me to the bedroom. He throws me on the bed and yanks down my yoga pants and panties. I kick them off while he unbuckles his pants and steps out of them. His cock stands proudly against his muscled abs. Zane grabs both of my ankles and pulls me to the edge of the bed, then places my calves on his shoulder. Roughly, he grips my hips and thrusts inside.

Pounds into me, using his hands to keep me stationary.

Grinds his pubic bone against me.

Gyrates to get as deep as my body will allow.

Fast and furious. Just how I—we— need it tonight.

"Rub your clit, Fee." He's nearly breathless from how hard he's fucking me. "Pinch your nipples."

I pull up my tank top and do as he asks. My breasts bounce from the force of his movement. My fingers dip to where we're joined and drag more moisture to my little pearl. I circle it feverishly in time to our intense rhythm and I get there.

We both climax with relieved groans.

Our orgasms help dissipate a lot of the tension we brought into the bedroom. He stares down at where we're still joined, his chest heaving. I watch him pull out real slow. Our release seeps out of me. He bends down and laps everything up, licking me clean. Sends me over the edge again.

Because, Zane.

A while later, I'm lying against him, satiated. My cheek is pressed against his chest. His arm is wrapped around my shoulders. I trace his rose tattoo with my thumb. "So what was your meeting with Carter about?"

"Ty wants to create a foundation to help bring music education to kids like him. Kind of formalize what Carter did for him in high school. He wanted our advice."

"Ohhhh realllly." I draw it out. "That's such a coincidence. Guess who I saw today."

"Who?"

"Someone from Ty's past who just so happens to be an expert in setting up nonprofits." I smile up at him.

And just like that, Zane and I concoct a plan.

Our own future might be up in the air for the time being.

Doesn't mean we can't help Carter right a wrong.

CHAPTER 32

TWO MONTHS LATER

Methodically, I rub my fingers along the frets of my old Gibson. Fondle the worn grooves and dings in the body. Every one of them battle scars. Memories of when LTZ was just a concept. I played this guitar at The Mission show. Shit, I've played it at every live show I've done all over the world. Not to mention rehearsals. Sitting on the tour bus jamming with Ty and Connor. Radio appearances. Sometimes just the two of us in a lonely hotel room. You can hear my guitar on every single LTZ song we've recorded.

My guitar is a part of me.

It's one of my limbs.

Someone told me recently it's valued at over half-a-million dollars. Who the fuck cares? To me, it's priceless. I never let it out of my sight.

All that's probably going to change, though.

Today, I learned it's been added to Corey Johnson's settlement demands. Fee texted me from her lawyer's office. She's there this afternoon trying to put an end to the madness. Doing whatever it takes to pay the fucker off so we can get on with our lives.

"Daddy, can we go to the beach?" Mia sits next to me cross-legged, oblivious to what's going on behind the scenes. Every time—and I mean every time— I hear her call me "Daddy," my heart clenches. In every respect of the word, I *am* her father.

Not Corey fucking Johnson, her shithead of a sperm donor.

Who, apparently, is so obsessed with being me, he's demanding my prize possession in exchange for his biological daughter. I mean, who does that?

It's certifiable.

I look into Mia's sweet face with her little bowed lip and push every murderous thought in my head aside. Nothing—not even my Gibson—is worth more to me than this little girl. Today, she and I have big plans.

"Let's make sandwiches first. Peanut butter and jelly or turkey?" I carefully set my guitar on its stand, and we head to the kitchen. I basically live at Fee's townhouse now. We plan to buy something bigger when all of this custody nonsense is over.

"Tu-key. Ju-key. Mu-key." Mia sing-songs behind me. I boost her up onto the counter where she helps me spread the mayonnaise and mustard on the bread. I slap on some turkey and Havarti cheese and we're ready.

It's Monday in the middle of March, and the weather is surprisingly warm. No one is out at Alki Beach, which is a relief. It's rare I don't need to put effort into disguising myself when I'm in public. Mia and I can just be a normal father and daughter today, if all goes well.

Her tiny hand clutches mine on our walk to a bench in front of the volleyball courts. Mia swings her feet and looks out at the water. I watch her. She reminds me so much of Fiona at her age. Long, dark hair. Creamy, milky skin. Red, bowed lips. Tiny black Chucks. Black-and-white checked pants. Red sweatshirt.

A little rocker kid, just like we were.

God, I love her.

"Are you excited for Disneyland, Meems?" I ruffle her hair. Fee and Mia are joining me in LA while LTZ finishes up the soundtrack to *Phantom Rising*, a sure-to-be blockbuster directed by Don Kircher.

"Yeah. I wanna see Cinderella." She grins up at me.

I wipe a bit of mustard from the corner of her mouth. "We can arrange that, sweets."

We spend the day walking on the beach looking for shells. It's one of our favorite activities we do together. Mia puts little treasures in her bucket. She'll use whatever she finds to create different types of art projects later.

I flip over a couple of rocks and she squeals with delight at the tiny crabs scurrying sideways across the wet sand. She chases me with a big piece of kelp and I pretend to be scared. We spot a mama sea lion and her baby sunning themselves on the boulders by the sea wall.

It's an absolutely perfect day.

Zeke is always close by. He's discreet, but I wouldn't care if he wasn't. I don't take chances with Mia's security. Not with all of this Corey shit we're dealing with.

We start walking back to the townhouse a couple hours later when Fee texts me letting me know she's on her way home. She won't feel like cooking after another trying day with her lawyers, so we stop to pick up some fish and chips from Spud's.

Anything to make her day easier.

Plus, delicious.

It's only after Mia goes to sleep that we're able to discuss what happened at her lawyer's office today. Fee curls up against me on the couch. I wrap my arm around her shoulder and kiss the top of her head. Keep her tight against my side. "I love you, Fee and I love Mia. If he wants my Gibson, it'll be worth it. Let him have it."

"No, Zane. We need to talk." She tilts her head up. "Trying to negotiate with Corey isn't going anywhere. I knew it would go this way, it's exactly how he handled this before. He's playing games. He wants five million dollars today. Ten million tomorrow. Today, he wants your guitar."

I shift so we're upright facing each other. "So the fuck what. Let him have it all."

"I *do* worry about it. This entire thing is a shit show." Fee pinches her nose. "I'm eighty grand in. It's time to stop the bleeding."

I take her hand. Caress her smooth skin. "Stop worrying about the legal bills. Let me just pay them. You shouldn't be delving into your nest egg. We should keep that for Mia."

"I know, and I appreciate it. But we can figure that stuff out later." She waves her free hand in the air. "My point is, today Skylar finally came around to my way of thinking. Corey has no interest in settling with me. He's been dragging all of this out just like I said he would. Finally, today she called his bluff. If he really wants custody, he has to file the Petition for Reinstatement of Terminated Parental Rights with the courts instead of using it as a threat. For now, we're all clear. I'm not spending any more days worrying about this. Let's all go to LA and just enjoy ourselves."

I stare at Fee's beautiful, determined face. "Wow. You're a badass."

She rolls her eyes. "Seriously, Zaney, I just want to live my life with you. On our terms. If he files, we'll deal with it then. If you want to adopt Mia, I think we should start getting the paperwork prepared."

"That's the best news I've ever heard." I trace her hairline with my finger, feeling more hopeful than I have in months. "Let's go to Vegas and get married. Then we can file adoption papers right away."

Her face falls. She averts her eyes. I tip her chin toward me so she can't avoid looking at me. "What is it, Fee?"

"You're such a trigger for him." She blinks at me. No judgment. Just truth. "I don't want to poke the beehive until things settle down. I think we should get the paperwork *prepared*, not filed. Let's give it a few months."

My heart falls. "Oh."

"Zane…"

"How is putting our own plans on hold living life? *Marrying* you. *Adopting* Mia." I feel so very agitated. Scared. "We're slipping back into dangerous old patterns."

Fiona throws her arm over her eyes. "I'm just so tired, Zane. My energy is zapped from the stress of all of this. I know you want those things. I want them too. It will happen. Right now we have this. Construction is underway at the Mission. I have my restaurant to work on. I just need to stay focused."

"So you want to postpone the most *important* part of our lives?"

She leans over and pokes her finger in my chest. "No. I. Don't. But us putting all of that in motion right now is not what is best for *Mia*."

"How is us not being a family…"

She puts her finger against my lips. Smooths my hair and gives me a reassuring smile. "Just hear me out. I don't think Corey will ever actually get around to petitioning the court. If we run off and get married, it will be all over the media, no matter how much we try to hide it. We don't need Corey's permission, because he terminated his rights. Adoption is a matter of public record. We'd be just throwing it in his face and he'll react. If we take our time. Plan. Be Fonzie, as you guys all like to say, hopefully we can outsmart him."

Fuck.

Maybe she's right.

The problem is, I have a bad feeling about it. Like Fee's keeping something from me.

My gut is gnawing at me.

It's persistent. Relentless.

Somehow, I know, if we don't act now, I might lose the chance to be Mia's father.

CHAPTER 33

AGE 30

SIX MONTHS LATER

Zane sits on a stool tuning his Gibson, a mess of dark curls hide his face. Ty paces back and forth. Jace tries to act cool, but he keeps his eye on the elevator. Connor is the lone wolf;, he's outside staring down at the Seattle waterfront.

LTZ just finished their sound check. Mom's watching Mia tonight so I could be here for Ty's party to announce his new foundation. This celebration is dope. A private LTZ show for a handful of friends and family, which will be broadcast live across the country on Sirius radio. They've taken over the entire Space Needle Loupe.

Zane startles me when he suddenly looks up from his guitar and shouts, "Shit, happy birthday, Ty!"

"It's a big day, I'm super excited about the kids we're going to help." Ty smiles, but is also distracted by how intently he's watching the elevator.

Jace mutters, "Or, you're super excited by a certain blonde lawyer. I'd tell you to be careful, but I can see you're going down the well again no matter what I say."

The guys banter back and forth like they always do. It warms my heart. Over the years I've watched these men become each other's brothers through and through. Outside of our relationship, Zane is never more fully himself than he is with these guys. Each of them in their own way are truly special. The fact that they've found each other and have spent a decade creating some of the world's most cherished music?

Incredible.

The guys giving Ty shit about—well, anything and everything— is par for the course. Tonight, though, the stakes are a bit higher. I'm told the famous Zoey will be here.

Yes. *The* Zoey.

God, this could be either the best thing to ever happen to sweet Ty. Or a total disaster. I'm pretty sure it was me who put things in motion. Carter—well, he just couldn't stop himself from interjecting himself into the mix after I told him I saw her at my lawyer's office. He's a meddling grandpa, God love him.

Oh well, it's not my business. Ty's a grown man, he'll figure it out.

LTZ puts on an incredible acoustic show. It reminds me so much of the summer before they first went on tour. Sitting around the firepit at Carter's house. All of the sing-songs. Back then, there was no way to know that LTZ would be the most famous band on the planet. It was a bunch of young guys with big dreams.

I had them too. Michelin stars. My own career.

I wouldn't trade Mia for anything, but now, with Zane back in my life, I have my dreams back. They're all coming true.

Zane is *my* dream come true. Always. God. I can't help but stare at this incredible specimen of a man who has been my everything for so long. As if he knows I'm watching, he lifts his head to catch my eye.

Purses his lips. Raises one eyebrow.

I smirk at him.

Telepathic. Our connection grows deeper each day we're together.

I can feel Zane in my bloodstream.

I think back to the days when Zane first showed his aptitude for music. He'd make up songs for me. Play the ukulele while we were on the phone. When we were older, the Gibson replaced the ukulele. Video chat replaced phone calls. As I watch the love of my life strum the final chord of the night, all I feel is gratitude.

Gratitude that this incredible man has loved me for so long.

Gratitude that we've survived so many life-changing events.

Gratitude that he loves Mia like she's his own flesh and blood.

Gratitude that he wants to spend the rest of his life with me—even after enduring all of the absolute shit we went through when Corey was at the height of his custody demands.

It's all died down now. Not a peep from the bastard once I called his bluff. Skylar feels we're in the clear. He had no legal leg to stand on. I'm not going to question it.

Zane and I aren't wasting any time. We're taking our future by the balls. Renovations have started at the new Mission. I'm planning the most incredible menu for the restaurant. Mia started kindergarten last week. We've finished all of the paperwork so Zane can adopt her.

Now all we have to do is set a wedding date.

On the way home, Zane and I sit in the back seat of the Escalade holding hands. He and Connor stayed behind to sign autographs and interact with the fans so Ty could make an escape. He squeezes my fingers. "Ty's still gone for that girl. I hope it works out for them."

I smile and nod. "He's come a really long way. He'll do what's right for him. And her."

"Yeah." He lays his head on my shoulder. "I'm so glad you were there, Fee. We don't have too many shows left before the break."

"Don't say that." I kiss his head. Wrap my arms around him. He's been such a rock for me throughout all of this shit with Corey. I'll do the same for him now. He's still sad about the band taking an entire year off. As much as he wants to be with me and Mia, LTZ is such a big part of who he is.

Zane will discover other parts of himself during his year off, I *know* it. Even if he doesn't right now. I want to give him biological children. Sooner rather than later. He's an incredible father to Mia.

He shifts to look up at me. His soulful eyes are filled with emotion. "Fee—it's been months since you've heard from Corey. I was thinking…"

God, we are so in tune it's scary.

"Yes. It's time. Let's do it." I've never been so ready to finally claim our happy-ever-after than now. We *deserve* this.

Zane sits up. Eyes wide. His body pulses with energy. "Are you serious?"

"I am." I lean over and capture his lips with mine. Wrap my arms around his neck to pull him closer. He grips my waist and yanks me nearly on top of him. We make out like teenagers. Complete with gnashing teeth and bumped noses.

Neither of us care.

Our kisses are passionate. Joyful. Celebratory.

We are all of these things. Every day.

As we near the West Seattle Bridge, Zane comes up for air. Reaches over and presses a button on his armrest. "Drive around for a bit, will you, Zeke?"

Zeke smiles at me in the rearview mirror. The glass shield closes and we have full privacy.

Zane slides his hand up my skirt. I throw my leg over his thighs. Grip his face between my hands. Our lips mash together. Zane slips two fingers inside me, finding me soaking. He scissors his fingers and presses deeper, finding the ridge above my G-spot. His lips fasten on the sensitive skin behind my ear that drives me wild. He licks and suckles. Zings shoot up and down my spine when he wiggles to add that crazy pressure deep inside of me.

Ohmyfucking God.

My hips buck against him immediately. The pleasure nearly insurmountable. Intense. Relentless.

"We can't do that in this car, Zane," I pant-moan because it feels so incredibly fucking good. "I'll make a mess."

Zane just grins and wiggles his digits.

"Zayyyyne…" I keen. Gyrate. Thrust. I have no control. I'm so close to drenching him with my release. Then, just as I'm about to go over, he pulls his fingers out and sucks them clean.

"Ride me, Fee," he mumbles against my lips. Yes! I fumble with his buckle. He reaches down to help, and together we manage to get his jeans open. His hard cock springs free, weeping at the tip. I pump him a few times. Climb over him on the seat and sink down on top of him. He squeezes his eyes shut, moaning, "Fuuuuckkk."

"Yes, I think I will." I place my hands on his shoulders. Cant my hips. Grind my clit against his pubic bone. When I find the exact spot I need, my body shivers uncontrollably. I cry out when he grips my ass to control my movement. He knows exactly how to keep the friction consistent on my clit while his cock hits my G-spot.

Torrents of ecstasy radiate through my entire body.

I give in to his control completely.

My head falls back against my neck as Zane pulls and pushes me against him.

Fast.

Furious.

A profound, vividly supreme celebration. Culminating in the most insane explosion of pure, true love either of us have ever experienced. It's spiritual, Zane and my connection. Every time we make love, it's intensified.

He and I are soulmates. I know that term gets tossed around too often, but for us it is really true. From the time we were born, we were meant for this. Everything we've been through seems predestined to bring us to this point.

He and I.

Mia.

Our children who haven't been born yet.

Everything.

CHAPTER 34

TWO MONTHS LATER

I'm fucking exhausted.

What should have been a relatively benign trip to New York turned into a complete disaster. Ty's still in the city dealing with it for God knows how long. Connor took off for LA to handle his own drama. Leaving me and Jace.

He hasn't spoken a word to me since we boarded our private charter home. He's not mad at me, per se. At least I don't think so. After all that happened on this trip, he's just plain spent.

Yep. The movie premiere for *Phantom Rising* and our private after show in NYC turned out to be quite the dramatic experience.

I tried really hard to keep everyone's spirits up. It was no use. I drove everyone nuts with my gleeful energy. It's so hard for me to control it though. For fuck's sake, I'm walking on air. Ty, Jace, and Connor were all distracted with their own shit the entire time we were in the Big Apple.

Legitimate shit, for sure.

Seriously fucked-up shit, actually.

But I really wanted to share my good news. There wasn't any appropriate time to do it though. When every one of my band brothers was hurting in some way? I can't flaunt my own blissful happiness. I'm not a dick.

Anyway, my big plan was to invite everyone to our wedding, but I never got the opportunity. Fee and I plan to get married in a couple of weeks. We're keeping it on the down-low. Friends and family only. No big announcements. When we get back from our LA Christmas show, she thought we could do an LTZ family holiday party at Carter's and then—wham! A justice of the peace will appear. We'll say our vows with Mia at our side.

Bing. Bang. Boom.

Happily ever after.

Now, I'm not even sure if any of the guys will even *be* in Seattle for the holidays.

I'll be sad if they can't be there, but nothing's going to stand in our way.

If it's just me, Fee, Mia, and our folks. That's fine.

We hit cruising altitude and I fire up the WiFi. If Jace isn't going to be much company, I might as well FaceTime Fee. When I log on, there are half a dozen messages.

Fee: 12:49: Call me as soon as you can.

Fee: 12:51: Call me.

Fee: 12:57: Please, Zane. Call me.

Fee: 1:04: God, Zane. Seriously. I need you

Fee: 1:05: Fuck, I'm sorry. You're on the plane. Call me ASAP.

Fee: 1:10: It's not life and death. But it's really important. I don't want you to freak out. Just call me.

Too late. I'm freaked out. I move to the back of the plane so I don't disturb Jace.

"Fee?" I know I sound frantic when she accepts my video call. "What's going on?"

Her face is streaked with tears. "I just got served."

"What do you mean?" I cock my head. I have no idea what she's talking about.

She holds up an official-looking document. "It's a lawsuit. Corey officially filed paperwork to reverse the termination of his parental rights."

"What the fuck?" The bottom falls out of my stomach. "Are you serious?"

"He wants immediate visitation." She shakes her head. Wipes tears from her eyes fruitlessly. "There's more. Tomorrow I have to appear in court. He's refiling that restraining order against you having contact with Mia until...well, whatever happens I guess."

I can't answer. I can't even comprehend what is happening. My entire body goes numb with fright. The thought of losing Fee and Mia is unfathomable. Not after we've made it through the worst of it.

Or so I thought.

"Zane, I'm so sorry," Fee sobs.

"Shh. Baby. It will be okay," I hear myself say, though everything in my brain screams that life as I've known it has ended. Somehow I've got to be strong for Fiona. And Mia. "We'll fight this."

"Skylar is preparing a response right now. Mom's coming over to stay with Mia. Can you meet me at the law office when you land?" Fiona props the phone against the kitchen counter and shakes out her arms like bugs are crawling all over them. "I just need to be with you."

"Of course. We touch down in about three hours. I'll head right over."

"Okay."

"I love you so much, Fee. Please don't stress. He's not going to win this fight," I say, though I don't know if I believe it.

I gaze through the screen at Fee's heartbreakingly beautiful face. Her lower lip quivers. She bites it, almost like she's annoyed that she's showing any weakness when she wants to be strong. Nods. "I need to get ready. Call me when you land?"

"I will. Text me when you get there. I won't be able to stand not knowing what's happening," I beg.

She grants me a small smile. "Okay."

"Fee?"

"Yeah?"

"Just remember, no matter what, nothing and no one will keep us apart. That's a promise." When I say the familiar words, I mean them with all my heart.

She nods. A tear seeps out of the corner of her eye.

When she hangs up, I stew for an hour. Do some mental KM exercises. Meditate. Visualize the outcome I want in this situation. It calms me. Makes me feel more stable.

Only then do I dial Carter.

He answers on the first ring.

I've had enough. Corey Johnson has pushed me to my limit.

As everyone who knows me eventually finds out, when I'm pushed too far, it's all over.

I'm getting to the bottom of this senseless vendetta once and for all.

Corey Johnson can fuck himself.

No one messes with *my* family.

CHAPTER 35

AGE 30

ONE MONTH LATER

I remember what my dad told me when Mia was an infant. That parenthood is a long game. A mother will do almost anything to protect her child. It's instinctive. My dad had faith I'd make the best decisions for Mia. When we talked about all the fucked-up things my mom did when I was in high school, he respected my mother's process, no matter how flawed it was.

I just hope that Zane will respect mine.

Zane's been distracted since he got back from New York. It hasn't been easy reading the litany of bogus allegations Corey has accused us of. He's used everything Zane did while we were apart as ammunition. Oh, there's a dossier. We're being painted as two people who should never be near any child. The lawsuit was designed to be a very public smear campaign against Zane.

Skylar put an end to that little game.

And the stupid restraining order.

For now, all of this is being kept out of the press.

Records are sealed.

Mia's a minor after all, she doesn't deserve to have to read about this when she's older. That was Skylar's winning argument to the judge.

Thank God.

Zane clomps downstairs from our bedroom. "I just got off the phone with the realtor, we can go out the day before I leave for LA."

"I told you to put that on hold." I sip my coffee. "Until things settle, we're fine here."

"Fee. We are being followed 24/7. We need to move. To protect you and Mia. I'm stressed enough about leaving you here when I go to LA for the holiday show." Zane blows the hair out of his eyes, exasperated.

"No, babe. Mia and aren't moving right now." Zane's eyes bug out a bit. He huffs and sinks into the gray suede couch. Watches me as I bring him a cup of coffee and sit next to him. "We need to talk."

"No good conversation ever happens with that as an introduction."

I smile and take his hand. Rub the top of it with my thumb. I love this man so completely. I'll do anything to protect him from this hell I brought into our lives. "Do you trust me?"

"Implicitly." He closes his eyes and sighs. "Doesn't mean I'm going to like what you're about to say."

"You won't."

But I have to trust my gut.

Mia's the most important thing right now.

Zane and me?

I really hope what I'm about to do doesn't blow up in our face.

CHAPTER 36

ONE HOUR LATER

I trudge up the walkway to Carter's house with my tour duffel and a box of toiletries and personal items. Of course, it's pouring down rain. Of course, I'm drenched. Because Seattle.

Mid-December.

Argh.

I've been working hard to clear my mind of rage. Corey's accusations of drug abuse, sex parties, child endangerment in his lawsuit are outrageous. Salacious. I want to bury the fucker. Find ways to torture him until he backs down. He's fucking with my family and I want to fuck with…

It's just…ahh, fuck it.

Anyway, Fee asked—no told— me to move back in with Carter until the situation calms down. As her lawyer explained it, Corey's challenge to an air-tight parental termination agreement will be nearly impossible.

Except, courts love second chances in parental custody cases.

The stakes are high.

And it will depend completely on the judge.

If Fiona wins, Corey's out of our lives forever. I'll be able to adopt Mia.

If she loses, he'll spend the next fourteen years of Mia's life trying to keep her from me. I get why Fee is pushing me away. She's trying to protect herself and Mia.

But also me.

Funny—but not funny—is how all of this feels like déjà vu. Fee and I have been stuck in this bizarre world of custody bullshit for our entire lives. When we were kids, our parents pulled us apart. I'm not letting history repeat itself.

No way.

Since this shit began with Corey, I've been terrified. Scared of losing Fee again. Scared of losing Mia. I've not been myself. Clingy. Snippy. Out of sorts. I know why, it's because I've acquiesced to everything she's wanted to do, even if I didn't agree with it.

Months ago, when this whole situation started, Fiona asked me if I was still practicing Krav Maga. I wondered why, but it got me thinking. The practice changed my life when I was young.

I'd let my daily physical training fall by the wayside. I came up with a million excuses. Touring schedules. Band obligations. Life in general.

But the truth is, letting my practice slip made me lose perspective. Lose a tool that got me through nearly two decades. I've been getting back in fighting shape. Both mentally and physically. The techniques of visualization, goal setting, positive self-talk, courage, determination, and relaxation are crucial to my well-being.

For fuck's sake, these mental KM skills helped me cope with

everything life has thrown my way.

Being bullied as a child.

When Fee and I were separated in high school.

Creating LTZ.

Dealing with Fee leaving for New York.

Her pregnancy.

Everything.

Now, with the fight for Mia?

I've got one objective:

Stop. Making. A. Fool. Outta. Yourself. Son.

"Jesus, Zane. Get the fuck inside." Carter swings the door open and motions me to start moving.

I plop my stuff in the foyer and peel off my raincoat. "I'm not going to miss this weather. Los Angeles is going to be a nice break."

"How's Fee?" Carter scrubs his goatee with his hand. "You getting through to her?"

"Um…clearly not. I'm moving my shit back in here for now." I drop my duffle, it thunks heavily on the floor. We move to the living room. I sink down into a cushy, oversized, navy-blue corduroy chair.

Carter sits on the adjacent matching chair and pats the arm. "What's going on?"

"Mia's court-appointed guardian ad litem is pushing for Corey to have visitation. He says Corey legitimately wants a relationship with his daughter. I call bullshit, but after everything Fee went through with Gus and Faye, Fiona doesn't want to repeat history. She doesn't want to deprive Mia of having a relationship with her father, if that's what he truly wants."

Carter coughs. Looks uncomfortable. Shifts in his seat a bit. He sighs heavily. "I think she's right to do that, Zane."

Oh shit.

Fuck. I didn't even think…

"It's not the same thing, Carter," I protest. "He willingly terminated his parental rights. Fiona and Corey never were together."

Carter holds up a hand. "I might not be the right one to talk to about this."

"No, I think you're *exactly* who I need to talk to about this." I point at him. "Help me understand what you mean."

He gets up and walks to the big picture window. He doesn't speak for a long time, but I'm patient. Somehow this moment feels profound.

"When I lost custody of you, it made me want to die. Oh, I was already well on my way with the amount of drugs I was using, but it kicked my path to self-destruction into overdrive. When your mom took you to Colorado, it felt like my heart was torn out. Like the light that shone brightly on my life went out. The thoughts of not seeing you killed me."

I bite the inside of my cheek. Dig my nails into my palms.

Let him speak, Zane.

Carter turns to me. "Your mother did the right thing then. And she did the right thing when it was time to send you back to me. When I was ready. When I wasn't a danger to you."

"Do you have any idea how many times I waited for you, Carter? Sat on Grandma and Grandpa's steps like an asshole hoping you'd show up, only to realize you weren't coming?" I choke out. "Only to hear Mom and Grandma fight about what was best for me? I don't want that for Mia."

Carter's eyes grow watery. He hangs his head. "I'll never be able to make that up to you."

"At least, despite all of your bullshit, you actually loved me." I get up and sit beside him. "This Corey fucker doesn't want Mia. If you read the legal documents—and I have—*kill me now*, you'd see he wants to get to me. So I'm really frustrated with Fee. Why does she want to give this guy a chance? *I'm* Mia's father. Not him."

Carter embraces me. No, he bear hugs me which makes me cry.

Release the tears I never cried as a young boy.

Tears for the years Fee and I lost.

Tears for the utter, paralyzing fear I feel right now.

I let it all out. To regain my mental strength for the fight ahead.

"Trust Fiona," he whispers into my ear.

"But..."

"No, my son." He grips my cheeks with his rough hands. Looks me dead in the eye. "Shh. Tomorrow, you're going to go to LA and do your job. However this plays out, you'll be there for Fiona. Whether it's to pick up the pieces or to rejoice at her victory."

My father holds me in his arms. Gives me strength. After a while, I move away and go back to my chair and fall into it. "I want to be the man she deserves, Carter. Fee's been through so much. When I can't help her, it makes me feel useless. Unwanted. Like..."

"Like you felt when you were a boy and I didn't show up."

I nod.

"You are a hundred times the man that I ever was or will be, Zane. Fiona wants you, it's always been you." He sits back down opposite from me. Points at me. Repeats, "Trust her. Follow her lead. It's all going to work out."

I stare at my father. We've come a long way over the past fourteen years. Outside of music industry stuff, rarely has he ever given me personal advice. Truth be told, his track record is terrible.

I get where he's coming from. I know he wants to help me feel better. Like a good father.

The thing is? I already trust Fee. Implicitly.

I don't need Carter to tell me that.

But follow her lead? Sure. Because Fee needs to feel like she's in full control. Especially during tough times. It's why I moved out without arguing. It was a mistake, though. Because now, more than ever, it's time for her to learn she can rely on me.

Every fucking time.

By the time I get back from LA?

She won't ever question it again.

CHAPTER 37

AGE 30

TWO DAYS LATER

It took a herculean effort to get here undetected.

No one knows I'm here. Other than my mom, who is watching Mia tonight.

Oh, and Ronni Miller. When I texted her a few days ago, she offered to fly me to Los Angeles. So I could be here for LTZ's final show before hiatus. She's had plenty of her own misogynistic assholes to deal with in her life and was more than happy to help me thwart mine.

In any case, there was no fucking way I'm missing this concert. Zane tries to play it off, but I know he doesn't really want a year off. He's fearful of the band splitting up. Add in everything that's going on with Corey. And me telling him to move in with Carter? Well, he's spinning.

He needs me.

At least my energy.

He'll know I'm here.

But I can't let him see me. Too risky. Too many eyeballs on every move I make.

While the guys' families get settled in the bleachers next to Zane at stage left, I slip undetected to the other side. I wear black from head to toe, including a black skull cap to hide my pink hair. Fake cat-eye glasses with clear lenses. I stand in the shadows to blend in with the rest of the industry executives who are lucky enough to be back here.

Ronni spots me. Nods discreetly.

Then looks away.

She's a badass bitch disguised by a sweet face and singsong voice.

You can feel the entire building pulse with energy. Everyone here is pumped to see LTZ. They've been promised a very special show.

One for the record books.

Connor lopes past me. Stands so close I can hear him breathe. He waits for his stage cue. If he looked down, he'd be staring at my head. I doubt Ronni would rat me out. Still, my heart pounds. I will myself to be invisible, while also trying to get a glimpse of who I came here to support.

Maybe it works, because Connor doesn't give me a second glance.

Phew.

All of LTZ's friends and family are on the opposite side of the stage. Suddenly, they become more animated. Ah, the other three are on the sidelines now. Ty and Jace joke with an older couple. Zane's off to the side with Carter, bouncing on his toes. Everyone seems to be in good spirits.

Then the venue goes black.

Completely and totally black.

I can't see a thing.

My heart stops when a single, blue spotlight shines on Zane, who is now alone on stage. Sitting on a stool, completely focused on the music he's creating. His fingers expertly dance along the frets as he plays a beautiful flamenco guitar solo that I recognize. He's been working on this piece for months. It blends perfectly with the backing track, a recorded sound of a river.

Everyone in the building, especially me, is completely enraptured.

Zane builds up his intricate melody from soft and feathery to dynamic and soulful. Heartbreaking. Joyful. His skill on the instrument is mind-boggling. I can't help but remember all the times he played songs for me growing up. How I've been the only one in this world to witness his evolution as a musician from the start.

He's effortless. Engaging. Completely immersed in what he's playing. His full lips part and close. Sneer and smile. Purse and curl. His eyes squeeze shut. His eyebrows raise and squinch. His face is a map of emotion as he coaxes the most beautiful sounds from his guitar.

I've never seen anything more riveting in my life.

Then the river sound fades. The lights begin to flicker. Sparkle.

Blues.

Greens.

Purples.

Aquas.

All the colors dance around the stadium. Almost as though we've been plunged into a pool of the most crystal-clear water. The effect is breathtaking.

Zane rarely allows himself to be the sole focus of LTZ. He's always conceded the top spot to his best friend, Ty. When I see him out on stage. On his own. It's where he belongs. He's the prodigy turned virtuoso.

I'm staring at him so hard my eyes are drilling a hole into the man I love with all my heart. I can't help it.

I love you. You're my other half.

The second I have the thought, he looks over. Right to where I'm standing. Like he *knows* I'm there with him. He turns and smiles at the crowd. Plays to the audience. He morphs his solo into little teasers of the opening notes for *Butterfly*. Just enough to make the crowd hold their breath...

Will he play it?

No, it's something else.

Wait, is it....?

Zane draws it out. Launches into an impossibly complicated run, then dramatically raises his hand above his head and throws the pick into the crowd. He flutters his hand around in the air like he does when he tells his Flea/Fly story to Mia, and stops when he's reached the neck of his guitar.

All is quiet as the lights go black again. Only for about five seconds until Zane starts the actual intro to *Butterfly* and a white light beams to the back of the venue. Like lightning, it pulls back revealing the entire band on stage with 3-D butterflies in every color of the rainbow, fluttering and flying around them.

Zane tried to describe the light show they had planned to me, but it doesn't do the actual experience justice. I've never seen anything like it. Despite all the trauma we're dealing with, Zane put his own needs aside to create this special moment for Ty.

His brother.

But I realize, also for himself. For me. Mia, too.

God, I love this man more than words can ever express.

Coming here was the right thing to do. I stay for the entire show before a car whisks me back to the jet, which is waiting to take me back to Seattle. If circumstances were different, I could be on Zane's arm at the after party.

Oh well. Hopefully, there will be plenty of other opportunities.

Although Zane's worried, I know LTZ isn't done. There's no way this will be their last show.

I settle back against the tan leather seat and shut my eyes. It's only a short flight back to Seattle, I should be in bed before midnight. I'll be there in the morning to feed Mia breakfast. We reach cruising altitude when the text comes in.

Zane: I know you were there Fee. I felt you.

Fee: ???

Zane: I fucking love you.

Fee: I fucking love you too.

Zane: I'm trying to understand. To trust.

Fee: I know.

Zane: We should be together right now.

Fee: I want to, but I can't risk it.

He doesn't respond.

I don't blame him.

It's better this way, though.

He'll see.

CHAPTER 38

AGE 30

PRESENT DAY

Fiona presses her lips to mine. Slips her tongue into my mouth. I savor her. One day is too long not to kiss my girl, let alone three weeks. My hands trail down her sides. Reach around and cup her ass to haul her against my throbbing, needy cock.

"I'm not staying away from you a minute longer, Fee." I pepper kisses along her jawbone. "I won't let anyone keep us apart. I know why you wanted me to leave. And I do trust you. But, you need to trust me too."

She rakes her nails through my hair. Her pouty lip trembles. "Zane. Stop. You're the person I trust the most in this world."

"I didn't expect you to be here. Where's Mia?" I say through kisses.

"In bed. Mom's watching her. I stashed her Christmas presents here. You know how insane she is this time of year. There's no safe hiding place."

I chuckle at the thought of little Mia, the scamp, unwrapping all the gifts under the tree last year. Three days before Christmas. I should be there for all of this. Not being with my girls isn't an option.

Ever again.

"We are spending the holidays together. You should have been at Ty's tonight, Fee." I press my lips to the hollow of her neck and lick and suckle the area that drives her mad. Press my knee in between her legs. She bucks against me.

Then pulls away. Abruptly.

"Just be patient. The hearing is coming up in a couple of weeks." She rubs her hands on her thighs. Almost like she's trying to get control back. "He's watching everything I do. Who knows what will happen if he sees you at the townhouse."

"He's not going to win, Fee. I promise you that."

"If he truly wants to be in Mia's life, Zane, you know that I have to make peace with it." She crosses her arms over her chest, almost protectively. "I'm just trying to keep you out of the mix right now. Take away the one thing that seems to be fueling this. Which is *you*. It's not forever. It's not permanent. Please stop worrying."

I close the distance she's put between us. "I'm not worried about that anymore. Not in the least. What if I told you that I hired my own investigator the day after you made me move out."

"You *what*?" Fiona narrows her eyes with anger. "How could you risk Mia like that? Skylar was adamant that we play this clean. Not to stoop to his level."

"Well, she was wrong." I'm defiant, but rightly so. "Maybe in normal circumstances, her advice would be right. Not with Corey Johnson. You're almost a hundred grand in, Fee. I've stepped aside for too long when we should be working as a team. Now that I know what I know…none of this would have gotten so far. We wouldn't be split up for no fucking reason. Again."

"It's not about the money. You know I'd spend any amount of money to protect Mia." Fee's chin juts out.

"Well, so would I. And I have."

She stares at me. I don't back down. Eventually, her face softens. She blinks up at me. "I wasn't trying to exclude you. Don't you understand that?"

I pull her to me and hug her with all my might. "I do understand, Fee. More than you know. Because I will do *whatever* it takes to protect the *both* of you. I'm just not scared of Corey Johnson. Or his bullshit threats."

"Tell me what you've found out."

"I'll do one better. Let me show you."

"Zane, I don't have a lot of time. I need to get back home." She breaks free from my embrace and heads back toward the office. "I've got to get Mia's presents under the tree."

"It will just take a second." I pull out my phone and open up the Dropbox files. She virtually flips through the document. Her eyes wide. Every now and then she looks up at me and shakes her head with disbelief.

When she is finished, she stares at me slack-jawed. "Okay, well, holy shit."

"I'll add you to the folder. You can send them to Skylar in the morning." I can't help but gloat, just a little. "I can't believe he's been willing to go to this amount of effort, all because of a chick he crushed on back in high school set her sights on me. Seems a bit extreme, no?"

"It's sad." Fee's shoulders hunch in. "The idea that he'd get back at you by doing what he did. It's batshit."

I step toward her and pull her into my arms. "I'm just sorry that he took it so far. My PI dug up so much information on his father's shady business dealings, I wouldn't be surprised if the entire thing is dropped before the New Year."

We kiss. Touch foreheads.

"Thank you." Fee wraps her arms around my waist and presses herself against me. "I never even thought to go after his dad."

"Disarm your enemy. By any means possible," I whisper in her ear. "Finding the emails about my stupid band room hookup? Well, that was just a bonus. And at least now we know why. I hope he gets the help he so obviously needs."

Fee nuzzles my neck. "Anyone would choose you over him, Zaney."

"Let's get Mia's presents to the car before I fuck you right here and now." I step away from my greatest temptation.

I follow her back to the office where she has a bit of a gift-wrapping station going on. We grab the packages and load them into her trunk. By the time I lock up the space, she's already seated in the driver's side of her car, starting the engine. Carter and my mom peer at us from behind the windshield of the Audi.

I wave at them and jump into the passenger side of Fee's Toyota.

"Zane, you know you can't come back to my place. Not right now." Fee sighs. "I'll send the stuff to Skylar tomorrow, we'll need a few days to sort—"

"Nope. We're done hiding. The three of us are spending Christmas together. With our families. Like normal people. Then tomorrow evening, we'll take Mia over to Connor's house for sherry trifle." I take her hand. "I'm not wasting one more minute, Fiona Reynolds."

I turn toward the passenger side and signal Carter to roll down the window. "I'll text you Fee's address. Be there tomorrow around eight a.m."

My mom smiles. Waves.

Carter drives off.

"Are you sure you know what you're doing, Zaney?" She leans back in her seat and shuts her eyes. "Even after seeing all of that evidence, I'm scared. He always seems to find a way to torture me."

"I promise I do. Let's go home. I'll take care of you tonight."

"I want that so much." Fee cups my cheek before backing out of the parking space and turning the car toward West Seattle. She glances at me when I reach over to massage her neck. Leans into my hand.

My strong, feisty girl is more than capable of doing anything in this life.

I'm just not going to let her do it alone.

Never again.

Our lives are meant to be lived together. Through thick and through thin. Through the good and bad parts. Through the ups and downs.

Through all the times of our lives.

Especially now, when the stakes are the highest.

We're not trodden-down cowards. She and I are warriors. We've fought too hard to be together to let some loser use a one-sided vendetta to fuck up the life of my other half. And my daughter.

I'll be right there by their sides. For now. For always.

She pulls into her garage and stops the car.

"I've got you, Fee." I squeeze the back of her neck gently. "Believe."

She looks deep into my eyes.

"I do."

"So we're in this together? From now on?"

She grabs my T-shirt and pulls me toward her. Her lips dance against mine. “Fuck yeah.”

“Thank God.”

EPILOGUE

TWO MONTHS LATER

I've been lulled into a state of relaxation I don't think I've ever had in my life. We're surrounded by a garden of lush, tropical plants. Mango trees. Hibiscus flowers in a myriad of pink, purple, and orange. A waterfall spills over rocks into the infiniti pool that overlooks a vast white-sand beach.

The Pacific Ocean gently ebbs and flows against the shore.

Mia and Zane are building an insane sand castle. She's very intent on building a huge turret. It's a race against time, the sand dries so fast in this heat. When the inevitable happens and it crumbles, Mia starts to cry. Zane rubs her arms from shoulder to fingers. Takes her little hands in his and shows her how to breathe.

Her tears give way to giggles in minutes.

She throws her arms around him and he kisses her whole face. Takes her hand, they're on their way back to me.

Watching the two of them together like this makes me so grateful that Zane stepped in to save me from myself. He brought our family together when we could have easily been torn apart.

"Did you see our sandcastle, Mama?" Mia is about to launch her sandy little body on top of me when Zane catches her in midair.

He carries her to the outdoor shower and turns it on. "Get the sand off yourself, Meems."

They rinse the sand off. Zane sits next to me and Mia nestles close to me on the lounger. "It was beautiful, were you sad when it crumbled?"

"Yeah, but Daddy told me that we'll build a new one tomorrow."

My heart. Zane will officially be Mia's daddy next week. For now, we're in Maui. At our new seven-bedroom beachfront house. The one we purchased with the settlement money Corey's father paid us to avoid further legal trouble.

The entire LTZ crew is here with us.

So are our families.

In a few short hours, Zane and I are getting married at sunset. With the people we care most about surrounding us. In many ways, it's just a formality. A ceremony to make what we've always known official.

Zane and I have that once-in-a-lifetime kind of love.

The kind of love that is innocent.

Yet also decadent.

Wanton.

All-consuming.

The kind of love that endures.

Through separation.

Misunderstandings.

Mistakes.

Our love is *everything*, and it will endure in this lifetime and in the next. I know this because what we have is something few people in this world ever get to experience.

A love that is timeless.

THE END

If you loved TIMELESS – I want to give you a FREE gift of RESTLESS,

the **FREE Prequel Novella NOW**

CONNECT WITH KAYLENE

If you have a couple of minutes, PLEASE leave an honest review! It really helps self-published authors like me to spread the word!

Keep Reading for an excerpt of ENDLESS (Ty & Zoey's story)

ABOUT THE AUTHOR

When she was only 15, Kaylene Winter wrote her first rocker romance novel starring a fictionalized version of herself, her friends, and their gorgeous rocker boyfriends. After living her own rock star life as a band manager, music promoter, and mover and shaker in Seattle during the early 1990s, Kaylene became a digital media legal strategist helping bring movies, television, and music online. Throughout her busy career, Kaylene lost herself in romance novels across all genres inspiring her to realize her life-long dream to be a published author. She lives in Seattle with her amazing husband and dog. She loves to travel, throw lavish dinner parties, and support charitable causes supporting arts and animals. The Less Than Zero Seattle Rocks Series is her debut in the world of Rock star romances. Kaylene hopes you'll love the gorgeous, sexy, flawed rockers and the strong, beautiful women who capture their hearts.

Email: kaylenewinterauthor@gmail.com
Website: www.rockerromance.com
Kaylene: https://www.instagram.com/kaylenewinterauthor/
Reader Groups: https://www.facebook.com/groups/rockromance/
Bookbub: https://www.bookbub.com/profile/2883976651
Goodreads:
https://www.goodreads.com/author/show/20367389.Kaylene_Winter
TikTok: @kaylenewinter
Twitter: @kayleneromance

BEHIND THE SCENES
LIMITLESS EDITION

I can't believe we've come to the end of the first installment of the Less Than Zero rockers!

Yes, you heard it first – the first installment!

As you know, at the end of each of my books I love to ramble a bit. Pontificate a little. Share a few thoughts. So, here we go!

A year ago, I released ENDLESS and had no idea where my author journey would take me. In one short spin around the sun, the experience has been so much more than I ever dreamed. It's all because of YOU! Yes, you – the readers who have shown me such love and support.

Thank you.

Let's get into Zane and Fiona, because man. I love these two so much.

First of all, I very deliberately dropped only a few hints about Fiona because she's probably the most like the women I knew from the Seattle music scene. Effortlessly cool. Extremely sensitive but strong. Hard working. Beautiful. Fiercely loyal. You may remember in ENDLESS, Fiona was described as having black hair. When I "cast" Fiona with Sophia Tomlinson, she had recently dyed her hair a deep purplish pink. I LOVED it and that is why Fiona dyed her hair in TIMELESS.

As for Zane, he's always been very special to me. Probably because I had the opportunity to work with so many well-known musicians throughout the years, I loved the idea of making Zane rock royalty – the son of someone famous from that time in Seattle's history. Because unlike a lot of the Hollywood celebrity kids, the Seattle kids who have celebrity parents are grounded. Humble. Sure, they have a lot of advantages in life. Privilege, you might even say. But seriously, every one of them are caring, loving, accepting and GIVING individuals. It's who we are in Seattle. Oh, before I forget, when I met Enrico at our photo shoot, I learned he is a master at Krav Maga – is an instructor coveted all over the world. I HAD to bring it into this story.

And no, Zane and Fiona are not based on anyone real. None of my characters are. I'd never do that. Ever.

Ahem. So, back to Zane and Fiona. God, haven't we all tried to outsmart our parents? To avoid making the perceived mistakes they made in raising us. Mistakes in decisions. Mistakes in their actions --- or lack of action. Anyway, the reality is EVERYONE makes mistakes and the question is, how can you overcome them? How can you allow someone to grow and evolve and fuck up, yet love them anyway?

In TIMELESS, I wanted Zane and Fiona to try to navigate their long distance relationship differently than the other couples. They saw what happened to Carter and Lianne and decided to give each other permission to be "free" when neither of them really wanted that. It seemed logical to try and avoid what happened in both of their broken homes, right? I think when people are young and have their whole lives in front of them, they don't have the necessary perspective to make fully-baked decisions. I know I was that way in my late teens and early twenties – boy I thought I knew everything.

And then you learn. And learn to deal with challenges together. As a couple. At least, that is what Zane and Fiona figured out. They were always better together. They were always each other's other half.

Anyway!!! Don't despair, you haven't heard the last of the LTZ couples yet. Audiobooks are coming!

And—. Each couple will get an ENCORE! I always find when I really love a book, I'm sad when it ends and wonder what happened to that couple and where they are now. I'm excited to learn about what happens to all of our LTZ rockers and their sig others, aren't you? Stay tuned for more news on that front.

From there, I'll be creating all sorts of LTZ spin-off worlds—including the McGloughlin brothers – yes! Each of Connor's brother's will be getting their own book! I have a lot of other tricks up my sleeve so make sure you sign up for my newsletter and follow me on social to be first to learn about it all.

Words cannot express how much it means to me that you've read this book and this series. I hope you have loved this first installment as much as I've loved writing it. If you haven't received your free book, please make sure to sign up for my mailing list and get it free here: RESTLESS.

Until next time,

Love, Kaylene

ACKNOWLEDGMENTS

This book was an absolute labor of love, and I couldn't have done it without the help and support of the following awesome rock stars:

Cover/Graphic Designer/Finder of hotties: Regina Wamba https://www.reginawamba.com/

Editor: Grace Bradley—https://gracebradleyediting.com/

Proofreading: Letitia Delan

Formatting: Cat at TRC Designs

Photo Crew: Debbie Murphy, Elena Chavez, Art of Shock, Laura Murphy

Executive Assistant: Krisha Maslyk

PR: Next Step PR (Kiki, Anna, Colleen and team!!) - https://thenextsteppr.org/ (LINK)

Website Maven: Sublime Creations https://www.sublimecreations.com/ (link)

Zane: Enrico Ravenna - Instagram: @enrico.ravenna
Fiona: Sophia Tomlinson Instagram: @_sophiatomlinson_

To two of my rockstar romance author inspirations who let me insert characters into Zane & Fiona's book:

- Jaine Diamond – Ashley Player
- Kenna Shaw Read – Flying Monkeys

My VIPs/Readers/Alpha and Beta Readers Sheila, Kris, Beth, Anna

OMG! To the readers, bloggers, bookstagrammers & my readers – I can't do this without you.

Thank you thank you thank you for helping spread the word—I'm overwhelmed by your love, support, kindness, etc. Thank you for making my dream come true!

OTHER TITLES BY KAYLENE WINTER

ENDLESS – LESS THAN ZERO Book 1 (Ty & Zoey)
"An absolute Rockstar Masterpiece!" – Anna's Bookshelf

LIMITLESS – LESS THAN ZERO Book 2 (Jace & Alex)
"#Utterperfection!" – The Power of Three Readers

FEARLESS – LESS THAN ZERO Book 3 (Connor & Ronni)

"I gave this book five stars which is something I only do when the story is perfect." - Maday Dearmus (BookBub - 5 Stars)

TIMELESS – LESS THAN ZERO Book 4 (Zane and Fiona)

RESTLESS – LESS THAN ZERO PREQUEL NOVELLA (Carter & Lianne)
"Rockstar Story, Rockstar Writer!" – Karen C

ABOUT THIS BOOK

Get ready for the gorgeous rockers of Less than Zero and the strong, feisty women who bring them to their knees.

TIMELESS

I vowed nothing would keep us apart...

Fiona Reynolds is my other half.
It's been that way from the day I was born.
I've dedicated my life to keep my promise.
Fate just laughs in our face.
She's always out of reach, this time for good.
I'll do anything to prove she's my destiny.
If only she'd trust me one more time.

After what I've done, how can I deserve him?

Zane Rocks is my everything.
There's no one I love or trust more than him.
It wasn't his fault when he left me.
I always knew he'd find his way back.
Fear overwhelmed me, and I broke his heart.
Will most celebrated musician on the planet.
Really give me another chance?

When a rash decision changes their lives forever, hope for their future is all but shattered.

Stakes are high.

But Zane's determined to prove a love this pure is timeless

DEDICATION

G—you are my biggest supporter and push me to be better in everything that I do. Thank you for encouraging me to follow my dream and publish my first book.

To Sheila and Kris, the inspirations for Alex and Ronni—before digital, before Kindle, back when we still typed on real typewriters—who knew that the book I wrote about all of our rock star "boyfriends" would lead us here.

EXCERPT FROM ENDLESS

PROLOGUE

I burrowed into my delicious rocker's side, breathing in his manly scent, a mix of leather and grapefruit body wash. I reached up to carefully brush a long, chocolate-brown wave from Tyson's full lips while he slept deeply. His long, silky hair cascaded over the pillow; his square jaw was covered with the beginnings of a beard because he hadn't shaved in a few days. It made my sweet rocker look slightly dangerous. Gazing at the three small scars nearly hidden in his thick, dark eyebrows, I still couldn't fathom how tough his childhood was and how anyone could hurt such a beautiful soul.

My breath hitched. I tried to memorize everything about him, to soak in every detail of my gorgeous man. I knew I was about to hurt him, and it destroyed me. When I traced my finger over a smattering of his rough stubble, he sighed in his sleep and pulled me in even closer. I held him tightly too, resting my head on his lithe but defined chest and gripped his hip, careful not to rouse him. I wished I could gaze into the pools of his deep-blue eyes one more time.

If only I didn't have to leave him.

I was moving to Bellingham to embark upon my new normal, living with a roommate in a dorm and working toward my college degree in social services. Ty's band departed for their first tour in a few hours, traveling cross-country in a small van for six months. Letting him sleep was important. It would be grueling enough spending long hours in such cramped quarters without the added weight of heartbreak. The least I could do was let him get some rest now.

So I laid for as long as I could against my love and listened to his heartbeat. My mind was a hamster wheel. Second-guessing. Third-guessing. Then—resolved. I had been asked by possibly the most influential person in his life to do something for Ty. For his future. As much as I didn't want to, leaving him now was the right thing for me to do. But it didn't make it any less devastating.

When my tears wet his chest, I knew it was time to go or I'd wake him. My heart seized in agony at the thought of never seeing him again. I wasn't sure how I'd survive. Yet, I knew that I had to set him completely free, without any ties to me, so he could embrace his shot at fame.

Maybe someday Ty would understand why I left him.

Maybe someday he'd forgive me.

CHAPTER 1

FIVE MONTHS PREVIOUS

"C'mon!" Alex pleaded with me. "We're going to be late!"

"I can't help it if I need extra time, you look amazing in a paper sack," I whined to my best friend since diaper-hood.

Even though my family had moved from Ballard to a big, renovated craftsman in the Wallingford neighborhood when I was eight, Alex and I spent time together most weekends and nearly every day during the summer. Our neighborhoods were close enough that we retained our sisterly bond, which was so tight we could finish each other's sentences. Now, with only a few weeks to go until graduation from our respective high schools, all we did was obsess over music and boys, sometimes not in that order.

Which meant on a Saturday night, as per our usual routine, we got ready at my house to go out for the evening.

"You look gorgeous, you always do." Alex surveyed my outfit, her hands on her hips. Tall and thin with supermodel beauty, my BFF looked fantastic in her simple getup of a black, V-neck fitted T-shirt, baggy boyfriend jeans with a beat-up brown belt holding them up, hoop earrings, a distressed, black motorcycle jacket, and black motorcycle boots. Her blonde hair styled with fringy bangs was effortlessly tussled as though she'd spent hours on it, when really all she did was run her fingers through it a few times.

I sighed, studying my image in the full-length mirror. As a short and slightly voluptuous girl, I tried to accentuate my curvy assets. Tonight, I wore a casual outfit of skinny black jeans with shredded knees, my favorite black, flat, suede knee-high boots, and a vintage Van Halen T-shirt with the sides and back cut out in a crisscross pattern, which gave a glimpse, but not full view, of my D-cup boobs.

"Well, this is as good as it's going to get." I shook out my long, thick blonde hair streaked in beachy waves, and turned to check out how my butt looked. I loved my curves, and thanks to the Kardashians normalizing a bit of tits and ass, I could hold my own even if I couldn't be bothered to paint on a perfect Instagram contour.

"Thank God, the Uber is here." Alex swooshed out of the room and bounded down the stairs, with me following close behind.

We had been waiting all week for tonight's show at The Mission, an iconic Seattle all-ages venue, which launched the grunge era over two decades ago. My parents had met there at a Limelight show, so they were surprisingly cool about my acute love of live music. The club, which lacked in charm, still featured an awesome lineup of up-and-coming bands and we loved nothing more than to experience live music up close and personal.

Even better, we were finally going to see Less Than Zero, a throw-back rock band that made actual real music and didn't rely on auto-tune or fancy production. We'd been obsessed with their YouTube channel and Instagram account because of all their hot pictures and crazy video snippets. Their music was amazing, driven by screaming guitar riffs, anthemic lyrics, and groovy beats. It also didn't hurt that all the guys in the band were tasty, tasty snacks.

"Are you staying over tonight, Alex?" my dad called out as we bounded past him in the living room.

"No, Mr. Pearson." Alex stopped to address him. "Mom and I have plans early tomorrow morning."

Alex's mom and dad were divorced, and she lived with her hilarious mother who had a successful mail-order pie business. If her sense of humor wasn't reason enough to hang out at her house, we were guinea pigs for her kitchen experiments, which turned out some delicious food. Her dad, a developer who had remarried, lived on Bainbridge Island, a suburb across Puget Sound.

"Alex, how many times do I need to tell you to call me Mike," Dad chastised good-naturedly. "Are you off to The Mission, then?"

"Yep!" I bopped over to give him a kiss on the forehead. "I'll be home by midnight."

"How are you getting home?"

"Jeez, Dad. Stop interrogating me like a lawyer. You know I'll take an Uber." I rolled my eyes. For God's sake, I was a dedicated 4.3 GPA student, it was annoying that he didn't think I could figure out a ride home.

"Zoey, I'm glad you're finally getting out of the house, you've earned some free time to go out and be more social." Dad hugged me. "I'm just happy you're not buried in books for a change."

"Is Mom home tonight?" I ignored his annoying comment. My

mom, Olivia, traveled a lot for her job as a pharmaceutical sales manager. She was flying in that night from a conference in Miami.

"Yes, I'm going to pick her up in an hour." Dad smiled cheekily. They were still so in love, I hoped to find that for myself someday. Maybe when I was thirty.

When we finally made it through the long line into the divey, dark club, Less Than Zero's melodic, guitar-driven, ass-kicking rock was already in full force. As was our usual M.O., we pushed our way to the front of the stage so we could see the band in action and, of course, dance. Our bodies couldn't resist moving to the music. LTZ was on point. By the time they launched into their third song, I felt electrified. The energy in the crowd was intense, as if we all knew we were witnessing something special.

All the guys in the band looked hot in the videos and pictures we had been poring over on YouTube and social. LTZ in person? Other-worldly.

Drummer, Jace Deveraux, played shirtless, lean with taut muscles, intense, piercing green bedroom eyes, and sexy dirty-blond hair that brushed just past his shoulders. He thrashed hard yet kept the most complicated groovy rhythm, his mouth moved in time to the beats he played.

Zane Rocks, a pretty boy with an infectious grin, dark-brown eyes, and a mop of jet-black, unruly hair that didn't quite reach his collar, played lead guitar. He bounced all over the stage but managed to make eye contact with everyone in the crowd, drawing them in. Effortlessly channeling classic Slash and Eddie Van Halen, his natural skill translated into his own unique sound.

Bassist Connor McLoughlin was the hottest ginger I'd ever seen, his thick, curly reddish-brown hair hung well past his jaw. He stared into the crowd with light, golden-brown eyes that were brooding and almost dangerous. Ropy, thick muscles bulged underneath his vintage Alice in Chains T-shirt. He was cool AF, popping and thumping in perfect rhythm with Jace's percussion.

As hot as the rest of the LTZ guys were, lead singer Tyson Rainier was the most magnificent-looking guy I'd ever seen in real life. His chiseled, square-jawed face with just a hint of stubble made him look like a young, rogue biker. His gorgeous long, brown hair hung in loose waves. He swung it wildly, scanning the crowd through sapphire-blue eyes rimmed with dark, long lashes. His lithe yet muscular body rocked tight skinny jeans and a frayed, fitted white V-neck. He stomped around the stage like a throw-back grunge rocker in duct-taped, forest-green Doc Martins. Ty's voice was mesmerizing—a mix of soaring range, complicated and unique lyrical phrasing, wolf-like growls, and passionate, emotional delivery.

He figuratively and literally mastered the stage and the audience, and I was hypnotized by him. There was no way not to stare. To me, he was passion personified. My body was consumed with what felt like an intense, gravitational pull.

While I was gaping at him, the beat changed to a slow, sultry low groove. At that moment, he looked down from the stage directly into my eyes. Like a lightning bolt, his look caused a *zap* straight to my core. My heart thumped so fast. I wouldn't have been surprised if it exploded. I glanced around and saw beautiful women everywhere having the same reaction to this magnificent rock god. Immediately, I felt foolish. He hadn't singled me out, specifically. I was nothing special. He just had that effect, which is why LTZ was destined for something bigger than a local club.

Throughout the rest of the show, I purposefully avoided looking at the sexy singer. Making eye contact was like looking directly into the sun. Smiling to myself at the ludicrous thought that I would ever have a chance in hell with Tyson Rainier, I immersed myself in the music. Alex and I swayed, danced, and cheered at LTZ's awesomeness. Hands down, they were the coolest band I'd ever seen.

After their encore, Alex and I were still a bit sweaty by the time we pushed through the crowd to find our friends, who were live-streaming their commentary about the show. Alex added to her Instagram story, and I flashed her some rock horns when she turned the camera phone on me. We couldn't stop squeeing about the band and how incredible they were. Despite my earlier insecurities, I couldn't shake the feeling that something about the lead singer had struck a chord deep inside me.

"I think he looked right at you." As if reading my mind, Alex nudged me and waggled her eyebrows.

"Uh-huh. There is no chance," I guffawed, "the lights were shining in his eyes, he couldn't see anyone in the crowd."

"No, I'm serious. He kept trying to catch your attention," she asserted. "You didn't see it? He was singing to you. My Gawd, you have to talk to him!"

"I can't do that." I wrapped my arms around myself protectively. "I'd die of embarrassment. I'd just be standing there looking completely basic."

The thought of it made me cringe.

"Holy fucking shit. Well, you better think fast because I'm pretty sure he's heading this way." Alex's eyes were wide with excitement.

I barely had the chance to turn around when a big hand clasped my shoulder and a distinctive, deep, husky voice asked, "Hey, um. Sorry to interrupt, but haven't I seen you before?"

Looking up into the deepest blue eyes I'd ever seen, for a beat too long, electricity once again crackled throughout my body. I managed to speak, if not eloquently, "Um—Umm. I just was watching your show."

I stared at his exquisite face, not able to help it. After a beat too long, I finally was able to look down at my shoulder where his hand rested. "You are amazing, I mean—the band was amazing— I mean—I loved it!" I stuttered, wanting to disappear through the floor at my ineptitude of being able to flirt.

"Oh, uh, cool. Thanks." Ty's cheeks visibly reddened and he looked at his boots almost bashfully. This took me by surprise, I hadn't expected any of the LTZ guys to be modest. Or nice. Or shy. They were all so, well, overwhelmingly hot. Brushing off the compliment, Ty looked at me intensely. "No, I mean it. I feel like we've met somewhere and it's driving me crazy trying to figure it out."

I couldn't find my words. With little dating experience, having such a powerful reaction to a guy was new. But then this was not just any guy—he was a fucking rock god, so maybe it was to be expected. "Oh-kay, but no, I think I'd remember you."

Realizing this came out somewhat snarky, I changed my tone, trying to be sexier and more confident. Unfortunately, instead, I sounded like a total nerd fangirl. "I mean, I'd for sure remember meeting you."

God, I'm an idiot. I blushed literally everywhere.

Some of the crowd swarmed around us when they noticed the singer of LTZ was among the masses. Ty didn't appear to be aware of his effect at all. His focus was solely on me, like I was the only person in the club. He moved closer in so he could hear me better. His fingers lightly stroked down my arm, almost like he was afraid to touch me but couldn't help it. "I'm not super good at this, um. Well, maybe I made up an excuse to say hello, so hello. I'm Ty."

Not good at it? How could this possibly be? Everyone wanted to talk to him as evidenced by the crowd of people pushing toward us.

"I'm Zoey," I answered, and then my mind emptied of all coherent thought because the world around us fell away and there was only me and him in the room.

We stared at each other, both of us with goofy grins on our faces, the silence between us embarrassingly long. I didn't know how to flirt with him. Apparently, he was in the same boat. Beautiful girls of every size, shape, and color surrounded us, batting their eyelashes, trying to catch his attention. Clearly wondering how to divert his attention from me.

"That's a pretty name for the prettiest girl here," he said before finally breaking eye contact to glance down at his phone.

My bullshit detector activated.

"Really? That's your line?" I cocked my hip and wrinkled my nose in dismay. Surprised, but internally cheering for myself, at my wariness. "I almost fell for it. This is actually how you meet girls after a show. Ty, I'm *not* a thirsty groupie, I actually genuinely loved your music."

A look of mortification passed through his eyes before changing into intrigue. His hand continued running up and down my arm slowly. "Hmmm, well, I admit—that sounded super cheesy." He looked back down at his phone but smiled up at me through his mane of brown waves, scrunching his nose slightly.

My arm was tingling, hyperaware of his touch. Could he feel the energy between us too? I studied him and challenged, "I was hoping you wouldn't be a pick-up-line guy."

His blue eyes snapped up from his phone, piercing mine again intensely. "I'm *not* a pick-up-line guy," he insisted.

A text lit up his phone that he read quickly before he shoved the device back into his pocket.

“I’ve gotta go help load out, Zo-ey.” His deep voice drew my name out, which sent sparks to my girl-parts.

“I didn’t mean—” I called out to Ty’s back. He was already stalking back toward the stage where the rest of the band was packing up their gear. Feeling deflated, I traced my arm absently, immediately missing the warmth and zing of his hand rubbing it.

“OMG are you SERIOUS?” Alex whisper-squealed, interrupting my trance. “He is the most gorgeous man I’ve ever seen in real life. Although . . . No. The drummer is delicious, more my type.”

“Alex, I just royally fucked that up.” I pouted dramatically. “I’m such a tool, I basically put the hottest guy that ever talked to me on blast. No wonder he bailed. I totally just missed my chance.”

“Shut the fuck up. Did you see the way he looked at you? He’ll be back, trust me. Let’s just chill and hang out for a bit more. Just look nonchalant, cool. As your dad would say, ‘Be Fonzie.’” She laughed.

I tried to be Fonzie. Unsuccessfully. Keeping an eye where the band was loading out, I hoped to catch a glimpse of the gorgeous singer and maybe make amends. Waiting around while Alex chatted with friends, I prayed Ty would come back. After a while, there didn’t appear to be any sign of LTZ, their gear, or Ty. Of course, I was so short it was hard to get a good look, even when I continuously stood on my tiptoes to assess the situation.

Dejectedly, when my curfew approached, I turned back to the group and pulled out my phone. After one more hopeful look, I opened my Uber app, tapped in the address of The Mission, and said my goodbyes. “Guys, I’m calling it. I’m heading home.”

Because the club was in the heart of downtown Seattle, a car arrived in under two minutes. I was a wannabe Cinderella, and the hourglass had run out for any chance at talking to Ty ever again. I didn’t exactly give up. I took one last, sad look around the club before dashing out the side exit to locate the car. When it pulled up, I jumped in and was closing the door when it suddenly flung back open.

"Hey, wait, did you forget about me?" Ty was nearly out of breath when he got into the car. "Can I catch a ride?"

"Tyson, uh, uh I-I— I'm going home. I have a curfew." I mentally thwacked my hand against my head, not wanting him to know that I was still some dumb high school kid for another month.

"Uhh, shoot. I had this great idea to ride home with you, Zoey. Maybe you'll give me your number and we can hang out sometime." Ty gave me a side look, his hair flopping over his eyes. "That's not a line. It's just what I hope will happen."

My smile stretched from ear to ear, and it felt like a thousand butterflies had been released from the top of my head. Holy shit, this was like a movie. Determined not to blow it again, I scooted over and patted the seat. Ty slid in next to me, pressing his long, lean thigh against mine in the tiny back seat of the car. He turned toward me and grinned, just a hint of white teeth peeking through his full lips. I turned toward him, my smile widening even more. The car sped off and I couldn't help but get lost in the depths of his piercing, blue eyes.

Crap, this guy's gonna break my heart.

I pushed the thought aside, beamed at him like a fool, and heard myself saying, "Pretty good comeback, rocker-boy."

Made in the USA
Monee, IL
06 September 2022